MOTHER

OF

ROME

ALSO BY LAUREN J. A. BEAR

◆ ◆ ◆

Medusa's Sisters

MOTHER

OF

ROME

· · ·

LAUREN J. A. BEAR

ACE
NEW YORK

ACE
Published by Berkley
An imprint of Penguin Random House LLC
penguinrandomhouse.com

Copyright © 2025 by Lauren J. A. Bear
Penguin Random House values and supports copyright. Copyright fuels creativity, encourages
diverse voices, promotes free speech, and creates a vibrant culture. Thank you for buying an
authorized edition of this book and for complying with copyright laws by not reproducing,
scanning, or distributing any part of it in any form without permission. You are supporting
writers and allowing Penguin Random House to continue to publish books for every reader.
Please note that no part of this book may be used or reproduced in any manner for the
purpose of training artificial intelligence technologies or systems.

ACE is a registered trademark and the A colophon is a trademark of Penguin Random House LLC.

Book design by Alison Cnockaert
Title page art: Mosaic tiles © FrentaN / Shutterstock

Export edition ISBN: 9780593818466

Library of Congress Cataloging-in-Publication Data

Names: Bear, Lauren J. A., author.
Title: Mother of Rome / Lauren J. A. Bear.
Description: New York : Ace, 2025.
Identifiers: LCCN 2024011521 (print) | LCCN 2024011522 (ebook) |
ISBN 9780593638941 (hardcover) | ISBN 9780593638958 (ebook)
Subjects: LCSH: Rhea Silvia (Roman mythology)—Fiction. |
LCGFT: Mythological fiction. | Novels.
Classification: LCC PS3602.E2477 M68 2025 (print) |
LCC PS3602.E2477 (ebook) | DDC 813/.6—dc23/eng/20240513
LC record available at https://lccn.loc.gov/2024011521
LC ebook record available at https://lccn.loc.gov/2024011522

Printed in the United States of America
1st Printing

For R, D, and S,
who made me a mama bear.
(Or should I say a mother wolf?)

'O daughter, first there are hardships to be borne by you; but after that, your fortunes will rise again from a river.'

—Quintus Ennius, "Ilia's Dream," *Annales*, Book 1

PROLOGUE

THE GODS WHISPER a girl's name; she curses them all.

On the night Rhea Silvia, Princess of Latium and favorite daughter, took her vows, five other women encircled her in the House of the Vestals, in its secret round room, enclosing the girl in a double loop of white robes and whiter stone. Rhea felt the heady mix of incense and energies—those of the women, the building, Vesta herself—some joined in accord and others at odds. Celebration, excitement, sisterhood. But also distrust and a bitterness bordering on enmity. Following the hallowed steps to the sacred hearth, she held all their empathies and judgments upon her young shoulders, obliging their ritual with the shallow reverence of an unwilling participant.

She kept her chin down but walked like a queen—even barefoot, even at her age. She had carried far greater weights than these.

When Rhea knelt before the fire, she imagined the unholy glee of her enemies, those who had killed and connived to bring her here, how they might revel in perverse satisfaction at Numitor's lofty daughter brought so low. She heard their giddy hate across the city, in all the cities, and inside the minds of some women present.

No queendom for her!
No wedding night!
No wealthy prince!
No jewels or servants or golden cups!

Someone must pay the price for Numitor's mistakes and losses, his wild queen.

Embrace this *future, penitent!*

Even the fire cackled.

But then Prisca, the eldest and ranking priestess, stepped forward, breaking the perfect symmetry of their circular order. "Hail, holy Vesta, living flame, center of our world!" she began. "You, holy Vesta of the Perpetual Fire, you stand on perpetual guard, your light protecting our city, our people, and banishing the darkness."

Rhea's fists clenched; what did these sheltered fools know of darkness? Any belief she'd once held in Vesta's protection had long since shattered. The goddess was either dormant or indifferent. Vesta had not intervened in any of the tragedies that had befallen Rhea's family. Vesta had done nothing to protect the land they'd ruled for sixteen centuries.

And the Silvian line, descended from Aeneas of Troy, had been pious enough, certainly. Had made the sacrifices and honored the flames only to be brought here: the end of the direct line. Fourteen generations of legend gelded.

But Rhea would not lay blame at Vesta's altar. *Focus your hatred,* she reminded herself. *Hone it. Keep it sharp and precise.* Her subjugation wasn't the goddess's fault. Nor was it Prisca's. Rhea was here, humbled on hands and knees in the ash, future burned, by the machinations of one man.

The taste of his disgusting kiss still lingered in her mouth. Bile rose in the back of her throat, and Rhea Silvia tasted rage.

She might choke on it, maybe suffocate.

This room was suddenly too small. And there were no windows, save for the smoke hole in the ceiling. And she knew she wasn't supposed to look up. From now on, she must keep her eyes low, honor the hallowed.

Obey.

The ceremonial chanting commenced. Prisca called and the other four responded, surrounding Rhea. Their voices targeted her from every angle: voices ranging from alto to highest soprano, voices that ordinarily giggled and inflected, soared and speared, all homogenized by ritual.

A drone of wasps.

"Vesta, you dwell in our hearth so we may be one with your eternal power. Recast us in the shadow of your radiant blaze!"

"Hail the illuminating virgin."

"Shine true in darkness—that of time and heart!"

"Hail the incorruptible virgin."

One unmistakable voice cut through the rest, however, gloating with pointed piety. It was that bitch who had taken Rhea's hair—her mother's hair, as thick and brown as deep forest wood. The priestess Tavia had lopped it off with a kopis, large and slightly curved, shearing Rhea like an animal, nicking her scalp more often than not and leaving her head like a forgotten stump, a fallen log dotted with clumps of moss.

Tavia hummed while she worked, so Rhea knew her voice well. Heard it now, with traces of that sadistic melody, as Tavia repeated the high priestess's call with a hint of singsong.

No, Rhea would not mourn her hair, not now, but she felt its loss, an empty shadow where it used to lie, down her back and almost to her elbows.

Oh yes, emptiness is its own weight, absence another burden.

Four members of the royal guard had escorted Rhea to the temple earlier that morning. *Four.* Apparently, her womb was that terrifying. After the soldiers left, the princess Rhea Silvia was taken apart, stripped, shorn, and reassembled as an initiate, ageless and shapeless. Covered in a white ascetic shift with a veil draped over her bare head. How her brothers would have laughed!

If she still had any brothers, that is.

"Vesta, wise and modest matron, accept this initiate, this offering, into your truth."

"Hail the virgin, immaculate through immolation."

Prisca, Virgo Maxima, Vestalis Maxima, sprinkled salt into the hungry flames. Rhea stared, letting her eyes go slack and unfocused, a practice that allowed her mind to escape from her body, to travel upward

3

with the smoke, through that hole in the roof. In her imagination, she hovered above the temple and spied—even in the dark of night—her former hair hanging from a bough of the stone pine at its entrance, swaying slightly in the evening breeze, saying hello. Or maybe farewell?

Down below, the priestesses continued to chant.

Pounding, incessant. A war drum demanding her surrender.

To dream herself away was another act of rebellion, and Rhea Silvia was no stranger to the subversive. She had made that abundantly clear in her final hours of freedom. And these prayers were long. Boring. Blood and fire and salt in repetition. Instead, Rhea thought of the sky, of secrets shared with the stars. The scandalous euphoria of the night before.

Dream Rhea, spirit and ghost Rhea, departed the House of the Vestals and their temple. She flew toward the Regia, the royal complex built by Aeneas's first son and the home where she was no longer welcome.

But in her mind Rhea could do whatever she wanted. Over the stone walls she bounded, to the windows where she could behold the wreckage: Her father's bed. Her cousin in tears. Gratia and Gratia's daughter, Zea, turning over her room. The new king on his throne.

And in her imagination Rhea made herself corporeal, leaping through this window and grabbing the Alban monarch by his throat. She held him down on the floor, thumbs pressed between the cords of his neck while his eyes bulged, and he sputtered and—

The splash of holy waters against Rhea's face returned her to an equally gruesome present.

"Be cleansed! First by water, then by fire!"

Rhea Silvia ground her teeth, desperate to wipe the droplets from her face but knowing she could not. She must temper her emotions, in her countenance and in her actions—even if they saw her naked, even if they took her beauty or doused her in freezing water.

Her stoicism would be a tiny victory.

She could fantasize, but tonight was not destined for her revenge but to celebrate his: Amulius, uncle and usurper, his victory and vengeance upon them all.

"Vesta," Prisca continued, setting down the ladle and pail, "we Latins survive by your favor and thrive within your love."

Love. What was love to one betrayed and outmaneuvered by her own kin?

Love. To someone who'd known such heartbreak, such loss?

Love. To one abandoned and alone?

"Rhea Silvia, only daughter of Numitor and Jocasta, do you accept Vesta as your true mother, the Vestals as your sisters, our order as your home?"

"I accept." And though Rhea lied, she could be proud, for her voice did not crack, did not shake.

"Do you accept our way of life? The standards we uphold to be worthy of this divine service? Do you sacrifice your years of fertility and transfer your maternal powers to Latium and the renewal of generations?"

"I accept."

"And you will accept the consequences should you bring shame to yourself, or shame to your true mother, your new sisters, and our order?"

Rhea's throat tightened. "I will. I accept."

The priestess laid a bundle of spelt and wheat before her, and her voice was warm: "Then, child, kiss the beginnings of bread, which we transform in Vesta's fire to sustain our bodies and our people. And let that seal your oath to the goddess and her Vestals."

Rhea lowered her face to the ground and placed a chaste kiss on one fragrant sprig.

Prisca regarded the others. "Priestesses, do we accept this woman into our midst, to be our sixth? To complete our circle? To tend the city's flames, prepare and cleanse the hearth, and observe the most inviolable rites?"

"We accept."

"We accept."

"We accept!"

"And we remember that to break these vows is to betray all of Latium."

"Honor your vows!"

"Live your vows!"

"Protect Latium!"

An instrument rang from the periphery, some sort of brass peal, a concluding note. The end of a dirge. Prisca placed her wrinkled hands over Rhea's inclined form in a final approbation. "Then let it be done."

Rhea Silvia, princess turned priestess.

Yet unbeknownst to all, she had already been unmade in the forest, where she would be remade over and over again—but not yet, not tonight.

Tonight, she would be the virgin sacrifice.

But she was no virgin.

She remembered his hands upon her just the night before, in the woods, in the waters.

The women around her began to sing.

And beneath her veil, head bowed, Rhea Silvia thought of tomorrow and smiled, showing her teeth.

TEN DAYS EARLIER

Chapter I

RHEA

RHEA SPENT THE night before the eclipse on the Regia's roof thinking about wolves and kisses. The top of the palace, above it all, away from it all, was the place she most needed when her restless mind would not rest, when the walls of the royal compound felt too finite and her thoughts required utmost freedom.

After a long day, Rhea climbed the bay laurel, scooting across its branches to where her hands could just make purchase on the rooftop. She pulled herself up, unrolled the blanket she kept stored between overlapping clay tiles, and lay upon her back. Breathing steadily, one hand on her ribs, the other on her belly, Rhea engaged the world above.

"Hello, beautiful," she told the moon.

This was no relaxation exercise, no passive observation—there was nothing passive about Rhea Silvia—but an active conversation between herself and the sky. For Rhea saw herself in the night, as if it were a mirror reflecting her own humanity, and she had so many questions.

What was I born to do and how shall I do it?

Though Rhea was not exceptionally skilled—not particularly musical, only adequate at the loom, and possessed no prowess with a bow or sword—she felt remarkable. She believed in her own importance, in her place in the universal plan.

And the stars surely held all the answers. They guided sailors home; they must know the direction of Rhea's life as well.

Below her, the Regia—the royal palace and all its environs—transitioned into nocturnal life. In her periphery, Rhea could see windows illuminated by lamp and candle; could almost feel the pulse of bodies moving across the tufa-paved courtyards, returning from their tasks to their rooms; could almost hear the timbre of each voice change as stress lessened and selfness returned.

And out in the beyond? Among the sleeping trees and hills, her people, the people of Alba Longa, ended their own exhausting days, and Rhea pictured other women, other lives, other dreams. Her mind found more possibility, more freedom, in the darkness. During the night, without diurnal distraction, memory and conjecture held equal rank. The present ceased pressing its priority, and Rhea could both imagine and remember at almost the same time. A confusing but delightful trajectory of thought. Thinking about her own thinking was a way to uncover herself, and there was no better place for self-discovery than the roof.

It was her older brother, Lausus, who had shown her how to reach this beloved summit. When she was too small to merely lift herself from tree limb to stone, he ordered her to jump.

"I will fall!" young Rhea cried in terror. "Carry me!"

"You can do hard things, Ilia."

He was stern but correct. She could, and she did, taking a wild leap and flying, landing hard on her knees. She'd punched Lausus furiously, and he'd taken her fists with a smile.

"You could have helped me," she fumed. "Nobody would have seen; nobody would have faulted either of us."

Lausus shook his head. He sat with his legs dangling over the edge and gestured into the shadowy distance. "Even when you cannot see them," he said, "the wolves and gods are always watching. I can't let you forget."

That memory struck a chord with another, for Aegestus had also mentioned wolves before he'd left.

Tend to my animals, Ilia. Watch out for wolves.

Aegestus was her younger brother—her only brother, now that Lausus was dead—and away on a summer hunting trip, a time-honored Latin tradition. A select group of unmarried princes from a handful of cities entered the Ciminian Forest, the feared and pathless wilderness between Latium and their contentious northern neighbor, Etruria. Both Rhea's father and her uncle had participated as young men, as had Lausus, who'd loved every part of the experience—sleeping outdoors, basking in the boisterous male camaraderie, mastering the techniques of tracking and trapping.

But Aegestus, with his affinity for animals, could hardly stomach the thought of the hunt. Her sweet brother, who cherished every goat, every sheep and bird and calf; who rode his stallion, Hector, with a horsemanship unlike any other, controlling the animal entirely with his legs and seat, never relying upon metal in Hector's mouth or a crop at his flank.

"I hate hunting," complained Aegestus when Rhea had helped him pack.

"I know, but Father is letting Lucian accompany you," she reminded him. "You won't be alone."

"I know," he replied, repeating her words crossly.

Lucian was an orphan, brought into the Regia's employ as a child by their mother, the late queen Jocasta. He worked in the stables and was Aegestus's closest friend.

Rhea sat beside her brother on his bed. "It could be exciting," she offered again, a bit more gently. "And you will experience a forest I've never seen. I want you to remember every detail so you can describe it perfectly to me when you return."

He'd rested his head against her shoulder, and she'd laid a kiss in his mussed hair. Her worry for her younger brother was a cyclone she couldn't control—all-encompassing—and it made her feel hard and soft at the same time. If she could, she would forever hold him in her arms, shield him from the worst of the world, but he was no longer a child. Aegestus was his own person and the heir to all thirty confederated cities of Latium.

"Do you remember Mother's brooch, the one with the three gems?"

Aegestus's eyes lit up. "For her three children. I could never forget it."

Rhea pulled it from her belt, where she'd kept it concealed. She offered it to Aegestus on the palm of her hand.

"Take it with you. Take us with you. And keep yourself safe."

His mouth curved slightly upward, making him look both happy and sad. "I might not give it back."

Rhea crossed her arms over her chest. "Do not overestimate my generosity."

Aegestus attached the brooch to the inside of his toga, where it rested, hidden, over his heart. And that's when he said it, when he mentioned the wolves. "Tend to my animals, Ilia. Watch out for wolves."

She scoffed. "I do not fear the wolves."

"You wouldn't, would you?"

"The only people who do are the ones who think like sheep."

Aegestus rolled his eyes affectionately. "Fear isn't passive or stupid. Fear saves lives."

Oh, she had many extant fears but would not speak of them. Fears for her father, for her younger brother, for their health, their hearts, their safety. But beasts? No. Rhea could care less about fangs or heights or spiders or storms, things other people lost sleep over.

She grabbed Aegestus's hand. "Find a wild boar or bear and come home to me quickly."

The hunting party had been gone for weeks, and she missed Aegestus more each day. Without him, she felt herself coming untethered and going adrift, for she was a boat in port, moored to her family. After two snapped ropes, she clung to her brother and father for purchase. Should they break, should they untie, she would be lost.

And their father, King Numitor, needed them together most of all.

The moon above her was a curved sickle, skinny and sharp. Tomorrow would surely be a new moon. A dark moon in a caliginous sky.

Black moon, black sky.

Her mind pulsed with those words, then devolved into the corresponding image that haunted her mind's eye.

Black wolf.

Rhea had first seen him at the Latin Festival in April: a wolf, darker than the stygian shadows, bigger than any wolf ought to be. Oh, she had spied wolf packs before, scavenging the Regia's goats during the transitional time when night met dawn. And, more often, she had seen their pelts, trophies of hunters, furs for the winter. But this wolf, its size and color, was unprecedented.

She'd stood frozen amid the tents and camps of Latium's most important representatives, those who met each year on the Alban Mount to pledge loyalty to her father, and stared into that pair of red eyes. A cry for help concentrated at the back of her throat. She should have alerted the guards, should have warned the others, but she recalled her mother's strange bedtime stories and their even stranger messages: *Never kill a wolf—it is disgraceful.*

The scream-in-wait faded as quickly as it had collected, and the wolf regarded her as it slunk backward, the embers of its eyes dimming out.

"Ilia?"

Scuffles in the bay laurel and her pet name in whisper. Rhea propped herself up on an elbow and watched as her cousin pulled herself to the roof. Antho, tall and slender and undeniably feminine with her wide doe eyes and small mouth.

"How did you escape Claudia?" Rhea asked by way of greeting.

"She was meeting the midwife," Antho returned. "Again."

"Is your mother pregnant?"

Antho nearly choked on her laughter as she settled beside her cousin. "What a horrific thought! No, I think that is very doubtful. They are preparing draughts for me," she admitted quietly. "Every month, to ready my womb."

Rhea sat all the way up, any thoughts of wolves vanished. "Is a betrothal so soon?"

"I will be the last to know." Antho bit into her lip, worrying it with her top teeth. "But I am sure my mother would be overjoyed should I marry before you."

"She'll have me presented as the bride's spinster relation."

"She will be insufferable."

Antho was one year younger than Rhea, almost to the date. Their fathers were brothers—only Rhea's father was the king, and Antho's father, Amulius, was his adviser. Though the royal children were raised together, a clearly defined and recognized hierarchy existed: first Lausus, then Aegestus, followed by Rhea and, finally, Antho. It never affected the cousins' relationships or fun, but it had soured any bond between their mothers.

And even though Rhea's mother was dead, the bitterness remained, lingering and festering like a bad taste or an open sore.

Aunt Claudia did not like Rhea, simply because she hadn't liked Queen Jocasta. Claudia seemed perpetually irritated by her niece's presence and offended on her daughter's behalf, for she saw the way people preferred dark and unholy Rhea, and despised the way her only child didn't seem to mind—though, in truth, Claudia didn't much care for her own daughter, either. Too soft, too sweet. Antho was honey—from her soft, oiled feet to her golden hair—and Claudia was a raw onion.

The Latin people had preferred Rhea's mother, too—preferred her even in death.

For Claudia, this was a living wound.

"Well," Rhea replied, reclining on her blanket and arranging her body into a more comfortable position, "nobody has asked for my opinion, but I think you should marry Leandros."

Rhea's cousin made no ostensible move, but Rhea was no ordinary bystander, immediately noticing the telltale rigidity in Antho's spine, the forced nonchalance in her face, the strangled sound of her breath.

"Why would you say such a thing?" Antho managed to ask.

"Because you adore each other."

Her cousin fell quiet.

"He's a guard, Ilia."

"He is."

"And Greek."

"Also true."

Antho sighed, looking away. "You say impossible things."

"At least once a day, I hope."

Then Antho lay back beside Rhea, and their hands found each other's. Rhea squeezed.

And because it was the uppermost thought in Rhea's mind, she let her most thrilling secret partially slip.

"I met someone at the Latin Festival."

"In April? Why didn't you say something before?"

"I'm telling you now," Rhea answered carefully, "because he isn't a prince, either, and it's important to me that you know."

Antho pursed her lips, blew air in a faint whistle.

"Who is he? Do I know him?"

Rhea considered. How much was she willing to share? The whole truth was delicious.

Nighttime on the Alban Mount, and Rhea danced before the altar to Jupiter. She followed the ecstatic movement of the crowd around the bonfire, the circular stream of energy, until a pair of strong hands grabbed her waist. Rhea spun to protest, but—

Oh.

A gorgeous man, hard and muscled and intimidatingly tall, with a glinting grin like mica in stone. A man she had not seen among the Latin representatives, had never seen before anywhere. Rhea felt an aura of invincibility, of detachment, of unadulterated power in the strength of his hands, in the charge of his gaze. Like black lightning, like toxins, like uncut wine.

Yes, this was a stranger in every sense and her instinctive sensibility understood why.

He was an immortal.

"You are not from the League," she observed dryly.

"No."

She pushed his hands away from her hips. "This event is for Latins."

"I am. In a sense. I live here now." He cocked his head. "Among other places."

This was a festival for Jupiter, but the man looking down at her was no Father Sky. How could she be so certain? She had already spied his other form, its four-legged silhouette, amid the tents.

"I saw you earlier."

"And you did not scream."

Had that been a test? Well, she wasn't afraid, and she was never impressed. He might as well know now.

"And yet you changed."

He held wide his arms. "It's much easier to dance on two legs."

Rhea stared at his chest, at the dip where his collarbones met his neck. She wanted to taste that patch of skin.

Stars! How much wine had she consumed?

"Prove it."

He grinned and took her hands in his own.

Rhea loved to dance, and this man moved with her and against her in alluring ways, to a song only she could hear: the drumbeat in her blood, the wild refrains of her soul. The bonfire incarnate. She had danced with others that night, lesser princes who lusted after her name, but those were cursory exchanges. Nothing like this: his perfect body, his breath on her neck, all of it leaving her lightheaded with a terrifying but rhapsodic thrill. Her father might be watching. Her uncle, Amulius, the royal council, or any of the very real, very mortal men dissecting her every move.

"People can see me," she whispered into his ear, forced to stand on her toes.

"Doing what?" he whispered back.

"Enjoying myself."

"Tell me to leave and I will."

She should say the words, make her excuses, and run far in the opposite direction. Instead, Rhea laced their fingers together and led him into the forest. When he murmured approvingly, even so far away, under arboreal cover, she felt the combined effect of him and the nearby conflagration burn her cheeks.

It felt like kismet; maybe she was kismet.

She stopped walking and faced him. "You are too old for me."

He smiled, and she saw them, undeniably. Wolf's fangs. "You knew that before you brought us here, just as you know who I really am."

His hand slipped through her hair to the back of her head, and Rhea murmured his name.

"Mars."

A growl rose from his throat, and his fingers gripped her neck. "Yes."

He had to stoop to bring their faces together, and oh, she had never been kissed in such a way and surely never would be again. No human boy could come close. Her heart soared, and so did her feet. Was she floating? Was she still corporeal?

Yes and yes, but the god of war had lifted her off the ground— so easily, so effortlessly.

She wrapped her arms around his neck, her legs around his waist. "If any of the Latin kings see us, I'll never marry a prince."

"Rhea Silvia, you were never meant for a mortal man."

She knew this, too, somehow, but it did not make his response any less exhilarating, and then his tongue was in her mouth, his hands passing beneath cloth, and Rhea became something hot and delicate. Molten gold.

Kissing, simmering, alchemical.

Where would this go? How far would she allow it?

Questions she never got to answer because Aegestus stumbled into the woods calling her name and Mars cursed, placed her on the ground, and disappeared.

Just recalling the memory brought heat to Rhea's chest. She was undeniably flustered—and caught, judging by Antho's amused expression.

"Well?" she prodded. "Who is the mysterious man that makes you blush?"

But as dearly as Rhea loved her cousin, she would not divulge her savory encounter with the god of war. Antho might not believe her, and if she did, would worry incessantly. Romances with immortals only ever went badly, especially for the mortal, especially for the girl—or so it went in all the stories.

"You do not know him," Rhea said instead, maintaining ambiguity. "I barely do."

"Whoever he is, they won't let you have him."

"They certainly won't," Rhea agreed, and then she sighed. "But it's a shame. I've yet to meet a Latin prince with a body like his."

"I think of Leandros's stomach all day long," Antho confessed. "The place below his navel, the line of hair that goes downward."

"Now which of us is keeping secrets!"

Antho bit back a smile. "We may have spent some time together."

"Time alone, apparently."

Antho laughed. "Just a bit, never enough." And then she became serious. "At least half the Regia's women watch Leandros with mouths hanging open like dead fish. But I can't let anyone else have him." She fingered the gold bangle on her wrist. "We should run away, Ilia, and live in the forest together."

"Or commandeer a small boat and take the Tiber to wherever it may lead."

"To anywhere. To everywhere."

"Drink as much wine as we want. Stop styling our hair."

"Disguise ourselves and pass unnoticed through villages, telling stories and singing songs for food."

"Bed every handsome man who pleases us."

"Oh, yes, all of them."

"We would need horses."

"New names."

"And sharp blades, for those who might stand against us."

And they continued to dream aloud, together and freely, in the time-honored manner of girls and women, in that safe space where desires can be revealed and choices seem possible. To imagine worlds without limit where love and adventure and knowledge are accessible to any who dare. Until Antho fell asleep against her cousin's shoulder and Rhea remained, still waiting, forever waiting, for the stars or gods or wolves to hear, and perhaps change, everything.

Chapter II

RHEA

RHEA AWOKE ON the rooftop alone. She was not certain when Antho had left—probably before dawn, before Claudia could catch her out of bed and commence her scolding. Rhea sat up and stretched. She was just about to reach for a sturdy branch and make her way down the tree when she heard her father's voice.

She paused, held herself still, focused her ears.

Not just her father but her uncle, Amulius as well.

Rhea slid back onto her stomach, lying as flat as the roof itself, and listened.

"Corinth has sent a tentative introduction," her father said. "And so have the Greek tributaries in the South. Cumae, Tarentum."

Her uncle scoffed. "If you are considering Greek offers, why not betroth her to the Volsci or the Sabines! Give your only daughter to our most immediate enemies!"

A betrothal. And hers? This might be a private conversation, but considering the subject matter, Rhea felt no shame in eavesdropping.

"I have answered correspondences, Amulius."

"You have given them hope. It suggests they have a chance."

"Perhaps they do. What if my Ilia could unite our peoples? Children of two nations might ensure a future full of peace."

"Peace is never assured."

"Of course not, but—"

"Latins are good at two things, Numitor. Farming and war. You forget this!"

"I could not call myself a diligent king if I didn't seek peace at every opportunity."

Rhea heard her uncle snort. "Peace is contrary to human nature, Numitor. It's an illusion. A myth."

But the king ignored his brother's philosophical baiting. "Other Latin cities have also requested permission to court my Ilia: Tibur, Praeneste, Gabii. But I cannot entertain any without first speaking to Ardea."

"You are too loyal."

"I owe them a queen."

Up above their heads, among the branches and birds, Rhea drew in a sharp breath.

Ardea.

Lausus, Rhea's older brother—and Numitor's firstborn son—had been promised to Princess Mariana of Ardea before his death. A strong alliance with the southeastern city was important for Alba Longa. Ardea, the Rutuli's notoriously autonomous former capital, was coastal and expansive. This alliance would have offered Alba Longa a piece of the lucrative sea trade with the islands. Years of negotiations had collapsed when Lausus died. Rhea and Prince Taurin would be a second-rate option, a way to salvage the agreement.

But did she want to marry him? Could she?

Rhea had met Mariana's brother a handful of times. Timid, plump, with white-blond hair and fine clothes. He brought to mind a well-dressed peach. She tried to imagine him climbing atop her in their marriage bed, but even the thought of their mouths meeting made her queasy. And he couldn't possibly find her attractive, with her thick dark hair and dirty feet and sharp mouth.

Could a pair be any less suited for each other? Would her father seriously consider such a match?

"You owe Ardea nothing," Amulius argued. "It was one thing to bring their princess here for Lausus, but if Rhea goes to Ardea and marries Prince Taurin, their children will have our bloodline *and* control of the trade routes. Ardea's strength would rival, if not surpass, Alba Longa's."

"It is only a conversation. It is the right thing. Do not worry yourself so much with Ilia's progeny."

"One of us should. If you match her with someone too powerful, it could potentially challenge Aegestus's claim to Latium and bring war to our walls!" From the way the volume of Amulius's voice fluctuated, Rhea knew he was pacing, though she did not dare look.

"I thought you advocated for war," her father teased.

"Yes, with the Etruscans. Not from within!"

"Aegestus is young still. His future children are not guaranteed. Maybe Ilia's children will be the best choice for Alba Longa. Do not close yourself off to the idea. Change is human nature, Amulius. Do not discount it."

"That is where you are wrong, brother. Humans do not change."

And something about her uncle's tone made Rhea shiver. She awaited her father's response, but Amulius spoke again, with a forced levity this time. "I only ask that you wait until Aegestus returns from the hunt, for the harvest to come in, and then make a decision about Rhea."

Her father chuckled, a sad sound. "I've already kept her longer than I should have."

There was a long, fraught pause and then: "You suffered a great loss two years ago."

Before Numitor could reply, and surely to his relief, a servant arrived requesting Amulius's presence, and Rhea heard the particular, syncopated click of her uncle's sandals in his departure. Rhea counted silently in her head, and when she hit a sufficiently high number, she climbed down through the tree.

Her father lingered on a stone bench below.

"How much did you hear?" he wondered, not looking up at her but studying a laurel leaf between his fingers.

He always knew; it felt impossible to deceive him.

Rhea smiled and closed the distance between them, sitting on the ground and leaning her head against her father's knee as she used to do. "All of it."

"No need for small conversations or summary, then. What do *you* think of Ardea?"

"The place or the boy?"

"Either. Both."

Rhea shrugged.

"You have been remarkably quiet on this subject, my girl, especially for one so typically loud." But her father misunderstood her silence, as evidenced when he gently added: "There are other princes, of course. Does one already hold your heart? The heir of Tibur or Praeneste?"

"One fights so often he's already lost half his teeth, and the other is younger than Aegestus."

"Taurin is of a similar age, at least," the king continued. "Though when he comes to see me, I will check his teeth like a horse."

She grinned.

"Is there an Alban man you prefer? Even if he is common, Ilia, you can tell me."

There was nothing common about the man she preferred. *Black wolf, black hair. Devouring each other in the black forest.*

"No."

She longed to ask him about her mother, to hear him tell the story of their betrothal, one she never tired of hearing. Jocasta of Satricum was a second daughter, a friend of her uncle's. Numitor was already engaged to another, but when he met this unconventional young princess, he was bewitched and would have no one else. His father, King Procas, had to cut many deals to placate the offended parties, but her grandfather respected his oldest son and heir's decision to marry for love. Lausus followed soon after their wedding.

The king placed a tender palm upon his daughter's head. In these quiet moments, when he was contemplative, the Trojan trauma he carried seemed heaviest. Numitor had been born with a tragic knowledge that existed in his marrow, that was passed down by a people who had witnessed their city burn, who wandered, starving and shelterless, for so many years. An inherited pain, an ever-present exhaustion in the depths of his eyes. Her father, more so than his younger brother, was a living relic, a soul-filled scar. And that was before he lost his wife and son.

"It will be a struggle to find your match, I am afraid." And Numitor ran his hand down his daughter's hair, for Rhea's hair was important hair. It was the same as Jocasta's, and it was Rhea's inheritance.

She leaned her head into his touch, and while she reveled in her father's attention and his love, Rhea hoped it did not pain his heart.

♦ ♦ ♦

RHEA MISSED HER mother so much.

Two years she had been gone.

Memories of the dead queen were precious, and Rhea sometimes feared that those she cherished were wrong, that she had changed them through some metaphysical process, some mental translation across time, in her desperation to keep them safe and perfect.

What, then, did Rhea remember?

The touch of her mother's hand on her chest, passing back and forth, tracing slow circles, humming when her daughter took ill or had a nightmare. Rhea could resurrect that haptic impression sometimes, a ghostlike sensation, an illusory return to safety.

And there were smells. The scent of the lavender-infused olive oil Jocasta rubbed into her body. The sprigs of rosemary she kept in her family's rooms.

Sounds, too. Her loud laughter at lewd jokes or the uncanny way she could imitate animals, delighting the children to no end.

Her cutting mouth, her smile like a curved blade.

Watching her mother nap outside in the sunshine like a satisfied cat. (This had driven Claudia mad: "The queen is passed out in broad daylight like a village drunk!" But the king had never woken her; he'd found all her idiosyncrasies endearing.)

Jocasta had cared little for propriety, and as the king's beloved, she'd gotten away with all sorts of mischief.

"Mama," Rhea had asked as a young girl, "why do you feed Aegestus from your own breast when the other mothers use nurses? Why do you wear your hair down and unveiled? Mama, where are your sandals?"

And when Jocasta had responded, she'd lowered her voice, as if imparting a great secret: "I cannot live the city ways, because I was born in the forest, a child of Cybele, 'the Great Goddess.' The king of Satricum found me scavenging with the bear cubs and scooped me up. He brought me back to court and raised me as his human daughter." She winked. "But I was always meant for the woods."

"That isn't true, Mama," Rhea argued, but they giggled anyway.

And always there was the golden brooch, the only fine jewelry Jocasta ever wore, dependably pinned above her heart. Rhea had loved to sit upon her mother's lap and finger its three precious gems—a garnet, an amethyst, a moonstone.

"Ilia," Jocasta would say, "do you know why your father chose three stones?"

And Rhea would nod. "For your three children."

"Yes, my three children, my jewels. Lausus is here, my bloodred garnet, and Aegestus here, an amethyst for his temperance. But you, Ilia, you are my center stone, my middle treasure, my moonstone, my only girl." And she would take Rhea's finger, press it to the stone—one small fingertip beneath its mother's, rolling against that milky blue and white—and recite her favorite line, her chant, her prayer, her spell: "To be a mother is to be alive."

Which wasn't true in the end. The cruelest memory of all.

The brooch had passed to Rhea after the funerals, but she'd never worn it, had only removed it from its wooden box to lend to Aegestus. Rhea thought of him on his trip and hoped he was keeping his promise to her—to wear it, to keep it safe. And she would honor the one she had made as well.

She would tend to his animals.

On her way to the pastures and pens, however, Rhea crossed paths with her uncle.

Amulius was a decade younger than her father, with a shock of black hair and a corvine face, and he walked with a limp, a permanent injury from childhood. He was a cold man—in his demeanor and expressions, in the frigidity of his voice—so Rhea delighted in any opportunity to shatter his saturnine stoicism. Amulius might not despise Rhea as strongly as his wife did, but neither did he seem to like her.

He noted Rhea's empty hands, and his eyes narrowed. "Shouldn't you be with my wife, cleaning or"—he waved a dismissive hand in the air—"attending to whatever you women do?"

Rhea forced a deep sigh. "Oh, Uncle, I needed to see the midwife for a tea and more rags." She cupped her hands at the bottom of her stomach. "But I remind myself that it is a blessing my courses are so regular."

And when Amulius's face flickered with disgust, she gloated.

"Because that's another thing us women do, Uncle," she added, glancing over her shoulder in flippant farewell. "Give birth to kings."

◆ ◆ ◆

RHEA FED AEGESTUS'S pets. She cleaned their pens. She wasn't affectionate with them in the way of her brother, but she attended to their needs faithfully. Outdoor chores on her own terms were invariably superior to indoor ones overseen by her hawkeyed aunt.

But one moment it was a typical Latin summer, thick with heavy heat, and in the next breath the sun had quit its post, abandoning the day to the darkness of dusk. Rhea looked up, shocked to find its cause: the moon passing between earth and sun, obstructing the day's light, dimming life in a sharp contrast to her own heart's acceleration.

The animals fell silent, the land itself muted—in color, in sound, in all its tones. A natural response to an ominous anachronism—an inversion of the order of things. When night falls during the daytime, what else can be upended? Will fish fly and mothers' milk turn to blood?

"A demon has eaten the sun!" screamed a voice in the fields, and hysteria ensued.

Shrieks and cries. Tears. Rhea's pulse beat with furious demand, reverberating in her ears, her head, her bones, as time itself seemed to pause.

Her first thought was that Aegestus would not want her to abandon his animals to the end of the world, but that was absurd. She should save herself and return to the protection of the Regia. But Rhea did neither; she waited, caught undecided in between what happened then and then what happened.

Was this the end? Would they never return to the halcyon days of yore? An extreme thought, surely, but what if, *what if?*

Eventually, the moon moved, the sun resumed its shine, and the shaken animals took tentative steps toward resuming the process of living. Field hands laughed off their nerves, clapped one another on the back, and made jokes of their trepidation.

"Only an eclipse, no need to panic."

"I saw your panic dripping down your legs!"

Rhea knew the lore, however: an eclipse was a signal, a symbol of powerful and unnatural forces at work. Alarmed, she raced home like a horse given its head. Only speaking with her father would ease this apprehension.

She groaned when she spotted Helvius standing guard outside the king's door. Her least favorite of the Regia's soldiers, Helvius had a lazy tendency to lean against walls, ogle servant girls, and make crude comments under his breath.

He was vile; Rhea loathed him.

"The king is occupied with the augur," Helvius jeered, barring the doorway with his body, and Rhea's hands itched for purchase on his stubborn neck. His upper lip, sliced in some past skirmish, had healed incorrectly, giving him a permanent, grotesque sneer. It suited him.

"Father," Rhea yelled through the door, "may I come in?"

A pause.

"Let her pass, Helvius."

Helvius muttered invectives, and Rhea shoved the guard with her shoulder as she entered her father's rooms.

King Numitor, sitting at a table with his brother and Sethre, the augur, was the only man to acknowledge Rhea's presence. Not with words, of course, but with the slightest nod of his head. For just a moment, Rhea wondered how it might feel to be offered a chair, an invitation to share her opinions openly, to ask her own questions. What would it be like to be welcomed like Lausus had been and Aegestus would be?

Instead, Rhea stood silently to the side, listening with her head down.

"An eclipse is a sign of war!" Amulius insisted. "The king must summon more soldiers to our borders with the Sabines and Etruscans."

"We are not at war, brother."

"We are always at war."

"I have consulted my texts," interjected Sethre. He was a strange man, with one long, dark eyebrow. "An eclipse is an empyrean omen, but what it portends I cannot yet tell. A natural disaster? A catastrophe? The end of a dynasty?" His lips tightened into a thin line as he offered his advice: "A sacrifice would be sage. One hundred cracked eggs in offering to the sun god, Sol. To ensure that his light will not leave us again."

"Do so with my full support," the king replied.

After the augur excused himself to perform the rituals and prayers, Amulius looked pointedly at Rhea and shot one final query. "Has our family lost favor with the gods, Numitor?"

"The moon and sun have met, then passed. This has happened before our family existed and will happen again, long after the last of us meets the pyre."

Rhea's uncle stood, bowed to his brother, and departed, while she remained, wondering at Amulius's question. Was it possible that the Silvian line of Latium had erred? Were mistakes and misbehaviors among her family enough to upset the planetary alignment?

What a horrifying thought.

Unlike the Trojans and Greeks, the Latin people maintained a respectful distance from their pantheon. It was a cold and practical relationship, mutually beneficial, and dependent upon the proper practice of word and action. The mortals provided worship and offerings in return for divine blessing. This was do ut des: *I give that you might give.*

And because of this, the Latin gods did not behave like Greek ones, chasing and tricking, using their omnipotence as an advantage in a cruel game. It was a good system, and devout family members like Antho and Numitor preserved the goodwill of the gods, the pax decorum.

But there was nothing holy in Amulius, and sometimes Rhea thought the same of herself—especially after what she had done with Mars at the Latin Festival. Could this somehow be her fault? What cataclysmic events might those illicit kisses have ushered in?

Numitor noticed her disquiet and reached for her, brushing his knuckles across his daughter's cheek. "There is no need for alarm, Ilia. The sun always returns."

Later, Rhea would recall this conversation and see its devastating irony: the sun, *the son.*

The augurs with their bromides and one hundred eggs, her father with his platitudes and faith. It all meant nothing. For there would be no return from what was happening—from what had already happened—as the eclipse passed over a forest far away and a beloved boy saw nothing, for he would not see anything ever again.

Chapter III

From *The Histories of Latium* by
Aetius Silvius Flavius

There was a Latium before the heroic arrival of Aeneas, but there was no Alba Longa.

Aeneas, cousin of Hector and Paris, was forced to flee Troy after the invasion of Odysseus's wily wooden horse. He left the burning city of Ilium with the family Penates—figurines representing the guardians of the royal house—strapped to his back. Though Aeneas lost his wife in the melee, he did not stumble, did not stop until he reached Mount Ida. There, with his son Ascanius and his father, Anchises, Aeneas led the survivors in exodus. The Trojans struggled for many long years to find asylum, tossed mercilessly by the sea. Eventually, after sojourns in Thrace and Delos, Crete and Carthage, Aeneas's few remaining ships and their browbeaten crews sailed up the Tiber into Latium.

This is it! sang Aeneas's beleaguered heart. *A safe haven at long last!*

Many gods and goddesses greeted him in dreams, but foremost of all was Tiberinus, the Latin god of the river. He called Aeneas forward to claim his destiny: a future empire to surpass any other in breadth, might, or influence. And when Aeneas first beheld the Alban Mount, or Monte Cavo, the

Trojan warrior saw his journey come full circle. Here was another fated mountain, just like Mount Ida, where he would collect life and preserve it against every resistance and setback until his dying day.

To solidify his people's successful immigration, Aeneas married the Latin king's daughter, Lavinia, but more war followed, for Ardea's Rutuli prince wanted the princess for himself. Men fought over a woman, and people died. Men fought for their pride, and people died. Men fought against outsiders, and people died. But eventually a baby gave these disparate groups a common cause to celebrate. Lavinia gave birth to Silvius, a son of Latium and Troy, and he was cherished by all. Here, finally, was the reason for Aeneas's divine protection, why the gods had guided him to this place: up this river, to this land, to this woman.

Silvius, so called because he was hidden from his enemies in the forest. Silvius, whose descendants would establish a great empire—the greatest of all—according to the prophecies.

Aeneas knew very few years of peace before his untimely death, but his two sons ensured the future of their family, claiming a new city, Alba Longa, on a lake between two volcanic mountains for their combined progeny. Though Ascanius died with no heirs, the Silvian line continued and flourished.

The Latin League, which precipitated the Trojan arrival, was originally formed as a mutual defense against the Etruscans. This changed with the advent of Alba Longa. Because of Aeneas's legend, because of Silvius's success, all thirty Latin cities came to acknowledge the preeminent leadership of Alba Longa and its high king. Alba Longa's adamantine rule went unquestioned for fourteen generations, for four hundred years.

Until Rhea Silvia, of course.

Chapter IV

ANTHO

CLAUDIA RAISED ANTHO in the same manner as her own mother, by one simple commandment: "Keep the house and work the wool."

Antho was meant to be simple, to be pleasant in conversation, to walk with grace, and to embody the virtues of a good Latin wife: obedience, industry, modesty, and piety. Claudia herself was so neat, so precise—made nearly lifeless through her cleanliness—and worn gaunt by her daily companion, anxiety. ("Anxiety over what?" Rhea had once asked. "Everything," Antho had answered, glumly.)

Her mother's fastidiousness made itself manifest in Antho's careful braids and trimmed nails and immaculate clothes. And though Claudia's daughter did exactly as she was told, this only made Claudia more demanding, more uptight. Antho was doomed no matter how flawlessly she performed her role.

If my perfection isn't perfect enough, Antho sometimes allowed herself to wonder, *why not be gloriously imperfect?*

Who would that Antho be? An Antho who never rose before dawn to prepare the mola salsa of spelt groat and brine, the sacred flour required by the Lares and Penates. An Antho who didn't refrain from a second cup of wine or kohl around her eyes or the stationed corridors of the Greek guard Leandros.

In short, an Antho who slept well, ate well. Laughed loudly. Felt good about herself. Felt real.

No. Claudia and Amulius would beat that Antho out of her without any qualms or hesitation.

For the majority of her shared childhood with Rhea, Antho had been secretly jealous of her cousin, not for her beauty or her title, but because Rhea belonged to a woman like Jocasta, a queen who caught every eye and breath. How would it feel to belong to such a mother, one so munificent, so adoring of children, so lively that even Antho's father smiled when she was present? Antho pictured herself in Rhea's family all the time, saw herself amid those adoring brothers, with Jocasta's nightly kiss on her brow. She used to imagine it so often and with so much ardor that now, even two years after their funerals, Antho still blamed herself for Jocasta's and Lausus's deaths. Maybe it was her own insidious envy that had poisoned their bodies. Maybe her ardent longing had upset their family's balance.

But Antho loved Rhea without any qualms or hesitation, for without Ilia's surplus of strength, Antho would be too weak, too dull and simple. She would become all the insults her parents regularly delivered:

Like a turkey in flight!

All the firmness of a jellyfish!

Soapstone against quartz!

In her heart and mind, Antho was none of these pathetic things. She had such forceful thoughts and feelings! But besides her cousins, nobody at the Regia had ever considered her as anything more than a wife-in-waiting. Not until recently, that is.

Until the soldier Leandros.

Who had come to Alba Longa in the past year, a Greek son working to free his parents from slavery.

Who didn't find her diffidence distancing.

Who had spoken words that she recited every night in irreverent prayer: "Your gentleness devastates me, Antho. You do not understand the power your kindness wields over someone like me, who has known only pain and punishment."

Was it true? Could tenderness be an attribute? She had been raised to believe the opposite.

But perhaps with Leandros, different realities were possible.

"Why do you stare at walls?" Claudia snapped, breaking Antho from her reverie. "Why was I cursed with such an idiot daughter? Antho, move!"

People were hungry, and Antho held back the meal. She finished her remaining tasks quickly and found her seat beside Rhea. All the Regia's women ate together—the royals, the servants, the foreigners who came to the compound through the sins of slavery. At the head of the long table, Claudia prattled on about a banquet she planned to host when her family from Tibur visited—the dishes she wanted prepared, the decor and entertainment.

"I will procure a peacock for the feast."

Claudia's most loyal women expressed their delight. A peacock was certainly a grand delicacy and would make a stunning centerpiece.

"Shouldn't such an expense be saved for a wedding feast?" challenged Agrippa, a councilor's wife and one of the late queen Jocasta's former attendants. "We have all heard rumors of the many suitors vying for Princess Rhea's attention."

Though Antho's mother regarded the woman with pinched disapproval, others shared in the excitement, winking at Rhea and laughing. Antho thought that her cousin's forced smile looked slightly ill.

"Who will it be, Rhea?"

"Yes, tell us, please!"

"The Regia is desperate for some fun!"

"And some fresh men."

"Princess Antho will also be entertaining suitors soon," Claudia remarked coolly, silencing the laughter. Antho's face flushed. *Please don't,* she begged. For there was nothing more embarrassing than her mother forcing her into competition with her cousin. It was so obvious a maneuver; surely everyone felt as awkward as Antho.

But then Ursan, a royal soldier, came barging into the women's chamber.

"Princess Rhea! Princess!"

Rhea dropped her utensils. The dinner table went still.

"Lucian has returned from the hunting party. He is . . ." The guard swallowed, then looked away, and the bottom of Antho's stomach turned over, as did the mood of the room.

"He is what?" Rhea demanded, standing, her fingers clenched to keep her from pouncing. "And my brother?"

Ursan shook his head. "Lucian arrived alone. You must come and see."

Antho pushed her plate away and joined Rhea, as did most of the other women, and they accompanied Ursan through the Regia at a hurried clip.

"I found him at the edge of the city, Princess," Ursan explained. "Riding Hector. Barely."

"Why would he ride Aegestus's horse?"

"I asked no questions, only brought him home."

"You did well, Ursan."

They traversed the many corridors to the atrium and its rectangular rainwater pool. There, in the corner, just past the formal entryway, were two figures. One lay wrapped in a guard's cloak and shivering on the tiled floor; the other, kneeling, was Leandros. His silhouette was already imprinted upon her. Antho would have known him in the dark.

"I didn't dare move him," the Greek guard said, looking quickly at Rhea, then Antho. She held Leandros's haunted eyes with her own, and she knew that Lucian was not long for this world.

I am sorry I cannot shield you from this ugliness, Leandros seemed to say.

Oh, my beloved, I require no protection from the truth.

Rhea dropped to Lucian's side, and Antho quietly followed. She watched her cousin clutch Lucian's hand in her own.

"Dear Lucian," Rhea began in her softest voice, "you are home now. You are safe."

Lucian murmured incoherently, seeming even younger than his mere fifteen years. A boy, really, a child. The orphan whom Queen Jocasta had rescued and raised alongside her youngest was bleeding out on the floor.

"What happened to him?" Rhea murmured to Leandros.

"It is . . . not pleasant."

Antho noticed her cousin stiffen, so Antho took a deep breath. She would be brave for Rhea, in her way. "Lucian needs water," she told the gathered servants, sending some of the crowd away. "Quickly, please! Clean cloth and wine!"

And then, with more privacy, Leandros pulled back the fabric of his own cloak, revealing a gaping wound in Lucian's stomach. Necrosis already circled the wound with its dark-blue-and-black gore, oozing and putrid. Someone behind Antho gagged, and truly, she understood the reflex, for Antho had never seen its like, and she hoped she never would again. Antho placed an instinctive arm around Rhea, who had clenched her teeth so tightly that the muscles in her jawline ticked. The cousins would face this together.

"Viper venom," explained Leandros, almost apologetically.

"The work of barbarians," denounced Ursan, the other guard. "Cowards who lace their blades."

"Find my husband." Antho turned. Claudia, lowering a shaking hand from her mouth, instructed anyone, everyone, to find Amulius. "And King Numitor."

But Antho was a listener. She listened to healers. She knew things.

"Mother, we need rue and myrrh. Tannin. Curdled milk."

Claudia regarded her daughter with open aversion. "You hapless fool. It is far too late for any of that."

"I will fetch them," offered Leandros, standing straight, and with a curt nod he made for the storerooms.

"Should I . . . should I suck out the venom?" Rhea shuddered, staring at Lucian's gored torso with equal parts apprehension and determination.

"No, Ilia. It would poison you as well." Antho ran a comforting hand across Lucian's forehead, over his matted blond curls. "It's Antho," she sang lightly. "Lucian, I am here, too."

"I know it hurts," joined Rhea, voice shaking, "but where is my brother? Where is Aegestus?"

Lucian's eyes were closed, his brow furrowed, but he began to speak, each word an act of fortitude. "The hunt was over," he rasped. "We headed home. Our party was attacked by a band of men. Swords and spears and arrows. Only I escaped."

Only Lucian, not Aegestus.

Antho did not—could not—meet Rhea's gaze, but by then a cadre of men had assembled, Antho's father at their lead.

"What men?" Amulius demanded. "What language did they speak? What did you hear? What names?"

Tears dripped down Lucian's swollen face, and his lips trembled with overwhelming agony. "No words, just screams."

"Think!" Amulius ordered. "Did they carry any colors? Any heraldry?"

"He *is* thinking!" Rhea snapped. "Look at him—he is doing his best!"

"There is no time to be gentle."

Beside Antho, Rhea flared with anger. "There is always space for compassion."

"By the weak wisdom of women."

"That is enough of that, I think."

Heads whipped around. King Numitor had arrived with the augur in tow, and Antho released a sigh of relief. The animosity between her cousin and her father had always made her nauseous, but her uncle, solonian and true, brought peace.

"Lucian, what you have done is heroic," praised Numitor softly. "You made it back, and you bore the message. I commend you, dear boy. But now I need you to tell me who hurt you."

"Thieves," Lucian managed. "In masks."

"What can you remember about these masks?"

"Long black beards. And pointy hats."

"Phersu," whispered the augur, Sethre, stepping forward with wide eyes. "The masked man who brings the executed to the underworld."

"I have never heard of Phersu." Amulius frowned. "From where does this tradition hail?"

37

Sethre bowed his head, weighed down by the impact of his response. "It is a custom of Etruria."

Antho's father sucked air through his teeth. "I knew this day would come. We have ignored their threats for far too long, Numitor."

"Enough," commanded her uncle. One word slammed downward, demanding silence, proclaiming authority. As definite as any hammer, any fist. The growl that sends a lesser dog back into the pack. Amulius obeyed.

(And, oh, it was so disloyal, but Antho thrilled at every rare occasion when her father was made to cower!)

"Where is my brother, Lucian?" Rhea entreated, bringing Lucian's hand into both of hers. "Please tell me where to find him."

Lucian's beautiful face crumpled. "He is dead, Rhea. Aegestus was murdered. Everybody was murdered."

Chapter V

RHEA

HOW DO YOU break a broken heart?

Just like this.

By severing the last string of hope, the final piece holding it together.

The tapestry unravels. The foundations collapse.

Rhea was no longer herself. She was a light extinguished. A flightless bird. A lone wolf.

All of them at once, and also nothing.

Aegestus was murdered.

Words that could not be recalled. Words that invoked an abyss—fathomless and lightless, unbreachable, insurmountable. She would drown here, surely. She would choke on the words that might express her grief. For there are some hurts that are unsayable. Rhea could circle around this pain with the language that she had, but it would never do the loss of Aegestus justice. Aegestus with his horses and easy smile, with Lucian, with her. Aegestus on their mother's breast, in their brother Lausus's arms, on their father's knee. Aegestus laughing, Aegestus thinking, Aegestus playing.

Aegestus, the baby—their baby, her baby—killed.

Killed meant dead, meant gone. Forever. Not ever. Not even one more day, one more hour. Not again.

She would never, ever see her brother again.

Rhea could not breathe.

She . . . could . . . not . . . breathe.

And her heart exploded.

A fist—her own—met her chest. Over and over, a battering ram.

Take it down!

Blood in her fingernails. A wet face. Wet dress.

But there was Antho, still beside her, always beside her. Antho's arms and hands and lips moving.

"In and out, in and out," her cousin commanded through her own tears. "Breathe, Ilia."

Rhea didn't want to.

Aegestus had joined their mother and Lausus, but she was still here in this stupid, senseless life. Rhea had believed she would never feel such devastation again. A childish dream. To think she deserved to be spared! No, to live was to hurt. To be real was to die.

But this was too cruel, too unfair.

"I am sorry," wept Lucian beside her. "I am so sorry."

Rhea vaguely heard Antho murmuring to Lucian, comforting him in her sweet way. But all Rhea could think was *I will not survive this*, and then came the memory of her mother in those final days telling her the exact opposite: *You* will *survive this.*

Rhea hadn't wanted to then, either.

Pain is fire, my Ilia, but it purifies as surely as water.

Losing her mother and Lausus had burned, scouring Rhea's insides. For a long time, all that remained of her was a stripped-down skeleton—blood and meat and heart consumed. Eviscerated. If that was cleansed, it was also empty. Incomplete.

But even that existence was more substantial than what she was now, than what she would ever be again.

Aegestus is dead.

Her brothers were dead.

And Rhea was cursed with life.

◆ ◆ ◆

LUCIAN DIED OF his wounds some hours later.

King Numitor dispatched a party of elite guards to the location that

Lucian had described. They went to search for survivors, to retrieve the dead Alban bodies, and to exact revenge upon the Etruscan bandits.

As Lucian was parentless and a pseudoward of the king, the Regia bore responsibility for his funeral. Rhea wanted them to wait until they could burn Lucian beside Aegestus, but the boy's corpse, riddled with toxins, decomposed too rapidly. They burned Lucian in a private ceremony. After his pyre had dimmed from flames to embers to soot, Rhea scooped a handful of ashes into a small cypress box, to entomb later with Aegestus.

Her brother deserved to have his best friend beside him in eternal life—assuming that the Regia's soldiers found his body. Until then, Rhea decamped to the Regia's roof, where she awaited the search party's return. Antho visited often, just to sit by her side. They did not speak of kisses or dreams, did not exchange any pleasantries at all. Rhea barely noticed her cousin's presence. Servants delivered up plates of bread and meat, jugs of wine. Rhea ignored them all; she liked the way hunger panged. It felt right.

Her father did not come, but she heard his cries both day and night.

Rhea wrapped her shoulders in a horse blanket and maintained her watch. Her hand found the hard spot on her chest, the very center of her ribs, where her mother's touch used to comfort her in repeating circles. Her own hand did not feel the same.

The people of the Regia kept moving, kept living, but Rhea remained still, intentionally stuck in the dark place, the void she had previously avoided for fear she could not pull herself out.

Remember it all. Why not? Hurt more, hurt better.

She did not fall into the abyss; she jumped.

Jocasta had brought Lausus to her home city of Satricum, a modest city in the marshlands, and while they were away, celebrating his impending nuptials, the rivers flooded. This alone was not worrisome. The river's moods were a part of Latin life, a cycle understood and respected. But when the earth is wet for too long, the bad air comes and brings with it the biting bugs.

Insects do not discriminate between rich and poor, important and inconsequential, and these infected the queen, her elder son, and their entire caravan on the return trip to Alba Longa.

By the time the company reached the outskirts of the Regia, everyone was infected or already dead, and the prince was grasping at life. Jocasta called for help, arms clutching her son, who was racked by plague. The Alban heir, sweating, dripping with fever. Body aching, head splitting. Eyes yellow.

Rhea, Aegestus, and Antho caught only glimpses of Lausus before he was hidden away, and only the queen entered that sick room, barring the door against others. She nursed Lausus until his last seizure, his final breath. And when he died, when Jocasta lost her oldest child, her howls rolled through the Regia.

There are many pains in this world, but none like that of a mother who outlives her child.

And then, inevitably, Jocasta succumbed to her own sickness, for she had been ill for almost as long as the others. Numitor smashed through the door to be with her, but Jocasta screamed for Amulius. The king's brother came rushing through, pulling Numitor back from the rubble and remnants.

"She is infected!" Amulius exclaimed. "You will die, too, if you stay here!"

"Good," the broken king moaned.

"You must live," Jocasta rasped. "Ilia and Aegestus need you."

And because she could not trust her husband to listen to reason when it came to her, Jocasta did what she had to do. She escaped the Regia by unknown means and pushed her dying body to the edges of the city, where she curled up beneath a fir tree and died.

A farmer found Jocasta's body, a smile upon her face, the bejeweled brooch in her hands.

Rhea had lost both her mother and her brother within days of each other. Without hugs, without goodbyes. The Regia had mourned, Alba

Longa and Latium had mourned, and everybody had seemed to believe that this was *their* tragedy—that *they* should be consoled over the loss of the queen and prince.

But it wasn't the Latin people's heartbreak; it was hers.

Only Aegestus had understood how that felt, and now he was gone, too.

On the third night of Rhea's vigil for Aegestus, she spotted the black wolf. It walked straight past the animal pens, uninterested in livestock, focused only on her. Her eyes met those red ones through the darkness, over the walls, and understood its offer, its attempt at coaxing her back to life.

No, not now. Maybe not ever again.

Still, the wolf remained until dawn.

And on that same morning, a troop of soldiers and a horse-drawn cart appeared in the distance. Rhea climbed down from the roof—so hastily that she nearly slipped multiple times—and ran her starved, exhausted body to meet the caravan.

"Where is he? Where is my brother?"

She could sense the mania in herself, could anticipate the others' confusion, but didn't care to explain. Rhea must kiss her brother goodbye. She pointed to the bodies on the cart, all wrapped in cloth from head to toe. "Which one is Aegestus?" she demanded. "Tell me now, or I will open each one!"

"Princess," began Leandros, coming forward. "I do not think it would be wise to—"

Rhea did not listen. Ignoring the embarrassed guards, who were too uncomfortable to stop her, Rhea climbed up into the cart. She would dig through these corpses and rip away every bloodied shroud until she found her brother. *I love you*, she would tell him one last time.

Nobody would take this farewell from her again.

But Leandros's strong hands were clutching her upper arms, picking her up, and pulling her backward.

"Let me go!" she screamed. "Let me go, or I will have you killed!"

"I'm sorry," he murmured over and over as they struggled away from the cart, from the reeking remains and the shocked and weary company. "But I cannot."

"Give her to me!"

Antho appeared, breathless, and threw her arms around her cousin, taking Rhea from Leandros. The force threw both girls to the ground, but Antho held Rhea firmly against her chest. "Oh, Ilia, I'm so sorry."

"He won't give him back," Rhea sobbed, feeling the wetness she made on Antho's dress. "I need Aegestus back. I need my brother."

"If she sees the body," Leandros argued, "it will infect her memory of him. It would be an iniquity."

"Take the cart directly to my father, Leandros. He will tell the king."

"I want to see my brother!"

"Ilia, no." Antho squeezed her tighter. "I love you, but no."

"He is all I have."

"No, he's not. You have me. You will always have me."

And Rhea released the tears she'd kept dammed up. Three days of sleepless watch, two years of mourning. They poured from her like a great deluge. Some part of her sensed that the cart left, the soldiers departed, and the skies dimmed, but Antho stayed. Saying nothing, Antho held her and let her cry, for she understood that no words could pretend to understand, could in any way provide a balm to soothe such an incurable wound.

"My father will never recover, Antho. This will kill him."

"But it will not kill you," Rhea's cousin whispered. "We will survive this together."

It was not lost on Rhea that Antho did not deny the truth about the king.

Unspoken awareness filled the empty spaces of their embrace.

It was just the two of them now.

Chapter VI

RHEA

RHEA SOUGHT HER father, but he sought oblivion.

Amulius ordered Sethre to provide the king with a jug of cretic wine, heavy with the milk of the poppy. The king drank until he drowsed, until he forgot who he was and what he had lost—and what he still had.

And Rhea shouldered this rejection, this neglect, next to her grief.

Because of the destructiveness of the poisons, the accelerated decomposition, and the contamination risks, Amulius ordered expedited embalming and funerals for the members of Aegestus's hunting party whose bodies had been recovered. The customary processions were canceled, as were the feasts, and the remains of Aegestus's servants and guards were hastily buried far outside the city. Only the prince would receive the public rites. Amulius sent missives borne by the fastest horses to the Latin League cities. *Hurry*, the messages said, *we will inurn the prince soon.*

A pig sprinkled with mola salsa was sacrificed in offering to Ceres, the divine warden between the living and the dead, as was Hector, Aegestus's stallion, so the prince could ride him into the afterlife.

Disgusted, Rhea turned away, recalling instead one of her final conversations with Aegestus, right before the last Latin Festival.

Aegestus was leaning against a fence post, transfixed. For there, amid the cacophonous rabble of goats, pigs, and sheep, stood a white bull. Alone and apical, he occupied the solitary top space in the hierarchy of beasts.

"Ilia," Aegestus murmured, acknowledging his sister's arrival.

"When did he arrive?" she asked, gesturing toward the bull.

"Only this morning. Father paid a northern farmer a small dowry for him."

The young bull was nearly perfect. Pink nose. Unblemished coat. Young horns growing, curving upward to form nature's most graceful weapon. A bull that had never known a yoke, an integral symbol of its purity.

"You sound nearly wistful," Rhea chided.

"Maybe I am, for there are plenty of other bulls, and I wonder at the need to kill what is most special."

Rhea considered the bull, considered her brother's words. "Is he sacrificed because he is beautiful or beautiful because he is sacrificed?"

Aegestus nodded. "We have done these things for so long; does anyone know anymore?"

The siblings stood in measured silence, watching the bull snort at the chickens, kick halfheartedly at a passing goat.

"He is frightened," explained her brother on a sigh, pointing out the bull's arched back, the way he lowered his head and shook it side to side. "See how his hair stands on end? And look at his eyes."

The poor creature's wide eyes throbbed, pulsing with anxiety.

"What would happen if I entered the pen?" asked Rhea.

"He would fight you. Or he would run."

"There is nowhere for him to go."

Aegestus gave his sister a half smile. "Then you have your answer."

"Do you think he knows what awaits?"

The altar. The knife. The blood. The fire.

"He can sense the change—in our smells, the heat, the grass. He knows he is away from home. But does he know he is about to die?" Aegestus shrugged.

"It's better not to know, don't you think?"

"Perhaps."

"We could set him free," Rhea whispered.

"Stop. You say useless things."

Rhea threaded her arm through her brother's, binding them together. "Father is merciful. It will be a quick, clean death." The king always told his children that you could tell a lot about a man by the way he killed. It was a justice to the animal to be calm and straightforward.

But Aegestus shook his head. "Death is never a mercy for the young and healthy."

Aegestus had been young and healthy, the best of all of them, and now he was dead.

A litter carried by royal guards brought the prince's body to the lavish multistoried pyre adorned with elaborate garlands of violets and roses. The flowers served a dual purpose—to cover not only the ghastly sight of toxin-suffused slashes and slices but also the odious smell of putrefaction. The wood was further fragranced with incense and aromatic herbs and leaves. In complete silence, Numitor lit the fire, and afterward, as if the act had exhausted all his resources, Rhea's father took a seat in the shadows, allowing Amulius to step into the flaming light and lead the orations.

It was a grand affair, full of formal and informal eulogies. Alban people of all sorts assembled to pay their respects, many in tears. They called Aegestus "the Bareback Prince" and praised his thoughtfulness, his compassionate ways.

"Our queen has her baby back," Rhea heard an elderly woman whisper, and that was precisely when Rhea stopped listening. She couldn't bear it. Not another condolence, not another prayer. She heard neither the invocations recited by priests nor the official speech given by her uncle. She focused solely upon the crackle of the flames, burning away her brother, his heart and mind and easy smile.

Later, much later, when the pyre extinguished itself and the priests poured wine across the smoking site, Rhea watched as they placed what remained of her brother in an urn, a human life reduced to ash and fragments of bone. Surreptitiously, Rhea added the ashy contents of a small cedar box.

Rhea still had Antho; Aegestus deserved Lucian.

In the days that followed, Rhea made countless attempts to speak with her father, but he was always sleeping.

"Has he eaten?" she quizzed the servants. "Has he attended council? Bathed? Left his room? Gone outside?"

No. No. No. No. No.

Those damn poppies! They were not a remedy but a getaway, and Numitor was escaping without her, from her.

It hurt.

"Do not let Sethre prescribe any more of that wretched drink without alerting me first," she instructed any and all who would listen, her tone frantic, her fists clenched. "Do you hear me?" Rhea only needed one person to acknowledge her, but the servants and enslaved stared at the floor in strained silence. They couldn't respond, even if they sympathized, for Amulius frightened them and Rhea was just a girl. All her efforts felt futile, further reminders of her impotence, and this made Rhea spiteful. She stormed through the Regia, breaking things and yelling at anyone in her path. Throwing a tantrum like a child. She should have been ashamed, but she wasn't.

She wouldn't be ignored; she would make them pay attention.

But it wasn't Rhea's father who came to speak with her later; it was her uncle.

"Leave," Amulius ordered Zea and Rhea's other servants before seating himself at her small table.

"Are you here to scold me?"

"Sit, Rhea."

A command, not an invitation. Warily, she joined him, and he studied her from across the wooden tabletop with those cold crow eyes. The subsequent silence dragged between them—a long and heavy rope made heavier by the distance. Who would drop it first?

Finally, Amulius began: "You are wrong to blame the augur. He soothes my brother's pain."

"The poppy seed is dangerous," Rhea returned, crossing her arms. "My father could lose himself in its oblivion."

"Give Numitor time; we will wean him off the cretic wine like a babe with milk."

"Do not liken your king to a child."

Amulius ignored her. "The loss of a son—*two* sons—is a grief I hardly expect you to understand."

She bit down on her tongue, too hard, and tasted blood.

"Do not be angry with him for abandoning you, for forgetting all of us. You are not alone."

"I'm not angry." A blatant lie.

Her uncle sighed. "Antho cares for you very much, which is why I am here. To speak with you directly before word reaches you upon the lips of others."

Something about the intensity of his gaze threw Rhea into disequilibrium. She was flushed and chilled simultaneously, her body alert—almost too alive—in warning.

"Your father is exhausted," her uncle continued. "He is beaten by tragic circumstance and no longer himself."

"He is in mourning."

Amulius raised his eyebrows dubiously, as if engaged in a conversation with a small child. "He has been declining in his duties for two years now."

"My father is beloved by his people," Rhea insisted.

"And he will continue to be, I have no doubt, but he will no longer be our king."

And Amulius said it so assuredly, his precision as lethal as any poisoned blade, cutting away her past, her future, and her very identity like fat and meat. A fatal, bone-deep laceration made by the most skilled butcher.

Oh, Father, what have you done?

But she held herself rigid with the restraint of a queen. Royals learn how to control their bodies at a young age—how to lower shoulders or relax fists in fits of rage, how to keep feet from tapping when bored, how to never nibble at a lip when anxious. And her father had taught her well.

Do not gasp. Do not react. School your face, your features. Give him nothing.

"I do not understand."

Amulius watched her intently, elbows on the table, fingers steepled—a maniac in repose.

"Numitor ceded the crown to me this morning before witnesses, and tonight I will be officially crowned."

"What witnesses?" she managed to say, though her voice cracked.

"Sethre, Calvus Flavius, and the royal council. The guards Helvius and Petronius."

Rhea's mind raced, but her uncle did not wait for her to process his statement; he continued speaking as if discussing insignificant matters—the weather, crops, or local art—and not a seismic shift in their family.

"Rhea, it is your wish to stay in Alba Longa, not to be married away."

"Yes, I—"

"Very good. As your king I will protect you. Keep you here."

He was moving the conversation too quickly, purposefully, for he must have known that she would have questions, objections. She needed to say something! But then Amulius leaned across the table, reaching for her. And she watched in disbelief as one of her uncle's hands grasped the ends of her hair, pulling a section toward him, holding it tightly in his palm.

She sat on her hands to keep from slapping him away, but in her mind, she dropped an executioner's blade upon his arm, and his filthy hand fell to the floor.

"Your father has told you about Jocasta and me?"

Oily revulsion pooled at the bottom of Rhea's stomach. Her uncle had her pinned in place—by his hold on her hair, by the suggestion in his words—but she swallowed carefully, remaining measured and unshakeable. "Everyone knows you were friends."

"We were much more than that." Amulius brought her brown tresses to his mouth and Rhea had no choice but to lean forward. He closed his eyes as it touched his lips. "I was her first kiss."

Though a deep cold crept upward, spreading through her chest and arms, she did not shiver.

"But not her last," she managed to say.

Amulius chuckled and released Rhea's hair, which swung back into place against her chest.

"Don't tell Claudia," he cautioned, standing and straightening his toga. "It would only upset her, and she is your queen now, after all."

Rhea watched him leave with a straight face, as stony and cold as any marble carving, but when he shut the door, she crossed her arms over the table and laid her head down, biting into the flesh of her forearm so that she did not scream.

If her father was no longer the king, what did that make her?

Rhea Silvia wasn't afraid; she was terrified.

Rhea Silvia wasn't angry; she was livid.

◆ ◆ ◆

RHEA RAN.

First to her older brother's empty room, locating Lausus's sheathed sword and strapping the contraption to her waist. It was heavier than expected, but she was so manic with exigency that she hardly felt its weight. And then she fled the Regia, racing out of the royal house, past the forges and market stalls and temples, and through the city gates. She ran toward the woods, running until she breathed fire, until she felt her whole self come aflame. She was some doomsday comet, streaming toward what? Eruption? Devastation?

The leather from the belt chafed, and she stopped, hands fumbling to remove it, to loosen its hold on her heaving, gasping torso. Finally, it dropped into the forest detritus, and Rhea bent forward, removing the sword from its hold and raising it above her head. Her arm shook.

"God of war!" she screamed. "Mars!"

But he did not come, and Rhea breathed heavily through her nose.

Should she have brought salt? Bread and wine? How does one summon a god? Antho would know the proper way; Rhea only had instinct. She brought the edge of the blade against her palm, eyes closed and jaw clenched as metal tore through skin, and then she slammed her bloody hand into the nearest fig tree.

"God of war!" she cried again. "Mars! Come to me!" And the longer she waited alone, bleeding into that trunk, holding a dead man's sword, the more pathetic she became. Rhea rested her forehead against the back of her hand and tried one final time, speaking to herself, mostly in defeat. "Mars," she moaned, "show me how to kill a man."

"I cannot make you a soldier in one afternoon."

Rhea spun. Mars stood behind her, exactly as he'd appeared during the Latin Festival: dark, disheveled hair, a commanding height, that twisted mouth.

"Not a soldier," she clarified, composing herself. "Just a murderer."

He raised an eyebrow. "And who is your target?"

"My uncle."

Mars ran a hand through his hair, sighing, and looked away from her. "No."

"No?" Rhea reeled. "I am strong. I am quick. Why aren't I worthy of your instruction? Because I have breasts and a womb?"

"Because you will get yourself killed."

"I won't," she replied stubbornly.

"Your uncle Amulius is a capable fighter, and he is guarded by a highly trained force."

"I must try. If I don't, he will take everything."

"Your life is more important than your father's title."

Rhea bristled. "Then return my brothers and they will fight in my stead."

"I have no authority over the dead, Rhea."

"God of war, god of death. I see no difference."

He frowned. "You are being insensible."

She recognized the truth; she was behaving atrociously—without sense, without boundaries. Admittedly deranged yet defiant. A mad, mad woman.

"If you fight your uncle now," continued Mars, "you will lose."

Nobody believed in her; nobody ever listened or took her seriously. She was thwarted at every turn, stymied in every effort, by all the men in her life. Rhea flung her brother's sword, and it crashed unceremoniously into the brush.

"I am so tired," she explained, lip quivering, "of feeling powerless."

"You called me, and I came," he answered, softening. "That's more power than most."

And, damn her, maybe she was weak, for when she met that beautiful face, her eyes sought his lips. She wanted to taste his mouth again. That she could long for a kiss when her life was falling apart only confirmed something seriously wrong with her head.

"Here," Mars said, as he handed her Lausus's sword, magically retrieved from the bush. "Do not summon me again unless it is a service I can provide."

And given the way he grinned, Rhea knew she had done no lasting damage to their relationship. Or whatever the forces drawing them together could be called.

Rhea watched him disappear, and after he vanished, she lingered beside the faint outline of his form and its scent of fire, of wood and ash and wildness. She rubbed her eyes with the bottoms of her hands, pushing her palms into the bones of her eye sockets.

Sighing, Rhea returned home, following a path along the Almone River, which ran from the sacred mountain of Alba Longa down to the Tiber. She cursed herself for the years wasted in idleness. She could have been toning and training, studying and strengthening. Turning her body into its own weapon, one independent of any male forger. Instead, she had been spoiled and lazy, assuming that her father and brothers would always protect her and their kingdom.

They were gone, and her time had passed. She was nineteen, with no real skills or allies.

"Now what can I do?" she mused aloud. "What do I have?"

"Tenacity."

The word arrived on a zephyr, and the light wind tugged at her hair. Rhea wondered if she'd heard it aloud or only in her head. She stilled.

"Who said that?"

But there was no one present. She stood alone, in silence, beside the steady babble of the river, the light rush of water over stone and branch.

"You will fight Amulius, Rhea Silvia, but not now. Not yet."

"Show your face."

A pause and then: *"Not now, not yet."*

But she had wasted enough of her life doing nothing.

"I have no talent for patience."

"Stubbornness is patience, in a way."

"Yes, I am stubborn," she admitted, "but I am also tired of waiting."

"He waited," chided the voice. *"That's how he won."*

A somber realization, but no less accurate. Attacking Amulius now in an imprudent act of passion would only derail her vengeance. Her father might lose his kingship, but he was still alive, and Amulius had promised to keep her in Alba Longa. There was time to plan and plot, to fix this.

If Amulius could wait, so could Rhea.

But then she laughed, just a little, because talking to the river did little to flatter her sanity, and in that moment of humor, she felt a fleeting warmth, like the sun before a cloud burst. Not lasting or lingering like a mother's touch, but enough.

Just enough.

Hope.

◆ ◆ ◆

BEFORE AMULIUS OFFICIALLY declared himself king, the goodwill of the gods must be ascertained. He convened in assembly the royal council, esteemed guests, and all the people of the Regia. To begin the proceedings, Sethre took the auspices, a form of divination. The augur removed a pouch from his belt and emptied it onto the floor, then retrieved a chicken, bringing the fowl forth in his arms.

"Should this sacred bird take its feed, Amulius Silvius shall be our king."

He deposited the chicken on the ground and stepped back.

Rhea scoffed. This was inane. A farce! But nobody shared her cynical amusement. The crowd watched with bated breath as the chicken took one step, two, then began to peck voraciously at the poured seed. The people rejoiced.

The people are idiots, Rhea thought, feeling increasingly despondent.

"It is auspicious!" someone cried.

"The gods have shown Amulius their favor!"

For the first time, Amulius accepted the oak-leaf crown and took his place on Numitor's throne. Claudia and Antho joined him, standing on either side, dressed in luxurious new clothes and covered in peridot, the evening emerald. Rhea stared hard at her cousin, who was pale-faced—marmoreal—a perfect statue, solely focused on the back of the room, where a row of guards stood at attention.

But even lifeless Antho seemed more animate than Numitor, who sat to the left of the dais, shoulders slouched, eyes glazed, face blank. He offered no reaction when his younger brother stole his birthright.

The Regia has inverted itself, Rhea thought. *And I live in an upside-down world where everything and everyone is vaguely familiar but flipped or twisted.*

"To live is to change," began Amulius, addressing his people as their king. "We are guided by the cycles of the seasons, the stages of the stars. A forward momentum replicated in our land and bodies. But to live is also to accept the inevitability of give-and-take. Providing for the earth so that we can reap its harvest. Sacrificing to the gods so that we maintain their grace."

Rhea recalled her uncle telling her father that humans never change. It was becoming impossible to discern his truth from his lies.

"Change has come to Alba Longa. Numitor, my brother, who has been the very best of kings, is without an heir. Our people are without a prince.

"Yet with trial comes transformation. Our royal family has been tested. My brother, above all, has been tested. He has given so much—too much—and now he must rest, passing leadership peacefully to the one who respects him most."

Placing one hand over his heart, Amulius bowed his head, affecting a humility that made Rhea want to laugh. She scanned the audience. Surely somebody shared her mirth. But no, the others were too immersed in the spectacle to question its validity. Why spoil such a good show?

"We will adapt, we will move forward, and furthermore, we will thrive. Because we are the chosen people of Troy and Latium, and we will not fail or flounder.

"While those Etruscan thieves who robbed us of our prince will be dealt with—I promise you, as a man, an uncle, and a ruler—what we must foremost prioritize is the reputation of our beloved city. When enemies strike at us, when illness plagues us, we must unite and decide how we will continue. How we will present ourselves to the rest of the world."

Amulius rose to his feet.

"Just as Numitor both honored and improved upon the reign of our father, King Procas, so, too, will I initiate a new era. One that is founded upon our traditions, but also our advancement. We will invest in our farms and our armies. We will send metalworkers to train in outside lands and bring them home to strengthen our tools and weapons. We will become the city Aeneas was promised when he first rode up the Tiber."

More clapping, cheering. Rhea wondered at how her father could sit through this nonsense with no reaction. Why didn't he care? Why didn't he stop this charade?

How much cretic wine had he drunk today?

"Henceforth and in perpetuity, I give myself to Alba Longa and all of Latium. I pledge myself as a servant of Jupiter, Juno, and Minerva, to provide my blood and bones and heart to the service of the people as their king."

Calvus Flavius began the chant: "Hail, King Amulius! Hail, King Amulius!"

Amulius opened his arms, and the crowd went silent. He wasn't done yet. Rhea nearly groaned; she was sick of standing, and her head pounded with fury. She longed for water and her bed and the end of this most terrible, humiliating day.

"There is one final matter I must discuss," Amulius said, and Rhea noted how his tone changed, felt it trigger some deep, endogenous alarm. "Our providence is dependent upon the gods and goddesses we worship. Latins are a pious people, from the moment we wake to the moment we lay our weary bodies in rest. Throughout our industrious days, we show thanks; we make the proper acknowledgments. Take, for instance, my daughter, Princess Antho. Has anyone seen her without her salt bag? Our Lares and Penates depend upon her devotions."

He cleared his throat.

"And then there is Rhea Silvia."

If those in the crowd hadn't noticed her before, they certainly did now. How many heads spun? How many pairs of eyes suddenly speared her with their curiosity, their distrust and pity?

Damn their pity most of all!

Amulius motioned to Antho. "Rhea has been a sister to Antho, another daughter to me and my queen, and as such, I have selected her for a great honor."

Finally, Antho's eyes met Rhea's in shock. She shook her head, just slightly, just enough, to tell Rhea that she was also unaware of Amulius's plan. Rhea's mouth parted; her lips were dry.

Would her uncle renege on his promise in front of everyone? Was he marrying her to the Prince of Ardea after all? Would he send her even farther away, to a lesser prince, an inferior city?

Papa, please, wake up!

"My niece has shared her wishes with me, and I have come to a decision. Rhea Silvia will not leave Alba Longa, will not serve her Latin duty through marriage."

She was not betrothed, then, but Rhea could not relax, could not ignore the latent threat in her uncle's voice. Why did she feel that what he was about to announce would somehow be worse?

"I have selected for her another righteous path." He paused, and the tip of his tongue licked his bottom lip. "Rhea Silvia will fulfill her obligations to Latium in supplication."

Rhea thought of his mouth on her hair; Rhea thought she might be ill.

"In my first official act as king, I commend Rhea to the Order of the Vestal Virgins, where she will take the vows of chastity, purity, and obedience, committing herself to the goddess Vesta for the next thirty years."

Chapter VII

RHEA

A VESTAL VIRGIN.
No husband. No children. No marriage bed.
No touch or kiss, communion. Milk, babies, blood.
Her future, her family.
All stolen.
Rhea was a fool. The politicos and plotters must've suspected Amulius's intentions long ago. They probably shared none of her surprise at such a proclamation, but she had been too distracted by undesirable marriage prospects and loss, by divine encounters that left her feeling chosen. Rhea was taken unawares by this shocking public reminder that she was just a womb, after all, and nothing more.

She recalled her father's conversation with her uncle. It seemed from another lifetime.

Do not worry yourself so much with Ilia's progeny.
One of us should.

Amulius's reign would never be certain if Rhea married and produced sons. He had pretended to be her savior, but he was only saving himself. And now he would punish her with a plan he'd surely had all along, a life of forced virginity; Rhea, indoors and isolated, chained to a prison of chores and worship. Alone. Apart.

If she had known this was the other option, she would have married some Latin prince months ago, but Amulius had advised her father to halt negotiations. She'd heard him on the roof.

Wait until Aegestus returns from the hunt, for the harvest to come in, and then make a decision about Rhea.

Her uncle's tricks were far more nefarious than she'd ever imagined. She needed to speak with her father, but the guards Ursan and Helvius were already upon her. An organized ambush. She flared up when their arms brushed against hers.

"Do not touch me."

"King Amulius ordered you to your rooms."

"I must speak with my father," she managed to say, grinding her teeth to stymie a scream.

"The king told us you would say that," Ursan answered. "The king says—"

"I do not care what the king says!"

Helvius pulled Rhea's wrists behind her back and held them together in his callused grip. "Walk," he ordered, thrusting her in front of him. Her shoulders strained at the force. He needn't handle her so roughly, but he enjoyed it. She could sense his excitement in causing her pain. Rhea thought quickly. How could she escape these men if she had no chance of overpowering them?

"Please stop!" she told the guards. "I am going to be sick."

Rhea lurched forward, coughing and hacking, and Helvius released her hands. She placed them on her knees, letting her back heave up and down in racking convulsions, and when the guards moved away in revulsion, she bolted.

Rhea had grown up between two brothers. She was fast, and she could dodge.

She dashed down the halls, pushing past guests and servants as Helvius and Ursan cursed and gave chase. Rhea flew down the passageways to her father's rooms, crashing into him just outside his door.

"Ilia!" he exclaimed as she collided with his chest.

Her fingers clutched the fabric of his toga, and a hundred questions, demands, and pleas struggled for purchase as Rhea buried her face into his familiar scent.

Where have you been?

Why did you forsake me?

Do you not love me enough?

You would have been strong enough for my mother. Why not for me?

Instead, she asked: "How could you let him?"

Numitor sighed. "I am unwell, Ilia. And weary. I do not want this, any of this, anymore. I do not want to be king."

"You love being king!"

"It's hard to love anything, anymore."

She closed her eyes, reeling from the sting, but her father didn't seem to notice how he'd wounded her.

"You don't need me, Ilia. You never did."

"My uncle is a spider. He spun this web to trap me."

Numitor frowned, shaking his head. "The temple is no trap, it is safety. No band of thieves, no plague will touch you. You will not die in childbirth or lose your children."

"But *nothing* will touch me. I will be *nothing.*"

"Hush. Do not disrespect the Vestals."

"I don't want to be a Vestal Virgin!"

She searched his hazy eyes for any semblance of the man she had admired for the past nineteen years. All she saw were clouds.

"What have they done to you?" she whispered, stricken.

Her words finally cut through the mist—she saw the flash of recognition like a brief glimpse of lightning—but by then the guards had reached her. Ursan drew Rhea back—civilly, of course, because Numitor watched, and he once was king.

"Father."

One word, hardly simple. Not an appeal, per se, but a call for action. She would not beg for his aid, but he could end this now. It was not too late. Numitor wavered, his indecision apparent in the rocking of his body, the crease along his brow.

Reclaim your kingdom. Reclaim me.

Rhea pleaded not with her voice but with the power of her mind. *Hear me.*

But then his shoulders melted, retreating into the curve of his back, his bowed body. Her father opened the door to his rooms, where Sethre's drinks—and their welcome amnesia—waited. He had considered his daughter, but he chose the dream, and closed the door on Rhea one last time.

Helvius chuckled.

◆ ◆ ◆

THE NEWLY CROWNED king positioned vile Helvius at Rhea's door because he knew how she despised him—how all the women did—but Rhea ignored the guard's leers, his crude attempts to bait her. *He's just ugly furniture*, she told herself.

Antho knocked, but Helvius refused her entry.

"King's orders," he boomed, delighted.

"I didn't know, Ilia." Antho's weeping voice came softly from the other side of the door. "Please believe me."

Rhea did not respond. She would not allow Helvius any access to her thoughts or feelings, even if that meant shunning her cousin.

But later the door did open, for even Helvius would not dare turn away Prisca, high priestess of the Vestal Virgins.

Rhea and Prisca had met briefly over the years. Though they'd exchanged pleasantries, they'd never engaged in a full conversation. Prisca had achieved a legendary status for completing her thirty years of servitude to Vesta and then opting to stay. Gray wisps escaped her six braids, which were wound about her head and wrapped with a white headband in the style of the Vestals. There was something flimsy about her, her eyes a bit too loose in their sockets, her extremities in constant twitch. She was like a thin branch rattled by the wind.

Prisca took in Rhea's lavish room, her lips moving but making no sound. Her hands stayed clasped at her chest.

"We have nice girls from nice families in our order, but you will be our first princess. My little birds are beside themselves." Her voice, high as it was, evoked its own kind of bird. One calling out from a precarious perch.

Rhea, standing and unsure of what to say, inclined her head. Despite her foul mood, it would be masochistic to make an enemy of the high priestess so soon. Crying and pouting would earn her no favors.

"When your uncle—now that is a godly man!—first asked me of our order's capacity, we did not have room for you. We are always six, as you see. But then we lost our little starling, Musa, so suddenly. A tragedy . . ."

Prisca pointed to Rhea's bed, where Zea had been stacking folded togas and collecting toiletries.

"Oh, you will not need those. We forfeit worldly possessions when we enter the temple. But do not worry, for Vesta provides." She held her hands up to the sky, a slight sway to her movement. "You must have many questions. You will learn in time what a beautiful opportunity you have been given. And you will gain sisters, a family to replace the one you lost."

Jocasta. Lausus. Aegestus. They were irreplaceable. It was an affront to assume otherwise, and it activated an animal-like rage. How Rhea longed to throw herself at this silly woman, teeth to throat, and rip out every asinine utterance she might make! But no, Rhea would not bite, she would remain as focused as any hunter.

Do not take an early shot at the easy prey, Lausus once told her, *or you will scare away the big game.*

Not now, not yet, the voice at the river had said.

This elderly priestess was not the trophy she had in mind.

"Your wisdom in all things precedes you," Rhea murmured.

It was the correct response. Prisca patted Rhea's arm. Her touch was as light and airy as her voice. "Tonight, starling, you must enter the forest and journey alone to the sacred oak forest, to the Vestal altar by the Ferentine spring. Do not be afraid. We all have done it. Once there, you must wash your hair and body in the consecrated waters. Then, you will pray. Answers will come—they always do—and when dawn breaks, walk to our door. We will be waiting to receive you and begin the ceremonies."

Prisca pulled a long pleated dress from a bag she wore over her shoulder. "After you are cleansed, put this on."

A sleeveless stola, the dress of an initiate.

This was truly happening. Rhea Silvia, Vestal Virgin. It was preposterous.

"Thank you," she managed to say.

Prisca nodded. "You will learn to forget what you have missed. After enough years, the longing for a man's touch disappears."

From his watch against the wall, Helvius snorted, but Rhea ignored him, and the high priestess did not seem to hear. Rhea accompanied her to the door.

"Your new life starts in the morning," Prisca trilled, patting Rhea's arm again before departing.

When she was gone and the door closed, Rhea exhaled, long and slow, but awful Helvius, remained eyeing her every move with a hungry expression.

"I could escort you to the sacred spring," he offered, smirking. "Help you wash."

"I would sooner be flayed alive," she replied dryly.

"You'll be desperate for more than my touch after a year in that place."

"You overestimate yourself and underestimate me. I'll be quite fine."

He shrugged. "It's the last night to change your mind."

Rhea stood straighter. "I am still a princess. My father will have your tongue for such insolence."

"No," answered Helvius, shaking his head, "I don't think he will."

And if Helvius was correct—which Rhea felt he might be—then she was in greater danger than she had previously realized. There was no security for her here, in her own home. Not anymore.

She pushed a chair to the wall farthest from Helvius and sat. Her last night in the Regia, caged like a beast or a common criminal. Once again, true to the grand theme of her life, Rhea would not say goodbye. But in her mind, she could still roam free. She pictured herself on the roof, eating dried figs and honey cakes, or sitting beneath the bay laurel. Rhea traveled down every hallway, considered each tile and fresco, and committed them to memory. In the women's gardens, where right now the plantings—mint and arugula, artichokes and capers—were ripe and full, she wandered, storing their scents beside their images.

Rhea could handle Helvius's derision, and later, when Amulius inevitably came to gloat, she would take his barbs and jabs in stride. For now, she had the palace at her imagination's full disposal.

She would reminisce, and she would enjoy.

Humans are made of memory and story as much as blood and bone.

Chapter VIII

ANTHO

HER FATHER WAS king.

Antho's father was King Amulius, ruler of Alba Longa and all of Latium.

What did that make her? The heiress of a nascent era, the offspring of an usurper? Both? Strictly speaking, Amulius hadn't betrayed her uncle, Numitor, but events had moved at a pace that left Antho more than unsettled. Not even a week had passed since Aegestus's funeral. Would her uncle have willingly ceded the kingdom if allowed more time to grieve?

Before the assembly, Claudia sent for Antho. Her mother had dresses laid out—ornate ones—and Antho fingered the fine cloth, wondering at the detail, at such an expense. When had her mother had these commissioned? How could she have been so prepared?

"Does Rhea know?" Antho asked faintly.

"Let your father handle her."

And during the production, as Antho stood behind her father on his quasi-stolen throne, she kept her head down—not out of respect but out of shame. She could not smile, could not celebrate the triumph of one part of her family at the expense of the other.

"Don't look so sour," her mother hissed in her ear. "The men watching you want a sweet bride."

Antho forced the corners of her mouth to lift in an approximation of a smile and raised her gaze to the back of the room. She let her eyes glaze over, her vision focusing and defocusing on the steady image of Leandros. In and out, in and out. To the crowd, she probably resembled her poor uncle, drugged and vacant, cast to the side. Numitor, who had always been kind to her. Numitor, who had submitted to grief and let it overtake him, despite all his virtue and wisdom. His soul crushed three times too many.

But Rhea had suffered the same agonies and still stood on two feet. Had kept her chin defiantly raised when Antho's father had publicly ordered her to the Vestals. As the person closest to Rhea, Antho knew best how much this would destroy her passionate cousin. A life without physical love would surely be torture. Antho wondered about Rhea's mystery man. Did he know? Did he hurt, too?

She needed to speak with her cousin, but Antho was immediately herded from the throne room to a celebratory party. She kept to the periphery, longing to disappear. Her parents were happier than she had ever seen them—carefree, even—and her father downed glass after glass of wine as if it were water, as if he could not quench his thirst.

Why am I here? she thought miserably, nauseated with traitorous guilt.

But Claudia dragged her sulking daughter away from the wall.

"Quit moping, or I'll give you a real reason to mourn."

"Rhea should be here, Mother, and Numitor. It would show solidarity."

Claudia pinched her arm.

"You ungrateful child. Your father made you the most desirable woman in the entire Latin League, and you would ruin this day with your whining? For that miserable girl?"

"She is my sister."

Claudia threw back her head, rolling her eyes to the ceiling. "She is no sister! Why must you perseverate on that smug family? You always have, trailing after those children like some stray dog. Accept that they are gone. Done. We've entered your father's moment and you will follow his lead."

She pinched Antho's arm again, hard and long enough that tears threatened the backs of Antho's eyes.

"Do you understand me?"

"Yes, Mother."

"Yes, *Queen*."

When Calvus Flavius entered, Amulius welcomed him with arms open wide. Calvus was the longest-standing member of the royal council, a group of elite men selected to advise the king. He owned nearly all the vineyards in the Alban Mountains, and his prosperous winery afforded him a unique prestige: Calvus was the wealthiest man in Alba Longa, even more so than the Silvian family. And he was old—*ancient*, according to Rhea—at least a decade older than her uncle, Numitor, who was a decade older than her own father.

"Go," urged her mother, pressing a palm into Antho's lower back. "Bring Calvus Flavius a drink and some comfort."

Calvus's wife had died unexpectedly this past winter. *Comfort* was a clear euphemism.

Though Antho's hand trembled, she carried a golden wine cup across the room without spilling a drop. Calvus accepted the drink—and Antho herself—with expectant eyes.

"Princess," he greeted. "Such a pretty girl with a pretty new life!"

Calvus was *not* pretty; he was a skeletal man with white curls and thin, purple lips.

Antho bowed her head. "You flatter me, my lord."

"Your father speaks highly of your compliance, your willingness to please."

She tried not to cringe at how he made these characteristics sound disgusting.

"And you have your mother's talent on the loom?"

"She sets a high example, but I do my best."

He nodded. "How old are you now?"

"Only eighteen."

"Only?" Calvus chuckled. "My first wife was much younger when we wed."

"I was aggrieved to hear of her passing. You must be distraught. My aunt Jocasta has been gone two years, and I know King Numitor still suffers greatly."

"Your *uncle* Numitor is more sensitive than most." Calvus took a long sip of the proffered wine. Truly, he was a serpent. Wine dribbled from the corner of his mouth, and his pink tongue flickered, licking at the remnants. Those stray droplets he didn't catch wiggled down the folds of his chin and onto his chest, staining his white toga. Antho tried not to stare. "I come to the Regia often, girl, to counsel with the king. You will attend me when I am here."

"Yes, my lord."

"What instrument do you play?"

"The lyre."

"Bah!" He waved a hand. "I prefer the flute."

"I have never learned it."

"You will. On my next visit, I will hear your progress."

She bowed again, hoping this might serve as her exit gesture, a cue that she was leaving the conversation, but Calvus grabbed her hand, rubbing the pad of his dry thumb back and forth.

"Such soft skin," he mused. "So firm." And his face twisted as he lifted her hand to his mouth. "Yes, a very pretty girl."

He laid a kiss upon her wrist and the touch of his flaky lips—like snakeskin—sent shivers creeping up her spine. She excused herself, hurrying away from Calvus's lascivious looks and his laughter, thinking only of her first kiss with Leandros—how he had asked permission!—and trying not to sob.

Leandros.

His arrival at the Regia had been a gift she'd never expected to receive. He'd come with the spring, and she would never forget the first time they spoke.

It was the ides of March, the day the Alban people celebrated the festival of Anna Perenna, the sister of Dido and the goddess of the wheel of time. Antho had always loved this day; it was an unassuming celebration, and she felt a small, secret connection to the Carthaginian queen's less exciting sister. People scattered among the fields outside the Regia, drinking and singing. Many couples huddled together, the men reclining in their lovers' laps. Others, like Aegestus and his friends, played games, wrestling with balls of animal bladder and leather.

Antho and Rhea watched the activities together, unsure of where they belonged, considering their age, their status. But then Rhea nudged her cousin sharply, and Antho turned, straightening as a delicate "Oh!" escaped her lips.

Walking toward the girls was Leandros, the new guard from the southern Greek colony of Locri. Though he had arrived at the Regia only a fortnight ago, he had already earned himself a reputation among the women, as much for his respectful ways as for his handsome face.

Because he was so good-looking, he must be coming for Rhea. Antho would try her best not to be jealous.

She had become quite adept at that.

"Princesses." He greeted them both with a smile and a slight bow, then held up a small, worn sack. "I noticed you haven't had an opportunity to participate in the games today. Perhaps you'd like to play knucklebones?"

Antho waited for Rhea to reply, but the guard's hopeful eyes were pinned entirely on her own. Antho opened her mouth, but in her surprise, could not speak.

"With pleasure," Rhea answered instead, motioning to the empty spot on their blanket next to Antho. "But do not be deceived. Antho has quick hands. She's a savage player."

"Hardly," Antho demurred, shooting her cousin a furious look. "You will play, too, Ilia?"

"I will keep score."

Rhea turned her body and moved slightly away, pretending to be invested in the outcome of a game of harpastum as Leandros settled down and emptied his sack onto the blanket.

"What a lovely set!" Antho exclaimed, fingering the six-sided pieces.

"I brought them from home," he explained in his deep accented voice. "They were my mother's."

"Did she teach you to play?"

Leandros nodded. "Yes. She always said, 'Leandros, when you play astragaloi, you entrust your fate to Aphrodite!' In Locri, we say a perfect roll is an 'Aphrodite throw.'"

"And Aphrodite is?"

"Our Venus, our goddess of love and beauty."

"I see." She felt her cheeks warm. "And you want to play Aphrodite's game with me?"

The guard, realizing what he had implied, matched Antho's embarrassment with his own. "Not that I meant—it is just a silly game, of course."

"Of course. Very silly."

But they played anyway, and Antho laughed louder than she normally did. This freedom, this honesty, must have alerted her father, for Amulius strode into Antho's line of sight, his face like iron, signifying bars, manacles. Violence. Despite the lilt in her father's gait, he could move with the speed of a raptor when provoked.

The happy smile vanished from her face, and she stood. "Hello, Father."

Leandros shot to his feet.

"Bows need restringing," Amulius said in that soft, humorless, and utterly devastating way.

Leandros rushed off, but not before glancing back at Antho one last time.

I will see you again. We will laugh again.

"You are too idle with your time," Amulius scolded, interrupting her subversive thoughts. "Cavorting with common men in the dirt is beneath you."

"Yes, Father."

"I invited Leandros to play with us," lied Rhea, interceding.

Amulius narrowed his eyes. "And yet I did not see you participate."

Rhea shrugged, unfazed. "Come, Antho, let us cavort with uncommon men, then."

Oh, it was a dangerous game that Rhea played with Antho's father!

While Antho was not as brazen as her cousin, she did find ways to be with Leandros after the festival, in the low times at the Regia—just before dawn, during parties or the chores she was trusted to do unchaperoned. Nobody suspected foul play when Antho requested additional errands, when Antho excused herself from a gathering. Because Antho never misbehaved. And in these stolen moments, she learned all about him: his joys, his ideals, his journey to Alba Longa and painful separation from his parents, who were enslaved in Greece. He listened to her stories in turn. Leandros did not find her boring or dim. He took everything she said seriously.

"I have thought about your lips since the day I first beheld you," he told her one day. "I imagine their sweetness, how they might fit perfectly with mine. May I kiss you, Antho?"

A breathless "Yes."

One kiss and she was his. He was hers.

He made her feel beautiful, made her world beautiful.

Back in the present, Calvus still watched her from the other side of the room. When he caught her eye, his tongue flicked once more between his peeling lips, and she heard him, even over the din of the gathering, the jests and arguments, music and gossip.

"Pretty, pretty girl."

Chapter IX

RHEA

WHEN AMULIUS FINALLY arrived in her rooms, Rhea recognized right away that he was drunk—on wine? on power?

On both.

"Leave," he commanded the servant girls and Helvius, in what was becoming a disturbing pattern. While the guard left with a lurid wink, Zea, Rhea's most loyal attendant, resisted.

"Go," Rhea repeated. *There is nothing more he can do to me,* she might have added.

Zea withdrew reluctantly, mumbling a prayer.

"I have been an excellent brother," commenced Amulius once they were alone. "The most forgiving! Supportive of every foolish decision Numitor made—and there were many. Now it is his turn to play the lesser brother."

Rhea stared silently at the redness in her uncle's normally pallid cheeks.

"You are mad at me for deceiving you, for sending you off with that sanctimonious hag when you are still so young and beautiful."

Still, Rhea kept quiet.

"Say something!" Amulius yelled, slamming his fists against a table. A vase tilted and shattered. Neither of them made a move to pick up its pieces.

"I have nothing to say," Rhea responded tightly. "And there is no need to explain yourself. I do not care."

"Of course you care. Don't lie to me." This was her uncle as she had never seen him before, neither collected nor calculated, nearly raving. Rhea crossed her arms, holding herself, while Amulius paced and muttered.

"Since I cannot marry you myself, there was no other option."

Rhea's fingers gripped her upper arms. Surely, he joked, or he had imbibed even more than she thought. Insults she expected, but this? This was dark; this was wrong.

It was evil.

"It is not evil to want," he concluded, and Rhea wondered if she had spoken aloud—or, worse, if her uncle could read her mind. Would it surprise her if he could?

"It might be," she replied evenly, stepping backward and away from him, "when what you want is not yours."

"You have always been a vain child. Numitor let you believe you were better than any other, that you were the best of us. But I will tell you the truth: You are the daughter of a whore. Your mother lay with me long before she met my older brother."

Liar.

Disrespect my mother again and I'll cut out your tongue.

But that was the reaction he wanted.

"It is not right to defame the dead," she replied instead, struggling to stay indifferent, to maintain her resolve.

"*Defamation* implies that what she and I had together was bad for her. It wasn't." Amulius's nostrils flared, and his eyes shone. "Jocasta was my secret. A nobody princess from a nothing city. And we loved each other. But when my brother discovered her, he could not see reason. He had to have her. She was mine! Numitor was already betrothed!"

"People are not belongings."

So lost in his storytelling, Amulius did not seem to hear her.

"I petitioned our father, telling him everything. And you know what he said to me? 'Stand down, Amulius.' Why couldn't he say as much to Numitor? Why couldn't he say, 'Do not do this to Amulius'?"

"My parents were deeply in love."

"Your greedy mother saw his throne and sold herself for a crown." Amulius paused, his chest rising and falling from the exertion, from the reveal. "I have always wondered if Lausus might have been mine."

"He looked like my father."

"And you look like Jocasta."

As Amulius walked toward Rhea, she retreated, eventually stumbling into the wall. Her back hit the stones, so cool against her flushed skin. Certainly, her uncle could smell her sweat, her fear.

He reached for her hair. "The very same," he murmured, and pressed his body against hers. "I was Jocasta's first kiss."

"So you have said." Rhea shot back, resisting the urge to squirm at his proximity. "And so I must remind you again that my father was her last."

Amulius laughed. "How fun you are sometimes! Rhea, I shall be your first *and* last."

His open mouth attacked hers, tasting of oak and sour grapes, and his hands roamed up her body. She almost detached herself, separated her mind from this assault on her body in an act of defense, but *no*. She would not accept this violation. Her uncle might have lost his mind, but she still had hers. Rhea's teeth clamped down hard on his tongue. Amulius howled and backed away, spitting blood onto the floor.

"Stupid girl." He held up a finger, a warning. "Be grateful I didn't ask for more than a kiss."

"You didn't ask," she snarled, and he slapped her once across the face. Sharp, bright pain, like a bee sting or a burn. She had never been hit in the face before, not by an adult, not even when play fighting with her brothers.

"I used to ask," he seethed. "Now I take."

He picked up one of Rhea's dresses and used it to wipe his mouth, leaving behind a crimson crescent. He dropped the soiled garment on the ground.

"All of this is your mother's fault."

Rhea's eyes narrowed. "Because she found a better man and left you? Do not blame my mother for all you have done and become. That is unfair, even for you."

"You understand nothing besides pride. Your mother never really left me. Who do you think fulfilled her dying wish? I distracted Numitor so Jocasta could escape and die in the woods the way she wanted. *I* heard her last words. *Me.*"

Before Rhea could stop herself, the question slipped through her lips in all its agonizing earnestness: "What were they?"

"You bit me, Rhea. You think I will share them with you now?"

She had never thought herself capable of the visceral hatred she felt at that moment. If she acquiesced to its rage, it would ravage her humanity, peel back her flesh to expose the creature of violence lying beneath, and she would break the world she'd known, the person she thought she was, to pieces.

But she could not forget Mars's counsel: with only her bare hands, she might hurt Amulius, but she would not kill him. Furthermore, an attack on the king would mean her execution and she wasn't ready to die. Not for a few punches and scratches. No, when Rhea laid down her life, she had to know that her enemy was thoroughly humiliated and defeated.

"I will return one day," she vowed. "And I will eat your heart."

She figured Amulius would laugh at her, but he didn't.

"There is nothing left to consume," he said instead, and with that admission, the mania broke like a fever. He became, once more, the uncle she'd always known, masked in sad severity.

"I have spoken with Prisca," Amulius continued, as if he hadn't kissed her, as if nothing strange had occurred. "Tonight, Leandros will escort you into the forest. I would send Helvius, but I cannot trust him alone with you. My virgin niece cannot be sullied."

Her virginity. His victory.

"It is unfortunate that it had to be this way, that you couldn't just die like your brothers."

He sighed, completely unaware that a tiny, seedlike idea was beginning to unfurl in the still-fertile regions of Rhea's wintery brain. Its possibility bloomed, and she gasped, quickly covering her mouth with her hand, lest her uncle see her reaction and suspect.

Yes, it was Amulius of all people who gave her the idea.

"Uncle, I will enter the forest and the temple peacefully. All I ask is that I may bid Antho farewell."

"Would you beg for it?"

Rhea quickly weighed the odds.

"Yes," she finally answered, and she lowered herself to her knees.

Amulius's lip curled in contempt; he threw up a hand. "Off the floor, Rhea. Humility doesn't become you."

She stood, relieved.

"For Antho's sake, not yours, you may say goodbye."

There would be no show of gratitude, for they both knew it would be insincere. Instead, Amulius left and Zea and Helvius returned to their duties. Rhea thought through her mad plan once, twice, a hundred times as she awaited Antho's arrival.

There were no guarantees, but if the cousins could pull off such a scheme?

It might change everything.

Chapter X

ANTHO

AMULIUS THOUGHT THAT by exiling Rhea and her influence, he could reform Antho into a better-behaved daughter.

The opposite was already proving to be true.

She rubbed the bruises along her arm and picked up the pace.

As she snuck through the Regia, holding her sandals in her hands, Antho realized that she had never been so aware of her own breathing. Each inhale, every exhale, sounded like a gust of wind in her surreptitious flight. Silence was paramount, even as she traversed the servants' corridors that led outside the royal complex and onto the streets of Alba Longa. Only then, free at last, did she take a proper breath, exhilarated by her exit's simplicity. Nobody stopped her or came running in her wake because she wasn't on any watch list. For all intents and purposes, Princess Antho slept soundly in her bed.

With or without her cloak pulled up, Antho knew how to be unnoticeable.

She sped past the city walls and all the fields and farms. The long exodus passed quickly, like any task when the mind is elsewhere. Antho barely perceived the changes in terrain, how the trees thickened and the air densified as she moved farther into the early-autumn forest at the base of the hills.

Her earlier conversation with Rhea had been guarded, coded in a way that only two girls who had grown up together could comprehend. Amulius kept spies everywhere, so they had to be vague, but Antho was almost sure she understood the message Rhea delivered between the lines as she bade her a tearful farewell.

Why Rhea made this request, how it—or she—figured into the night's events, remained a puzzle.

Should Antho be caught aiding Rhea in some act against the king, she might as well run away now. But Antho recalled all too vividly the way she had felt when Calvus Flavius leered at her. Exposed. Commodified. Gross. And she remembered how her father had overseen their interaction with his own self-satisfied grin. If Amulius would sell his only child to that decrepit lech for wine and gold, she owed him nothing. Rebellion was warranted.

And she wasn't committing treason; she was just meeting Ilia in the forest. She could always pretend it was a coincidence, right?

Rebellion might be warranted, but she was still a little scared.

Antho halted, at last, in a place she knew from childhood.

Remember the old ironwood tree, where the hops hang? How I wish I could see it one more time.

They used to play here, collect the hops. Lausus and Rhea would compete, climbing higher and higher into the ironwood's branches, slinging taunts at each other. Meanwhile, on the ground below, Antho would tend to Aegestus. He'd let her hold him like a baby, and she would practice being the mother she wanted to have and would one day be.

Antho sat, leaning her back against the tree's mighty trunk, her knees pulled into her chest. All she knew of Rhea's machinations was this, the tree. And afterward? Well, Rhea could have any number of mad ideas in mind. Would she attempt an escape—and what did she expect of Antho?

I cannot say no to her.

Her mother's voice came in ready reply: *Subservient. Submissive. Spineless.*

But *subversion* was certainly not obedience. Antho listened to her parents because she feared them. She would help Rhea because she loved her and because supporting her cousin might ease the guilt she would always carry, the bequeathed burden of her father's betrayal.

And then two figures entered her line of sight: Rhea, holding a torch, beside an armed soldier. As they came closer, Antho overheard Rhea tell her guard, "This is as far as we go."

He replied: "I must escort you to the hallowed grove and spring."

Antho covered her gasp with a hand. Leandros? She hadn't known, hadn't even suspected, that he was assigned to Rhea's watch. Had he always been part of Rhea's plan?

"These are my last hours of freedom," Rhea returned. "I must spend them alone."

"I cannot allow that, Princess."

"You can, and you will."

After listening to their exchange, Antho understood her role. She wasn't called here to be with Rhea but to serve as a distraction. Should she be offended? No, Rhea was using her in a mutually beneficial way.

A night alone with Leandros was more than Antho dared to dream.

"What am I missing?" he questioned. "Why would I do that?"

"Because I will be with you, Leandros."

Antho rose to her feet, letting the cloak fall back, and Leandros finally noticed her presence, cursing under his breath, and glancing back and forth between the cousins in disbelief.

"Let Rhea go," Antho urged. "And be with me."

"Accept this night as my parting gift," added Rhea with a smile, eyes twinkling in the light of her torch.

"It would be negligent . . ." he insisted, but it was a flat protest, lacking substance; Leandros could barely remove his eyes from Antho. "And it is dangerous in the woods."

Rhea demurred. "After the last few days in the Regia, I'll take my chances in the forest."

"If something happens, I will lose my position," he argued, appealing to Antho. "Or my head."

"Ilia, you must promise him—and me—that he will not be held responsible for whatever you intend to do."

"I promise," Rhea vowed, gravely serious, "on the tombs of my brothers, I will not run away. I will not kill myself. Come dawn, I will enter the temple without fuss."

Leandros rubbed his hands across his face, torn and discomforted.

"Rhea would not lie to me, and we haven't much time." Antho pulled away his hands, replacing them with her own, her palms on either of his cheeks. "Let us not waste what is left of this night."

Leandros groaned, but when Antho murmured, "Stay with me, please," his face finally softened. One of his own large hands moved upward, covering Antho's, so gently yet so protectively.

And Antho's heart ached for him, for Rhea, for all of them, doomed as they were.

"I will meet you both here," Rhea concluded, "when the first bird begins its song."

"I pray you find your peace this night, Ilia."

"In my own way."

Antho gave her cousin a small smile. "No other way."

◆ ◆ ◆

"WHAT HAPPENS TO us now?"

"What do you mean?" questioned Antho. A pretense. A platitude.

They walked the woods with hands clasped, fingers intertwined. Never before had Antho and Leandros displayed their affection so openly, and Antho hadn't known that such a freedom could feel so exhilarating, so euphoric.

"Your father is high king. With Rhea a Vestal, your child will become heir to all of Latium."

"I suppose."

He stopped her. "Antho, be serious."

Tears filled her eyes. "Would you have me say what we both already know? I will be married to the man who makes the most strategic alliance for my father. I will leave the Regia and bear children; hopefully, I survive the ordeal." She paused. "Or maybe not. Maybe I will die, and then I won't have to suffer a loveless bed."

Leandros closed his eyes. "Never speak of your death to me. I cannot bear it."

"I cannot bear *this*. Leandros, I want to be with you." She had never expressed herself so ardently before. It was terrifying. It was glorious.

"You are a princess," he replied, quiet and dejected. "I am a Greek soldier in a Latin army. They treat me like a well-trained dog, tolerable only if I follow orders. Stay quiet, keep clean, obey."

"In that way, we are the same." She wrapped her arms around his neck, forcing him to look at her. "Neither of us dreamt tonight could be possible, and yet here we are. Rhea breaks rules and makes things happen, but so can I."

"Antho, this night is exceptional . . ."

"So are we. My father might send me away, but I will always come back. I will always come back for you."

His sadness subsided as he kissed her, as she alleviated his pain, as if she were his sustenance, and she returned his kisses in the same way, for he was her source of strength.

"We will need a signal to meet," Leandros said, when their mouths paused to breathe. "A way to communicate that will not garner notice."

They discussed using the most innocuous items, the least charming locations before settling on a code. A vase in Antho's windowsill meant convening in the larder when the moon was at its highest.

"The larder is hardly romantic," admitted Antho, somewhat shyly, "but it is never used at night."

"I think excitement is romantic," he said, pulling her closer. "And when I am near you, when I get to talk to you, or—gods—touch you, I am overcome with excitement."

She smiled, and he leaned down, placing his mouth just above the curve of her neck, making her skin tingle.

"When I say the words that make you happy," Leandros murmured against her ear, "I feel I've done something heroic."

She shuddered, deliciously, as Leandros lowered them to the ground, bringing Antho into his lap. Though she luxuriated in their closeness, in the open enjoyment of his lips and smell, her mind perseverated on Leandros's words and a subsequent realization: Happiness shouldn't feel heroic. Why had the parameters of her life excluded joy, made delight something she had to steal for herself? Shouldn't happiness be her right as a living, breathing human? If she could, she would shatter the system that restricted happiness. Because it wasn't just about her and Leandros. A generation denied love only perpetuated lovelessness.

"Is something wrong?"

She saw the evident worry in Leandros's face, she felt it in the way he held her. Antho knew she should remain in this moment while it was still hers, not lose herself to larger problems—the roots of all their suffering—but her mind had already traveled too far into that center of crisis.

"Not with you," she replied, resting her head upon his shoulder, "never with you. I was only thinking that the ability to speak freely with you is almost as precious as the space to share my body."

Leandros nodded and pulled back, just enough for Antho to sense a change, a firmness in his resolve.

"I fear I may spoil our night," he admitted, "but there is something I have kept from you, something I can only say outside the Regia's walls."

"You have a wife and children in Greece."

And how did Leandros react to her foolish, besotted outburst? With laughter. Cascades of it, washing away all her anxiety. She could not help but grin.

"Gods, no, Antho! Nothing of the sort."

"Well then, anything else I can certainly handle."

"It is an item, something I have kept on my body since I first discovered it."

Curious, Antho watched his hand reach into the satchel at his side and return in a fist, closed around some object that fit fully within his grip. "Prince Aegestus was wearing this on his toga the day we recovered his caravan."

Leandros's fingers unfurled, and there, on his palm, sat Queen Jocasta's brooch. Three stones for her three children: garnet, amethyst, and moonstone. As luminous, as vital, as ever. Antho's eyes widened.

"If the prince and his men were truly beset by thieves," he added carefully, "why leave such a fortune behind?"

Antho saw where he was going, and though she reined in her galloping heart, hard, she asked the necessary question: "Then who attacked my cousin?"

"I think they were mercenaries, hired to murder in Etruscan masks."

"Why?"

"To destroy a king. To start a war."

And a third unavoidable question, in no more than a hush: "Who do you believe hired them?"

Here, now, was the threshold. What Leandros insinuated was not only treasonous to the Latin king but also slanderous to Antho's father. Leandros was taking a great risk. Would he dare to cross this line, not knowing if Antho would meet him on the other side?

She would not give him the choice.

"You believe this was orchestrated by my father," Antho answered in his stead.

"I do."

She sighed, then said the three words she could never take back: "I do, too."

I think my father had Aegestus killed. I believe it. I know.

My father isn't just mean, isn't just manipulative—he is a murderer.

"I am so sorry," Leandros said, brow furrowed.

"It isn't your fault."

Unhappiness had deformed her father. He had grown up wrong, through some misery or agony that bent his soul more permanently, with more consequence, than could any fractured leg. Forget the limp; beneath his kingly robes was a man composed of scar tissue.

"Will you tell Rhea?"

"Later. This knowledge will only devastate her, and she needs all her strength for what is to come." Antho returned the brooch to Lean-dros's satchel. "Keep it hidden. We will have need of it someday."

"When that someday comes, I will be by your side." He brought her back to his chest, clutching her tighter than before. "And until then, we have the larder."

And despite all the night's dark epiphanies, Antho laughed.

Chapter XI

RHEA

RHEA SILVIA FELT inevitable.

The night thus far had gone to plan. True, Rhea had summoned Antho to the forest with ulterior motives, but she'd left her cousin and Leandros with their fingers interlaced, a picture of precious sweetness. She hoped that meant Antho would forgive her.

For only without a guard could Rhea seek her vengeance against Amulius.

She followed Prisca's directions and easily found the Vestals' sacred altar in a clearing of trees between the Ferentine Spring and a mountain cave. A stone table, nothing ornate. Rhea ran her fingers across its rough, cold surface and found a holding place for her torch, which she stowed there. It hit her then with full force—the emptiness of her hands, the lack of company, her aloneness in her own person, in her one and only life.

She swallowed. Stepped back from the altar and the flame's light. Listened for a woodpecker.

Nothing.

Would he come again?

Might as well fetch the water, then. Rhea retrieved the large earthenware jug from beneath the altar and walked to the spring, an outlet of Lake Nemi. She brought the jug to the stream and crouched down, catching the mild current over the rim, listening to the sibilant whisper of the waterfalls against rock wall. When the vessel was full, she hefted it back to the altar, then set it upon the stone.

The hair on the back of her neck lifted, and gooseflesh prickled her upper arms.

Somebody watched her.

"I know you are here," she called, circling slowly, searching the understory of trees for a specific silhouette.

The wolf passed through the shadows, a sentient, dynamic blackness breaking free.

A wolf like no other, before or again, who walked noiselessly on padded paw despite its enormous size. A galvanizing sight, lifting Rhea's spirits, raising her pulse.

Can a wolf grin?

This one did.

And then the wolf became both something more and something less. Rhea watched in amazement as the beast before her recast himself into the man she'd kissed at the Latin Festival, the one she'd argued with only the day before. Mars, wearing no tunic beneath his black toga, bare chest exposed.

"In the woods," rasped his voice as it resumed human form, "it isn't safe to be so lovely and so alone."

"I'm not alone. You are here."

"Indeed, I am. Yet you remain unafraid. No mortal could stare war in the face like you do."

For he was a predator, she could not forget. Surely he noticed the intensity of her heartbeats, how his nearness heightened her senses—the hitch of her breath, the scent, the heat of her own skin.

"I become a Vestal tomorrow," she told him.

Mars scowled. "It will be a waste of you. Like telling a lion to be a barn cat."

She wore his praise like armor; it made her bold.

"You told me to call when I needed something you could provide." Rhea wet her lips, suddenly dry, with the tip of her tongue. "I will not go a virgin."

First an eyebrow lifted, then a lazy smile. "Ah."

"My uncle would control me, would take away my choices." She stood straight, as tall as she could be—which was negligible beside his imposing height. "I want you to lie with me. Tonight. Now."

"Here I was, daring to hope for a goodnight kiss."

"I do not jest."

Mars pulled her to him like the moon tugs the tides, like they themselves were a force of nature. He tucked a piece of her hair behind her ear, searching her face for any doubt. "Then you are certain?"

Rhea felt she had been perfectly clear, but to demonstrate her seriousness, she let her simple dress fall to the ground, puddling at her feet. When she stepped out of it—baring everything to him, offering all—his eyes widened, and a flash of wolf betrayed his countenance, a momentary blend of man and beast that Rhea found particularly thrilling.

"I didn't know human girls did things like this."

"Human girls are more capable than most."

She kissed him first, to replace the one from the night before, but as Mars hungrily accepted her mouth and her body, any memories of the Regia dissipated. The god of war moaned into her neck, by her own invitation; Rhea Silvia was invincible.

The kisses continued—lengthening, deepening—until her legs were lifting and Mars was carrying her into a cave. Thick furs covered the floor—had any of this been here when she arrived?—and she was on her back, Mars growling into her ear: "You are so beautiful."

It hurt for one moment, two, but passed. Rhea's tolerance for pain, in all its forms, had strengthened with her resolve. She approached their joining with a kind of fascination.

I am doing this.

With him.

And afterward they wandered down to the spring to bathe, submerging themselves fully in the cool waters. Rhea thought he might be done with her now that it was over, now that she was no longer a maiden, but he could not keep his hands from her, reaching for her waist as she swam languorous laps around him, long hair floating in her wake.

The moon was still high, and it reflected on the surface. She swam into its light, claimed its shine for herself.

"How do you feel?" Mars asked.

"Fine," she answered honestly. "I only thought it would be . . ." She paused, searching for the right word. "*More.*"

"More," he repeated incredulously.

"More worth risking everything." For she was familiar with the great love affairs of the past, recalled how Dido self-immolated after losing Aeneas, how Paris started a war for Helen.

Mars stiffened. He turned away.

She had upset him.

"It was nice!" she insisted, inwardly cringing at that ingrained pressure to always be polite, to coddle the feelings of others—even when those others were infinitely more powerful.

"Nice?!" He whirled back around, and the look on his face was so charmingly boyish that Rhea couldn't help but giggle. She clapped a hand over her mouth.

"And then she laughs." He narrowed his eyebrows to a dangerous point. "You are a difficult woman, Rhea Silvia." And he traversed the water between them, head lowered like a crocodile, his desire chasing her through the water. She bit her bottom lip when he caught her.

"Come," he demanded, and his voice was deliciously rough. "Let me show you why men and women risk everything."

And he showed her.

Oh, how he showed her.

◆ ◆ ◆

BACK IN THE cave, Rhea spent the last moments of moonlight naked on a wolfskin with her god. They lay on their sides staring at each other, and Rhea promised herself she would remember every detail: the stretch of skin over taut muscle, hair falling across those burning eyes. How he smelled of fire and salt.

"I suppose we made two enemies tonight," she confessed, watching their fingers play in the space between them. "My uncle and Vesta."

"Nobody will fault me for what we did here, Rhea. Only you."

She fell onto her back and looked fixedly at the granite rock above. The world worked in the same way for mortals and gods. If their affair was discovered, Mars would be irreproachable. A god doing as a god does, the prototype, the aspiration, of every human man. But Rhea would be ruined. A whore—like her mother, if Amulius was to be believed.

"I can handle what may come."

"I am glad my son will have such a strong mother."

Rhea shot up. "Your *son?*"

There had been many shocks over the past ten days—reveals and disappointments and heartbreaks that made her cry, made her angry. But this? Rhea nearly laughed aloud. Here she was, at the apex of comedy and tragedy: a virgin potentially carrying a god's baby, a woman so bent on revenge that she had cursed herself in the process.

How did I fail to consider this possibility? Why did it never enter my mind?

"I can't be pregnant after one time!" she proclaimed in abject denial. Mars raised an eyebrow, and Rhea sighed, correcting herself. "Alright, many times. But only one night."

Mars laid a reverent kiss against her navel, but it failed to appease her. "Men pray to me for virility. We will see soon enough if my reputation holds."

Oh, she was the worst sort of fool! *There are consequences to lying with men,* she scolded herself. *Obvious ones.*

Obvious ones she had clearly ignored.

(*You knew,* a tiny voice insisted. *You always knew. Your revenge was twofold.*)

She would ignore this, too.

"And then what am I to do?"

"I am an immortal, Rhea. Humanity's standards do not concern me."

Rhea pushed him away from her stomach.

He frowned. "You cannot understand my existence."

"No more than you understand mine."

"As I have said before, if there is something I can provide, you may call upon me. I will come if I can."

Vague half pleas and half promises. An incomplete conversation about a dreaded hypothetical that intersected two incongruent worlds. But more than enough damage was done. The mirage faded: this was not love, nor was it lasting. The cave was too warm, too cloying, and Rhea too wracked with nerves. She began the search for her dress. "I must meet my cousin."

Mars sighed. He rubbed the palms of his hands against his eyes.

"Will you regret me?" he wondered aloud.

Soft words from a hard man; they moved her. Rhea dropped once more to her knees beside him, grazed her nails against his chest, and lowered her face to his. "You have made me more animal than not tonight, and beasts do not repent."

He laughed, low in his throat. "Beautiful mortal girl."

She nodded and stood, dressed now in the drab gown of a penitent. She pushed that long, important hair back behind her shoulders and walked out into the almost dawn.

And she refused to look back.

Chapter XII

NUMITOR

THE KING—THE *former* king—slept. For too long he had carried on without realizing his exhaustion. But the bone-weariness had steadily accumulated for years and years, and now he was too far in its debt. Numitor was tired—from bearing the crown, from years of living under the legacy of Troy's greatest soldier and Latium's greatest queen, from surviving while his most beloved died. His shoulders slumped like a much older man's. Inheritance is a weight; family, an anchor. Both weighed him down.

And that was before he was worn to the bone by grief—over his wife, his sons.

And now over Ilia.

Dead. Killed. Taken.

In pitiful moments, he wondered what he had ever done to merit such woe. But this line of thinking led only to pointless conjecture. There was no cosmic equation, no balance between justice served and justice done. He had tried to do right by his people. He'd listened to the augur, his council, his dreams. Honored the gods in the ways he'd been taught.

Regardless, this had brought suffering.

Once, he had loved being king almost as much as he loved his family. But now he was done with both. It felt nice to sleep. And didn't he deserve a bit of rest?

Dear Sethre and his tonics—elixirs of peace!

When Numitor drank, he felt nothing. That was bliss; that was paradise. Not excess but its opposite. An abdication of emotion. He forgot it all—his people, his duties, even his hunger. Who needed food? Another foul obligation of the flesh. He was done with love and lust in all its permutations. He had transcended.

Numitor settled into his bed of wools and dreamed of sheep, soft and meek. But a wild dog with Ilia's eyes came and barked in his ear.

Wake up! or *Notice me!* or *Help!*

She is the strong one, said a sheep.

She doesn't need you, bleated another.

She is safe.

Good, good. He rolled over, away from the canine and its anxiety. The right choice—for him, for now—for it was easiest.

His obsession: ease.

Easing of pressure. Easing into stasis.

Is it easier to remember truth or lies? It is easiest to remember nothing at all.

His mind was liquid, his human form blurred. There were no more edges; everything was soft.

Numitor disappeared.

Chapter XIII

RHEA

THE COUSINS REUNITED in the mists of morning, cutting through the forest fog to clasp each other. Bodies that had slept beside each other, played together, grown together, held each other for years and years. Bodies that bore a unique empathy, an infinite, innate understanding of the other, one born of shared blood and circumstance.

I will miss you.

Do not leave me.

Can I do this without you?

I cannot do this without you.

Once Rhea let go, she would release not only Antho but everything this moment represented. They would never be these two women again. When they met next, they would surely be different. Changed by experiences neither could comprehend. Strangers. So she held Antho tighter, at the edge of the woods, beneath that ironwood tree. Rhea clung to the only remaining soul who understood her childhood in the Regia.

This goodbye, away from Amulius's eyes and spies, was Rhea's wish; she hadn't anticipated its difficulty.

Finally, Rhea stepped away. She cleared her throat and pulled her shoulders back, hoping that was enough to relay her message: *Antho, be strong. If you break, I will, too.*

Antho nodded, understanding. She sniffled but held back her tears. "Was it good to be alone?" she asked, ever polite.

"Yes." A simple answer for the most complicated night. "Was it good to be together?"

"I love him, Ilia," Antho replied softly, shooting a look backward to where Leandros waited, scanning the road, running a hand through his thick hair.

"Then find a way to be together!" Rhea leaned forward, knowing that the impending separation gave more import to each word. "Cling to this love, Antho. Let them pry it from your bloody fingers."

"I am. I will. I promise."

"Soldiers approach."

Rhea followed Leandros's line of view to a distant party of approaching soldiers. Even from this far away, she could distinguish the full panoply, and . . .

"Is that a donkey?" Antho asked.

"One final humiliation," Rhea replied, steeling herself.

"You must leave, Antho," Leandros entreated. "Now, before you are seen."

Antho turned to her cousin, tear stricken.

"Do not say goodbye to me," Rhea warned, holding up a hand. "I cannot handle it."

Antho pulled the hood of her cloak back over her head.

"Go!" Leandros demanded, and Antho fled, as light on her feet as a deer under pursuit.

Thank you, Rhea thought, eyes closed. *Be safe.*

The guards arrived soon after, grunting greetings to Leandros. Helvius grinned at Rhea and gestured to the donkey.

"Our wise king thought you might be tired from your night of prayer and arranged for a ride, one befitting your humble new station."

But Rhea only smiled, forfending the insult, because her legs *were* tired and the thought of Amulius knowing why brought her great mirth. Her secret was her strength; knowledge gave her courage.

Rhea strode forward, stroked the creature's gray muzzle. "The donkey is Vesta's chosen animal," she explained, "for it turns the millstone, grinding the grain for the bread baked in the sacred hearth. He and I will make a blessed entrance. How thoughtful."

She would undermine every cruelty they showed her.

Keep them coming. Rhea smirked. *I am quite at my leisure.*

A consummate bully, however, is not so easily deterred. "From the battle stallion to a barnyard ass . . ." Helvius whistled. "The children of Numitor have fallen."

Rhea rolled her eyes. "Oh, the only ass here is you, Helvius. And we are all so tired of your braying."

Ursan coughed into his hand while Helvius sputtered.

Rhea mounted the creature without assistance, trying her best to appear dignified. She tapped her heels against the beast's ribs, urging him forward, but he would not budge.

Oh, you stubborn beast! Not now!

But before she could panic, Leandros came forward and slapped the donkey's rump, prompting him into a steady walk. The soldiers fell into line behind her.

"The king instructed us to use force if you resist," Helvius announced, his voice creeping across Rhea's back like the insect he was.

"There is no need for threats."

And because she presented herself so peacefully, he was forced to pivot, to change the angle of his attack.

"How old will you be when your commitment is complete? Fifty? Rhea, the crone." Helvius grimaced, his scarred lip twisting his face into a grotesque visage. "Old hags are barely more attractive than lepers."

Fifty. A crushing reality. She would not enjoy another night with a man until she was *fifty*. But that was Amulius's intention: Rhea would be released from service when she could no longer bear a child. To him, she wasn't a woman, a conscious person with a heart and mind. She was just a womb.

"And where will you be in thirty years, Helvius?" Rhea quipped.

"At home with children who despise you? With a wife forced to lift your wine belly to locate your limp manhood?"

Ursan winced. "Princess . . ." he cautioned, for Helvius had pulled a dagger from his side.

"She's no princess," Helvius spat, with a hatred so thick, so tangible, that he nearly choked upon it.

"What would you do?" Leandros interceded. "Stab her? In full daylight, before us all? Be reasonable."

Helvius glared at the Greek guard but lowered his dagger.

"So angry," Rhea tutted.

Too soon, far too soon, the Temple of Vesta came into view. Round and austere, with the more modest House of the Vestals tucked behind it. Five women waited at the bottom of the steps leading to the wooden portico. They were cantillating—Vesta this and Vesta that—all robed in identical white dresses, with white wool scarves wrapped several times about their heads.

"Eerie," Ursan muttered.

Rhea recognized Prisca, but the others were strangers. Two were much older than Rhea, and two seemed of similar age.

Her new family, the head priestess had said. Her eerie new family.

The benedictions ended, and the priestesses greeted her with a line of compulsory smiles—all except one. A young woman with mousy brown hair, cut just below her ears. She held a ceremonial bowl of fire, and her scowl burned through the flickering flames.

Such hostility! Who was this girl? Was Rhea's name alone so ignominious, so inspiring of contempt?

Rhea dismounted the donkey and passed the lead rope to Leandros. She brushed her hands down the front of her shift, smoothing and dusting, for something to do. The guards and priestesses regarded one another, Rhea standing awkwardly in between.

"Four soldiers," Prisca said dryly. "This is a first."

"King's orders."

Prisca turned to Rhea, inspected her from toe to head. "Do you breathe fire or fly? Does your gaze turn mortal men to stone?"

Rhea stifled a grin. "No, I am only an ordinary woman."

Difficult, Mars had called her, with delight.

"You may all go home," Prisca informed the guards. "I think we Vestals can handle this ordinary woman on our own."

Leandros and the others seemed relieved to be finished with their odious chore, but Helvius faltered, frustrated. Cruel, simple men need the last word, but even boorish Helvius didn't dare make a final jab in this holy space.

Rhea caught Leandros's eyes before he departed, conversing in the way of two people with a shared secret.

Love her for me.

Always.

"Come." Another priestess beckoned, laying a hand on Rhea's arm, and Rhea turned away from her past, allowing it to recede as she followed the line of white robes into her future.

"We won't perform introductions in public like some gauche theater," a third priestess informed her.

They led Rhea into their house. Inside the vestibule, the five women removed their headscarves and shared their names.

Prisca, unquestionably the eldest.

Horatia of the silver hair.

Valeria with the ready smirk.

Aemilia, who had the kindest eyes.

And frowning, fuming Tavia.

"I am Rhea," she added unnecessarily.

"I must ask you about last night," Prisca said, and Rhea's fists clenched, her fingernails imprinting waning crescents onto her palms. For the first time, she wondered if the Vestals sent spies to the sacred grove. If so, she was doomed already. Rhea prepared herself for interrogation, quickly readying her lies, her defenses, her excuses.

"You prayed?"

To war.

Rhea nodded.

"You bathed?"

With him.

A nod.

"And washed your hair?"

Her head arched backward when his hands found her under the surface.

"Yes, High Priestess."

Prisca clucked, and Rhea eased the tension in her hands. Her answers were accepted so easily. Maybe she was wrong to judge these women, this life. Perhaps this was a warm home, trusting and fair—a burgeoning hope further nurtured by friendly, young Aemilia, who guided Rhea in a brief tour of the house. There was a kitchen and a garden. Hens and goats and plants to tend. A small bathhouse.

Here is where we eat, where we pray, where we sleep.

We.

There were three bedrooms. "The largest is for Prisca and Horatia," Aemilia explained, "for they have been here the longest. Next is Valeria, who is in her second decade of service."

Rhea frowned, confused by the hierarchy.

"In a Vestal's first ten years, she learns her duties," Aemilia continued patiently. "In the next ten, she does what she has learned. And in the final ten, she teaches others."

"You and Tavia are in your first decade," Rhea said.

"Yes," Amelia answered. "And we will share our room with you. I have served longer than Tavia. I will begin my second decade and move in with Valeria soon."

The mention of decades sent Rhea's head spinning. That, combined with lack of sleep, made her dizzy, made her legs shake.

"Oh, but you have gone pale! Sit for a moment." Aemilia brought her to the third room, pointing to a bed near the window. "That will be yours."

Rhea sat, ran her hands along the thin blanket. She struggled to remember the name Prisca had mentioned, the name of the dead girl, and then it came. "Was this where Musa slept?"

"You do not get to speak of her."

Rhea whirled. Tavia stood in the doorway.

"I was only asking a question."

"And the answer does not concern you."

Aemilia's jaw dropped. "Tavia, don't—"

But Tavia paid her no mind. She stepped into the room, steaming, boiling over with heated hate. "You could never replace her."

"If you expect me to apologize for my presence," Rhea replied, standing, "I will not."

"I expect nothing from a royal. They don't acknowledge their selfishness or greed. They only take."

"Tavia!" Aemilia chastised again, but her dismay did little to mitigate the other priestess's anger.

"Titles and ancestors mean nothing here. *You* are nothing here."

Certainly, no other woman had dared speak to Rhea with such cruel candor. Though shocked, Rhea felt more irritated than infuriated. Tavia was a gnat compared with a venomous snake like Amulius. So Rhea chuckled, softly under her breath, and closed the distance between them, hoping haughtiness would add a few inches. Though they were of the same age, Tavia was much taller. Might this come to blows? Rhea had wrestled her brothers before.

And won.

"You cannot hurt me," she purred, almost smiling.

It would become Rhea's first mistake. Because Tavia returned the smile.

"I hope I won't." Tavia raised the knife she'd hidden behind her back. "Because Prisca has tasked me with cutting your hair."

❖ ❖ ❖

IT IS ONLY hair. Just hair.

And what is hair? It is neither person nor memory, neither an identity nor a lifeline.

Only hair.

And yet this was the most distraught she'd felt since Amulius had announced her fate.

"It will grow back," Aemilia murmured, as she oversaw Tavia's hacking.

Rhea could not respond, for tears threatened, and she would not cry before these strangers. Everything about this situation hurt. Tavia pulled Rhea's head back so severely that her neck screamed. A piercing agony shot through her skull as her hair was ripped out by its roots.

Aemilia gasped. "Tavia, enough! She's bleeding."

Tavia only grunted, tossing handfuls of deep-brown hair and their bloody ends to the floor. Aemilia quickly swept them up, whispering, "Stop this. Let me do it."

But then Aemilia was called away by Horatia, leaving Rhea and Tavia alone in their new rivalry.

"Nobody wants you here."

Rhea laughed. "Myself included."

"You don't believe in our work. I can tell by the look on your face."

"You can no more judge a heart by a face than you can judge a mind by a head of hair."

Tavia yanked, the blade sliced, and Rhea's last lock hit the floor.

◆ ◆ ◆

RHEA WAS BROUGHT to a spartan room to fast and pray until night fell, and her initiation ceremony commenced. She had nothing to say to Vesta. Instead, Rhea curled inward on herself upon the stone floor like a cat.

A hairless one.

She clutched her knees to her chest. Alone at last, she abandoned the bravado; Rhea had never felt so small. The Vestals were about to take her name and her body and her next thirty years.

Also, she was dreadfully hungry.

"You are Rhea Silvia," she murmured, cheek pressed against tile. "Then, now, and forever."

She must have fallen asleep, for she woke to a sharp kick in her stomach. Rhea groaned. Tavia stood over her holding a lamp, face illuminated like one of Pluto's foul creatures from the underworld.

"Get up. It's time."

Tavia tossed down a veil.

"Cover your head. It's unsightly."

They did not speak as Tavia led Rhea through the House of the Vestals and outside into the night. When the evening air hit her skin, Rhea felt the urge to run, a tickling, tingling, and thrilling call to freedom.

But Rhea did not flee. She allowed herself to be brought to the temple like a sacrificial bull. The other four Vestals waited at its steps like somber statues, laurel crowns holding veils over their own faces, made uniform through ritual and role. Rhea could hardly tell them apart, a disconcerting observation. Soon outsiders might say the same of her.

One form came forward, and when she spoke, Rhea recognized Prisca's airy voice.

"I take you, Rhea Silvia, into our temple for the most hallowed of our rites. I take you to your vows, to the sisterhood therein, and the goddess herself."

Unsure of the decorum, Rhea bowed.

"As you enter the atrium of Vesta, you emancipate yourself from your father and forefathers. You rescind your name and royalty. You will be Rhea only. A priestess. And one of ours."

A tickle, a tingle. A thrill.

She would find her freedom again, no matter what they called her.

Rhea Silvia followed the Vestals into their temple.

Chapter XIV

ANTHO

CHANGES AT THE Regia occurred in the same creeping manner as aging. No person notices the slow spread of wrinkles until they are nearly wizened, for time is easy to track by the steady sun's rise and fall, but far more difficult to register on the body; the act of living is so all-consuming that only on the day one is forced to stop and consider how their reflection has changed do they understand that they are old.

Amulius's tenure as king began as a natural response to a pressing need, not as a cataclysmic shift. The earth did not break its relationship with the skies, life continued, and the people kept so busy that nobody noticed the changes until they were done, cracks in the firmament, built into the day.

In short, everyone went back to work.

But nothing escaped Antho, the people's remaining princess. She noticed it all. With each update and upgrade, she anxiously calculated the cost. With every turn of phrase or shift in tone, she analyzed the ulterior meaning.

And when Rhea's belongings were moved to her bedroom, Antho wept, bereft.

"I don't want these," she told Zea and Gratia, Zea's mother, through her tears.

Old Gratia held Antho tight, rubbed circles on her back. "Sweet girl, where else would they go?"

There had been four heirs, and now there was one. Antho remained, the vessel holding all hopes for the future, and she had never been more miserable.

This is all so disingenuous, Antho thought, over and over, with increasing urgency. *How does nobody else see it? Feel it?*

For power alone could not sate her greedy parents; they were creating a legacy. And everything that followed the acquisition of their kingdom felt contrived in the same way.

Queen Claudia celebrated her promotion with coin. A new wardrobe featuring expensive dyes. Commissions for tapestries and pottery. Phoenician cists and silver dishes from Cyprus. The Regia was redecorated to fit an aesthetic of luxury, of modernity, and Antho recoiled at her mother's repeated—and favorite—explanation: "Jocasta was lovely herself but lacked any sense of style." Then came the obligatory laughs, the murmured agreement. "Yes, yes, Queen. So true!"

All of this was paid for with the king's treasury, with increased taxes on imports and exports, with more and more resources being claimed for Alba Longa and the reputation of Latium.

As for Antho's father, well, King Amulius's priority was simple: the supremacy of Alba Longa. His city must reign premier.

Antho watched how he set his plans into motion and marveled at his ingenuity, just as she cringed at the artifice. Incentives were offered for innovations, for discovery. Latium needed to produce more copper and iron and tin to compete with the foreign market. Rumors of external threats spread—the Etruscans! the Aequi! the Volsci! the Sabines!—which merited an expansion of the royal guard. There were more skirmishes along the borders, more raids. Battles brought bounty—enslaved people and loot. Amulius made speeches lauding the "Latin glory in death."

Antho disagreed. She didn't think death meant anything. Life, however, might—if you could use it in the pursuit of something good and true. Antho was eighteen years old, subsisting under parents whose values were completely antithetical to her own, so she survived in the best way she could: by armoring herself in honesty and kindness. She controlled so little in her life—not her clothes or her diet, her activities or her surroundings—but despite their best efforts, the queen and king could not choreograph her core self.

And to remind herself that she was real, she met Leandros in the larder.

It took all Antho's willpower not to raise the sign every night. But he mattered too much; she had to exercise caution. In the storeroom, they shared words, their bodies—but not too far, never to the point where Antho would be changed.

"I don't care," she insisted, clinging to him. "Ruin me."

Ruined was real, at least.

"I care. Your father will punish you in ways I am loath to imagine."

And he will punish you, too. It went without saying, but if she lost Leandros after losing Rhea—her sun and her moon—she would surely float away. Dandelion fluff, indifferent to gravity. Drifting and done. So Antho was careful. Quiet. Kept her midnight rendezvous to a minimum.

She thought her subterfuge successful until one horrid day when the vase went missing. Panicked, her heart aflutter, Antho scoured her rooms, under the bed, in her chests. Questioned every servant.

"Your mother, the queen, took it," Zea confided. Sick with foreboding, Antho went to her mother to receive her sentence. Claudia held court at her loom, shattered pieces of Antho's clay vase scattered across the floor. Claudia did not look up from her weaving.

"The vase broke, Antho, and it will stay broken."

Though Antho's voice trembled, she kept her back straight, her chin up. "It meant something to me."

"It is just a vase, and you are an incredibly stupid little girl."

She could almost hear Rhea's voice in her mind, could almost find comfort in her cousin's confident rebuttal: *You are not stupid, Antho. Do not let them use your youth or sex to disparage your value.* But Antho bowed her head. "I am sorry, Mother."

Claudia set down her shuttle. Her mouth stretched so tightly that her lips nearly disappeared. "Are you still a maiden?"

The question scalded, leaving Antho raw and exposed and *angry.*

How dare her mother pry and judge! She did not ask because she cared about Antho's well-being; Claudia's only concern was the commodification of Antho's body—the return she would make on her daughter's innocence. A rebellious part of Antho longed to lie, just to see her mother's reaction when those matrimonial schemes collapsed, but Antho was too conditioned to behave. She told the truth. "Yes."

Some of the tension left her mother's jaw. "You will not see that man again."

"Will you tell my father?"

"I already have."

Later that night, King Amulius entered his daughter's room carrying a flute.

"Calvus has requested you learn to play this instrument."

Antho stiffened. "I play the lyre quite well."

Amulius slapped the flute against the back of her head. The unexpected impact threw Antho to the floor, and she covered her head with her arms as she sobbed.

"Alba Longa needs Calvus's wealth to remain in our city. Did you know he speaks with fathers across many lands? He could take his wines and gold to Aricia or Laurentum. He is a desirable man."

"He is disgusting," Antho attested.

Her father crouched beside her, brushing back her hair from her eyes, her ears. "You will make yourself attractive to Calvus. You will master the flute. You will accept his petting, and you will marry Calvus, or I will have the Greek guard killed."

The tears she'd held at bay released and Antho raised an imploring hand. "Please do not hurt Leandros. Send him away if you must, but I beg you, do not harm him."

Amulius's lip curled. "You thought I would send him away?" He chucked softly. "No, I will keep him close to keep you in order."

My father has never loved me, Antho realized with some astonishment. *But why does he hate me so much?*

"I will do whatever you ask to keep him safe."

"Yes." Her father smiled, a cat with a bird. "I can see that you will."

Chapter XV

RHEA

THUS BEGAN RHEA'S life as a priestess.

There were temple chores and house chores, day and night. Though strict, Prisca was hardly a tyrant, for she was no disrupter, just a product of a system. Prisca, not unlike Claudia, knew one way of living; she repeated the lifestyle passed down to her by the Vestals before, likening herself to some avian mother, calling them all her little birds, her starlings—even Horatia, who couldn't have been much younger than Prisca herself.

Of greatest import was tending the perpetual fire, Vesta's eternal flame, in the temple's hearth. It was dull, hot work, with constant sweeping—a never-ending fire creates a never-ending supply of ash. Rhea spent most of her days covered in soot, a grimy, gritty second skin. It burrowed beneath her fingernails; she found it in her teeth. If she still had hair, it would surely smell of constant smoke. She could almost pretend to be glad she was bald.

Almost.

Besides fire tending, there was the daily cleansing of ceremonial objects. Sweeping out the storehouse. Fetching water from the sacred spring—the same one where she had met Mars—for ritual sprinkling and purifying. Baking the salt cakes used as offerings. Roasting and grinding the parched spelt, the wheat grown in the Alban Mountains, into flour. As the resident novice, Rhea was tasked with the most physically demanding and noxious chores. She cleaned the henhouse. She prepared food for the goats and milked the ornery beasts. Her work started so early in the morning that by night she collapsed upon her thin cot and slept like the dead. For this alone, she was grateful to Vesta.

Because when Rhea wasn't sufficiently exhausted or distracted, her mind inevitably narrowed in one of two directions. The first? Revenge fantasies, ruminating on the many glorious ways she could ruin Amulius's life. It always began as an entertaining pastime, picturing her uncle covered in oozing boils, chained to Prometheus's rock, or cut into thirty-odd pieces and sent to every city in the Latin League. But such imaginings eventually ended in frustration. Rhea, trapped in a holy prison, with no money or weapons of her own, had as much opportunity to kill the high king of Latium as a domesticated goat.

The second train of thought began with a memory: *She was my secret . . . And we loved each other.* Were her uncle's accusations true or just another manipulation? Had her mother truly lain with Amulius in their youth? Did her father know? Worst of all, had Jocasta loved Amulius in return? Had her uncle received her mother's last words when Rhea hadn't even received a goodbye?

How could Rhea ever reconcile what she thought she knew about her parents with what she had learned?

Stop, she would scold herself. *You cannot change what happened, so don't perseverate on the past.* But the past persisted regardless; it mattered. Whatever had occurred between her mother and uncle had polluted Amulius against them all. Wasn't Rhea here, scrubbing temple floors on raw knees, to clean up her mother's mess?

It is a turning point in every young person's life when they realize that the generation before them is composed of complicated, fallible people. Rhea had always taken it for granted that her elders were intelligent and capable, in full control of their decisions and the consequences. But her illusions had cracked open like a bird's egg. Age and birth order don't guarantee wisdom. The people Rhea assumed knew what to do were guessing their way through life, as well; she had placed her confidence in a charade.

To be human meant pretending that you weren't fumbling, that you didn't see the others when they slipped.

And Rhea had never been a good actress.

◆ ◆ ◆

BEFORE BECOMING A Vestal Virgin, Rhea had given the order little consideration. The Vestals were religious ornaments to her, not blood-and-bone women. Such a dismissal embarrassed her now, for the priestesses were vibrant personalities, each with a distinct story.

Slowly, piece by piece, she learned more about their individual histories. To be accepted into the Vestals, a girl had to be freeborn, from a respectable line, and possessed of no physical or mental defects. Joyful Aemilia had been sent to the Vestals because her parents—an old Alban family—simply had an abundance of children. Tavia had been promised in an oath: her desperate father pledging her to Vesta if the goddess would bless him with a son. Valeria, with her acerbic tongue, had been conscripted into the order by a greedy brother who refused responsibility for her dowry. Horatia, considered too ugly for marriage, had waited and waited for a proposal that never came, then found a home here instead. And Prisca, the priestess who chose to stay, had been there for nearly fifty years and remembered no other life.

"Vestals are the best of Latium," Prisca liked to say.

"No sinners, no fornicators," Horatia added.

Horatia's mantra, her favorite phrase, made the others smile (Valeria with a roll of her eyes), but Rhea always pretended not to hear. She had sinned, she had fornicated, and yet she was here, worshipping in their temple, living in their house, as an initiated priestess. The fire reminded her of Mars, not Vesta. When she recited her prayers, she thought of the war god touching her in the forest. A Vestal is supposed to dedicate herself to the safety of the city and its people, but Rhea continued to romanticize danger.

She might not be a good actress, but she was certainly a fraud.

At night, when Aemilia slept, Tavia whispered across the space of their beds to Rhea's waiting ear: "You think of this place as an asylum, but it is not. It is an institution and there are rules, there are terrible repercussions for Vestals who misbehave. Naked skin whipped with laurel branches. Beatings until you forget your own name, deny your own body."

"Your bedtime stories leave much to be desired," Rhea returned, dryly.

But Tavia wasn't finished. She lifted herself up on her elbows, angling her body so that Rhea could better see her face in the room's scant moonlight.

"For the worst transgressors, there is a special punishment." One side of Tavia's mouth curved upward in fiendish glee. "You cannot kill a Vestal directly, for the body has been blessed with sacred oil, but there are other, more sinister ways to kill a woman.

"Vestals found to be unchaste are brought into a subterranean chamber. The ladder is drawn and the priestess left with only a bed, a cup of milk and water, bread, and an oil lamp. There she must live until the food is gone, the liquids consumed, and the oil burned." Tavia's voice was soft and light, a voice most appropriate for soothing a child in the night, not delivering violent messages. "In the dark, she will exist—for how could it be considered living?—until, starving and thirsty, her body begins to collapse. And it will be so slow, so excruciating. But because she is alone, no one will hear her beg for the merciful blade to hasten her own death."

"You find delight in women brutalizing other women, Tavia? I thought you believed in sisterhood."

Tavia bristled. "I believe in justice."

Justice. Rhea snorted at the word, then yawned, feigning ambivalence, a royal nonchalance she certainly did not feel. "Perhaps tomorrow night I shall tell you the stories of my grandfather's grandfather, Allocius, the vilest king in Alba Longa's history. You Vestals have a lot to learn about depravity."

But Tavia's account chilled Rhea to the bone. If Prisca or the others checked her body, it would be clear that she was no longer a virgin. What if Tavia suspected and voiced those suspicions? Amulius would not intervene on her behalf; in fact, he'd probably be delighted with a death sentence for which he would bear no direct blame.

A long, drawn-out death sentence.

Tavia couldn't know; it was not possible. Rhea's vivid imagination betrayed her, for Rhea had not dropped a single hint, and she never would. She turned in her cot, away from Tavia, and traced the curves and lines of her stomach—still small and firm. Everything was fine; she was fine. Nobody got pregnant after one night. It had taken her aunt Claudia years to conceive Antho!

Still, relaxation was inconceivable when she recalled Mars's boasts of virility.

When Rhea did sleep, she entered a dreary dreamscape of dirt and fire, choking on both.

◆ ◆ ◆

TAVIA AND AEMILIA performed different tasks than Rhea, ones commensurate with their rank and experience. These responsibilities took them off the Vestal property, much to Rhea's envy. But one day, Prisca, whether by an act of obliviousness or sly observation, assigned Rhea to help.

"Accompany Tavia on her errands today, starling. It'll be good for you to see."

Rhea's excitement over a change in scenery neutralized her distaste for the selected company. Any place besides the henhouse sounded like a grand time, even if she had to go there with the least fun person in the history of Latium.

"I don't need your help," Tavia snipped as she finished loading the cart they would pull through Alba Longa.

"The high priestess clearly disagrees."

Tavia laughed. "That's not what this is about, you fool. She's teaching you a lesson."

It'll be good for you to see.

And that easily, Rhea's high spirits plummeted.

Tavia offered no explanations as they departed the temple grounds, and Rhea would not give her any satisfaction by showing trepidation or asking further questions. Soon enough, their task became obvious: the priestesses were delivering food to people in need. Rhea settled into smug complacency. This wasn't scary! Still, Rhea let Tavia do most of the talking, not just because she was new to all this but because *she was new to all this*. To her chagrin, Rhea knew precious little about poor people, had barely interacted with any in her life, and that awareness created an uncomfortable distance.

And if Rhea felt awkward and ignorant, it was her own fault. She had never tried to understand the people outside the Regia; she had always assumed that some people had less because they didn't work as hard as her own family did, or simply weren't as worthy of the gods' favor. But those suppositions went up in smoke like softwood. The Latins she met that day either had employment that paid them unlivable wages or could not work due to circumstances beyond their control. A Latin doing their best and unfairly tossed aside by the people in charge.

For instance:

A man with a cane. "Iulius worked in the vineyards," Tavia began, offering explanations in a somber tone, "but after an ox trampled his leg, he could not move fast enough to meet daily quotas. Calvus Flavius let him go and replaced him with an enslaved Aequian, a prisoner of war gifted to him by the Regia."

A woman, half-asleep and filthy, huddled in a shaded space between two shops. "Drusilla grew up in the brothels, becoming dependent upon wine as a young girl. She fell asleep halfway through one of her assignments, and when they tried to wake her, she vomited on her client. He was Hadrian, a member of the royal council. She was thrown out of the only home she'd ever known. Now she services men on the streets to make enough coin for more wine."

"Wine dulls the pain," Rhea murmured, more to herself, thinking of her father.

There were so many others, injured or ill, some innocent—others less so, but no less deserving. Judgment came less naturally now that Rhea herself was a liar. Soon, the cart was nearly empty. "We have one final delivery," Tavia said, a glint in her eye. "A widow with five children. The husband left them with little, and they are quickly running out of everything—food, clothes, coin."

"She could remarry."

"You do understand what a univira is, don't you?"

To be univira, a woman must only marry one man. It was the Latin ideal. This meant that widows could not remarry, and should one get too close to another man, even with her first husband a corpse, she could be accused of adultery.

"Yes," argued Rhea, "but remarriage is legal, despite the connotation. I know many women who have."

"Just because it is allowed does not mean it is done. Second marriages are an upper-class privilege. Paulina has no rich father, no widespread connections. She's using what's left of her dowry to feed her babies."

"We can help her find work."

"And who will care for all those children during the day?"

Giggling, barefoot children, playing with a bony dog outside a shared home. Inside, the priestesses met Paulina, an exhausted woman no older than they were. She held a plump baby in her arms, one with angry, rubescent cheeks. It fussed.

Paulina accepted the food with much relief. "Thank you, Tavia. The high priestess has been so good to us."

"This is Rhea, formerly Rhea Silvia." And Tavia spoke her name with eyebrows raised, emphasizing each syllable. Paulina paled, clutching her child tighter.

"Your children are beautiful," Rhea offered, but the widow turned her face away.

Tavia opened her arms. "Paulina, rest a moment. Let me take him." The widow, grateful, passed her young son to the priestess. Tavia rocked from one foot to the other, rubbing the baby's back, while Paulina sank onto a stool.

"Sweet Marcellus," Tavia cooed, and then, more pointedly: "He never met his father, did he?"

And by the way Tavia asked, Rhea suspected she already knew the answer.

"No." Paulina wiped her wet cheek against her shoulder. "He died before I knew I was pregnant."

Tavia clucked her tongue. "A tragedy for him, for all of you."

Paulina hung her head, miserable, her arms folded around her stomach.

"We should be going," Rhea insisted, glaring at Tavia, who returned the child with an innocent shrug. They bade the family farewell, promising to return with more goods soon, and Tavia gave each of the children a piece of hardened honey as a treat. Rhea, livid with the way Tavia had poked at this suffering woman, headed back to the temple, stormy and silent.

"Paulina's husband was a soldier," Tavia called after her, relentless. "He died on duty."

"I am sorry to hear that."

"He didn't die on a military campaign."

"Hmm."

"In fact, he was brutally murdered here in Latium, on his way home, while guarding a young royal on a frivolous hunting trip."

Rhea halted. She felt it return—that horror, that heartbreak, when Lucian had arrived with the news.

"Yes," Tavia seethed, "those children's father was killed so a spoiled little boy could play Orion with other spoiled little boys. Paulina has not been compensated; her family was not even invited to view the body before it was tossed onto a pyre in a mass funeral."

"My brother died, as well. Do not—"

"Yes, he did," spat Tavia, "but you think your pain is the greatest hardship. The prince's death doesn't mean more than any other death, but wealth only acknowledges itself."

Do not engage, Rhea. Do not give her what she wants. Keep moving forward.

"You think your suffering is exceptional when it's the one thing we all have in common. That's what Prisca wants you to see. But what I want you to know is this: You are a selfish girl, blind to anyone besides yourself and your family. You are no better than your drugged father or cruel uncle, and certainly no better than the rest of us."

Rhea's instincts when pushed were to fight back, but one long look at Tavia stole her resolve. The priestess was distraught. Standing in the middle of the path, tear stricken and flushed, eyes wild. The spite she always carried replaced by righteous anguish.

And whether Rhea wanted them to or not, Tavia's words resonated. Rhea had always equated selfishness with greed, but maybe selfishness wasn't about material possessions. Maybe it was a mindset. If Rhea was honest, she hadn't once considered the families of the guards who had died with Aegestus. Just as she'd never thought of the people who had also died on the caravan with her mother and Lausus. All those lives forfeited so the royals could visit relatives, go on a ceremonial hunt. Did their sisters and mothers and daughters hate the Silvian family, too? How many Latins blamed the Regia for their past losses, their persisting agony?

"What would you say to these people, Rhea?" A plea disguised as a demand.

What did Tavia expect, an apology? Recompense? A confession? There was nothing Rhea could do about any of this now. She held no power, no influence.

"If you have complaints," she said calmly, "bring them to the royal council."

Tavia laughed and laughed.

The shame of it burned.

Chapter XVI

RHEA

AUTUMN ARRIVED, COOLING the nights and sprinkling light rain, dropping hints of the winter to come. Rhea enjoyed the change in weather, for it broke the tedium of her Vestal life. Months had passed with no messages or visitors from the Regia—as Tavia loved to mention—and Rhea longed for home. She wanted to hug her father beneath the bay laurel, to lie with Antho on the roof sharing one of Gratia's honey cakes, to have harmless gossip with Zea. Did nobody miss her? Had she meant so little? And she wondered about occurrences behind the Regia's walls; Rhea had become an outsider to her own home, peering in and speculating. People on the streets spoke of King Amulius and his council with wariness but remained hopeful. Though taxes had increased significantly, Latin pride was strong.

On the ides of October, Rhea reunited with her family for the first time as a priestess, and it did not undo her. Quite the opposite; she hardened. The Vestals were required at the ceremonies of the October Horse. This was an annual celebration in Latium, a festival for Mars to conclude the farming season and military campaigns. In the main event, chariots raced through the city, and then the right-hand horse on the winning team was speared through the side and decapitated. The horse's tail was removed by the victor, dipped in the horse's own blood, and brought to the Regia to burn in the sacred hearth.

Aegestus had despised this day. "Why must the best horse die?" he once cried to their mother. And Rhea remembered another conversation—more recent, more painful.

"I wonder at the need to kill what is most special."

"Is he sacrificed because he is beautiful or beautiful because he is sacrificed?"

"We have done these things for so long; does anyone know anymore?"

As the Albans assembled outside the Regia, Rhea watched the crowds watching her, waiting for a reaction. Bitter and proud, she refused to give them one, aligning the movable parts of her face into a veritable mask. The royals proceeded to a raised and decorated dais, arranging themselves like the dramatic characters in a tragic climax—Amulius, the crowned usurper, beside his severe queen and dour daughter. Her family could orate and act and preen; Rhea would be stone.

Stone does not emote, nor does it perform.

Neither Calvus Flavius nor the royal council acknowledged Rhea, not with a wink or a smile or a smirk. Men she had known her entire life behaving as if she had never existed. Was Rhea Silvia a forgotten question or a problem solved? Did it matter when either option gutted her?

"I matter," she whispered to herself, and Tavia shot her a scathing look. But at least that was something. Rhea would rather be hated than ignored; what did that say about her character?

Last to arrive was Numitor, drugged and drowsy.

Oh, Papa.

He had always been a dignified man—broad shouldered, regal in his baldness, his bearing—but this Numitor was malnourished. His clothes hung awkwardly against his yellowed skin. Worried she might run to him, Rhea pinched her thighs hard—a physical reminder to stay put, to remember who she was now. But that did not mean she couldn't watch him. *Look at me, Papa, please. Just once, to show me you still care.*

Numitor did not seem to watch anything with his bloodshot eyes, half-closed in world-weariness. He did, however, speak a word to the guard Petronius, who frowned but handed over a drinking vessel obediently.

Rhea felt her nostrils flare as she breathed hard and fast through her nose. *Really? Still?* Noble Numitor, who had once stood for everything righteous in Rhea's estimation, felled by a damned cup.

In that moment, she hated the royal congregation, the way they stood above the masses like they were superior when they were a disastrous example of humanity. In that moment, she imagined herself stealing a torch of sacred fire, tossing oil and flames on the entire presentation—not just the offerings of food and bone, but the ostentatious clothes and unnecessary wreaths and leather and flesh. An agent of chaos, Rhea would rip off her headscarf and—bare and shorn, feral and free—incinerate the reign of Alba Longa. She would become the volcano of old made manifest, burning everything to the ground, the complex itself and all it stood for, all the people who perpetuated its deceit. Crackling heat and dying screams and Rhea, raging with retribution.

No, Ilia. You are not fire today; you are marble.

More than a stone, she was a statue—etched in meaning, intentionally stoic. White and sterile, celibate. Vestals did not burn people alive.

Only bury them, countered a cynical inner voice.

Rhea felt like a disaster today, too.

Without actually listening, she obeyed the calls of the priests, sprinkling salt at the designated moment, laying fig boughs in the fire, reciting prayers. Words that sprang from her mouth, not her heart. You can worship without meaning it, and if the gods knew, Rhea didn't care.

At the conclusion of the ritual, the elites dispersed first. Antho departed behind Calvus, her head down. Claudia and Numitor followed with the council and bodyguards, and then only the king remained on the dais. Amulius, finally, regarded Rhea with his beady, birdlike stare, those disconcertingly still eyes, and she met his gaze. Did he remember her promise to return one day and eat his heart? His face told her nothing, but then he raised his fist, just a slight upward bend in his elbow, and Rhea saw it: a lock of dark hair tied around his wrist.

Her hair, which had swung from the stone pine outside the temple. Her hair, which reminded him of Jocasta, which he'd held in his fingers when he'd gripped Rhea's head and kissed her mouth. Her hair, now his property.

She was going to be sick.

Then, a shadow of a smile playing on his lips, her uncle moved on, walking into the crowds, into the adoration of the masses. For kings feed upon worship as surely as gods.

The Vestals exited in their own line, Prisca at the front and the rest in hierarchical order. Rhea came last, and she let the space between her and Tavia increase, let the crowds come between them. She purposefully dragged behind, disappointed and disheartened, disgusted. This had to be her worst day since becoming a Vestal. But she was abruptly cut off from her self-pity when a stray hand grabbed her arm, yanking her sideways into an alcove. She yelped, but the stranger hushed her with a finger over her mouth.

She knew his smell, the taste of his skin.

Mars.

"What are you doing here?" Rhea whispered, overcome with delight.

"I am the guest of honor." He grinned, pinning her to the stone wall. "I've been trying to catch you alone for weeks."

"At the temple?"

"Nearby. I got as close as the chicken coop one day."

Rhea laughed, then covered her mouth with one hand.

"A wolf in the henhouse," she jested in a softer voice. "You are terrible."

"I am."

"We are terrible."

"We are perfect, Rhea Silvia."

Did he know what he did to her when he spoke her name—her full name, her true name—with desire and not disdain? It was like he cast a spell with just those words.

"Again," she murmured, and at first, Mars did not understand, but then he leaned closer, knowingly, until his lips were just above hers.

"Rhea Silvia."

She closed the distance, kissing him until she became Rhea Silvia again. The princess who laughed in war's face, defied kings, wrestled her brothers, and dared to dream.

"You only like me because I'm forbidden," she managed to say, scooting away to catch her breath.

"I could say the exact same of you."

She smiled, welcoming his touch, but when his hand slid up her dress, she paused. "Just a kiss. I can't. I shouldn't."

His voice in her ear: "What's done is already done."

Threats seemed existential when she was here, present, alive in this alleyway, engaged in the most scandalous pleasure. Rhea acquiesced; her body wanted this, too. It thrilled at the feel of him, at being squeezed and held and filled and real.

"Be quick, then!"

He growled, nipped at her neck.

There is nothing more they can do to me, she told herself.

But there was.

And they would.

Chapter XVII

ANTHO

THE FESTIVAL OF the October Horse marked Antho's worst day since her father had become king. The Regia hosted a feast that continued long into the night. Antho, exhausted and uncomfortable, yearned for the privacy of her room, but her mother would not grant her leave.

"As long as the important unmarried men remain, so do you." Claudia frowned. "And stop fidgeting!"

Antho's intricately braided hairstyle itched, and the weight of the precious stone and gem jewelry she wore made it difficult to maintain her posture. Her sore and swollen ears were probably infected at this point. She wanted to curl up in her bed—hair down, naked—and sleep.

Preferably with Leandros.

He was stationed at the dining hall's entrance. Antho tried not to glance at him, just as she had tried not to look at Ilia during the earlier ceremony. She was not maliciously avoiding either of them, but her parents monitored her every move. By now, she had learned that even the most insignificant gesture, a smile or a nod, could be used against her and the few people she loved. Since her mother had shattered the vase, Antho had not met Leandros in their hidden place. At night, she lay awake, wondering what he thought. Did he think she was upset with him or, worse, tired of their relationship? There had been no opportune time to explain herself.

During the party, her one godsend was Calvus Flavius's inattention—a new move in whatever game he was playing with her father. Thus far, she had not been forced to interact with him, as Calvus was happily engaged elsewhere. He seemed wholly preoccupied with the other men, presumably discussing war and weather and whatnot. And with each hour that passed, every food course and fresh pour of wine, without Calvus requiring Antho's attendance, Queen Claudia became more enraged.

Relax, Mother, Antho wished to say. *You're looking apoplectic.*

But *relax* was not part of Claudia's vocabulary. She leaned her head slightly toward her daughter, issuing instructions in Antho's ear: "Go to Maximus Ectorius. Welcome him to the Regia."

Maximus Ectorius, a visiting prince of Lavinium.

"Mother, please—oh!"

The queen's heel dug into Antho's toes under the table, and they were stinging, straining, singing with pain. Antho closed her eyes, stilled her trembling lip.

"*Go.*"

Antho caught Leandros's eye as she moved toward the empty seat beside Prince Maximus. The torment in Leandros's beautiful face was so dangerously obvious. Antho instinctively looked downward. A sardonic laugh rolled through her head: *You are developing quite a relationship with the ground, Antho.* The voice sounded like Rhea.

Well, Ilia, sometimes it is easier that way.

Talking to Maximus was painless. He spoke of the salt flats along the Tiber, which Antho found somewhat interesting, and, best of all, she could sense he had no romantic interest in her. It wasn't often that Antho could enjoy a conversation at court that had no ulterior motive, and she actually relaxed.

But Claudia's scheme worked, and a servant girl knelt at her side with a message.

"Calvus Flavius has requested you, Princess."

"Yes, of course. Thank you."

The servant moved on, and Maximus surprised Antho, laying a burly hand atop hers with a surprisingly gentle pat.

"Be well," he told her.

Because Antho had become so accustomed to cruelty, acts of kindness always astonished her. Meanness was hardly surprising. But compassion? A rarity in her world. She left Maximus Ectorius reluctantly, and as she approached Calvus's company, he opened his arms.

"Ah, Princess! Come, girl, sit on my lap."

She forced a smile but made no move. Surely, this was all in jest.

But when Calvus cleared his throat expectantly, she sat.

"You are skin and bones," he remarked, his hands pinching at her ribs and hips. "Far too thin."

Hair rose along Antho's arms, at the back of her neck. "I have always been this way."

"It's not what men like. You have a pretty face, but I want you soft beneath the cloth."

"Beneath him!" a man joked, leaning in from the other side of the table. They laughed, drank from their cups.

She should not be here; it wasn't safe. Antho recognized the instinctual warnings at her core, those passed down through generations of women who had survived situations just like this. "I should congratulate the victor on the race."

She attempted to stand, but Calvus's hand gripped her dress, and he pulled her back down.

"Not until you eat something."

He tore a piece of thigh meat from the roasted goose dish and held it before Antho's face.

"Open," he commanded.

And she didn't know what else to do. Her jaw dropped just a fraction, enough for Calvus to jam his greasy fingers inside, shoving animal flesh against her tongue. She chewed, breathing through her nose to keep the air coming, to stop herself from gagging or crying, and when she swallowed, the nearby men cheered.

"Now the princess needs a drink."

Calvus instructed a servant to pour Antho a cup of his wine, filled to the rim. She was forced to lean forward from her position on Calvus's lap and sip from the brimming cup on the table until she could hold it without spilling. She was aware of how she appeared: lapping wine like a dog. Her parents did not intervene, but that wasn't the worst part. Leandros remained in the room, witnessing her degradation.

I will never get over this humiliation, she thought. *I will never be the same again.*

So she kept drinking. And drinking. Endless rounds of the Flavius varietal. She might have joked with Calvus's companions; she might have sat quietly. In all honesty, she was too hazy to discern exactly what was happening. She didn't know if she said wild things aloud or only in her head. But she did recall standing up to go relieve herself and immediately crashing to the floor.

"See," Calvus pointed out, annoyed. "If you ate more, your body could hold its wine."

See, echoed her mind, *you are developing quite a relationship with the ground.*

Calvus returned to his associates without offering her a hand. But Zea had arrived; Zea was there on her knees radiating trust and practicality, helping Antho to her feet. When had she come? Had she always been at the feast? Antho couldn't remember seeing her before.

"The princess will rest now," Zea told the men, affirmatively, then carefully led Antho from the dining hall and up to her room. They stopped often; Antho was much taller and tilting precariously. Then strong hands scooped her up from behind, one arm under her knees, the other around her back. There was no need to look; she knew who it was. Wine drunk and not caring who might see, she nestled her face into his chest.

"You were right to find me," Zea told Leandros.

"Thank you for coming."

"Did you see?" Antho mumbled. "Did you see when he fed me?"

"I did."

She began to cry. "You think I'm weak. I disgust you."

"Princess," Zea warned, "be quiet."

The muscles in Leandros's square jaw clenched, but he did not respond.

"My parents know about us, Leandros, and the vase. My feelings have not changed."

"Hush, Antho. Please."

All too soon, the trio arrived at the door to Antho's room. "Stay with me tonight," she said into Leandros's ear, but he placed her feetfirst on the ground, keeping one hand on hers to hold her steady. Zea entered the room, ostensibly to prepare Antho's bed but actually to give them privacy.

"I cannot stay with you, and you could never disgust me." He ran the knuckles of his free hand against her cheek. "Antho, you are resilient, something beautiful that has bloomed in impossible terrain." And then his touch was gone, but he was presenting a flower that he had pulled from inside his uniform. A sprig of small whitish flowers, the yarrow that grew throughout the countryside.

"The king will notice I'm gone. I must leave." He passed the stem into her hand and laid a kiss on her forehead. "Dream of us. Keep dreaming of us."

He turned. Antho watched him walk away until he turned the corner. Then she stumbled into her room, slamming the door behind her with all her might, hard enough to shake the wall. An exquisite *bang*. Antho collapsed on her bed, no longer caring about the earrings or the braids, and when she woke the next morning, her head splitting and her stomach threatening to revolt, she still held the yarrow in her fist.

Chapter XVIII

RHEA

RHEA'S MONTHLY CYCLE stopped, but her stomach remained the same. She knew because she checked it obsessively. *If anything*, she comforted herself, *I've* lost *weight since entering the Vestals.* Pregnant women had big bellies. Her bleeding had merely been affected by changes in diet and activity. No way was Rhea with child.

But she had been undeniably reckless with an immortal more than once. Of course she was with child.

Her mind volleyed back and forth in this way—*I am pregnant, I am not*—throughout each task and service, all the days and nights. She thought she could hide her anxiety, but living with five other women in intimate quarters made every mood obvious, and Rhea's uneasiness was misinterpreted as melancholy.

"She misses home," Horatia asserted.

"Wouldn't you," Valeria commented, "if you had been the king's only daughter?"

Prisca offered a solution. "This little starling needs to spread her wings. Birds that fly are the most grateful for a nest."

As the priestesses prepared for the Bona Dea—the Vestals' covert, curious celebration of the Good Goddess—Prisca tasked Rhea with a special assignment.

"The Bona Dea is our best day," Horatia crowed.

"Why?" Rhea wondered aloud, genuinely curious.

"Because it requires the sacred relics of *Aeneas*," the elder priestess answered, lowering her voice in reverence.

"Before fleeing Troy," Prisca explained, "Aeneas rescued his Penate, the household deity that protected his family, from his burning home. He carried it on his back over land, stowed it safely on his ship, and—despite loss and hardship—brought it to Latium."

Rhea knew all this, of course, but nodded politely.

"Over generations, as our capital city changed from Laurentum to Lavinium to Alba Longa, the Penate of Aeneas was believed lost. But that was a lie." Prisca lifted her head a bit higher. "Because of its value and desirability, a king of yore entrusted the Vestal Virgins with its care."

Rhea's eyes widened. Did her father know? Did Amulius?

No, for they would have taken it back.

But this begged another question.

"At the Regia, we honored the Penates, our guardians. Yet you speak of the Penates as 'it,' as one."

The Vestals shared a secret smile.

"The Penate of Aeneas," Valeria responded, reveling in the enigma, "is singular."

She might have been too proud to admit it, but Rhea was intrigued.

"You and Aemilia will retrieve the Penate; it is essential for our celebration of the Bona Dea. We keep the relic hidden in the Egeria Spring, in the sacred grotto of the Caffarella Valley. It is a very long walk, five hours to the northwest. To get there and back will take an entire day."

A day away and a mystery! Rhea cared little for another ritual but would never denounce such welcome distractions.

"Thank you, Virgo Maxima, for this confidence."

"You've been so out of tune, little bird. Time outside will restore your song."

◆ ◆ ◆

ON THE MORNING they left, Valeria passed Rhea a knife. "Not everybody respects the white stola," she explained. "If any man dares to touch you, gut them like a fish." And she pointed to a spot below her navel, tracing her finger up to the bottom of her ribs. Rhea nodded, tucked the blade into her belt.

Valeria was easily her favorite of the Vestals.

As Rhea and Aemilia traveled farther from the house and temple and city, Rhea became more open and unencumbered—despite the heavy cloak she wore for the December weather. Positivity came naturally on a journey so splendid, as the thick woods broke into pastureland and the women descended colorful hills into the river-run valley.

They walked and talked, sharing innocuous stories from childhood— legends and games learned around hearth or campfire. Aemilia had been a Vestal since she was very young, so her memories of home were precious. Mythic. Not unlike the way Rhea memorialized her own mother.

"I am happy we were chosen," Aemilia said. "Last year Tavia and Musa collected the relic."

Rhea was not one to shirk an opportunity, and here was her moment to ask the question that most bothered her. Who was the specter haunting the house and the temple—the dead girl who had once slept in Rhea's bed?

"Aemilia, what happened to Musa?"

The other priestess sighed, blowing air through pursed lips. "There is not much to say; she died."

"But how?"

Aemilia recounted an illness of vomiting and nausea, cramps and blood, then incapacitated sleep. "It was horrible. To see Musa in such pain . . ." Aemilia paused, adjusted the strap on her bag, and then completed her thought: "But also to see Tavia in such pain. She did not leave Musa's side until Prisca pronounced Musa dead and Valeria had to pull her away, crying and tearing at her face."

"They must have been extremely close."

"Inseparable. Many nights, they pushed their beds together to sleep side by side, like sisters but also not." Aemilia cleared her throat. "They were a bonded pair, more like . . ." She stopped. "I must be honest, Rhea. I would rather not talk about this anymore. It does no good."

Yet it did. Rhea knew how it felt when death took someone you loved, both in the awful moment and in the doomed thereafter. She knew how hard it was to witness replacement; Rhea had seen her mother's queendom taken by Claudia and Lausus's heirdom passed to Aegestus. Rhea's presence among the Vestals reminded Tavia of all she had lost, a constant poking at her bruised heart.

Nothing could justify the hateful way Tavia treated her, but perhaps Rhea could understand it.

They passed quietly into the lush vegetation of the wetlands, its maples and holm oaks, acacia and poplar, nettles and reeds. Among the rushes were groaning frogs and rustling snakes.

"We are almost to the grotto," Aemilia declared.

The atmosphere shifted as they approached the acqua santa of the Egeria Spring; a lightness in the air, suspended, like an intake of breath. The sense of an apex. Here, in the mist, the presence of holiness and history met in perfect balance and blend. Though it brought gooseflesh to her exposed skin, she was not afraid.

Aemilia pointed out a discreet cave across the pool of blue-green water, disguised by rock and shadow, its entrance further obscured by a small waterfall. Rhea never would have found it unaided. To enter, they were going to have to get wet.

"No wonder Prisca sent us," Rhea muttered, eyeing the narrow, watery tunnel ahead with some disbelief.

"I will retrieve the relic," Aemilia offered as she removed her cloak and passed it to Rhea. "And call for you if I need help." Rhea watched her wade into the venerated spring, paddling her arms when the depth increased. Before she disappeared through the rock face, Aemilia turned and waved to Rhea. "It is so cold!" she squealed, laughing.

Rhea grinned.

She sat at the water's edge, waiting, her fingertips skimming the surface, making ripples in the infinite glitter. When a man's face materialized beneath Rhea's hand, she gasped. He gazed up at her with sapphire eyes bluer than the water. Reeling backward, Rhea blinked, once, twice, then looked again. His image remained. If he wasn't a hallucination, a trick of the light, than what was this—a river god? A ghost?

"It seemed the right time to show my face," he said simply.

Recognition sent shivers through her upper body. She had heard this voice before, at the Almone River after Mars had refused to teach her how to fight. Steadying herself, Rhea peered closer. It was a nice face. A slightly aquiline nose, a light beard. Short hair standing in every direction.

"Have I been patient?" she asked. "Am I still tenacious?"

A softly crooked smile sent his eyebrows into an up-furrow, an expression of endearing alertness. But before the man could answer, Aemilia emerged from the rock face, splashing and hollering, oblivious. Rhea looked up. Tucked against the other priestess's chest was a wrapped statue the size of a young child.

"I have it!" she called out. "Come see!"

Not now, not yet. Rhea disregarded Aemilia, returning her attention to the spring. The image dissolved. Frustrated, she thrust her hand into the water, hoping to grab hold of him, to keep him there, but she found nothing. Water streamed out of her grip, leaving Rhea awash in emptiness, in a peculiar yearning. Why had he revealed himself? Why did he care? Something about these encounters, brief as they both had been, brought Rhea something close to serenity. It must have been strong magic; Rhea's life was anathema to peace.

"Rhea, can you take it?"

Shaking herself, Rhea entered the pool up to her knees and accepted the Penate from Aemilia, whose lips were quivering from the chill. She wrapped her arms around herself, rubbing warmth into her body. Though the sun remained on high, it was still winter. Together, they trudged up onto the bank and while Aemilia dried herself and donned her cloak, Rhea recommitted herself to the moment. She should be appreciative. By roundabout means, she had been reunited with the guardian of her Trojan ancestor. If she ever spoke to her father again, she would have to relay every detail.

"Ready?" Aemilia asked, her eyes sparkling.

The women unwrapped the pieces of white cloth, taking their time as a show of respect. Removing the final layer revealed a woman carved in stone, a woman who sat upon a throne wearing a crown in the shape of a turreted city wall. An attendant lion stood at her side. A civet and a drum rested in her lap.

Rhea's eyes widened. Aeneas's household guardian was a god*dess*. And not just any goddess, either.

Cybele, the Mountain Mother, the Great Mother.

Jocasta's favorite.

Beside her, Aemilia beamed. "She's perfect, isn't she?"

"In every way."

Chapter XIX

RHEA

RHEA AND AEMILIA brought Cybele into the Vestals' home, not their temple, for though observation of the Bona Dea and the recondite "Good Goddess" was a responsibility of the priestesses, it contradicted, in some ways, their worship of Vesta. They kept the goddesses separate.

Though the other women saved the details of the ceremony for a surprise, the excitement on the grounds was palpable—and contagious. This day, Rhea surmised, was less about hearth and hard work and more about being a woman—a celebration, not a duty. Cybele's statue was placed at the center of their house altar, and the Vestals dedicated an entire day to decorating and cooking. Aemilia wove flower garlands and crowns. Tavia draped vines across the ceiling and along the walls, until their home resembled a Latin garden of the Hesperides. Valeria retrieved a box from storage, and Rhea watched her unpack one exotic item after another. She placed a drum and dried fir branches at Cybele's base, then revealed a long, luxurious lion pelt cape.

"This is for Prisca," said Valeria, with more than a note of jealousy.

"It is magnificent."

The decadent aroma of roasted pig wafted out from the kitchen, where Horatia held court, taking no breaks yet exhibiting no fatigue. She sang offbeat, off-tune melodies that made Rhea laugh and Valeria groan.

"Don't encourage her," Valeria snapped when Rhea clapped along.

Once night fell, the six priestesses assembled for prayer wearing masks of hawk feathers and snakeskin. Lit candles covered every surface, casting syncopated flickers around the room.

Prisca began: "We are the Vestals of Alba Longa, who tend the flame that warms our hearth and cooks our bread. We honor Vesta in our role as women through our purity, service, loyalty, and humility, which is the Latin way."

Horatia brought forth a large jug. "Is it time for the milk, High Priestess?"

"I have not finished our first prayer yet!" But when Horatia sighed so dejectedly, Prisca conceded. "Oh, it's fine. Go ahead, Horatia."

Smiling again, capricious Horatia filled cups and passed them around. Rhea sniffed hers and pulled back. Horatia's "milk" was extremely strong wine—not the second-pressed kind they typically imbibed—and the older priestess was already quite drunk, spilling as much as she poured.

"Is it that potent?" Rhea whispered worriedly to Valeria.

"Only when you've been sneaking it all day," she muttered back.

Rhea took a sip and flinched. Too much of this and she would be dancing naked beneath the stars.

Prisca continued: "For one night of each year, however, we honor a different feminine, the one that existed before the order of city and home. The woman of the wilderness, the womb of the world. Creator and protector. Mother bear, lioness, crocodile, wolf spider, vixen, and sow. The Good Goddess—whose name we do not reveal—is also the Great Goddess rescued by our Trojan father and brought to Latium. Tonight we honor her."

Horatia banged a drum, and the women began to shriek. Rhea startled. This was no hymnal but a bestial choir of screams, of war cries and animal sounds. She stared, wide-eyed, as one Vestal after another began to move to the atonal music, circling Cybele with arms waving, hips shaking, eyes closed.

It looked somewhat insane; it looked like a bit of fun.

Rhea laughed, took a deep drink of her milk, and she danced, because she loved to do all these things and it had been so very long. She spun, held hands with Aemilia and Valeria. Rhea twirled and crowed, downed cup after cup of Horatia's milk.

Even Tavia smiled.

Yes, tonight was a different sort of night.

♦ ♦ ♦

LATER, VALERIA AND Rhea rested on the floor, leaning against the wall, as they ate pork meat with their bare hands. Rhea licked the grease from her fingers.

"Jocasta loved the Bona Dea. Every December, she would sneak away from the Regia with your father's best wines."

Rhea gaped. "You never said that you knew her."

"You have been so sad, Rhea. I would not make it worse." Valeria paused, and the glaze of recollection slid down her face. It was a look Rhea knew well, the one people wore when they remembered her mother, when they remembered she was dead.

"My mother honored Cybele above all others."

"Indeed." Valeria chuckled. "Vesta was never the goddess for her. Too stationary."

Her wild, storytelling mama, who had claimed she came from the forest. Her mother had been here, in these rooms, with these songs and flowers and food—even some of these women. Her mother had seen Aeneas's Penate as well, but she had honored the Vestals' confidentiality and never shared that knowledge with her family.

"Why didn't she bring me with her?"

Valeria frowned, but not without empathy. "I could not say."

Yet another of Jocasta's many secrets. How many more would Rhea uncover in her lifetime? And how many more would she never know? Jocasta in the woods. Jocasta with the Vestals. Jocasta as queen, as a mother. Jocasta and Amulius, in bed together, possibly in love? Her last words given to the man who despised Rhea above all else.

Suddenly, the room felt unbearably hot, the air too thick with sweat and incense. She stood, neck and face burning, and rich food and drink boiling urgently in her belly. Rhea made for the exit, clamping a hand over her mouth, but it was too late.

She was sick down the front of her dress, splashing the floor by Valeria's feet with purple wine and pig flesh. The drum stopped mid-rhythm, leaving the room quiet and off-kilter.

More nausea rose, coming up out of her with brutal force, and then Valeria was standing at Rhea's mortified side, one hand on her back. "Oh, you poor child."

Horatia brought fresh water. "It was my milk!" she bemoaned, flushed.

"Yes," shot Valeria. "Your 'milk' could intoxicate an elephant!"

"Starling," Prisca murmured, joining them, "you should lie down. And somebody clean this mess!"

"Not me," muttered Tavia. "It better not be me."

Rhea pushed the jug away; even water made her nauseous. "No, I only need fresh air."

Aemilia put her arm around Rhea's waist. "I will help you outside."

What is wrong with me? I am seasick on dry land. Maybe she had the illness that killed her mother and brother. Perhaps it was finally Rhea's turn to die.

But as they passed the Penate, Rhea swore she saw Cybele's lips move.

"You know, Rhea Silvia, you've always known."

Rhea's body went very still, then began to tremble in a way she could not control.

"Oh, you're shaking!" Aemilia exclaimed.

"I'm fine."

With Aemilia's assistance, Rhea made it to the stone pine at the front of the temple. "I'm fine, Aemilia," she repeated. "Please go back inside."

Aemilia frowned, wrinkling her nose as she considered the proper thing to do. Finally, she shrugged. "Call out if you need me." And then she left, content to continue the night of devotions.

Alone at last, Rhea closed her eyes and pulled her knees to her chest, holding herself in a tight, protective lock. Her mind raced with prayer and memory and image, of the gods, of her mother and Aeneas.

You were never meant for a mortal man.
The woman of the wilderness, the womb of the world.
To be a mother is to be alive.
What's done is already done.
You know, Rhea Silvia, you've always known.
I am glad my son will have such a strong mother.

She would need to be strong.

Rhea was not drunk, and she was not sick; she was pregnant with the war god's child.

❖ ❖ ❖

BECAUSE THE VESTALS still felt the tragedy of Musa's death, they treated Rhea's illness with seriousness. Her chores were suspended, and she was allowed to lie in bed for the next few days—days that ran the longest of her life—as she tempered bouts of queasiness with debilitating dread.

She was a pregnant "virgin," and she was going to die.

Not quickly but slowly, through thirst and starvation, alone and in the dark.

But they would kill her; there was no debate.

Horatia insisted they send for a healer—the very last person Rhea wanted poking about her body. She appealed to Prisca with a convincing litany of half-truths. "Please. Healers have only hurt my family. Those who came for my brother and mother left them worse. I drank too much wine on an empty stomach. It's embarrassing, but it's nothing."

Talk of medical intervention was suspended, and Rhea learned to hide her sickness, her bone-weary exhaustion, and return to her duties as if nothing were wrong.

Time is neither kind nor cruel; it simply is. For Rhea, however, time became her enemy. With every day that passed, her child grew. With each bite of food, with each night of rest. She counted the months. A baby conceived at the end of summer would come toward the end of spring. Could she make it through the winter before her stomach began to show? Rhea cursed herself for not paying more attention to the women

136

at court! She longed for Antho, who always listened, who knew about these things.

Rhea could run, but where would she go? She lacked the skills and resources to survive in the woods. She had nothing of value to trade in the cities besides her body, and were pregnant women even desired as whores? Her father didn't care about her—or anything—anymore. He had made that abundantly clear.

Mars had made her no promises, implying that he would assist *if* he could, *if* it was a service he could provide. Too many ifs. It humiliated her to need him, especially when their love was not true. Not in the way of Aeneas and Lavinia, Paris and Helen—even her cousin and Leandros. Rhea loved his body, certainly, and the physical way they connected, but she saw no future for them. Rhea would only call on Mars as a last resort.

There was another option, of course. She could end the pregnancy on her own. When Rhea was still young, Jocasta's dearest friend had fallen from a horse and lost the child she carried. Rhea would never forget the sound of that woman's sorrow when the blood came between her legs. The horrific cries. Her mother had slept in baby Aegestus's bed that night, refusing to let him go.

How could Rhea mimic such a fall? The Vestals owned no horses. But then, fetching water one day, she passed a persimmon tree in fruit. It would make a believable story—she climbed up to collect the winter fruit and lost her footing. When the blood came, she would dismiss it as a particularly bad cycle. Inspired by her idea, feverish with intent, Rhea rose easily through the tree's branches. Near its high point, she closed her eyes, imagining for just a moment the world laid out before her like the maps in her father's study. Where would she go if she could leave this place?

Egypt. Cyprus. Phrygia. Thrace.

There were so many foods to try, languages to hear. Foreign clothes and aromas and stories.

She looked down, found the ground through the interlacing leaves and branches. It was a significant drop. Falling might kill the child; it might also break her spine.

Not now, a voice inside whispered. *Not yet.*

(Soon she would regret not jumping, but not yet.)

Rhea climbed down from the tree, both of their limbs shivering.

She forgot to pick a persimmon.

◆ ◆ ◆

ONE DAY, AS Rhea worked in the yard repairing a broken fence post, Tavia appeared, arms crossed, blocking Rhea's line of sun.

"You have a visitor."

Rhea had never had one before.

Expectations had the potential for heartbreak, so Rhea prepared for disappointment. It would not be her father, come to his senses, come to fetch her home. It was most likely Amulius, here to deliver bad news in person so that he could personally witness her pain. Naturally, Tavia's face betrayed no hints. Rhea brushed the dirt from her hands as best she could and followed wordlessly.

A lithe figure waited before the house steps. Golden hair in perfect braids.

Antho.

Rhea stumbled, tripping on the instinct to tackle her cousin in a crushing hug. What was the protocol for a reunion between the crown princess and a Vestal Virgin?

"Do not tarry. The fence must be fixed by nightfall."

Though Tavia left, Rhea suspected that she lingered somewhere nearby to listen.

Antho wore finer clothes than ever before, but even the prettiest trappings could not conceal her troubles. She was too thin, purple circles rimmed those large eyes, so full of mournful intelligence, and her lips trembled as she took in her cousin. Rhea ran a self-conscious hand down the back of her head, against the uneven new growth, and attempted levity. "For what it's worth, the haircut wasn't my idea."

"You will always be beautiful, Ilia."

"I have missed you every day."

"I was not allowed to come before. But then Mother heard you were ill and sent me to check on you."

"To spy on me."

Antho inclined her head in silent agreement, but then Rhea frowned and lowered her voice. "How could Claudia know of my sickness? Who does she speak to?"

"Oh, Ilia. She tells me next to nothing besides where to sit and when to smile."

"Tell her I am quite well. Healthier than I've ever been."

"Of course."

"How is my father? Does he still take the poppy seeds?"

Antho nodded, ashamed.

"You could do something to help him."

"It is very different now."

"Do not speak to me of different." Rhea stood straighter, callused hands turned upward, daring her cousin to acknowledge the soot on her cheeks, the uneven remnants of her once-glorious hair.

"I'm sorry, Ilia. I didn't mean . . ."

Rhea sighed. "None of this is your fault, Antho. Tell me of Leandros."

Antho responded by turning her head, stretching her neck so that Rhea could see the bruises along her cousin's collarbone. Rhea gasped, but Antho put a finger over her lips.

"My father must remind me of my position. I have misbehaved in the past, but no longer." She said it loudly enough that no eavesdropper needed to strain their ears.

"What has he done to you?" Rhea demanded, infuriated. And then she asked her next question with reticence, as she feared the answer: "Is Leandros alive?"

"So long as I fulfill my responsibilities as a Latin woman and the king's daughter."

Protocols be damned. Rhea clasped her cousin in a tight embrace, not caring if Antho felt the taut bulge of her stomach and aware that letting go would be excruciating.

"Has he promised you to Calvus?" Rhea whispered.

"Not yet," Antho returned, just as softly. "He dangles me like bait before sharks."

"We should have run away, Antho."

"I wish that every day."

Chapter XX

ANTHO

RHEA WAS WITH child. Antho noticed right away. Her cousin's face had changed. Rhea's lips were fuller, her breasts larger. Antho couldn't begin to understand the *how* or the *who*, but neither changed the fact that Rhea was a decidedly deflowered Vestal Virgin.

Oh, Ilia. What will we do now?

"Well?" Claudia charged when Antho returned to the Regia. "Is she truly sick or faking it?"

"Neither, Mother. She seems well. It was an ordinary illness, and it has passed."

Claudia's mouth twisted. "What else did you notice?"

"She has no hair."

"Besides the obvious, stupid girl! Has she made friends? Could she be influencing the other priestesses, manipulating them with her lies? Does she speak against your father?"

"She seemed quite lonely."

The queen nodded, clucking her tongue. "Good."

Soon, Rhea's pregnancy would become common knowledge, and a Silvian child—even a bastard—would push Antho's father to act in ways she was loath to imagine. Bad times were coming to the Regia, and Antho felt overwhelmed by dual apprehensions: concern over her cousin's condition along with her resident worry, the one pulling constantly at her heart, needy and urgent—Leandros.

She had avoided him since the night of the October Horse, terrified that someone might have witnessed her foolish behavior in the hallway. If her love for Leandros never left her heart, her father's threats of future harm certainly never left her mind. A man who would beat his only daughter would demand vicious retribution against a lowly soldier. Antho couldn't allow the man she loved to pay such a penance.

Amulius had failed to control Rhea's body; what wouldn't he do to control his daughter's?

But circumventing Leandros was no easy feat, especially with a love so young and vibrant, so recent and ravenous. Every day he was so achingly close—living in such proximity its own kind of torture—but she continued to evade any interactions. She didn't trust herself around him anymore, and this was terrifying. If she made another mistake, it could very well kill him.

Their separation was never going to last forever, and Leandros found her first, stopping Antho in a corridor outside the women's quarters as she fetched more water. He must have stationed himself there, hoping for such a moment.

"Hello," he said simply.

"Hello."

"Allow me." He took the jug from her hands and filled it from the well. "I know the vase is broken, Antho," he told her quietly, "but do you remember what we said to each other in the forest?"

Every day she replayed that night, when they spoke of making things happen, of being exceptional. But before Antho could answer, she heard a shuffle. Her head shot up. In a far corner, a guard pulled his body farther out of sight. A spy, and she had a very good guess as to who it might be. There was no way to warn Leandros; she would have to present an alternative narrative, one that reinforced her parents' rules, and hope he saw through her lies.

"I must be candid with you." She took a deep breath. "I have not been myself lately. After Aegestus's death and Rhea's departure, I acted in audacious, inappropriate ways. It was wrong of me to extend you such attentions when I will be married soon." She swallowed. "I must focus on the future, on my children who will be kings and queens."

He was hurt. She had hurt him. The evidence was etched in the broken lines of his incredulous face.

His perfect face. Her favorite face.

"I don't believe you, Antho," Leandros managed to reply. "You can barely say the words."

He was right, of course. Nor could she look at him, but she would finish this. "I am the crown princess. You should address me as such." Antho drew herself higher and projected her voice loudly. "You need to end this preoccupation with me. I apologize if I entertained your delusions. That wasn't fair."

Leandros stiffened, as if he had received a blunt blow to the stomach, but he nodded once, firmly. "I hear you, Princess. I always have." He cleared his throat. "I will not bother you again. I wish you a healthy life."

He bowed to her before turning and marching away, every bit the soldier. A healthy life, he'd said—not a good one, not a happy one—and yet it still felt like more than she deserved. She had done this wretched thing for her parents' ears, sure that Helvius overheard, but now she found herself in a quandary. Though it was intended as an act, she had just ended her relationship with Leandros, something she never thought she would be able to do. Should she let it be, let him go? He would be delivered from all of this.

Antho wrung her hands. Commit to the ruse or confess?

Yes, they had spoken once under late summer starlight, and she had promised to always return, to always come back for him. Such gorgeous folly. Antho had believed it all.

Henceforth she would believe in nothing. Hope, the hardest love, hurt too much.

When she returned to her room, the jug of well water waited by the door.

Chapter XXI

RHEA

IN THE FIRST months of her pregnancy, when she was still willfully oblivious to her condition, Rhea lost weight as food lost its appeal. Flavors that had once charmed now repulsed her, and she picked at the meals around the communal table, eating only enough to remain inconspicuous. But then her appetite returned with fervor, and she could not be satisfied by such humble portions. She salivated over memories of sea fish stew, oysters, wild game, and stuffed dormice. Mushrooms and artichokes and honey. None of it made sense, but she wanted it all together all the same.

Only when completely alone could Rhea marvel at the physical changes to her body. As her breasts swelled and the bottom of her stomach curved, she thanked Vesta for the unexpected boon of formless stolas, which gave her figure the space and seclusion to change.

She knew she shouldn't draw attention to her belly, but it was becoming harder and harder to keep her hands away.

As Rhea swept the hearth, she thought of her child. As she fed the chickens and stocked the storehouse, baked the bread and spread the salt, she wondered about him—his eyes, his laugh, the feel of his hair. Yes, he was a child of Mars, but he was also *her child*, a child of Rhea Silvia. She hoped he resembled her brothers, with Lausus's fortitude balanced by Aegestus's gentleness. Would he have Jocasta's imagination? Numitor's patience? Her own ferocity?

Insane questions. This baby was her death sentence. She would never know him. They were both doomed. She had never been one for crying, but Rhea was forever at the edge of tears.

Delight and denial and dread. All at once, all the time.

Because this was no ordinary child, of no common man, it seemed to grow at an abnormal rate, and by six months, Rhea could certainly no longer disrobe in front of her roommates. She either rose and dressed before either of them woke or pretended to fall asleep fully dressed. She stopped washing, as the bathhouse became too risky.

Her stench was noisome.

The temple's eternal flame could never go unattended, so one Vestal always took the night watch, with the younger priestesses assigned most shifts. When Rhea's turn came, she knew what she had to do: while the others slept, she could sneak a quick bath.

Did she dare?

Rhea took one sniff of her armpit and cringed.

Yes, she dared.

Rhea Silvia *always* dared.

But she wasn't careless. She ensured the fire's stability, loading it with plenty of wood to keep it burning, and then she crept to the bathhouse at the edge of the Vestal property. She did not risk lighting the brazier that warmed the water, but by this point, she would have gladly bathed in the stormy frozen waters of the Far North. Anything to feel clean again. She tossed her dress to the side and applied a handful of oil to her naked skin, massaging it into her arms and hands, her swollen feet. She groaned as her knuckles dug into her lower back, into every sore, neglected part of her body.

Next, she removed the strigil hanging from the wall, the curved metal tool used to scrape away the dirt and sweat accumulated in the oil. Scrape and flick, scrape and flick. Removing detritus like a snake shedding its skin.

As Rhea lowered herself into the pool, she bit her fist to keep from crying out. It wasn't too cold; it was too *good*. A catharsis, a cleansing. She fully submerged, letting the water lift the short strands of her hair, and blew out bubbles, then broke through the surface and flipped onto her back. Rhea rested and recalled hot summer days on the river with her brothers. For a brief moment, she reclaimed that bliss. She loved swimming; she loved the river.

She thought of the man in the Egeria Spring, how he had brought a similar feeling of contentment. How curious that just a face and a few exchanged words could make such an impact! It was a silly desire, improbable, but she wanted to meet him again.

The small bulge of her belly popped out, and she took a long look at her navel, at the curious brown line leading downward. When had that appeared? In another life, she would have had the peace of mind—and physical safety—to delight in these changes. But this was not that life, and she had already dawdled too long. Summoning all her self-discipline, Rhea forced herself from the bath, pausing only to stretch her back and shake out her hair. Droplets of water flew against the walls.

Rhea smiled at this moment, stolen for herself, the happiest she had been in many, many days.

"I knew it."

An insidious exultation, invading Rhea's serenity, breaking the night.

Fully nude, Rhea spun around. Tavia stood at the entrance to the bathhouse, eyes wide and incredulous, one hand pointed at Rhea's telltale stomach.

"Whore."

◆ ◆ ◆

A PRETERNATURAL CALM descended upon Rhea as she scooped up her dress and pulled it over her head, then navigated her way toward Tavia in the same way she would approach a feral animal.

"Listen to me, Tavia," she implored. "Let me tell you my story. The truth."

Tavia seemed jittery, as if hit by lightning and charged with its destructive, cataclysmic energy.

146

"I don't care," Tavia said, shaking her head, amazed to find herself finally validated, her enemy defeated. "Even if you bribe me, even if you beg."

Rhea had nothing to gift. She considered dropping to her knees but could not do it. Perhaps Tavia had been right about her all along; she *was* too proud for this place. But Rhea had almost begged once before, and she never would again.

Humility doesn't become you.

"Why must you hate me so ardently?" she asked instead. "I would have welcomed your friendship."

It was the wrong thing to say.

"I had a friend," Tavia spat, heat returning. "She made this life worth it. I loved her. And they killed her to create space for you."

"They? I don't understand, Tavia. Who killed Musa?"

"Your people! Musa was perfectly healthy. I would know! But then that wizard came to dinner, and the next day, Musa was dying. He poisoned her. I would stake my own life on it."

Rhea's mind spun, struggling to process, to keep up. "Sethre? The augur?"

"Yes, the one with the hideous eyebrow stretching across his forehead."

"If what you speak is true, Tavia, then our enemies are the same. The new king and his allies plotted against me as well."

Tavia crossed her arms. "Yet you are alive, and Musa is not."

Rhea held out a beseeching hand. "You owe me nothing, but I need your help, Tavia. If you keep my secret and we share what we both suspect, we might be able to right a great number of wrongs. We might be able to save Alba Longa from a heinous traitor."

Tavia pulled her lower lip between her teeth, and tears filled her eyes. Indecision. Emotional misery. Rhea barely dared to breathe.

"Tavia . . . ?"

The girl rubbed the back of her hand roughly against her face. "No. I cannot help you, not when you are the reason Musa is dead."

And Tavia turned away, racing into the night.

◆ ◆ ◆

RHEA FOLLOWED BEHIND, cursing her own stupidity and Tavia's stubbornness as the priestesses dashed into the House of the Vestals.

"Sleep no more!" Tavia cried. "Wake and rise! You must all bear witness! There is a heinous traitor in our midst!"

Rhea flinched at the use of her own phrase against her.

Wearing a disgruntled frown, Valeria arrived first in the central atrium. "What nonsense cannot wait until morning?"

"The matter is too grave. I cannot speak without the high priestess present."

"And I am here."

Prisca stepped forward. Behind her waited Horatia, wrapped in a shawl. Aemilia entered the room last, glancing nervously around the room. Tavia was formidable, a woman possessed, completely committed to the havoc she would wreak.

"Rhea is no virgin."

Aemilia gasped.

"Sinners and fornicators!" Horatia cried. "Sinners and fornicators amongst us!"

"That is a serious accusation, starling," Prisca warned. She raised the oil lamp in her hand as she came near, head cocked to the side, inspecting Rhea. "What proof do you offer?"

Tavia held a kopis in her hand, the same blade she'd used to take Rhea's hair, and now she used its edge to slash the ties at the top of Rhea's dress. "How dare you!" Rhea seethed, longing to shove the priestess back but needing her arms to clutch the butchered cloth to her chest, hiding as much as she could.

"Rhea is the proof. She is with child."

"Show me," Prisca commanded, her tone like iron.

Rhea closed her eyes, summoning her mother. Jocasta's voice was worn by time, but her message remained, as clarion as ever: *You will survive this. Pain . . . it purifies.*

Rhea dropped the dress.

Valeria moaned, and Aemilia openly wept. Horatia clapped her hands over her eyes. "I cannot look!" the old woman keened. "I cannot handle such depravity!"

Was this the most humiliating moment of Rhea's life? Standing exposed before these women, judged and shamed while a woman who despised her stood exultant?

Yes. In any life, in any lifetime, yes.

Prisca swallowed deeply, seeming to struggle for words. On a deep breath, she began to speak: "This is a dark moment in the House of the Vestals, perhaps the darkest. A priestess fouled under my watch." Prisca lifted her arms, palms up, in supplication. "I feel Vesta's approval diminish. I feel the goddess denouncing me, abandoning all of us—" Prisca's gasp cut her off. Her eyes widened like twin moons. "The flame!"

Two words, but more than enough to send all six Vestals rushing barefoot from the house and into the temple. Rhea wore her torn dress in a hasty wrap.

The inner sanctum's blackness spoke to Rhea's transgression—yet another one, and one of paramount consequence. This was the flame that guarded all of Latium.

"Check for embers!" Prisca shouted, to anyone, to everyone, frantic. Valeria and Tavia reached the circular hearth first and poked at its ashes with rods.

"Nothing," Valeria reported in a hushed tone. "The light of Vesta has gone out."

Prisca ululated, a dying sound, harsh and terrible. She collapsed to the floor, and Horatia fluttered to her side.

"You have cursed us all," the head priestess wailed.

"I—"

Rhea did not finish—her defense? her apology?—before the walls began to shake. Tiles fell from the ceiling like fatal hail, and the pillars holding up the roof trembled.

Vesta was displeased.

The Vestals screamed, clutching one another in what must be their final moments.

I have cursed them all, Rhea agreed, succumbing to guilt and grief. *I deserve to die.*

But clearheaded Aemilia held fast and steady. She ripped Horatia's shawl from the old woman's shoulders and flew to the fireplace, sure-footed despite the earthquake. She flapped the fabric outward—once, twice, again and again—with the force of both arms.

"Return, Vesta!" she enjoined, calling the flames with wind and word. "We who serve you are fallible, human, and endlessly complicated. We need your strength now more than ever. Come back to us, though we may err—against you and each other. I beseech you, holy Vesta, please return."

And whether it was the air Aemilia fed to that last dying spark or the divine will of Vesta offering them a second chance, the fire returned. A single flame at first, but a tiny light is more than enough for trained priestesses to support with kindling.

Prisca laid her face in her hands.

Outside, a lark sang.

Chapter XXII

RHEA

NOBODY, NOT EVEN the Virgo Maxima, dared to beat Rhea. Not because any of the Vestals liked her so much, but because her father was still very much alive and had been the king of all Latium for most of their lives. But the priestesses, her so-called family, turned on Rhea quickly enough. Even Valeria, even Aemilia.

The priestesses tied her hands behind her back with coarse rope. Linked her ankles together. They covered her eyes with a dark cloth.

"You should beg for leniency," advised Valeria.

"You know I will not."

"Lock her in the barn!" Horatia shrieked. "Fornicator!"

But the barn had too many openings to shutter, too many possibilities for escape. Instead, Rhea was placed in a windowless storage room of the house, door barred and Tavia on guard, while Prisca journeyed to the Regia to alert the royal council.

It was well within Prisca's power to dispose of Rhea however she saw fit. Still, politics prevailed. Because the Order of the Vestals received funding and protection from the crown, the high priestess would not jeopardize her other four birds for the one who had strayed from the nest. Until King Amulius was consulted, Rhea would remain unscathed.

Imprisoned but unscathed.

"There is nothing I can do for you now," Aemilia, her former friend, conceded from the other side of the door. "You should have known better."

Sweetness gone sour. A rotten fruit.

Tied down and blind amid the pots and brooms and rags, Rhea girded herself for the imminent taunts. How Tavia must relish in her righteousness after so many months of suspecting and waiting!

And yet none came. Not a foul word.

It was a surprise that Rhea couldn't fathom, so neither could she enjoy the quiet. It was a strained silence, a calm before the impending storm. By now, her sins were known throughout the Regia. Her reputation was ruined, her death arranged. Was there some relief? Maybe. Secrets are heavy, and she had carried this one, by herself, for a long time. But mostly she'd gone numb. Rhea supposed it was her way of defending her soul against abject devastation.

The one benefit of pregnancy? Her body always craved sleep. Despite the precariousness circling her—or maybe because of it—Rhea dropped into a deep, dreamless slumber.

◆ ◆ ◆

SHE WOKE LATER—how much later, she could not say—to Tavia's emotionless announcement: "He's here."

Amulius.

There must have been a time when Rhea trusted him. As a child, perhaps? But he had always been a monster, lurking behind her father, sniffing out their weaknesses, planning his attack on her family. She knew she should ready herself for battle, but she was so dispirited that it was impossible to summon her usual courage.

The storage room door creaked open. Her blindfold was removed.

"Ilia."

"Father?!"

His presence confused her, as did his diminished physical appearance. Rhea recognized Numitor while still noting all his changes. His skin was bleached of color as if he had eschewed the sun since the October Horse, and his hands seemed too large for what his body had become. But his watery eyes looked more alert than when she'd left the Regia. Less dazed, more focused.

"Let me see you," her father said roughly, as if sound itself moved along a path not recently traveled.

Rhea rose, struggling in her bindings. She had become accustomed to slouching, for bad posture best covered her belly, but now, with her wrists fastened behind her back, she stood straight. There would be no more hiding. This was who she was.

Numitor's eyes closed on a sigh, as if it hurt to look at her. "Who did this to you?"

"I did it, too."

That snapped his eyes right open. "Be serious, Rhea. Who is the father?"

Finally, the question. *The* question. She could certainly lie, but there was hardly a believable alibi. Everybody knew she entertained no sweethearts, and the truth might be her savior.

"Mars."

Numitor's brow wrinkled.

"Mars, Father. The god of war."

In the corner, Tavia gasped, but Numitor only frowned.

"It is not like you to play these games."

"I play at nothing. I lay with Mars in the woods."

"He was not Mars. Many men would call themselves such to bed a girl like you."

"I'm no fool, Father. After I watched him transform from a wolf, I had no doubt."

Numitor shook his head. "We are not like the Greeks. Our gods do not step into our lives."

"He certainly stepped into mine."

"You are serious? Mars is the father?"

"Yes."

Numitor clutched his chest, and Rhea worried his heart might stop.

"Oh, Ilia. This must be my fault. I angered Mars at some point, did not properly honor his altar, maintain the sacrifices. I have erred, indeed, for a god to force himself upon my daughter . . ."

"Father," Rhea began softly, "Mars did not hurt me. I called his name."

If Numitor had been near tears, they dried up after that proclamation.

"Rhea, that isn't done. Such impertinence, such brazen indecency!"

It should have been horribly awkward to discuss such intimate matters with her father, but he had not acted like one in such a long while. Their separation had removed a sense of filial propriety, or maybe Rhea's rapidly approaching death had made her brash.

"Father, a woman craving a man's touch is hardly novel."

"But didn't I raise you to respect boundaries? To observe and maintain the proper relationships between worlds—ours and theirs?"

"I have watched you do everything right, perform every ritual with the utmost care. And what has that awarded you? You lost your wife, your sons, your health. Your younger brother sent me away, and nobody raised a finger to stop him. So I sought the powers available to me in a different way."

He gestured to her stomach. "And this was your way? A pregnant Vestal under penalty of death? No husband? Rhea, you could have married the Prince of Ardea and been a queen. Why did you not accept his offer when you could?"

She could hardly believe her ears. "Where were you with such counsel—with *any* counsel—in this past year?"

"I suffered a great agony."

"I grieved Aegestus, too! Yet I did it alone, and with a clear head."

Numitor shifted his gaze away from his daughter.

"I always found you so brilliant," she continued. "I worshipped your mind, your ability to always cut through the noise to the just cause, the right path. But you have strayed, Father." She knew Tavia listened and was glad. "When Aegestus died, Amulius instructed Sethre to ply you with poppy milk, a drink that takes you further away from me, from Alba Longa."

"Sethre is an augur, not a poisoner, and he serves the rulers of Latium."

"And its current ruler? The brother who usurped you?"

Numitor sighed, rubbed at the sides of his forehead. "Rhea, Amulius did what was necessary for our family's legacy, for Latium. I allowed it."

"He drugged you and stole your throne!"

Why did he trust Amulius more than her? Such misplaced loyalty! Such severe injustice! Rhea's toes curled against the stone floor; she clenched and unclenched her fists. She had raised her voice, as well, breaking all the rules of proper royal decorum.

"Ilia, I thought I taught you to take accountability for your own actions. The world is not out to get you; it is a lonely life when you have no faith in others."

"Placing faith in the wrong people cost us everything, Father."

Numitor examined his remaining child with utter melancholy. "You find me an ineffectual father, and this might be my gravest failure of all, but I will speak to the council on your behalf. I would not have you punished for the act of a prurient god."

"Then you will bear false testimony. I was just as prurient."

He exhaled sharply. "I would spare your life, daughter, even if I struggle to recognize you as such."

His harshness stole her breath, but he was already departing, and the conversation had concluded. Rhea's bruised and battered soul—or whatever force had been holding her numb pieces together—collapsed. Tavia caught Rhea before she crumpled to the floor, then dragged her back to the storage room, setting her down inside with far more care than Rhea expected. Tavia paused like she might say something but then reconsidered; still, she did not retie the blindfold.

Tavia shut the door.

Indifferent to their circumstances, the baby kicked.

Chapter XXIII

ANTHO

WHY DID THE Virgo Maxima consult privately with King Amulius?
Why did the old king, Numitor, depart the Regia shortly after?

Whispers filled the royal compound, flying through the hallways, upstairs and down, over trays of food and carts of stone, between tapestries and trees.

Did something happen to Rhea Silvia?
What did that girl do now?

Antho caught the rumors and stopped short. She had a strong suspicion as to why Prisca consulted privately with the king, and why Rhea's father would need to immediately see his daughter for himself.

Rhea's secret had been released—Antho's worst fear realized.

She snuck away from her mother, feigning a stomachache, and went in search of Leandros. As a king's guard, he would best know her father's whereabouts. She found Leandros outside her father's tablinum, where Amulius had plotted and planned his kingship. Antho had been inside only once. The surfaces were covered in maps, in sheets full of tally marks and numbers. His conquests in land and gold.

Though Leandros undoubtedly noted every step of her approach, he did not break countenance and kept his shoulders square, his spear held tightly across his body.

"Is my father occupied?" she asked, knowing that it was awful to approach him like this after their unresolved conversation by the well.

"Yes, Princess."

"With my uncle?"

"With Calvus Flavius, Princess."

"Ah." She licked her lips nervously. She had betrayed Leandros; she did not deserve his assistance, yet she needed an idea of where and when Rhea's fate would be decided. "I wondered if my father—"

"The king has called his council to session in the reception room after the midday meal. To discuss the Vestal Virgin, I suspect."

Though Antho hadn't finished her sentence, Leandros understood what information she sought, and he wanted to help, regardless of how she had hurt him.

You are the best man I have ever known.

"Thank you."

He gave her a stiff nod, and then Antho fled in search of the servant Zea. Antho would repair the damage between her and Leandros, she knew that now, but it would have to be deferred until she learned more about Ilia. She pulled Zea from the laundry room.

"I need your aid," she whispered, leading her away from the others, "and your discretion."

Zea gripped Antho's hand and squeezed. "You always have both."

Antho prayed to Fortuna as the two women slunk toward the council room, and surely the goddess had listened, for it was still empty. Against the wall, there was a trunk where the servants kept spare furs for visiting dignitaries. Antho opened it and handed bundle after bundle to Zea, loading her arms with pelts.

"Please hide these for me. I will return them later."

Zea looked around the room nervously. "What are you planning?"

"There must be room in the trunk for me. I intend to listen to the council meeting."

Zea's eyes widened, but there was an approving slant to her mouth. "You have gotten quite willful since Princess Rhea left, but I can't say I disapprove."

Antho stepped into the trunk and lowered herself. She was tall but thin enough that she could fold herself into its confines. "Close the lid, Zea."

"It's heavy; how will you get out?"

"If you haven't seen me by nightfall, come get me."

Zea shut the lid, and Antho was entombed. It was a horrifying sensation, and she counted her breaths to keep herself sane. Thankfully, men entered soon enough, already engaged in hushed conversations that Antho could not discern, but when they all fell silent, she knew her father and uncle had arrived.

"Is it true, Numitor?" a voice asked, unofficially commencing the council. "Your daughter is with child?"

"She is."

Did the other men blush in discomfort at the common ugliness of family matters that transcended rank? Or did they secretly relish it? A princess brought low. A king humbled. The thrill of spectacle, of another man's scandal.

"It was by no fault of her own," Numitor continued. "Her innocence was violently taken by one much older and stronger."

"So says every woman with her life on the line."

"I have never known Rhea Silvia to be wanton."

"Then name the villain and bring him forth to provide testimony!"

It was difficult for Antho to match the voices with the other council members, though she had known them all for years. Calvus and Hadrian, Messina, Drusus, and Gallus.

"I may name him," Numitor replied hesitantly, "but he will not attend our summons."

"Is he mute?" Amulius challenged. "Lame? Dead? I am his king. I shall have his words or his tongue."

"You are not his king. Nor was I or our father before us. It was no man who came upon my daughter in the sacred grove." A long pause followed. "My daughter was violated by Mars."

Mars?!

Antho gasped, then covered her mouth with her fist, biting into her knuckles. Ilia and Mars? Could he have been her mystery man all along? Knowing Rhea as she did, it was not inconceivable. Outside the trunk, the councilors refrained from speech. They waited, holding back their reactions until receiving the king's signal. It was how all courtiers were trained to respond within the hierarchy.

Finally, a laugh. Loud and long.

"You are too old to remake yourself a jester, my brother."

"I would not joke with my girl's life, Amulius. Mars forced himself on Rhea and filled her womb."

"Another Aeneas," a voice mused in wonderment. "A child born of mortal and immortal blood. Rhea Silvia has been chosen by fate!"

"I pride myself as a man of reason," another countered. "This isn't plausible."

"In Greece, the gods impregnate maidens with abandon."

"But that is in Greece!"

"We are Latins, and the punishment for a Vestal who breaks her vow of chastity is clear." By the instinctive way her skin crawled, Antho knew Calvus spoke. "We would not meet to discuss any fallen Vestal if she weren't formerly of the royal family. If we go against the Vestals' tradition, we set a dangerous precedent."

"It will be more dangerous to offend Mars!" refuted another. "He has chosen the girl!"

"King Amulius, you have no sons. This child of Rhea Silvia and Mars would be a legend. If it be a boy, name him your heir."

"My daughter's son will be heir," Amulius replied in a bloodless voice, cold and reptilian.

Antho shuddered.

"Brother," implored Numitor, "you have always done what is right for me and for Alba Longa. The high priestess of the Vestal Virgins awaits your word. You alone can save my daughter. I stand before you not as your former king but as a humbled father. Do not condemn Rhea. Allow her to renounce her vows and go live somewhere safe and small with her child, in a place as far away as you choose. Do not jeopardize the Latin people with a god's wrath or break your brother's heart."

Numitor has done well, Antho thought. *Rhea has a chance.*

"King Amulius, I would ask your permission to speak."

Gasps from the assembly. A new voice! Who could it be? Familiar enough, but Antho's mind could not picture its face.

"You are no councilor!"

"Nor will I ever be. I am a soldier, the son of a farmer, but I hold information that must be shared. Forgive my intrusion."

A soldier? And then, with a sinking realization, Antho knew the speaker's identity. She pictured his mean, scarred face, saw him lurking in the shadows, following her and Leandros. Her father's henchman, Helvius.

"Well, what is it, boy? And be quick."

"Rhea Silvia's baby is mine."

A crash. Something clattered against the stone floor.

"No." A whispered refute.

"Before Rhea Silvia left the Regia, I was stationed in her rooms. We had . . . relations."

Antho grimaced, nearly gagged. Rhea hated Helvius—every woman at the Regia hated Helvius! The royal council, composed of Alba Longa's most intelligent men, would know this. They would find this testimony ludicrous.

"The princess and a guard? *This* guard?" someone muttered, and Antho's heart lifted. "It is unbelievable."

"Why would he lie? How would it benefit him?"

"These proceedings disgust me," groused Amulius. "Helvius, whether your disclosure is determined to be true or false, there will be punishment. Ten lashes and removal from your position within the Regia."

"I accept the consequences of my actions. I was a man tempted by a very beautiful young woman. But my duty is to the truth and my king."

"You are dismissed." Antho heard her father sigh. "I cannot deliver this judgment alone. To condemn my niece, regardless of her crimes, would weigh too heavily upon my heart. If you believe Mars, the divine, the immortal god of war and fertile lands, is the father of Rhea Silvia's child, then we must pardon her sins. But if you think that Rhea's condition is the consequence of a tryst between her and a young guard who frequented her rooms, then the Vestals must pursue retribution in their way."

"The child belongs to Mars," Numitor insisted. "I know this as surely as I know the sun will rise tomorrow from the east."

"I concur. Let Rhea birth her child. It shouldn't take long for its sire to be made apparent. I would not risk Mars's wrath."

"I wish I could agree with you two," another lamented, "but common sense must prevail. The child is mortal. Rhea is yet another young woman seduced by a soldier."

"Agreed."

"I must concur, as well. My apologies, Numitor."

"Then it is two for Mars, three for Helvius. Calvus, how do you reason? If we are tied, King Amulius must cast the deciding vote."

Calvus, keen as ever, now kept tight-lipped as he calculated the value of his decision. Antho shivered, chilled to the bone, for this was a man who knew the power of hesitation and used it to his advantage.

"My king, you made earlier mention of your daughter, Antho," Calvus crooned. "She will be married soon and her son named heir."

"And with a wise, decisive man as her husband, their lawful child shall be well worthy of the Latin crown."

Antho imagined the words passed through the ether between Calvus and Amulius, an entreaty answered with a nod. A treaty forged in silence, signed with a grin.

And then Calvus's careful, crafty verdict: "A child more deserving than the ill-begotten offspring of a false priestess and her bodyguard."

The deciding vote was cast, and with it, Calvus had both condemned her cousin and claimed Antho for marriage. Her heart flapped against her chest like a screaming swallow. Frenetic and repeated, overlapping. Her ribs, this chest, this palace—all a cage.

I will never be free. I will never forget or forgive.

"This council concludes. Rhea Silvia's fate will be determined by the Order of the Vestals."

"Her death, Amulius. Just say it. You release her to her death."

"It is the will of the goddess Vesta."

Sandals against the tiles as men exited, all clip-clops and shuffled steps.

"I'm sorry, brother," Antho's father said to her uncle, a gentle but meaningless offering. Numitor did not respond.

And for the first time in Antho's life, after eighteen years of practicing goodness with her whole being, she vowed revenge.

Chapter XXIV

RHEA

RHEA REMAINED BLISSFULLY unaware of these deliberations. She could not know that her father had stood up for her, albeit with half-truths, in a way he believed preserved her dignity. Similarly, she had no knowledge of Helvius's declaration, the actual besmirching of her reputation. Rhea Silvia would never regret her decision to lie with an attractive man outside of marriage. She did not care that people might deem her promiscuous. But that she would offer herself to a man like Helvius?

The ultimate disgrace to her name.

Rhea awaited her fate in the storage closet, sore from the cramped surroundings and needing to relieve herself again—a constant and inconvenient pressure in this changed body. Otherwise, she felt surprisingly tranquil. She should have been frightened, but *her father had come, and her father still loved her.* This inspired a certain optimism. For most of Rhea's life, Numitor's word was law. He might not have advocated for her before, and he might be disappointed in her now, but he would never let them kill her.

This was her tragic flaw; she still considered herself a princess.

A commotion broke out on the other side of the door. The pitch of the voices, their tension and tremor, triggered Rhea's nerves, and she sat up, leaning an ear against the wood, desperate to catch any word.

Now they would liberate her, and she would seek asylum in another city. Her father would give her money to start another life. Somehow, all would be well. Maybe, after enough years passed, she could return to Alba Longa, and her child could grow up beside Antho's.

Names cut through the clamor—her father's and uncle's—and then Aemilia cried out, and Rhea knew she was going to die.

Had she really thought her father would rescue her? The stupidest mistake in a series of stupid mistakes.

Rhea's mouth went dry, and her tongue became too large in her mouth. She could not swallow. The dryness of her lips became unbearable, as did the pressure on her bladder. Her stomach revolted in a flurry of movement. A reminder: *they* were going to die, not just she.

It was time—if there was any left—to call for Mars.

"Mars, perhaps I should have said something sooner," Rhea beseeched with a slight quiver, feeling especially desperate and pathetic that her final moments might be spent praying in a storage room. "But I was proud. I'm not anymore. Help me. Help us." Her knees ached against the harsh stone, but she remained, hands clasped to her chest. "Mars, you are our last chance."

Without the blindfold on, she watched as the air shimmered, flickering shades of silvery blue, like the most central part of a flame. From the ethereal fire, a petite figure in a chaste stola and veil materialized.

Not Mars but Vesta. Rhea's heart dropped; she had just hastened her execution.

Oh no, Rhea lamented to herself. *What have I done?*

"You dare call for Mars in my home?" The goddess's voice might have been sweet, but her tone was the very opposite.

"He is the father of my child."

"He is the father of many children."

Rhea's mouth set in a hard line.

"He is not welcome here, in my jurisdiction. Not while you belong to me." Vesta shook her head, on the edge of pity. "He was never going to help you."

Nearby. I got as close as the chicken coop one day.

He should have told her. His "other children" hardly mattered;

Rhea had never expected fidelity or romance from Mars, but because of this, she'd assumed her heart properly guarded. She thought knowing who he was, what they were, kept her safe. Yet this was a devastating blow. By skirting the truth, he'd made a fatal omission. Rhea wrapped her arms around her belly.

"Why haven't you apologized to me?" Vesta demanded.

"If I did," Rhea responded, regaining her composure, "would you pardon me?"

"No."

Rhea shrugged. "Then you have my answer."

Vesta's eyes widened. "Such impertinence! You should plead for my clemency regardless, mortal girl. You defiled my temple with your filth, nearly destroying its foundation! Your negligence lost my flame!"

Oh, Rhea was done with this conversation! If she was condemned already, she had nothing to lose. She laughed under her breath. "I didn't crack the temple—your tantrum did."

"Apologize immediately!"

"I am so sorry that I was born a woman and that I refused to be herded like a sheep." If Rhea still had hair, she would toss it over her shoulder. "Because women aren't your sheep, Vesta. We are wolves."

"Sheep, wolves—they both die." Vesta snorted. "And so do foolish girls. Sooner than you think."

The goddess's words met their mark. Rhea felt the bravado seep from her body like blood from an open wound.

"Nobody cares about you, Rhea Silvia, and nobody is coming."

And the rest of Rhea's confidence evaporated with Vesta, leaving Rhea alone and very, very angry.

"You've seen my smile," Rhea whispered aloud—to herself, to nobody, to everyone. "Remember my teeth."

It could not have been Vesta's intention, but their meeting invigorated Rhea's will to live. Maybe she'd lost her insouciance, but she hadn't lost her drive. She didn't need her father or her baby's father; she only needed herself. However, this required a weapon. There must be something of use in this damned closet. If she had considered this earlier, she could have amassed an arsenal by now. Neither of her brothers would have committed such a foolish blunder. In fact, Lausus would have already broken free, and Aegestus would have charmed his way into escape.

Apparently, Rhea lacked brawn *and* brains.

Beside her sat a clay pot. Even with her hands tied behind her back, she could clutch it and slam it down against the floor. Barley seeds spilled outward amid the shattered clay, releasing a slightly sweet scent. Rhea dug frantically through the remnants, searching for a suitable shard, anything sharp enough to break skin.

And then what? She'd stab an old woman? Slit a Vestal's throat?

Rhea's head drooped as the courage left her once more. Was she brave enough to be violent? She gripped the clay piece too tightly, felt the bite, the warm blood blooming upon her own hand. Her emotions vacillated so unexpectedly. Was this due to the pregnancy or her imminent death?

When the door opened, all five of the other Vestal Virgins awaited her, knives and ropes in every hand. Prisca, in her formal headdress, was awful to behold, a holy terror, Vulcan's handmaid, her sagging and swollen eyes underlit by the torch she carried.

"The Regia has chosen not to intercede on your behalf. Your fate belongs to the dictates of our order, as they have passed down through generations of Vestals. My opinion of you as a person is negligible; I must honor our ways."

Rhea wished for words, for strength, for courage, but fear robbed her of them all.

"I will not parade you undressed through the city; I will not subject you to the jeers of the people. That is my weakness but also my gratitude for your mother, who supported our order." Prisca turned to Valeria, and the other Vestal gave an encouraging nod. "My debt to the late queen Jocasta is paid."

The high priestess withdrew, and Horatia beckoned Rhea forward.

"Rise, sinner! Beneath the cover of night, while Alba Longa sleeps, we escort you to the underground."

Rhea's parched mouth could barely form a question. She forced a swallow, licked her lips. "Now?"

"Yes."

Aemilia untied Rhea's foot bindings but gasped when she moved to Rhea's hands.

"What is this?" the priestess murmured, prying the shard from Rhea's grip.

"A weapon?" Horatia keened. "She would kill us all!"

"No, I wouldn't . . . I wasn't—"

"I will handle it," Tavia interrupted. She took the shard from Aemilia and pocketed it, then held her kopis at Rhea's lower back, at the soft spot directly over the organs. "Your hands will remain tied. Walk or my blade will remind you."

Prisca led their troupe out of the house and into the city. A haunting funeral procession, ghosts in white. The living and the damned.

Rhea walked as if stumbling through a dream, through a nightmare. Could any of this be real? How could these be her last moments aboveground? Should she be memorizing each smell and sound, breathing as deeply as possible? How much life could she take in, take with her?

Their entourage halted at a low hill just past the city's edge, in a place so nondescript that Rhea had never noticed it before. And this was the point. The tomb had been built at the distance necessary to shield the Vestals and the Alban people from any condemned priestess's screams.

At the base of the hill was a square slab of gray tuff—the entrance. *Or a lid*, Rhea thought, *and I am to be the message, placed into this earthen bottle and sealed up forever.* What was the message? *Keep your knees together!*

Valeria and Aemilia joined forces to push the stone, but it would not budge.

Horatia motioned to Rhea. "Rhea, go h—" But then Tavia stepped forward, cutting her off. "I'll do it."

The combined strength of the three priestesses shifted the massive slab, leaving them huffing from exertion. The opening released a stale odor: dirt and rot, the aroma of the underneath. And the six women stood in awkward silence, in loaded witness, for they were aware—perhaps for the first time—that no one was safe. This was no sisterhood but an ancient religious order. If the old king's daughter could go down, each of them was one tiny sin away from a similar fall.

Prisca cleared her throat. "This has not happened since I became high priestess. It did, regrettably, when I was a young Vestal, but I had hoped to never see it again." Rhea felt Prisca's indignation, and it wasn't because Rhea was pregnant; it was because that pregnancy had forced the high priestess's hand into such a dirty business.

"Before you descend, know this: The father of your child has confessed. King Amulius stripped him of his sword and station and exiled him from Alba Longa."

Rhea startled. "My child's father?"

"Yes," Prisca answered, almost impatiently. "The guard with the lip scar."

Helvius. Should Rhea laugh? Scream? Cry? The confusing onrush of emotion threatened to burst her open. *Helvius* had claimed her virginity? That despicable man? Oh, she had been outmaneuvered once again! Amulius was no ordinary enemy.

"That is a perjury orchestrated by the king," responded Rhea. "I lay with Mars in the sacred grove. I bathed with him in the sacred spring. I knowingly spoke false vows to Vesta, and to all of you, the following day. But my child was sired by a god, not a guard."

Their reactions were varied. Valeria pursed her lips. Horatia covered her ears and hummed. Aemilia bit her fingernails. And Tavia? Well, Tavia already knew, but the lines of her firm, tight mouth quivered.

"Oh, starling," Prisca sighed. "If this is true, let us hope he has some plan to spare you."

Horatia presented the supplies.

"This basket contains bread, milk, water, and oil," Prisca said. "And I will provide you with this lamp. It shall light the chamber until it dies . . ." She let the final word resonate.

Valeria raised her own lamp over the hole and Rhea peered down.

A rope ladder descended into a subterranean chamber where a simple bed waited.

"Valeria," Rhea pleaded. She had always thought she would leave claw marks on this world, and here she was, pleading in a whisper. "Don't do this to me."

"*We* are not doing anything," Prisca clarified, interceding. "It is the rules."

How quickly those in power absolved themselves of responsibility under the cloak of tradition!

Aemilia cut the bindings around Rhea's wrists and placed the basket in her hands. Then Tavia surprised Rhea by pulling her into a close hug; when Rhea resisted, the basket jostled between them. Rhea couldn't be sure, but she thought she saw Tavia's hand slip inside. Neither woman mentioned it.

"Go," Horatia ordered, pointing at the rope ladder. "If you don't climb, we'll push."

Would a broken leg even register, considering what Rhea was about to endure?

"Your mother would be grateful you had nineteen years," Valeria murmured, her eyes wet. "That's more than either of her boys got."

"Do not speak to me of my mother," Rhea snapped. And with as much dignity as she could muster—and the basket over her arm—Rhea clutched the rope ladder as her feet found purchase. She moved downward as slowly as possible, not only because she wanted to delay the inevitable but also because her legs shook too badly to move.

"Faster!" Horatia urged, and somebody above shook the rope. Worried she would be thrown off, Rhea leaped the rest of the way down.

"Do not do this!" she exhorted one last time from the bottom of the pit. "You aren't murderers!"

Her pleas sounded thin in this stagnant air.

Five heads peered down at her. Five versions of the same look. And then Horatia said what they all probably thought: "You did this, fornicator!" she warbled. "Liar!"

"You are no longer a Vestal," Prisca denounced. "Rhea, you are released from your duties, your title, our governance and protection."

The Vestals pulled up the ladder. The stone slab slid back into place.

Her father had not come. Antho had not come. Mars was never coming. There was nobody left who cared for her.

And despite everything she had promised herself she wouldn't do, Rhea screamed.

◆ ◆ ◆

ONCE THERE WAS a princess with two brothers and two parents. She loved dancing and lying on the summer rooftop—those cardinal moments between bursts of wind when the sun warmed her body—and imagined a future of communion, the joy of coming together. Nieces and nephews, her own dark-haired children, and a husband who adored her spirit as much as her body.

But then the institutions she'd been raised to honor—the thrones and the altars—betrayed her humanity and hid her away like an unwelcome thought. Buried her like a burden.

"I have failed at everything I have tried to do," Rhea professed to the gloom.

She inspected her barren surroundings. A round dirt hole, perhaps two of her in height, one and a half of her in length. There was a thin mattress, no blanket. No table or chamber pot. Because of her pregnant body and its most pressing needs, Rhea dropped to her knees and a dug a pit latrine with her bare hands directly across from the end of her bed. She would position everything in relation to the cot so that when she lost light, she would know where to find things. Then she wiped her filthy palms against her dress, picked up the lamp, and circled the chamber, inspecting the surface of the dirt-packed walls, holding the light close to her face. She traced the tomb with her fingers, beginning to learn every change in texture, hoping—ludicrously—that she might commit each groove to memory.

And she also searched for remnants of the women before. Had they made notches, left any messages? Who were these sisters of hers, bonded forever in the solidarity of their shame?

Nothing, not a mark indicating that they had ever existed. Rhea hoped this meant they had died quickly.

Tour complete, Rhea sat cross-legged upon her bed, hugging the basket as closely to her chest as her bulging belly would allow. She had not eaten since before the bathhouse, and though hungry, she would avoid temptation. This mild discomfort was nothing compared with what would come. But the basket triggered the memory of Tavia's strange farewell, and Rhea had to peek inside: a loaf of bread looking too delicious, a small jug of water, a stopper of oil.

And the clay shard from the closet.

Rhea picked it up, pressed its point into her thumb. What was Tavia's purpose in sneaking her this weapon? To defend herself against ants? Moles?

To kill herself and end the misery. An extension of charity.

But then came that accusatory kick in her stomach that always seemed to follow her most macabre thoughts. Her decisions affected them both. If she slit her wrists, would the baby bleed out, too? Or would it carry on, left to die a slow, suffocating death inside its own tomb within her?

A single tear fell down her cheek. Rhea wiped it away.

"No," she scolded herself. "Conserve water."

Rhea lay down on her side and watched the lamp, waiting in morbid vigil for it to be extinguished, too. At least the flame would go out quickly. A luxury. She had never been truly alone before, had never experienced true quiet. Not in the bustle of the Regia—the servants and the duties and the gossip—or in the tempered business of the temple, reserved but continual. The silence made her conundrum more surreal: How could Rhea feel so alive yet also so close to death?

She could imagine no feasible way to save herself. She could neither reach the top nor move the stone slab by herself. If she attempted to dig, the walls would certainly collapse upon her. Surely a gradual death by starvation was better than suffocation, a frenzied final struggle to breathe as she choked on soil?

Small rocks littered the ground beside her filthy cot. Rhea selected one and used it to sharpen the edge of her shard, servicing it into a fragile but piercing point. It would crumble in battle, but could it still sever an artery? Absolutely.

Rhea continued feeding the lamp a steady diet of olive oil. The flame cast her silhouette against the earthen walls in surprising detail: a pregnant woman huddled on a cot, her scalp covered in uneven patches of new hair. Rhea ran a hand over her head.

"You are a shorn beast," she told her image, and then she howled, a feral call that ended in laughter, for she was communicating with her own shadow and well on her way toward insanity.

She clutched the shard tighter.

◆ ◆ ◆

RHEA WAS STILL awake when the light burned out. Forlorn and alone, she waited for gruesome deliverance.

In this chasm devoid of hope.

In breathtaking defeat.

Inhuman. Ignominious. Inglorious.

In the deep silence, a darkness compounded by the desolation of her soul.

"I am so sorry," she told her baby, to the tiny heart clinging to hers. It was her first real apology, the only one that mattered. "I love you."

Chapter XXV

ANTHO

HELVIUS WAS WHIPPED, stripped of duty, and then provided a fine piece of farmland and a house in Tibur. The servant Zea relayed the news to Antho, trembling with umbrage.

And Rhea was dying, wherever she was. No amount of prying on Antho's part had unlocked the location of the clandestine Vestal chamber. And should she discover it, what then? Antho would set Rhea free? Hardly. Antho was weak of body and mind. Pathetic. The lowest sort of soul. For when the king had announced her betrothal to Calvus the night before, she had kissed his proffered hand.

"Thank you, Father."

Antho burned with shame, blistered and branded, scalded and scorched by it.

Another woman might have screamed or cried, broken things, threatened. But what would any such behavior achieve? A beating, assuredly, but also restricted privileges. Antho would cling to the freedoms she had left. The adamantine agreement between Amulius and Calvus could not be broken by hysterics. She would only waste her energy. And worst of all, Leandros would be sent away on some perilous mission, leading a one-way vanguard into certain doom.

This was her life now. Antho would marry Calvus and bear his children and disappear, just like so many Latin women before her. Nobody would remember who she had been before. The child Antho, the young woman Antho. The dreamer. The believer.

She poured salt at the altars of the Regia's Lares and Penates. Who would honor the household and ancestral deities when she was gone? She should teach a servant the prayers before she left.

Prayers.

Antho covered her mouth with one hand as the thought struck her, salt spilling on the floor. Antho's own fate was signed and sealed, but there might be one last appeal to make for Rhea's. And if it helped, the irony was too rich. Hadn't her father boasted of his "pious girl"?

He might live to regret it.

◆ ◆ ◆

ANTHO DEPARTED THE Regia with Zea as her chaperone.

"To pray at the Temple of Juno," she told her mother, knowing that Claudia would approve, Juno being Claudia's patron goddess.

"What will you bring her?" the queen inquired.

Antho removed the lid of her basket. Inside lay a dead cuckoo bird. Claudia nodded.

Antho did not lie to her mother; she *did* go to the Temple of Juno, but Antho had become a master in partial truths. She gave the priests her cuckoo to burn and then hurried to her ultimate and ulterior destination: the Temple of Mars, just outside the city gates.

She removed the gold bangle from her wrist, and her arm immediately felt exposed. Lacking. For the sacrifice to work, it needed to mean something, and this was Antho's most treasured possession. Rhea had chosen it from Jocasta's effects after the queen's funeral.

My mother would want you to have something of hers. She loved you, too, Antho.

Antho placed it with the other offerings on the altar, and then she knelt.

In all her years of devotion, Antho had never made an entreaty to Mars. He was not the god of well-behaved virgin girls. But he had been the god for Rhea, and that was enough for Antho. She did not know the proper words of supplication, so she created her own. Antho would so-licit Mars with honesty if not formality.

Mars.

Mars Gradivus, man of war.

Mars Quirinus, man of peace.

Mars Ultor, the avenger.

When I consider the demands others place on you, my own appeal seems minor. I do not ask for victory in battle, absolute destruction to an army of my foes. I need no military conquest, no border, no scalps. I only ask for the life of one woman.

You wanted her, and I want this: save Rhea Silvia.

Do not let them kill her for living. Do not let them bury another woman who deserves to rise. Do not let them punish one for the acts of two.

Once Antho began, she realized how much she had to say.

What was right for you and Ilia was wrong for Vesta, so how are we mortals to act? How do we walk the shaky line between right and wrong when that line continues to bob and weave?

And if Rhea has fallen from your grace as well, preserve the child that rests in her belly. Your child, one of destiny, mixed with ichor and the blood of Aeneas.

Free Rhea, Mars. Release her to this world and its people, who need her.

And then, because she was not too proud and it mattered so much, Antho said *please.*

Chapter XXVI

RHEA

DAYS PASS, OR so Rhea assumes in the eternal gloaming. What is time to the nearly dead? A prolonging of pain, a false hope? The food is long gone, and only a few sips of water remain. When the living are buried, it disrupts the sequence of life, the proper order of things. As such, Rhea's thoughts are disordered, muddling how she processes what is happening to her. In the dark, she is every tense, unable to differentiate between past and present, split between life and death. For she is both there and not there, apart and a part of it all.

When the others arrive, she participates and spectates in a way that is only possible for a blinded person who sees solely with their mind. For when one uses their eyes alone, they never perceive the ghosts.

The mothers meet, beneath the earth, in a theater of queens, composed of memory and song, of soil and root and fossil and woman:

RHEA (aloud, her weak lips struggling to form the necessary
shapes). What was I born to do and how shall I do it?
(She wanted to run with the river, to love a man who
deserved her, to hold her family close. She wanted to nur-
ture, to save, to survive. Power? Perhaps. But justice? Al-
ways yes.)

The biggest spider Rhea has ever seen enters the cave, but Rhea barely recoils. The spider transforms, and there is Lavinia, Aeneas's queen, for she must come first.

LAVINIA. Rhea Silvia, child of my line, we are so alike! I, too, made decisions that my people did not understand. I chose the windswept outsider over a proper Latin prince, and it made all the difference.

RHEA. How?

LAVINIA. It led to you! To the catalyst and the crucible. Within your belly is the House of Aeneas of Troy and Lavinia of Latium, joined by gods both old and new.

RHEA (miserably). I am none of this. I am nothing. Why celebrate the condemned? It is too late for me.

LAVINIA. I am the ancient mother, and I will remind you who you are and who you need to be.

Animals materialize, lucent in the absence of all light. A crocodile slithers up to Lavinia. A bear and a lion appear, too.

LAVINIA. We are all wild first, Rhea. Call it back, call it up. Claim it. Choose it.

RHEA (incredulous). There is no "we." These are animals.

LAVINIA (smiling). We are women. We are both.

A woman Rhea barely remembers emerges from the crocodile: her grandmother Xanthe, wife of King Procas.

XANTHE. My child. You were a baby when I saw you last, and now you are so beautiful!

RHEA. Grandmother, I have never been uglier.

XANTHE (chuckling). I refer to your soul, Ilia. It shines.

RHEA. I am dying, and I am afraid that it will hurt. It hurts now.

XANTHE. That's not the dying, dear. It's the life inside you that hurts. Death is much easier than life.

LAVINIA. The history of our land is written in the blood of brothers. When my husband died, my stepson, Ascanius, became king. He was too battle-scarred to rule, and I worried he wouldn't be strong enough to hold Latium together. I did what I must. I brought my own son, Silvius, to the forest and raised him away from court. He returned to Latium a better man, the best man. He took the throne.

XANTHE. Are you beginning to understand?

RHEA (in frustration). No.

LAVINIA. This is the first lesson, Rhea. Men think they create the empires, but both are born of women. You will be a mother of kings.

RHEA (aside, more to herself). I said as much to my uncle once.

XANTHE. Which leads us to the second lesson, my lesson. Ilia, my sons put you here, not Mars. Be careful how you raise your boys. We worry too much about our daughters, ensuring they are pretty and polite, virtuous and hard-working. I should have expected more of my sons.

RHEA. I don't blame you, Grandmother.
(But she thinks: There is another woman I blame.*)*

The third animal, the bear, steps forward and transforms. It is Jocasta, of course.

JOCASTA (issuing from the bear's fur). My treasure, my moon-stone.

RHEA (in disbelief, with some guilt). Mama?

JOCASTA. Yes, my girl. I must also speak to you of brothers.

RHEA (stubbornly). Lausus and Aegestus were good, Mama.

LAVINIA (to Xanthe). We should leave them.

Lavinia and Xanthe, the spider and the crocodile, evanesce. Mother, daughter, and lion remain.

JOCASTA. It is different between us now; I can sense it. You have learned things about me, but maybe not this: Ilia, I loved them both.

RHEA. I did, too.

JOCASTA (gently). Not your brothers.

RHEA (stubbornly). I don't want to hear this.

179

JOCASTA. You must. I loved Amulius so deeply—he was my dearest friend—but I noticed the cracks in him. The obsession, the possession. His view was too narrow, too singular, and I realized he would make a terrible father. I made a choice. I left Amulius for his older brother, and it was terrible, but I knew that Numitor would be better for my children.

RHEA (suddenly cross). He was until he wasn't.

JOCASTA. You are so full of hate, and I understand why. But hatred is unnatural. Love is not. Love is wild, and what is wild is true.

RHEA. You were reckless with love.

JOCASTA. I was, and it hurt what mattered most. I did not respect love the way I respected the wilderness. That was my mistake.

RHEA. One of many.

JOCASTA. Do not be impenetrable, Rhea. I might never get this moment again. I can apologize to you until the earth crumbles to dust, and it will not be enough. I hope you can forgive me.

RHEA (sobbing). You are my mother. I will always forgive you. I miss you.

JOCASTA. I love you, Ilia.

The lion slinks forward, nudging Jocasta.

JOCASTA. I must be quick. The third lesson is this: Ilia, you are most equipped with our collective ancestral wisdom. Reclaim your wildness and you will go forth in power.

RHEA (frustrated). What does that even mean? I am dying.

JOCASTA. You will be a mother, and to be a mother is to be the most alive.

RHEA. But who is the lion?

JOCASTA (smiling). My goddess, our goddess.

RHEA. Cybele?

There is a scuffle in the earth overhead. Dirt falls like a light rain.

JOCASTA. He approaches.

RHEA. Who?

JOCASTA. A time will come when you must decide quickly. If the goddess offers you a chance, take it. Answer the call to fight, my moonstone, and take back what is yours.

RHEA (shattered). Do not abandon me, alone here in the dark. Can't you stay with me until the end?

Jocasta does not respond; she is already fading. Not instantly, like the others, for her image holds on. And for a brief, flickering moment, she is a bear again before she's gone altogether.

RHEA. Mama!

The lion holds Rhea's gaze for an extended moment.

VOICE OF CYBELE (in Rhea's mind). When that time comes, when you are ready, I will return.

Then the lion disappears, too. All the queens and all the animals are gone, and Rhea is not sure they were ever there.

Above Rhea's head, a grunt. The stone shifts, then slides out of place. The rope ladder descends.

One word in a familiar male voice. *Hurry!*

Chapter XXVII

RHEA

RHEA SILVIA DID not care what man held that ladder and what he might demand of her. She would've done almost anything to get out of that hole. She had discarded her personal standards with her faith in humanity.

But, first, she retrieved the shard.

The forgotten muscles in Rhea's arms and legs quivered as she lifted herself onto the first rope rung. Though the ladder shook, she ground her teeth and climbed, one step at a time, breathing furiously. She would not fall. Above her, the pitch-black night sky waited. She could almost feel its breeze, a freshness so shocking after days spent trapped in the fetid fug of her own stench and refuse.

A hand gripped her wrist and pulled—up, up, up. She twisted so that her belly didn't scrape the rim and then collapsed sideways against the grass, panting. Likewise, the man fell onto his back. She could not see him; even the moonlight was too bright for eyes accustomed to the grave. Squinting, Rhea spun, pointing the shard at her rescuer, only to lower it, dazed and amazed, as her vision adjusted.

Mars?

She opened her mouth but could not form his name with lips so cracked and dry, a throat so parched. Down in the hole, assuaging her thirst had been the most precious dream besides achieving freedom. She had tortured herself with memories of the river and the Regia's rain basins. Of diving into the crater lakes.

Mars passed her a leather canteen.

"Slowly," he warned. "Give your body time to accept it."

While she drank, Mars stared at her belly, and Rhea, feeling uncharacteristically modest, lowered the canteen to cover her protruding stomach. He must find her disgustingly changed since the last time they'd been together. Swollen. Grotesque.

But that wasn't it at all. Wonder lit his face.

"May I?"

It took her a moment to comprehend what he proposed, for nobody had yet asked. Mars wanted to touch her belly; he would be the first. Rhea nodded, suddenly shy, and he laid a cautious hand at the top of her stomach.

"No," she demurred, guiding his hand lower, to the deep curve beneath her navel. "Here. Now wait." Moments of stillness passed, but his patience was rewarded with a flurry of light kicks. Mars's wide eyes found hers.

"Brilliant," he whispered.

"I would hope so, after all I've suffered."

Her response dimmed the joy in his, like the snuffer of a candle's flame. Mars removed his hand.

"I am surprised to see you," Rhea said, and it sounded more like an accusation than a confession.

"I could not intervene while you remained under Vesta's authority," he responded defensively. "But when I heard the calls in my own temple and learned that your bond with Vesta had been severed, that the high priestess had expelled you, I came as soon as I could."

"Vesta's authority didn't matter much when I met you in October."

"The Regia is neutral territory!"

Mars was as handsome as ever, but she regarded him now with confusing sensitivity and irritation. After all that had occurred, was she disillusioned by their past? Had he failed to meet expectations she wasn't aware of holding? He was here now, after all. She owed him her life and should at least offer him thanks.

But it is the least he can do.

"Well, I would be lying if I said I wasn't happy to see you now."

She could give him that; it was something.

Mars removed his own cloak and handed it to Rhea, for the night was cold. He also passed her a laden sack.

"You must run, Rhea."

Her mind spun; her body reeled. Mars spoke with reason—she needed to go—but where? To the nearest city? To the port at Ostia? Should she seek sanctuary outside of Latium, with the Etruscans, perhaps? Trading insider knowledge of Amulius for their security?

"I have no boat, no horse."

"I cannot help more than I already have. Vesta will know soon, and even though you were excommunicated from her order, she will consider this an offense. She will appeal to Jupiter . . ." Mars frowned, ran a hand through his chin-length hair. "I know you are tired," Mars said, more gently than he'd ever spoken to her before. "But you are a warrior."

And maybe what Mars called a warrior was what her mother and the others called a wild woman.

She nodded. "I am." And then she said it a second time, louder. "I am."

He grinned at her, some of the spark between them revived, and then he moved to the rock slab that had held her captive. Mars stomped once, shattering it to pieces beneath his sandaled foot.

"Run, Rhea."

With the sack over her shoulder and Mars's cloak tied about her neck, Rhea turned toward the forest and fled. The Latin woods felt right—or at least preferable to laying her life before the jurisdiction of a foreign city.

In her hurry, Rhea stumbled, and her stomach cramped. She worried for her baby. He must be starving, too. *Hold on, little one. This is our chance. Stay with me.*

Rhea escaped Alba Longa to the north, entering the pasturelands of the wealthiest homes, the farthest villas and vineyards bordering Tusculum. She shivered. Had it been this cold the night she descended into the burial chamber? Had the weather turned while she lay in the earth? She was a seedling, sprouting in the wrong season.

Even the elements were stacked against her; Rhea pushed harder.

When forced to stop and catch her breath, she opened the sack from Mars. At the top was a type of meat pie, looking like a divine feast. She tore off a piece and shoved it into her mouth.

Oh, stars. Oh, gods.

This was the best food she had ever tasted. It took all of Rhea's concentration to exercise moderation; she resorted to counting her chews, one to ten, before swallowing each bite.

When you are safe, you may eat more.

The ultimate motivation.

Guided by her instincts, a destination selected by her subconscious, Rhea entered the volcanic woods around Lake Albano, a crater lake beneath the sacred mountain, Monte Cavo. On this fertile ground, amid the dogwood and oak, was a provisional woodcutter's hut she knew from childhood. She used to play there with her brothers and cousin, pretending they were Lavinia and Silvius, Aeneas and Ascanius. It belonged to the king and was used by workers felling trees for the crown, but it would be abandoned for the season. Nobody used it until summer.

She hoped it would not occur to the Regia that she would seek shelter in such a place. For Rhea to hide out at a royal outpost was too preposterous, too brazen to bear consideration.

Under the dim light of a crescent moon, Rhea struggled to locate the hut. Every part of her body hurt, and frustrated tears sat scorching her eyes. Still, she did not stop. She fought her way forward with a savage strength, growling and grunting as she battled through bush and branch, taking more than one scratch to the face and arms. Blood warmed her skin. She'd been barefoot when the Vestals buried her; shoes hadn't mattered then, but they certainly did now. Her feet were mangled by rock and root.

Death is much easier than life.

Just when she was sure this harrowing night would never end, Rhea spotted the hut's outline through the trees. Her breath caught in her throat, and she ran the remaining distance, heart pounding, elation warring with exhaustion. The sigil of Alba Longa was still there, carved into the front door, a warning against trespass. She leaned her weary forehead against the wood, smiling. "I made it," she said aloud, nearly giddy. "I did it."

And she was no interloper; this property was her baby's birthright.

She entered, pushing the stubborn door hard with her shoulder. The dirt inside the hut lay many months thick, but her accommodations hardly mattered. Rhea would happily live in a pigsty rather than die in a hole. She smelled dust, the time-honored odor of all things forsaken, but nothing dire. Nothing she couldn't clean. Rhea deposited the contents of the sack onto a wood table coated in grime, itemizing the gifts from Mars. Bread and cheese, dried meats and berries. Precious olive oil.

Oh, how her cold, weary body longed to light the hearth! But to do so at a time like this would be ludicrous.

The Vestals would soon return to the tomb to retrieve her body, and when they found the stone shattered, the hole empty, they would immediately alert the Regia. Amulius would dispatch his best soldiers across Latium to search for her, moving upon the land with demonic fury. The reward he would levy for Rhea's whereabouts would surely tempt even the most neutral of men.

And if the gods became involved because of Mars's intervention?

Rhea rubbed her face with both hands. Her list of enemies continued to grow.

She had to remain hidden, discreet, and judicious. This was her second chance, a divine gift, and she would not take it for granted. There would be no fire tonight, and she would conserve her food. A hot meal meant little next to a life returned.

Rhea dropped onto the woodcutter's bed and reached for her swollen feet. It was becoming hard to navigate around her protruding belly.

She rubbed one foot, then the other, and groaned. She would sleep first, and when she woke, she would clean and wrap her feet, then plan for food and water and warmth, for labor and delivery and motherhood and vengeance and—

So many plans—too many to consider right now—but at long last, a purpose.

Her hand drifted to her belly, and she could have sworn that somewhere outside, in the surrounding pines and cypresses, a wolf howled.

◆ ◆ ◆

THERE WERE NOT many hours between Rhea's arrival and the sun's rising, but wrapped tightly in Mars's cloak, she slept better than she had in months. In the morning, when the sun's power illuminated each crack in the wood and straw and stone, she rose in full appreciation of her sanctuary and its blessing of light. Even with the windows shuttered, it was sublime. Still abed, she watched dust motes float and twirl in the daylight's glorious golden rays. As free as a windswept dandelion.

The woodcutter's hut was certainly provincial but entirely perfect. There was a proper bed and a chest full of lambskins, a table and stool. A hearth, of course, with a large cauldron. Sufficient cooking supplies. Axes, saws, and hammers. Hunting accessories: nets, a rudimentary bow, a small skinning knife.

All old—archaic, even—but serviceable.

All perfectly capable of killing a man, should Amulius or his men take her unawares. She added her clay shard to the makeshift armory.

She also found a man's toga in the chest and put it on. With her stomach so large, the garment nearly fit. Her Vestal dress stank of judgment—of her sweat and shame, the filth of the grave. Though she longed to burn the thing, she needed its fabric for swaddling cloth when the baby was born. When she dared light a fire, she would boil it, then cut it down. Until then, Rhea shoved it deep into the chest and slammed the lid.

She positioned herself beneath a closed window where the sunlight angled downward. She needed to feel it on her face, to absorb it into her person, to store it in her core like a winter flower.

Rhea Silvia was on her own, impoverished and impregnated, with no clear strategy for survival. And yet . . .

Sanguine.

Expectant.

Ready.

Chapter XXVIII

ANTHO

WHEN KING AMULIUS heard of Rhea Silvia's escape, he wasn't mad—he was livid. Antho watched with a combination of fear and fascination as he issued frenzied orders: sending out soldiers as mercenaries, issuing bounties and bribes, and turning all the Latin people into spies.

The reward for information was high, but the one for Rhea's actual discovery was more than a farmer earned in three healthy seasons. And the punishment for abetting the criminal? Amulius's edict was clear: *Lend a hand to the disgraced priestess and I will have that hand.*

With the king incensed and the Vestal Virgins in disarray, the entire countryside was either searching for clues about the runaway's whereabouts or spreading gossip.

The princess's deliverance is a miracle!

She has been born again.

They say Mars took her in the sacred grove.

Her child heralds a new age of Latium.

Aeneas returns!

In public, Antho's father seemed primarily concerned with the violation of Vesta's sanctity and the dangerous precedent of eluding justice, but in private, he perseverated over every fabulous rumor. He treated Rhea's breakout like a personal attack on his right to rule.

"Where is she, Antho?" Amulius demanded, storming into his daughter's rooms.

"Is that rhetorical, Father? How could I know?"

He slapped her face. "Do not be pert. You know Rhea better than any. Where would she go?"

Antho ignored the sting—a pain to which she'd become increasingly accustomed—and considered the power he had just inadvertently provided. She would strike him back. "To Satricum, maybe, to her mother's people," she answered, feigning reluctance. "Or to Ardea, where they loved her older brother and considered her for the prince's bride."

Amulius frowned. "All that way? She is pregnant."

"Rhea is determined, and she knows she'll be safest outside Alba Longa. She would never stay here."

But Amulius did not seem convinced. How could she get him to trust her? It came to her as the best ideas do—on wings, like lightning, with a sharp intake of breath.

"Father," she added, keeping her eyes properly cast downward. "Rhea has erred over and over. I barely recognize her as the girl I knew. The sooner this mad hunt is finished and Rhea captured, the better for us and Latium."

"She has always been a problem, Antho. An aberrant child, an ungodly woman."

"I am ashamed to admit this aloud, but you are my father." She swallowed tightly, emphasizing her struggle. "If Rhea's child lives, it will threaten my future family."

Amulius cocked his head, just slightly, to the side. She had his attention.

"As much as I love my cousin, my son should be king, not hers."

"I am relieved that you finally understand."

"I apologize to you—and to Calvus Flavius—that it has taken me so long."

He studied her face for any tell, and when he appeared to accept her deceit, Antho wondered, *Does he consider me incapable of falsehood? Or does he miscalculate his own ability to spot one?*

Hours later, soldiers were dispatched to both Satricum and Ardea. Antho attended to her chores, her loom, her bag of salt. She helped her mother assemble her bridal wardrobe and began work on a wedding gift for her husband, a robe embroidered with grapevines. She talked openly of her marriage, of becoming a mother, of her relocation to the Villa Flavius, Calvus's vineyard on the northern border with Tusculum. All with girlish excitement.

There are a myriad of ways to rebel, and she would use the tools most at her disposal—that is, her upstanding character. Antho was already obedient, but she would be *the most* obedient. She would be placative; she would be boring, invisible, and forgettable. And while the Regia was preoccupied with both a high-profile fugitive and a royal wedding, Antho placed a new vase on her windowsill.

She needed to speak with Leandros immediately for two reasons, but the first of these was the most time-sensitive: Antho knew exactly where Ilia would have gone.

◆ ◆ ◆

ANTHO WAITED IN the larder amid the containers of dried peas and lentils, the hanging sprigs of rosemary, thyme, and fennel. Time dragged, torturing her heart. She stood, then sat, then paced the narrow diameter, considering every possibility or excuse. He hadn't seen the vase. He had, but he hated her. Amulius's spies had intercepted him on his way; Leandros had been beaten, imprisoned, killed.

Who needs enemies when the mind can be so wicked?

When the door opened and Leandros finally entered, she clasped her hands together to keep from reaching out for him too soon. She hoped he would accept her embrace again, once he heard what she had to say.

"Your cousin escaped," he said. "You must be happy."

Antho nodded.

"But you have been cold to me," he continued. "That day at the well . . ."

"I was incorrigible."

"Yes."

She took one step closer, her movements as soft as her voice. "But you came tonight anyway."

Leandros rubbed at the beginnings of a beard. "Of course I did. I cannot deny you, no matter how you treat me."

Another step toward him. "That day at the well, Helvius watched us. I said what I did to keep you safe from my father."

He seemed incredulous. "You didn't want me to be hurt, so you hurt me?"

"What is a wounded heart compared with a corpse?"

Leandros set his mouth in an ominous line. "He may try . . ."

"Enough, Leandros. It is dangerous to underestimate him."

He scoffed, then looked away.

"And you are to marry Calvus Flavius." He turned his head to face her, his own expression hardened. "So if you called me here to break the news, don't bother. I already know. Everybody knows."

"I should have told you myself, but I've needed to be careful." Antho cautiously moved forward, taking a third and final step. They were only an arm's distance apart now. Leandros tried not to respond to her proximity, but Antho sensed his defenses weakening. "I summoned you because I have two questions, and your answer to both could put you in terrible danger, but I know I need to stop making decisions for you."

"Ask me." His voice was husky and low; Antho's stomach fluttered.

"I know where Rhea hides."

Leandros lifted his eyebrows.

"Winter begins, and she is heavily pregnant. She does not know how to hunt, how to forage in the woods. She escaped that tomb only to die on a cold mountain." Antho paused, swallowed. "Will you bring her supplies?"

"I owe Rhea. For that night."

And then Antho was both in the present moment and back in the woods beneath the ironwood tree, remembering the way Leandros had held her, their shared optimism. Could she summon the spirit of that hope now? Before she asked this second preposterous thing?

Antho lowered to her knees, keeping their gazes locked.

"Leandros, my father has promised me to another, but I would first promise myself to you."

"I don't understand." He stared down at her glistening eyes, shocked and uncertain.

He is scared to understand me, Antho thought. *He is afraid I will let him down a second time.* She had to make her intentions clear.

"Leandros, my love, will you marry me?" And how she trembled! Her clasped hands shook.

A muscle in his jaw twitched. "You are a Latin princess. My parents are Greek and enslaved."

"We are more than where we came from. We are more together."

"Off the floor now, Antho. Please."

He offered her his hand, and as their skin touched, as her little hand slipped so perfectly into his, a little gasp escaped her mouth. It was always like this between them, an intoxicating rush, the alchemy of passion and genuine, tender love.

He lifted her back onto her feet and then brought her hand to his mouth. When he kissed the tips of her fingers, Antho's body swayed, her legs gone unsteady with desire.

"You are a revelation, Antho. An unexpected surprise, every day of my life."

"Kiss me," she managed to murmur, and that was enough to bring their mouths together. They hadn't been close in so many weeks, and this embrace was the culmination of all that longing. Antho kissed him in apology, but she also kissed him with a promise.

"We can have our own wedding, in private, before the public spectacle with Calvus." She placed her hand against his chest, where the beat of his heart matched the pulse in her palm. "And I would be your wife," she added shyly, as he still hadn't officially consented, "if you will have me."

Leandros brushed an errant lock of hair from her face. "I already said I cannot deny you."

She beamed. "I could command you regardless."

"At your command, my princess. For all of this life and whatever is to come."

Chapter XXIX

RHEA

DAYS PASSED, AND no soldiers marched through her woods, no Latin hunters neared her cabin. But Rhea did not celebrate. She exercised caution—only lighting her paltry fires in the dead of night, when nobody would see the smoke, and only leaving the hut for short walks when the moon's light was murky with cloud cover. Rhea Silvia, wanted woman of the woods, became a nocturnal creature. Vespertine. Living in darkness, tracing time by the night sky and its passing constellations. The stars were different here. Brighter, more essential.

The longer Rhea spent in the forest, the less familiar it became, for such is the way of wild places. To know them is to accept their mystery, their ever-present evolution. Yet Rhea did not fear the woods. The trees were gentle giants, and even the fiercest animals were honest about who they were, killing for survival, not out of hatred. Her mother was right about that.

Despite her childhood associations with this place, Rhea understood that she would not be another Lavinia raising her Silvius in the woods. This was no idyll. Amulius would find her eventually; she could only hope to remain until her child's birth. Once her son was old enough for the journey, they would truly disappear, and Rhea daydreamed of the places they would visit on their great adventure.

She would raise him away from the Regia's politics, its betrayals and jealousy and underhanded dealings. His education would be the world in all its manifestations—its humanity, its elemental nature, its cycles and dangers and potential. They would return to Alba Longa only when he was a man, and he would step into his reign with far better preparation than either Amulius or Numitor.

As a king, her son would be pure, unbiased, authentic.

Those were her happy moments, when she pictured only the joy of the life ahead, buoyed by the thanksgiving of a life reclaimed.

Other times, she saw a bleaker scene. A mother and son in rags, unsheltered and underfed, forever roaming. What did she know about survival without friends and family, wealth and name? She had made it this far upon the courtesy of others, the relationships she had built over an easy life. How could she begin again without any connections or resources?

Rhea did not have any answers to those questions, but she reminded herself of what she had already endured and whispered, again, her mantra: "You can do hard things."

For her baby, she could. And she would.

◆ ◆ ◆

A COVERED BASKET arrived at the woodcutter's hut, deposited outside the door while Rhea slept, and she nearly tripped on it when leaving for her nightly walk. All thoughts of a stroll abandoned, Rhea brought it inside but was otherwise afraid to touch it. Was it a trap? A test? She tried to ignore its temptation but eventually succumbed to curiosity.

Food! Rhea gasped, then clapped her hands in delight. Wheat bread and cheese. Nuts and meat. Salted fish. Beans. Grains to boil for porridge. Fresh eggs!

How? Why?

Maybe it was laced with one of Sethre's poisons, or maybe this was all some trick of the gods—like forbidden fruit that would leave her forever craving more after one bite. If she ate, would she die? Be transformed? Commit herself to eternal damnation? She groaned and returned all the supplies to the basket.

But then she saw the honey cakes, her favorite, so familiar in shape and smell, exactly like the ones made by the servant Gratia. This was Regia food.

Antho.

Antho knew about this place. She must have guessed that Rhea would venture here, and somehow, someway, orchestrated this delivery. Rhea ate the entire cake standing before the table. Afterward, she licked every sticky drop and lingering crumb from her fingers, moaning with delight.

Truly, Antho was her own kind of divine.

◆ ◆ ◆

THE AWARENESS THAT Antho knew where she was made Rhea feel much less alone, but so did a certain trip to the river. Retrieving water one night at the Almone, she encountered the mystifying man again. She was just lowering her jug into the stream when his face appeared, and Rhea yelped, falling backward and landing hard on the silty riverbank.

She cursed, then crawled forward on her hands and knees, glaring at the water's surface.

"Must you always do that?!" she snapped.

The face frowned. "Do what?"

"Appear without warning! I nearly went into labor."

"Ah . . . I apologize."

Rhea sighed, rubbed a dirty hand against her forehead. She was being rude. "I've forgotten my manners," she admitted, relenting. "It has been a while since I've spoken to another."

"I do not speak with mortals often myself, but wanted to see how you fared."

"For what reason?"

"Because you are important to Latium, which means you are important to me."

Her eyes narrowed. "I'm a fornicator and an outlaw."

"So?"

And because he seemed genuinely bewildered as to why that might matter, she laughed. For she was similarly bewildered by this baffling man—spirit? entity?—who reappeared, whose presence provided such comfort.

"This isn't my river; I cannot stay. But I will return if you would like. To say hello. With a proper warning."

Rhea bit back a grin. "Try bubbles."

His face twisted in confusion. "Excuse me?"

"Next time we meet, send bubbles before you arrive. Then I will know you're coming."

"Bubbles." He nodded, and his eyes twinkled, as if reflecting the stars themselves. "I do enjoy bubbles." And then he faded into the current's ripples.

As if the night weren't momentous enough, while Rhea returned to the woodcutter's hut, she saw a wolf. Not the black one but a mortal wolf, young and female, blocking her path. Rhea stilled, relaxed the tension in her muscles, her stance. Any hint of aggression could mean her death. Where there was one wolf, there was sure to be a pack, but despite how long they stood in a nervous standoff, no others came.

Another lone wolf.

No, not quite, for Rhea noted the sagging belly, the extended teats. This wolf was a mother, and from the look of her protruding ribs, she was starving.

"I see you," Rhea told the animal, reaching carefully into the pack she always carried in case the hut became compromised and she could not return. "And I know how you feel." She found a large strip of dried meat and brought it to her mouth, tearing it in two with her teeth. She tossed half to the wolf, who growled when it landed in the space between them.

"Go on," Rhea urged. "I can share."

But the wolf continued to snarl, lowering her shoulders and head.

Rhea sighed. "Fine." And she threw the remaining half. "I'm going home now. Don't kill me."

Then, in a possibly insane display of trust, Rhea turned her back on the wolf and walked away. She counted each step in her head, and when she reached a high enough number, she looked back over her shoulder.

Both the wolf and the meat were gone.

◆ ◆ ◆

SOON, RHEA WAS too large, too uncomfortable, and in far too much pain to walk the woods with such frequency. As much as she longed for fresh air and the river, her body simply would not obey her will. She alternated between lying on her side and pacing the hut, desperately wishing she could crack open a door or window, just to appreciate the smell of passing seasons. She felt feverish but not sick. Exhausted but restless.

Sometimes she studied her bare belly, its pulsing, engorged, ultra-human existence, and worried that something was wrong with her baby. She was too big; the baby moved too much. Rhea was a mortal woman birthing an immortal's child; how could she not be in danger?

She wondered, in these somber moments, *Will I die before the last of the winter snow melts upon the mountain?*

To keep her hands and mind busy, she carved figurines out of wood with the tools she found in the hut. Images from her most golden times to share with her child. Aegestus's horse, Hector, and Lausus's sword. A bay laurel. Aeneas's ship. She tried to re-create the Regia but ended up feeding it to the fire. She did not want her baby exposed to royalty, not even in toy form.

She prepared for the baby in the best way she could, forced to utilize every available resource in the hut. Repurposing was a new kind of creativity, one she'd never needed in her pampered former life. Was she a mother bird piecing together a nest for her eggs? Hardly. Birds were spry and light of foot. She felt more akin to some massive, hibernating animal.

Rhea slept a lot.

The baskets continued to arrive at irregular intervals, and one came with a different sort of supplies. Honey and oil. Wool bandages. Sacred salt and lemons. A scalpel with a steel blade and bronze handle.

"For cutting the cord," Rhea murmured aloud.

These were the items she would need to deliver her own baby.

"Oh, Antho, you perfect soul. Why couldn't you send yourself? I need you."

At the bottom of the basket lay two golden bullae, two childhood amulets, and Rhea fingered them delicately, remembering the boys who had worn them for guidance and guardianship. These had belonged to her brothers; they were removed from their bodies before the funerals and presented to her father. Antho must have stolen them from Numitor, deciding that Rhea needed them more. If this basket was any indication, Antho was becoming quite the rebel.

Rhea let the tears fall and did not wipe them away, for she was already placing the amulets around her own neck. She spoke to her son: "Your uncles are with you. My brothers are with me. Our family continues."

In her happiness, Rhea allowed herself one exultant lick of honey, sucking the golden sweetness from her fingertip. It left her parched and she remembered, with a moan, that her jug was empty. Rhea sighed; she would have to put it outside to collect the icy rain that still fell on occasion. However, when she went to collect the jug, she beheld a wonderful surprise. It was filled to the brim with cold, clear water.

"Magic," she murmured.

And then, in reply, the water's surface began to bubble.

Both Rhea's hands covered her mouth, hiding a smile that did not burst.

Chapter XXX

ANTHO

AT HER FIRST wedding, her true wedding, Antho wore a plain white sleeping tunic because she was supposed to be sick. With Zea's help and sworn secrecy, Antho faked a stomachache that kept her abed. As it was an embarrassing illness that required privacy with the chamber pot, Zea slept outside the princess's closed door on a straw pallet, ready to assist should Antho call, and the rest of the Regia kept away with wrinkled noses. A humiliation, but well worth it. She was getting married, and such an occasion deserved a better location than the larder.

As she awaited Leandros's arrival, Antho retrieved the items she'd hidden beneath her bed: a wreath of winter blossoms and white yarrow that she'd made herself, as well as a wool belt.

Nerves affected her movements, making her twitch and jump. She could barely contain her excitement.

At the designated time, long past the final meal of the day and when most of the Regia already slumbered, the door creaked open, and her beautiful soldier slipped through. Antho heard Zea coughing loudly to cover the sound of the door locking back into place. When Leandros stepped into her room with a nervousness that reflected her own, Antho broke into a bright smile and dashed forward, nearly leaping into his arms. She felt him loosen, soften, as each of their bodies eased into the other.

"I am so happy," she whispered.

There were no lengthy speeches, only love's solemn regard in the candlelight. Two souls in secret accord, covert harmony—the theme of their relationship.

"I love you," Antho said simply.

"And I will always love you more," he vowed.

In the Latin tradition, Leandros broke a loaf of stolen bread over her head.

"And for Aphrodite, I burned a lock of my hair."

She raised her hand to the nape of his neck, found the missing piece. He closed his eyes as her fingernails scraped his scalp. Then Leandros untied the Hercules knot in her wool belt, and Antho slid out of her dress.

No matter how desperate her want, she could not give her virginity to Leandros. If Antho did not bleed on her wedding night, Calvus would cancel the marriage, and Amulius's rage at such a public, political, and financial embarrassment would put many lives in danger. But there were other ways the lovers could demonstrate their adoration. Leandros would still be Antho's first: the first to see her fully naked, the first to give her pleasure and receive it from her in return, the first to call her *wife*.

Antho lay in her bed, in Leandros's arms, and wondered at her inability to be sated. She could not get close enough to him, would never get enough. She longed to burrow herself into him completely.

"I am trying not to think about sharing you," Leandros murmured. "I thought I could handle it, but now?"

"You are my husband. He will never mean anything to me."

They both avoided saying Calvus's name.

"But when I picture him touching you—"

"Stop." Antho laid a finger against his lips. "I beg you. This is our night, not his. Let it remain so."

He exhaled, his brow furrowed in pain.

"Instead," she cooed, her fingers winding lazily down the muscles of his chest, "imagine the ways you'll get to touch me the next time I am here."

That brought back his smile, and he called her a dirty name in Greek that made her giggle.

"I think this is what marriage means," he told her gently, his voice lulling her into gorgeous sleep. "Cling to me, and I will cling to you, and this life might carry us through together."

She could only murmur her agreement, as she was nearly asleep, but her hands gripped him tighter.

The morning came far too soon, and when she woke, her arms might have been empty, but her heart was full.

Chapter XXXI

RHEA

AGAINST ALL ODDS, Rhea made it to the other side of cool days and colder nights, to the glorious warmth of full spring.

The new season settled in, and its sun transformed the forest from sky to ground. Trees grew leaves, bushes made berries, and the mossy floor sprouted with wild mushrooms and sprinklings of color—blue periwinkles and fuchsia anemones and purple cyclamens.

Outside it rained, a promise of growth, pleasant with petrichor.

But inside Rhea was racked by sharp, shattering agony and rumbling, booming pain. Wet with sweat and tears, the waters of life pouring out from between her legs.

Labor had begun in the night. Rhea had woken to an unfamiliar sharpness, but she'd become so accustomed to the ongoing war in her abdomen that it did not alarm her.

At first.

But as the frequency increased, so did her apprehension.

It was time—really and truly—after all the judgment and condemnation and infamy. Rhea Silvia, unwed and unwanted, was having Mars's baby, and she would have to manage this on her own.

Between contractions, Rhea collected the supplies from Antho, but she could hardly focus or remember any of their uses. She had heard countless delivery stories before, but was the honey for her or the baby? Was she supposed to rub the lemon or smell it?

Just breathe, Ilia, she told herself. *Breathe through this pain.*

How had women continued to do this for generations? Why would anyone, after experiencing such torture once, willingly do it again? She understood why more women died in childbirth than soldiers died on the battlefield, and if Rhea survived, she was done with men. She swore it on everything she held dear.

People still scoured the countryside in search of her, so she knew silence was paramount, but what woman could go through such back-breaking agony without a voice? Bear the nearly unbearable without making a sound? Rhea's whimpers turned to moans, then cries and curses and, finally, shrieks. With morning, Rhea let loose her first scream and could not take it back.

"I can't, I can't," she gasped, tears streaming down her cheeks and entering her mouth.

"You can."

And there was Jocasta in a bearskin cape, smiling proudly at her daughter.

"You aren't real," Rhea whispered accusingly. "You are just me. My mind, a wish, a dream."

"Yes, I am you. And you are all you need. Your body was meant for this. Breathe down; push deep."

"Help me." Rhea's voice cracked under the agony.

"I cannot. You must do this."

"My back will break."

"Ilia, my wild girl, show me your teeth."

Rhea Silvia labored alone in that hut for another day and night and day again. And, yes, Rhea screamed—the wind took the sound and spread it across the fields, filling the ears of a farmer with nothing to lose and everything to gain—until she passed out, her right hand clutching the amulets at her breast.

◆ ◆ ◆

WHEN RHEA CAME to, she could not determine how long she had been unconscious. The sky seemed similar—had it been only a few moments or a full night and day? But the overbearing pressure on her pelvic bone was different, like a boulder forcing her open, and she worried she might split in two.

She moaned, sounding more like a calving mare than a woman raised in a castle. Rhea felt transcendent, ancestral and primal. Feminine. She had been imprinted with an animal's awareness by her mother and grandmother and great-grandmother and every mother before her. She knew what to do.

Push.

Rhea rose from her bed. She did not have a birthing stool, but that was a human comfort, and she wasn't sure she was human anymore. She crouched by the side of her bed, elbows propped up on her knees, and obeyed her body's demands.

Rhea pushed. And pushed. Pushing when it hurt, against the hurt, through the hurt.

Rupture.

Blood and mess splattered below her as the pressure hit its apex, and then she didn't break, because the pressure lessened—so quickly!—and out slid her baby, so fast and slippery that she barely caught him in time. A boy, her boy! Red and purple and wet and so very small. Rhea laughed and cried, holding him in the trembling crook of her arm.

"Hello, you."

His little face frowned and fussed in that newborn way as Rhea took in all his miraculous details. Dark-black hair and gray eyes like limestone, like stormy skies or owl feathers. Rhea reached for the knife and sliced through the cord between them. If it hurt, it wasn't enough to break through her numb euphoria. She pushed herself up onto her bed, collapsing backward with her baby clutched to her chest. Skin to skin.

"We did it," she whispered.

He did not cry, but he breathed, and they breathed together, two beings that were once one. *Alive, alive, alive.*

But then another contraction had Rhea shooting upright. *The afterbirth.* Rhea calmed herself, took a deep inhale. One more push; she could do that. She could do hard things, anything, and she was so close to being done. She placed her baby in the basket she'd prepared as a cradle, aching at even such a minor separation.

"I'll be right back," she assured him, then resumed her crouch. If it had worked for the baby, it would surely work for whatever liquids came next. Rhea massaged her palms down her stomach, hoping that would help, but nothing came forth. Her legs shook beneath her from the exertion. Was there supposed to be this much pressure again? Her frazzled, exhausted mind imagined a blockage. Maybe she had broken something? A bone or an organ? Something was not right.

And the contractions in her lower stomach continued, that same staggering pain.

Rhea put a hand to the sore place between her legs and gasped.

Her heart raced as she prepared herself for another push, and this time she was ready. The second baby emerged straight into their mother's hands.

Two! All these months, there had been two inside her. Two together, two entwined. Two listening and living.

Awed, humbled, and full of the most surprising joy, Rhea conducted the rituals a second time, cutting the cord, sticking the tip of her finger into this boy's mouth. More dark hair, but when this child let out his gentle cry, she met eyes as green as the vine. She placed him beside his brother in the basket, and they rolled into each other, reuniting in perfect symmetry. Rhea sat back, astonished by this immediate, overpowering love.

"My babies, my boys. Brothers."

Her twins.

She would need to feed them soon, and clean them, but for just a moment, she would lie here. She curled herself around the basket and, with just a fingertip, touched each baby's nose, stroked their tiny hands.

"Mine," she whispered. "You are mine and I am yours."

She removed the bullae from around her neck and tucked them into the blankets of the basket. Now, with the symbols of her lost family nestled among her babies, Rhea recognized the blessings of this new one.

"You already know each other, but do you know me? I am your mother."

She liked saying it aloud: "I am your mother. I am Mama." It made Rhea feel powerful and whole and luminescent.

To be a mother is to be alive.

Which is why what happened next was so difficult.

Rhea heard human voices outside the hut, coming closer, approaching her sanctuary.

"Here." A female voice. "This is where my husband heard the cries."

Rhea sat up and pulled the basket behind her as terror—hot and tingling, like a death fever—spread up her tender body. She grabbed the knife she'd used to cut the cords, still bloody, and angled it toward the door. She knew she should stand, should run or hide, but her legs shook, still far too weak to make a move.

After so much waiting, everything now happened too fast.

A parade of people entered the hut, buzzing with violent excitement. The vanguard in battle. A couple of farmers she did not recognize and a pair of royal soldiers.

The male farmer gestured triumphantly at Rhea, at the grisly mess of labor and delivery on the cabin floor. "It was her screaming! I knew it was no animal!"

One guard whistled at the other. "Helvius's whore and his *two* bastards? The king will pay well for this!"

"I am Rhea Silvia. These are *my* sons, and they will start an empire."

A pause.

Then everybody laughed.

Chapter XXXII

NUMITOR

NUMITOR HAD ALWAYS believed that there was no one way to experience the divine. Just as every human relationship was different—between lovers, siblings, neighbors, and so on—the same was true of humans with their gods. His wife, Jocasta, had needed the physicality of worship—the dirt, the wind, the invocation of the senses—but Numitor made contact with the immortal realm in his dreams. Only within the stasis of sleep did he actively touch a higher power. His dreams became the hallmark of his kingship. Within these subconscious encounters, Numitor received guidance, foreshadowing, messages. Perhaps that is why he did not fight Amulius's move for the throne—Numitor had seen it already, ordained in fragments of sleep imagery.

Some mornings, in the before, he consulted with Sethre, who'd been the Regia's resident augur for decades. An outside source provided a perspective stripped of the personal. But other times, he spoke with his wife. Jocasta, who had not read the holy scrolls or memorized the histories but moved with the cadence of the earth. A natural intelligence.

But his queen was gone, and so was his kingship. The augur attended to Amulius now, and Numitor, widowed and childless, whispered his dreams to the bay laurel.

"Mad old king," people lamented. "Lost his mind to tragedy and the poppy."

The dreams had gone dormant for a long while, especially after he'd begun drinking cretic wine, especially after they'd taken his daughter, his Ilia, and placed her in the ground with their rules and their lies. But then, with the new season, his visions returned like spring flowers. Bright, powerful, aromatic, and as vivid as they had been when he still had a full family.

This was what he saw:

A wolf in a cave, heaving and panting, in dire need, near death. Distressed.

A mob outside, armed and chanting:

"Kill it! Kill it now!"

"Wolves are dangerous, ravenous, aggressive, devouring, and devious!"

No, *Numitor thought.* Wolves are devoted, adaptable. Stalwart, strong, and brave.

But he said nothing. He tended to say nothing these days.

The wolf moaned—so conscious, so human—and then came the universal miracle. A shift, a schism, and then a head. Life emerging, pushing and pulling, aching, throbbing, pulsing into existence.

She was in labor, her baby stuck.

Help! *the king prayed.* Somebody, anybody!

A long-haired man appeared with a sword. A man grizzled and scarred, handsome in the way of an older age. A warrior. A legend.

Aeneas.

Numitor watched in amazement as Aeneas laid one massive hand upon the wolf's head. He spoke to her. "My heir," *he said proudly, and with careful precision sliced open the wolf's belly, bringing forth not a wolf pup but two birds.*

A vulture turned eagle. And an eagle turned vulture.

A metamorphosis in a moment, miracle upon miracle. A transformation natural to the order of destiny.

Twin birds. Brothers.

When each bird's beak found suckle, the wolf closed her eyes. Aeneas, kneeling, bowed his head. When the nourished birds took flight, the wolf eased into a pool of water and slowly faded.

Aeneas looked up, right into the eyes of the king, and delivered his message.

Numitor awoke. Sweat soaked his armpits, his shoulders, the top of his back. Even his face was wet. He wiped himself dry, panting and knowing. No augur necessary.

"Ilia lives."

Chapter XXXIII

RHEA

THE TALLER OF the two soldiers addressed the farmers and held up a small sack, presumably filled with coin: "Your service to king and country is noted."

Neither husband nor wife gave Rhea any mind; they could hardly suppress their greedy smiles. Did they not care what they had just done to Rhea and her children? Why would complete strangers hate her?

Or was it not about Rhea at all? Maybe they were only doing what was necessary to endure this brutal world.

But then the shorter soldier came up behind the male farmer and slit his throat.

Sputtering, spurting, in the throes of betrayal, the man plummeted gracelessly to the floor. And when the shocked farmer's wife attempted to retreat, the taller soldier jammed his own knife into the woman's lower back. She screamed and fell forward, bleeding out, facedown.

"You are monsters," Rhea cried, horrified.

The taller guard shrugged. "We are following orders."

"So says every monster," Rhea shot back, recalling Prisca's similar defense.

The taller guard pulled his knife from the dead woman. "Xeno, get the babies."

As Xeno stepped forward, Rhea flung her body over the basket.

"Move," he ordered. "Give them to me."

"No."

Xeno barked for his partner. "Hold her for me, Gnaeus!" And then both men were pulling Rhea up and back and away. She bit down hard on one of the hands, and Gnaeus, howling, punched her in the face.

Rhea spat a mix of their blood onto the front of his tunic. The soldier named Gnaeus looked down, disgusted.

"I promise," she seethed. "Release me and my sons, or I will kill you both."

Gnaeus rolled his eyes, and then he and Xeno bound Rhea's body with coarse rope. She could not walk, could barely move, without the fibers tearing into her skin. They gagged her and placed a blindfold over her eyes, so Rhea could only listen as the guards divvied up responsibilities: who would drag which dead body outdoors, who would carry the babies, who would handle Rhea.

Blind and mute as she was, Rhea could not tell which soldier mounted his horse with the basket and which one laid her across the front of his saddle.

It didn't matter; they would both die for what they had done.

The horses walked, poor beasts, unknowingly complicit in such a terrible crime.

◆ ◆ ◆

THE SOLDIERS BROUGHT Rhea and her sons into the Regia as its people slept. She had no way of knowing how they entered or who might have witnessed their arrival. But she still had her ears, and they were trained on her babies. The boys, who had yet to taste her milk, were too quiet, and Rhea could barely control her panic. Were they starving? How long could a newborn babe survive without nourishment? Rhea calmed herself by remembering their provenance.

These are the sons of Mars and me. They were born strong.

With the blindfold at long last removed, Rhea blinked, rubbed her bleary eyes, and found herself in the lowest reaches of the royal compound, inside a cistern turned dungeon, where oak stalls became death cells, holding people the Regia needed to disappear. The basket holding her babies rested on a crude table in the farthest corner.

And he was there, of course, standing over her, as austere as ever. Amulius at last.

"Finally, Uncle, you have me where you always wanted."

Heavily armed guards stood behind the king: Xeno, Gnaeus, and Petronius, a soldier from Numitor's personal retinue.

Her uncle surveyed her with his characteristically blank expression. "Untie her," he ordered, as if bored.

Xeno hesitated. "With all respect, my king, she—"

"Soldiers who must hear my orders twice never hear anything again." Amulius's hushed tone had the power of other men's invectives. His soldiers rushed forward to remove the ropes constricting Rhea's body.

"Don't be stupid," Petronius whispered in Rhea's ear as he undid the knot that bound her arms.

"Two," Amulius murmured in amazement, gazing into the basket. He reached a hand down and stroked each boy's cheek with his finger. "What a terrible waste of sons."

"Get your murderous hands off my babies," warned Rhea, struggling against the guards' hands holding her in place. "It is a crime against the gods to kill your kin."

"The gods, the gods." Amulius paced the length of the cell. "You and your father and your monotonous talk of gods. There are no gods, girl. Just us. Just this ugly, meaningless world." He halted before her. "Why can't I rid myself of you? How can *this*"—his eyes scoured her short, uneven hair and the bruises on her face with revulsion—"be my worthiest adversary?"

"Because this *person* is the only one unafraid of you."

He scoffed and gestured to her body in its stained men's toga, the liquid still leaking from the place between her legs. It coated her feet, the stone floor—her lifeblood betraying her. "Not for much longer."

Rhea swallowed tightly. "I will die, gladly, if you pardon my children their existence." She lifted her chin, exposing her neck. "Execute me—end this—but let them be. A life for a life."

"That is one for two, an unfair deal." And then his face slowly broke into a dark grin. "Or you could choose which one gets to live."

"You are sick."

He chuckled, and that was enough motivation for Rhea to rip herself free from the soldiers—so savagely that she wondered how the muscles in her arms hadn't torn—and leap upon her uncle. Clawing and kicking, tasting skin, gripping hair. Rhea fought bravely, but she was messy, moving erratically, hampered by postpartum wounds, and distracted by the presence of her sons. And she could not overpower four grown men. The guards peeled her off the king, and Amulius, inflamed and alight, struck her in the face over and over. His rings tore open her cheeks and lips. Her nose crunched. One of her eyes dripped red and her teeth splintered.

Amulius stepped back, chest heaving, and released her to the guards. Rhea took a punch to the stomach so severe it knocked her to her hands and knees. Endless feet kicked her like a dog on the floor. Ribs cracked.

They will beat me to death in front of my boys.

In their basket, the babies began to cry. Their shrieks pierced Rhea's heart and every mother's heart—the ghost mothers floating between the edges of the world, the living mothers who woke, sitting up in bed and clutching their chests. Perhaps even the first mother, who resides at the core of the world.

When children cry like that, no matter their age, every mother hears.

"Shut them up!" Amulius commanded. He wiped his face with the back of his hand. "You have whored, Rhea, and you have run. Now you have been caught. It was always going to end here."

It hurt to breathe. Rhea could scarcely see through the carnage of her face. Death waited in her bones; she felt the tingle of its anticipation and knew that if she succumbed to its demand, there would be no more suffering. Though surrender would be a mercy to her broken body, Rhea was more than limbs and organs, and her mind was set on living. If she died now, nobody would protect her sons.

And so she had to get up, had to keep fighting, because there was no other option.

"The gods are real," Rhea managed, spitting out one of her teeth as she pushed herself into a sitting position. "And so are the spirits. I have seen my mother, Uncle, and I know she watches you."

Doubt crossed her uncle's face, a momentary dismay that he shook off as easily as a fly. "Even if that is true, which it isn't, it is too late for me."

The tip of Xeno's sword pierced the back of her neck. Rhea tried not to flinch.

Amulius set his mouth in a line, then gave a tight nod. "Kill the bitch."

"No!" Rhea lifted her hands—purple and red, skin torn, nails shredded—and called for her goddess. "Cybele!" she cried, in petition, in offering. "Avenge me!"

Xeno brought the blunt edge of his sword down against Rhea's head, and her body collapsed forward, hitting the floor with a thud. The resounding peal, the final gong. A gory ceremony concluded.

◆ ◆ ◆

BUT THE GODDESS listened.

She accepted Rhea Silvia's blood.

And she came.

Chapter XXXIV

ANTHO

ZEA FLEW INTO Antho's rooms, waking her from the beginnings of sleep.

"Wake up!" she hissed.

Antho sat up, clutching her blanket. "Is it Leandros?"

"No, he is fine, but he sent me to alert you." Zea grabbed Antho's shoulders, shaking her with nervous, frantic emphasis. "You must hurry! Two soldiers brought Rhea Silvia home. She is in the dungeon with the king."

Antho grabbed a shawl and ran.

◆ ◆ ◆

ANTHO FOLLOWED THE lamplight to the pit of the Regia's underground, a place she had never traversed before. When she heard the scream—Rhea's scream!—she sprinted to the very last cell, where her father and three soldiers stood over a prostrate body.

Though bright blood spilled from Rhea's head, her chest continued to rise and fall—a body, a woman, *Ilia*, stubbornly clinging to life.

"She's not dead," the king declared with some exasperation. "Run her through!" The guard lifted his sword, but before he could thrust it into the former princess, the current princess made herself known.

"Stop!"

Antho rushed forward, arms outspread.

"Father, stop this!"

Amulius's head spun, regarding his daughter with genuine shock, a look she'd never elicited from him before. "How did you . . . ?" he mused, then shrugged a shoulder. "No matter. Antho, remove yourself now."

Antho scanned the room. In the far corner lay a rustic basket, rustling with the sound of infant life, and splayed in the middle of the room was the child's mother—Antho's cousin and sister and friend, who'd ended up here even after she and Leandros had kept her alive all those months. Rhea Silvia, beaten beyond recall, her short hair the only identifiable feature of the proud, beautiful woman she had once been.

Two guards glared in Antho's direction. The third, Petronius, kept his eyes down. *I have borne witness to what they have done; I remind them of their sins*, Antho thought, and the realization gave her the righteousness required to hold firm. "Father, I will not."

"I remember a very different conversation with you, daughter, in which you told me Rhea Silvia deserved her punishment, that her child might one day threaten your own."

"Yes, but I am not cruel. No crime deserves such ruthlessness." She directed the following words to the assembled soldiers: "My uncle Numitor always says you can determine a man's character by the way he kills. This isn't justice. It is savagery."

"Go to your room if you cannot watch."

Antho bit her lower lip; there was one final move to play against her father, kept in reserve should she need leverage for Leandros, but her hand had been forced. Amulius would never forgive her for doing this in front of soldiers, but she would never forgive him for so much more. Their relationship was unsalvageable.

"I will kill every child Calvus puts in me if you hurt Rhea."

A sound shot from the king's mouth, some hybrid of laugh and scoff. "Antho, please. Enough."

Her heart somersaulted when she met her father's face, thrown by the depth of his hate. It was a look she would never forget, that would surely haunt her, but she wouldn't let fear stop her—*I won't let him scare me*—and she persisted. "I know all the ways to kill a baby before its birth." She listed them with her fingers: "Silphium leaf. Pennyroyal tea. A suppository of lead—"

"You dishonor yourself, Antho."

"Do I? Or do I dishonor you? Kill Rhea and I promise your legacy ends with me."

Parent and child stood in open standoff, in deadlock, while a young woman bled out on the floor, newborns awaited milk, and a trio of soldiers wished they were anywhere else.

"I concede," Amulius finally responded, surprising everyone. "I will not hurt Rhea."

Antho stilled; she had expected far more resistance. "Neither you nor your guards," she clarified.

Amulius bowed his head. "We will not touch her."

She awaited a sense of victory, but none came. What else was she missing?

"Then we have an agreement. Petronius," the king ordered calmly, "take the basket and toss it in the river."

Horrified, Antho realized her mistake. "Father, no!"

"You said nothing about Rhea's mongrels, daughter." His eyes twinkled; he was enjoying her humiliation. "Your skills in negotiation, just as most of your skills, are lacking."

Antho keened as Petronius retrieved the basket and exited the cell as quickly as he could without running.

"Nobody will touch Rhea, for there is no need. She's nearly dead." The king instructed the remaining guards: "Leave her here to bleed out."

Antho knelt beside Rhea's body and wept. "Ilia, I love you. Ilia, I'm sorry."

"Xeno and Gnaeus, escort the princess back to her rooms. Station a man to be sure she does not leave until I see fit. Then return here to monitor the criminal until she dies. When it happens, come straight to me in the tablinum."

Xeno grabbed Antho beneath her shoulders and half dragged, half lifted her from the cell floor with Gnaeus in their wake. Antho fought against him and heard the indignant snap of torn cloth as her tunic ripped open, laying her flesh bare.

"I will bear that old man no children, Father. I swear it!"

The guards paused.

"You are disloyal, and I should have you whipped, but Calvus won't want an ugly bride." Amulius closed his eyes, and when he opened them, he seemed tired and far older. "You will bear Calvus a child—a son—or I will cut your Greek soldier open and send his heart to Villa Flavius wrapped in garlands."

Leandros must return to Greece, she thought. *I must remove him from this madness, or my father will use him against me for the remainder of our days.* But Leandros would never desert her, not after their wedding.

Antho no longer struggled in Xeno's arms, and his grip had loosened enough that she was able to shake him free. Xeno allowed it; they both knew there was no fight left in her.

"Was Rhea's baby a boy or girl, Father?" she asked quietly.

"Boys."

Her eyes watered for the many souls lost this night, and for the irreparable damage done to those who had survived. How would any of them look one another in the face again after participating in such violence? As Xeno and Gnaeus led Antho out through the doorway, she turned back one last time. In the cell, a tableau vivant made an eternal impression upon her person: the king positioned above the unconscious body, staring at the stone wall, running a bloody finger across his lips.

Chapter XXXV

PETRONIUS

PETRONIUS HEADED TOWARD the river, walking quickly and trying not to look at what he carried, but it was impossible to pretend the basket was only a package when the package was hungry. When the package cried.

He was a man who followed commands, who prided himself on trusting what he was told. The king knew the right course for Latium. The correct people, the divinely chosen people, were in charge. Even the orders that felt bad didn't make him a bad person. They only made him a good soldier.

Today, though, he was tasked with placing Numitor's grandsons into a coursing river, surely to meet their immediate death. It wouldn't take much for the basket to flip, and then—

He imagined the babies drowning.

Choking.

Sinking, then floating, swollen and bloated.

Precious corpses, nibbled by fish.

Petronius stopped. He vomited, turning to the side so he didn't mar the basket.

"Sensitive fool," he muttered, scolding himself. How many Latin infants were exposed to the wilds? These babies were no different than any other bastards or undesirables. He wiped the filth around his mouth with the top of his shoulder.

Petronius approached the river, but in its babble, he heard accusation.

Baby killer. Betrayer.

He loved Numitor with his whole being. The old king was like a father, certainly better than the one Petronius had been provided at birth. The old king believed in him, trusting Petronius in his personal guard, and he spoke to him—to all the guards—like they mattered. Petronius had heard the rumors, of course, and though no one knew for sure who had fathered Rhea's boys, their grandfather's identity was certain.

But Amulius was king now, and Amulius determined right and wrong. These babies, not even a day old, were apparently *wrong*.

Petronius laid the basket in the Almone before he could question himself again. He watched it drift away, waiting on the banks until the sounds of the panicked babes began to recede. But he prayed, in breviloquent yet subversive terms.

"River god, help them."

Rhea Silvia's sons were on their way, but Petronius had lost his own path. He lowered himself, splashed water across his stained face and shoulders, then stood, shook off, and began the journey back to the Regia, wondering how it could ever be home again after all he'd witnessed that night.

◆ ◆ ◆

BECAUSE PETRONIUS DID not follow the basket, he did not see it enter the Tiber. He did not witness its warm welcome by the great river, its acceptance into invisible arms. The boys and their basket were lifted—safely bypassing rocks and trees and eddies, the detritus of the Latin countryside—and guided to the Seven Hills, where in the shallow waters of the left bank, the river purposefully, intentionally snuggled them into the roots of a fig tree. A temporary refuge.

Two newborns, one of eyes so gray, the other of eyes so green.

Watched by the river.

Waiting for their mother.

Chapter XXXVI

RHEA

THE BACK OF Rhea's head throbbed something fierce, but she managed to find her balance and stand. Her mind was more than dazed, more than drunk, and wouldn't follow her instructions, wouldn't recall how she'd gotten here—wherever that was. Her inner self pressed against a barricade, pushing and probing to no avail. Hands she barely recognized as her own pressed down upon her belly, swollen but empty. No blood, no pain, but no babies.

Gone!

"Where are they? Where are my sons?"

Her first question. The only question. Where she had gone, what would happen to her, no longer mattered. Only them.

"Down the river," answered a woman's voice, as melodious as a cat's purr, as natural as a waterfall's resound, but entirely inhuman.

Rhea stood in a cave. Moonlight shot down from a skylight in the rock, and the speaker stepped forward, aglow in a milky halo. Rhea knew her, had carried her likeness to the Bona Dea. The divine statue. The Penate of Aeneas.

Cybele.

More beautiful in the flesh, auric, majesty made manifest. She had the palest skin and hair so dark it shone blue. An ancient power radiating from a youthful face. An enigma, a paradigm. She was love but also impossibly wild. A goddess without definition in the limited human vocabulary.

"Where are we?"

"In the space between things, which exists at the edge of time, at the edge of the world."

"So this is not real?"

"The mortal understanding of *real* is frustratingly limited. This is not a flesh-and-blood conversation, if that is what you mean, but it is a conversation. And it can still have consequences."

"Where am I, though? Where is my body?"

"In a dungeon. You will not last the night."

Icy dread traced its fingers down Rhea's spine, the caress of death, but Rhea shook it off. "No, that cannot be."

Cybele placed a hand on her chest, imitating a mortal expression of compassion. "If you were not almost dead, you would not be able to come here. Your soul is barely tethered to your form."

"But my boys need their mother."

"Everybody needs their mother."

Rhea spun, eyes searching the cave for an exit, but there was none. "I need to go!"

Cybele tsked. "You aren't remembering, Rhea. Think! After you delivered your babies, Amulius's men found you in the woodcutter's hut."

But it hurt to think, even more so to remember! Rhea squeezed her eyes closed, rubbed at the sides of her head, and images returned in piercing fragments. *The murdered farmers. The ropes, the gags. Her uncle's fists, the soldiers' feet. The boys in the basket, bawling for her.*

Rhea's heart lurched. She gasped as all the pieces came together in awful attachment.

Her final cry: Avenge me!

"I called for you with my last words," she remembered, slowly.

Cybele nodded, pleased. "And you have yet to say what you want."

What didn't she want? Rhea wanted it all.

"I want to undo time. I want Amulius destroyed, Numitor restored.

I want my children and myself to live and thrive." She brought her palms together in the posture of prayer. "I want to be avenged."

But the goddess shook her head. "Impossible. There are parameters, a limit to earthly possibilities, even for me. I cannot upend an entire kingdom. I work with what naturally exists in this world, not humans and their cities and their politics. I cannot remake you, Rhea Silvia."

Rhea's arms dropped to her sides. She stiffened, raised her chin. "Then make Rhea Silvia something else."

Cybele raised an eyebrow. She moved closer, inspecting Rhea from foot to crown. When she cupped Rhea's face in her hand, Rhea tried not to squirm. An impossible feat, for she felt Cybele's blazing eyes inside her body, searching and analyzing. Judging.

She will see the truth of me, Rhea feared. *That I am not worthy of her grace. That I have been selfish for far too long. I am irredeemable.*

"I see earth from your mother," the goddess mused, "air from your father. The fire of Aeneas and the water of Lavinia. You, Rhea Silvia, are somehow every element."

"Can you change me?"

"Hmm." Cybele pursed her lips, tilted her head to the side in non-answer.

But Rhea was done with the gods and their cryptic communications. They had all the time and every age to play and ponder, but this was her only life! She would force directness, and if that made her demanding, so be it. "If you cannot help me, Cybele, say it and release me."

"I would release you to your death, child."

Rhea laid her face into her hands. She was dead regardless. The fight was over.

"But if you care more about living than your life, I might have an idea."

Rhea lifted her head. "Whatever you offer, I accept."

"I cannot give you a different human life, but you can do as the wilderness does to survive. Adapt. Change." Cybele leaned forward. "What would you sacrifice to be with your boys again?"

Rhea looked the goddess straight in the eye, answering truthfully and without hesitation: "Everything."

Cybele's entire being lit up , and the lion that lurked in the shadows slunk forward—the very same lion from Rhea's vision in the Vestal tomb. When the goddess's hand found its head, the creature purred like a kitten. "All women have an animal that walks behind them," explained Cybele. "I see yours, clear as summer days or fresh water. It is your true soul, your wild soul."

Rhea knew it, too. Felt it always.

A wolf.

"Yes, Rhea, a wolf. And I can give your inner wolf a form, but only if you forfeit your human existence for a wolf's life." For a moment, Cybele was the lion, and the lion was Cybele, in mystical meeting, a shimmering superimposition. Rhea, watching in wide-eyed amazement, could not discern where one ended and the other began. And then Cybele emerged, separate, a goddess with a lion by her side. "The wolf is an uncanny predator—swift, strong, capable—but not without limitations. A wolf cannot speak or sing. A wolf has no hands to write her story."

If Rhea became a wolf, she could not hug her sons or kiss their bellies, could not tell them stories or teach them to speak her name.

"I only care about keeping them alive."

Cybele nodded. "And a wolf has an expected lifespan of less than twenty years."

Rhea's weary mind raced. Two decades with her sons? It was not much to a mother, but it was a lot to a dead person. And she supposed that's what she was. But what if Rhea made this deal and her boys had already been killed?

If the gods offer you a chance, take it.

Her mother's advice. How would it feel to have Jocasta back, but only as a bear? Rhea considered the question seriously.

It would still feel wonderful. Knowing a life without her mother, Rhea would take her back in any form, gladly.

And that was the answer.

"Great Mother," she asked, "is it too late for me to change?"

"Not if you are as strong as I believe you are."

Tenacity.

Before, when she'd resisted Amulius, she had thought herself strong. Her enemy would have forced her into perpetual maidenhood, would have closed her womb, so she fucked a god. And despite all the repercussions, hadn't she prevailed? Hadn't she outlasted the stigma, the contempt and derision, the horror, the lonely, loneliest pain?

Yes, Rhea Silvia had proven her tenacity.

But now, with Cybele, at the precipice of their agreement, in the genesis of her motherhood, Rhea understood—finally—the power of love and its dependency on sacrifice. She could be selfless after all.

Rhea Silvia, Latin princess and Vestal Virgin, would choose to become a wolf.

Maybe if she'd been less frantic, more physically present, Rhea would've weighed other options. Searched for loopholes. Added provisions. But, in truth, all her mind held was the recent memory of two sets of eyes—gray and green—beholding their mother for the first time.

Were they looking for her now, believing she'd abandoned them?

Such a question could make any mother do crazy things.

"I understand everything," Rhea declared. "I accept your gift."

For that's what this was. A chance is always a gift. And with it Rhea would transfer her rage and resiliency and devotion into a new body, one with fur and claws and fangs. An act of redemption, but also of magic. Wolves, after all, are the witches of the natural world.

"Rhea Silvia, you do your ancestors proud." Cybele lifted her chin. "Aeneas returned for me, though his city burned. You cannot imagine the smell, the screams. He came back, and so will you. On the new moon, on the darkest night of the lunar month, you will return to your human form. From sundown to sunrise, you will be Rhea once more."

Rhea barely dared to breathe. A boon. Glorious and unexpected. She pictured herself kissing her boys, laughing, holding their hands. Tears spilled down her cheeks as she bowed her head. "Thank you, Great Mother, thank you."

"Do not be so grateful quite so soon, child. None of this will be easy."

Cybele's drum materialized at her feet. The lion picked it up by mouth and brought it to the goddess's hand. She began the ceremony. "When my hand hits this drum, you will wake in the form of a Latin wolf. Are you ready, daughter of Jocasta?"

Yes. No. Never. Of course.

And Rhea had already decided, hadn't she? This was just a formality. Rhea wasn't one to change her mind.

"Yes."

Cybele raised her right hand, preparing to strike the drum, but before her palm could connect with the goatskin, she paused.

"Look for your sons at the Seven Hills."

One beat of the drum and Cybele, her lion, the cave, and Rhea Silvia disappeared.

Chapter XXXVII

From *A Natural History of Latium* by Aetius Silvius Flavius

The Latin wolf is a special breed, smaller than other wolves and far more isolated. It feasts on deer of the forest and woodlands but can also habituate in wetlands and pastures. It has gray fur that reddens in the summer, and dark bands decorating its back and tail tip. The eyes are almond-shaped and amber. Beautiful creatures, perfectly formed.

Our wolves are religious. The Sabine people have a cult of the wolf. There is a taboo against killing one, which is why wolves are allowed in cities and sacrosanct areas—unlike, say, the wasp or the ox. Spotting a wolf before going into battle is considered a powerful omen.

We have heard the fabulous tales of men turned into wolves and back again, which we must confidently regard as untrue. In our native tongue, they are called the versipelles, or skin-changers, and they change with the full moon. Their clothes turn to stone until they return from their escapades, which involve stealing sheep for illicit meals and consorting with the dead. Stories for children, perhaps, for entertainment on a winter's night around the hearth fire. Men cannot be wolves.

(But I ask, then, what of women?)

Chapter XXXVIII

RHEA

RHEA WAS SPARED the pain of transformation. She awoke and was a wolf.

A wolf in the Regia's windowless, stone dungeon. The same but different, not unlike Rhea herself, for this was a familiar place made unfamiliar with new eyes, new ears, a new nose.

New paws.

She returned, overwhelmed by the disorientation, the trauma, the shock, the explosion of her senses. And then came the screams.

Xeno and Gnaeus, staring at her in abject horror. These unforgivable, unethical men who had hurt her, who had stolen her children.

"What? How?"

"She's a wolf!"

Oh, she certainly was.

The wolf growled and sneered, hungering for warm flesh and hot blood. The beast wanted to eat, but Rhea only needed to kill. The soldiers had no time to draw their swords before the wolf pounced, her jaws clamping down on one throat and shredding, then leaping upon the other's fleeing back, claws digging through flesh, snapping a neck.

Such unbridled power! She panted, heart racing. Where was Amulius? She could still smell him, and the wolf wasn't done hunting. She leapt over the bodies and through the open door of her cell, racing down the corridor, empowered by the howls and cheers of the other prisoners.

But then she came to a crashing halt, a tumble and tangle of unfamiliar limbs.

There is no time for Amulius!

There is always time for revenge.

Rhea was part of the wolf, but she butted against the instinctual animal—the wolfness that was now part of her, too. Two entities in wary distance if not opposition. Rhea needed to impose her will over the other, assert her dominance.

We must leave!

We must kill.

Or maybe it wasn't about overpowering each other as much as joining together. Rhea tried something different. She pictured her twins and imbued that image with as much love and protectiveness as she could muster, praying the wolf would understand.

Ours.

Ours?

Ours.

And motherhood is one of the universal urges. Not a feeling or an emotion but a physical need. Something in the marrow.

Take me to the river.

The wolf and Rhea settled into each other, merging in full cooperation, and they—now, more or less, *she*—began to move.

Rhea didn't overthink her body—the second pair of legs or the view from this height. She simply relaxed into nature, into pace, into rhythm, leaving the Regia behind. A few Albans on the streets, out of bed for the usual nefarious reasons, saw her sprinting and exclaimed. But she was soon past them all, past the taverns and brothels. Out of Alba Longa entirely and into the woods. How quickly she moved! It had once taken Rhea half a day to reach the Seven Hills by foot. No longer. Oh, to travel at such speed, impeded by nothing! In this body, she could handle any terrain, any obstacle. Powerful, pulsating muscles. Unaffected by cold.

Traversing the terrain, Rhea was barraged, almost berated, by scent. She smelled each bird in the trees, every rabbit and mole in the mossy ground. She could smell what had died and what was dying, the aroma of a branch after it snapped, the fragrance released by flowers trod underfoot. She could smell running water, the way it scented the air as it splashed against rocks.

Her human body might have needed hours to find the Tiber, but wolves know the path to water by heart, and the susurrations of the stream sang in her ears long before gracing her vision. She raced into the sound and along the riverbank, searching for her young.

Instead, she found the guard Petronius, returning from his heinous mission.

Another unforgivable, unethical man.

With his face down, his defeated posture, he never saw the wolf coming.

And, in that way, a woman who had never killed anyone before became a wolf who had killed three.

This was a new life, surely, an existence founded on one simple principle: *If you are against my children, you are my enemy.*

She followed the Almone to where it joined the Tiber and pushed northward, nose to the ground. *I will not be too late. I will not be too late.* Repeating to believe. She passed the Aventine Hill, trekking through the muck along the river, every sense made vigilant, but stopped in the marshy valley when the river bent west at Tiber Island. She smelled . . . *herself.* Her human body. Her hands, which had woven that basket for her boys. Her blood, still matting their hair.

The basket waited just ahead, trapped in the tangle of a fig tree's partially submerged roots.

And above it stood a man with a face she knew well. The one she had wondered about during so many lonely hours in the woodcutter's hut. She had never seen him whole before! Though he stood in the water like it belonged to him, his skin and fine blue-gray linens were perfectly dry.

He gave the wolf a slight smile, a respectful nod, and then disappeared.

How did he always know?

The wolf shook herself, then splashed into the Tiber, paddling to where the fig tree rose from the water, to where the fibrous, threading roots formed a messy net. She gripped the basket's edge in her mouth and tugged it free, pulling it back into the river, through the currents, and up onto the bank.

The wolf poked her nose inside the blankets, inspecting the tiny naked forms. They were so frightfully cold! The gray-eyed baby reached for her muzzle. The other did not move, but it breathed. *Alive. Both alive.* Yet the predator within her could sense the babies' weakness. While one of the boys had enough energy to mewl with kittenish rage, the other was dying. Too long without food, too long exposed, when he should have been fed and warm and safe.

Would either of her boys have survived this ordeal without a divine father?

Or without the stranger—her friend?—in the river?

Rhea had no way of gauging how long she'd been separated from her sons—how much time had elapsed since she'd been knocked unconscious, met with a goddess, transformed herself, and made her way back from near death—but it hardly mattered anymore. She was here now, and she would find them all sanctuary. The wolf pushed the basket into a bush, hiding it as best she could.

Mama will be back soon, she would have said if she could speak. *I promise I will not leave you again.*

She had reached the Palatine Hill, the centermost of the seven, and began her search along the base of the flat-topped rectangular summit, the most logical place for a cave. Eventually, she spotted an empty den in the hill's southwest corner. The wolf bounded back to the bank, retrieved the basket, and dragged it to shelter. Even with her newfound agility, it was difficult work. The twins were so fragile, and each rock and bump, every twist along the basket's path, frayed at Rhea's nerves. The green-eyed baby still stared ahead and past her, without recognizing or registering, eyes dimming.

Finally, they arrived at the cave, and Rhea heaved the basket one final time over the threshold. If a wolf could shed tears, she would have sobbed with relief, but there were even more difficult tasks at hand. She still needed to remove the twins from the basket without human hands, without jointed fingers or soft arms. The wolf wrapped her lips over her sharp teeth as best she could—like a hunting dog—and picked up the gray-eyed baby by the back of his neck. It was hardly a graceful maneuver, and the boy yelped. She gently laid him on the dirt. The second baby hung limply, without protest, his pulse a whisper as she placed him beside his brother. The wolf positioned herself around them, nestling their faces into her stomach, where swollen teats waited, as ready as any human mother.

Canus, as she had begun to think of the gray-eyed baby, latched immediately, sucking with fervor in solid commitment to survival. But Viridis, of the green eyes, remained motionless. His face rested against the soft skin of her underbelly, but his lips did not move.

Please, baby. Please. I'm trying.

She had no magic words, no spell, to make him obey, only a most honest plea.

I know it is hard. I know how it can hurt. But do not go so easily. Fight, precious one. And maybe it will be worth it.

Maybe it wouldn't. Life was not always beautiful, but there was beauty in trying.

She nudged her son, poked and prodded with paw and nose and head. She whimpered at him, just like a begging cur at the Regia's kitchen. Nothing. Her gray-eyed boy had eaten his fill and already fallen into a deep, contented sleep. If the green-eyed baby did not suckle soon, he would die. Afraid and frustrated, the wolf resorted to her base nature: she growled. Harsh and menacing, sending vibrations down her spine. She lowered her head, looked her green-eyed baby in the eyes, and bared her fangs.

The message was clear: *Eat or face my wrath.*

Mama was mad.

And, finally, intimidated into action, the damned difficult baby did as he was told. His tiny pink lips closed around one of the wolf's teats, and he began to suck, halfheartedly at first but with abandon once the milk came free and those rich nutrients hit his belly, filling the child with energy and life and all their associates—greed and self.

Wolves do not outwardly sigh, but Rhea's mind did. She sighed with relief and anxiety—for every mother understands that it is possible to hold both at the same time. And she was exhausted. After little Viridis finished his first meal, he nestled back against his brother and slept. The wolf curled herself around them, wrapping them in her fur and heat and love.

This was a miracle.

They were a miracle.

The wolf slept, too.

Chapter XXXIX

ANTHO

RHEA WAS GONE, dead from her injuries. Her babies were gone, dead from exposure.

All three murdered at Amulius's command.

Antho could reiterate the truth in any number of ways, but sitting on her bed that night under armed guard, holding her knees to her chest, she knew she would never close her eyes again and not see it: Rhea, mutilated and hemorrhaging on a dirty floor, and those poor babies crying in their crude basket.

A person can cry so much that their cheeks sting. A person can cry so hard that their chest aches. If Antho hadn't had Leandros's love to live for, she might have jumped out her window. She had walked to the sill, considered the height, the fall, but being in that spot reminded her of setting out the vase.

The Greeks had a story about a girl who opened a vase and released all the horrors of humanity. But Antho's vase was its opposite. Hers held a bouquet of lovely moments, the ones she had gathered amid hardship and abuse. Her head on Leandros's chest, his kind words in that alluring accent: *Antho, you are resilient, something beautiful that has bloomed in impossible terrain.*

Killing herself wouldn't return Rhea or Rhea's sons, but it would ruin Leandros.

The fires began in the distance, pyres blazing on human fuel. Her father had wasted no time. Sick at the sight of smoke, Antho shuttered her windows and crawled into bed, vowing not to move until the pain stopped.

Dawn arrived with the king's orders: the princess would not be permitted to leave her quarters until her wedding to Calvus Flavius. Antho returned to her bed, recalling one of her father's despicable final statements: *I should have you whipped, but Calvus won't want an ugly bride.* He should have held his tongue, for he'd given her the key to resistance. She would not bathe, would not eat until her wedding, either.

Amulius placed her under constant surveillance, day and night. Any news that Antho received came in terse whispers from Zea as she delivered the meals Antho refused to eat.

"He has issued a royal edict announcing Rhea's death. He claims she was found dead and pregnant in the forest near Monte Cavo."

"How do the people react?"

"Those in advantageous relationships with the crown cheer," Zea brought her voice lower, "but those loyal to Numitor mourn."

"And how is my uncle?" she asked, afraid of the answer.

"Inconsolable. Confused. He refuses to accept her death, claims he had a vision." Sadness clouded Zea's features. "The king sent the augur to convince him."

Antho imagined her uncle's anguish and Sethre's "convincing." Plying him with poppy-laced wine and any other number of poisons.

A few meals later and Zea had more news.

"The guards from that night in the dungeon are gone."

"All three of them?"

Zea nodded.

Antho considered this information. "Is that why the pyres lasted so long? Did the king burn their bodies with Rhea's?"

Zea shrugged. "I couldn't say, but Princess? If you do not eat, I will have no choice but to alert Leandros."

Antho gripped the servant's wrist. "No."

"Three bites."

"I'm not trying to kill myself, Zea, but since a marriage to Calvus Flavius is my death sentence, I may as well play the corpse bride."

237

Zea shook her head wistfully but said no more.

She left Antho to wonder: What had happened to those soldiers? Was her father removing the witnesses to his crimes? Antho's testimony would count for little, if it counted at all. Either nobody would believe what she'd experienced in the dungeon, or worse, nobody would care.

Antho took one bite of the bread on her dinner plate, then crawled back into her filthy bed.

◆ ◆ ◆

THE DAY OF her wedding, then.

Since Queen Claudia adhered to every tradition—tradition being her dogma, her aesthetic, her favorite word—the nuptials were held on the first of June in honor of Juno. But when the queen entered her daughter's rooms that morning, trailed by innumerable serving girls, she stumbled backward in shock. Antho sat cross-legged on the floor, blonde hair tangled, nails overgrown. She had not cleaned her teeth or washed her body in days. And she was sallow, all protruding bones and sharp edges.

"Good morning, Mother."

"What have you done to yourself?" shrieked Claudia.

"Father had me locked in here for so long . . . I guess I lost track of the days."

Both Claudia's nostrils and pupils flared. She pounced upon Antho, pinching the backs of her arms and dragging her upward.

"You thankless, insubordinate brat," she hissed in Antho's ear, but to the women gathered, she issued commands: "Bring shears, sponges, oil and a strigil. Lavender, rose petals. A pumice stone. Oh, and fresh water. Don't bother warming it. A cold bath will do my daughter good."

It took hours for Claudia and her company to undo the damage Antho had wrought on her skin and hair. The queen forced watery wine down Antho's throat, to fill her belly and give her face a hint of flush. It didn't make any difference, so Claudia ordered Zea to cut her own hand and rub the blood into Antho's cheeks.

"I am so sorry," Antho muttered, as her friend drew a knife along her palm.

Claudia ensured that Antho adhered to every ceremonial detail. Her hair was parted with an actual spear, then braided. She wore a yellow veil and multiple necklaces of roses. As was the custom, Claudia dressed Antho in her long white tunic and tied the wool belt around Antho's waist with a Hercules knot.

Antho remembered Leandros's hands on that same knot. Safe hands, strong yet soft. Hands that worshipped, hands she trusted.

Before their group left for the great hall, while most of the women were double-checking Claudia's dress and hair, Zea discreetly handed Antho a wrapped package, small enough to pass between the palms of their hands.

"He says it's safer going with you."

Her aunt Jocasta's brooch. Indirect proof that Aegestus had not been murdered by thieves. With the others still preoccupied, Antho placed it in her trunk, hiding it beneath her collection of bridal clothes. She promised herself that she could collect more items, more clues and documents, and that one day this trunk would be filled to the brim with confirmation of her father's treachery. And Antho, Amulius's weak and stupid and uninteresting daughter, would be the one presenting the facts to publicly end his reign.

"You have seen him today?" Antho breathed. "He is well?"

"He is as to be expected . . . and quite drunk."

Her love, her husband. She wished to comfort him, but what could she ever say to ease his pain? *Try not to think too much about Calvus in my bed, in my nightclothes?* Ludicrous. If their situations were reversed, Antho would be sick with jealousy. Leandros with another woman? Just the idea made the bottom of her stomach collapse.

"Remember, Zea, to keep an eye on him. And send word to me if you feel he might be in trouble."

"I won't forget."

Claudia had offered Zea's service to Antho at Villa Flavius as a wedding present, but Antho needed an ally to remain at the Regia. Because he never gave servant girls any credence, King Amulius did not question Zea's loyalties, thus, as much as Antho hated to leave her, Zea had to stay behind to watch over Leandros.

Claudia bid her daughter to take her place in the procession. "We are late. Make haste."

As Antho traveled the short distance to the great hall and everything that awaited her there, she wondered if Calvus might look more handsome in his wedding robes.

He didn't.

The ceremony had songs and torches. Endless prayers. The Antho of old might have cried or arranged her face in a pretty smile, but the Antho of today felt nothing, only a hardening combination of mourning and resentment. Antho thought her father would appear triumphant, but he looked as disenchanted as she did.

Her poor, dear father, exhausted by all his murder.

The bride and groom exchanged their formal vows. Antho recited the required words: "When and where you are Gaius, I then and there am Gaia."

One sentence and Antho officially belonged to Calvus Flavius.

The Regia hosted a splendid feast with endless platters of meat and fish—fresh, salted, warm, and cold—and Claudia finally got her stuffed peacock centerpiece. Because of Calvus's notorious sweet tooth, the bride's family made sure to supply apricots in sauce, pear patina, a massive wine-soaked cake, and stuffed dates, fried in honey.

Antho ate little, nibbling at only a piece of cheese and slowly sipping at her drink. Calvus, sitting by her side, did not seem to notice. He hardly talked to her at all, spending most of his time gloating and fraternizing with similarly aged men and the royal council. Calvus's children—all far older than Antho—introduced themselves, kissing her hand and calling her "Mother."

It was wretched. She'd never been so embarrassed.

Antho scanned the edges of the crowd for Leandros, torn between terror and her desire to see him. There were dozens of soldiers on guard that night, but he was not one of their number. *It is for the best*, she told herself, *especially if he has been drinking*. What might he do if he saw her like this? And what about herself? Would she throw off the flowers and veil, leap over the banquet, and run to him? She entertained fantasies of different escape scenarios until Calvus rose, beckoning her to his side.

"The time has come for my young wife and me to depart and—"

"Consummate the marriage!" a drunken reveler shouted, to much hollering and applause.

Bright, hot shame lit Antho's cheeks, but Calvus chuckled. She despised his laugh, she realized. It was too airy; it rattled the apparatus of breath, as if even momentary delight were too great a taxation on his frail form. How could this insubstantial body exert such power and influence?

She was too young for him; this was not right.

The bride and groom were led to separate carriages.

Her mother bade her farewell with an awkward public embrace. Antho could not remember the last time they had hugged, held no childhood memories of her mother's arms or lap. But Claudia's eyes watered with some unidentifiable emotion. And then the king laid a hand upon Calvus's shoulder and exchanged a final pleasantry before he came to kiss his daughter on the cheek.

"A son," he reminded her, "or the Greek dies." The coldness in his tone made her shiver.

The caravan departed the Regia, and Antho burrowed into her cloak, eyes closed. But then an impulse overtook her, and she sat up, leaning out the window.

Her carriage passed the ironwood tree where the hops grew.

Leandros was there, waiting for a final glimpse of her with one closed fist over his heart. She caught herself before she exclaimed.

Her love, her husband.

I will be back; I will always come back for you.

The carriages reached Villa Flavius just before the sun. Calvus was too elderly to carry his new wife over the threshold, but she did enter holding her spindle and distaff in each hand. Antho prayed that Calvus would be too tired, too old, to lie with her, but that's all it was—wishful words. Worse, a delusion. She was an eighteen-year-old virgin, and she was his property. He would have her immediately.

Mostly, Calvus wanted to look at her naked and touch himself. Then he climbed on top of her in a bed scattered with flower petals. She shut her eyes, tempted to imagine Leandros, but no, she would never bring her beloved into this horrible act.

"Look at me," Calvus demanded.

Afterward, he noted the blood on the sheets with approval.

"You did well today, wife."

Unsure of what to say, she thanked him for the compliment. Then he got up to order a bath in his own room.

Antho lay facedown on her bed, bit into her blanket, and cried.

Chapter XL

RHEA

SOMETIMES THE WOLF caught human voices on the wind. Always male, the shepherd boys of the region. On such occasions, if the babes were awake, Rhea forced them to nurse. If they were eating, at least they were silent. As long as Amulius did not have her body to burn, he would still be searching for her. Rhea could afford no risks.

Sometimes she wondered how her uncle interpreted the events of that night. How did he react to his fallen guards and missing niece? Did he suspect her transformation? Did he believe that some divine intervention had spirited her away? Or did he presume that she had risen from the dead? That even with broken bones and a bleeding head, she had killed those guards with her bare hands and fled? Whatever he thought, she hoped insidious suspicion had wormed its way into his brain and now lived there, slowly devouring his peace and sanity. She hoped her disappearance plagued him. Ate him alive.

Eventually, her own hunger forced the wolf from the cave. If Rhea didn't hunt, didn't feed herself, her body would stop producing milk. And now that they understood the system, these boys were ravenous. Feeding two babies at once would deplete any mother, no matter her youth or stamina.

With her teeth, the wolf pulled a blanket over the twins and left the cave. In her human life, Rhea had never hunted wild game. At the Regia, she'd taken for granted that somebody else provided meat for the kitchens. As a Vestal, she had eaten animals that were already domesticated and penned. Chopping the head off a captive chicken was hardly an act of valor.

In and around the Seven Hills were sheep and goats aplenty, but these belonged to flocks, and taking one would alert the shepherds to her presence. There were fish in the river, frogs and turtles and otters, but she didn't feel she could brave the currents. Birds abounded, but those seemed hard to catch. And then she sensed the rabbit. It was quick, but not for a wolf.

When Rhea had given birth, she'd allowed her maternal instincts—the muscle memories she'd inherited from the mothers before her—to take control. The wolf knew how to hunt in the same way, with knowledge in the blood, passed down from survivor to survivor: *This is how you stalk, pounce, attack, kill. Snap the neck, split the skin, and feast upon the warm, wet meat.*

The rabbit did not stand a chance.

It was a gruesome act, perhaps, but direct. *I am the bigger animal. I require your life to sustain mine. You and I have always known this; it is the way of things.* There were no deals, no bartering or ulterior motives, no poisons or outsourcings. Nature is what it is; a sheep cannot trick its way into becoming a fox.

Killing, she learned, is not the same as murder.

(And those soldiers? What did you do to them?)

She fed on others to feed her children.

(And I killed others who would murder my children.)

What had she known about wolves before she became one? Precious little. And with no elder to show her the way, Rhea learned on her own four paws, turning inward and feeling the tremors of this strange body. The urges to hunt, to seek, to hide. To lower or raise her head or lips. To protect her belly and her den.

Always to protect.

Days passed, and already the boys were changing—making little movements and facial expressions, adorable gurgles and coos. Is there anything more charming than an infant's yawn? They kept their eyes open for longer and longer, those gorgeous gray and green eyes. And if they weren't gripping tightly to the wolf, they were connected to each other, always touching, affirming their pair, their twoness. Rhea was so glad they had each other. In those long months of pregnancy, she'd never considered twins, but now that she had them, she could not imagine any other possibility.

One baby would've been too easy. And Rhea's life was anything but.

The boys remained naked; she had neither clothes nor the ability to dress them. But she kept them clean, licking away the messes they made and, more than once in the darkest hours of night, lifting them back into the basket and pulling it down to the river, where she dunked each boy, one by one, into the cool water, holding them at the nape—a maneuver she had perfected by now.

Once, as she returned Viridis to the basket and to his brother, the wolf caught her reflection between the high moon and the water's surface. The image staring back was no beast but Rhea Silvia, beautiful and long-haired. The face of a proud princess she barely remembered.

How?

"It is the way I see you," the river murmured.

The river man, the river god. His face appeared beside her likeness.

In her heart, she knew who he was. Had heard his name in story many times. The implications were overwhelming, and now that she was a mother—and no longer fully human—she would avoid that conversation while she could.

The wolf hurried away with her basket, not returning to the Tiber for a long while.

◆ ◆ ◆

THINKING ABOUT HERSELF as a woman was complicated.

There were harsh memories of her journey here, to this den in the Hills.

Tavia's accusatory finger. Horatia's screamed threat: *If you don't climb, we'll push!* The eternal darkness of the tomb and the freezing winter of the hut. Those farmers who had betrayed her location and been betrayed in turn. Her uncle's acute hatred. All the different hands and fists on her body, mere moments after splitting herself open in childbirth. Beaten mercilessly to the brink of death, then rescued by a divine deal in the final moment.

After so much vicious humanity, Rhea preferred being a wolf. She liked the quiet, the feeling of being so healthy and strong, and the safety of her den under the hill. And between hunting and nursing, washing and nurturing, she could dedicate little time to worrying about her past life. Even now, her babies, her Canus and Viridis, wailed in hunger. There was no more time to pause and process. The wolf arranged herself around the boys, their needy mouths greedily latching on to her teats.

Viridis blew a spit bubble at his brother, and Canus giggled.

The first laugh.

A marvel! Had there ever been a laugh so perfect and precious? Rhea doubted it. And when the new moon rose, she would laugh again, too.

There was nothing complicated about this, how deeply she loved her sons.

◆ ◆ ◆

AND THEN ONE night, the black wolf appeared.

Mars waited outside, his massive silhouette filling the entire entrance to her den. She hadn't seen him since he'd released her from the tomb, smashed that horrid rock to pieces. She had been distant that night, and she wasn't sure how she felt about him anymore.

Not love, but it had never been love. Not hate, either, not at all.

Would she allow him in now? Clearly, he sought her permission.

She felt possessive of her den and her children. *This is mine. I fought for this! It belongs to me.* But her babies stared at him in wide-eyed awe, sensing some uncanny connection, perhaps. Canus pumped his pudgy fists. Just as so many doting mothers before her, Rhea could deny them nothing. She relented, nodding her head. *You may join us.*

The black wolf moved to her side with that stealthy grace she had come to know him by. He lowered himself to the ground before her, twisting his head in a way that exposed his neck. Rhea did not bite. She accepted his submission by easing her own guard and assuming her favorite position—curled around her babies, tucking them into her stomach. And Mars joined her, completing the circle with his own massive body, keeping the two boys safely locked between them, the wolves' heads touching.

"They are beautiful," his voice said in her mind. *"Just like us."*

"I know."

"You should sleep."

An unexpected luxury. Nothing would happen to them while Mars was here, and Rhea was so very tired. Though the black wolf did not shut his own eyes—could not, in fact, keep them from his human sons—Rhea drifted off to welcome sleep.

But she could have sworn, just before she went under, that she again heard his voice in her head.

"I fear I might like this too much."

When the sun's rays broke into the den, hitting Rhea's face and waking her, the black wolf was already gone.

He did not come again.

◆ ◆ ◆

OTHER CREATURES CAME to the cave, intrigued by the new arrival to the Hills. One day, still at a distance but unmistakable: a lynx.

Even with wolf ears, she wouldn't have heard its silent stalking, but she smelled its distinctly feline urine, even from a deep sleep. The scent woke her. The lynx was marking its territory, claiming its prey.

Her sons.

Rhea emerged from the den, and the lynx froze. It thought it hunted human babies; it hadn't anticipated the mother wolf.

It was a lovely creature, its tawny coat marked by black spots. Long white fur descended from its chin like a short beard. Tufted ears. Long, powerful legs meant for climbing and leaping. A male lynx, a bit taller than Rhea's wolf form, but she might outweigh it. Lausus had seen a lynx take down an adult deer once, but could it best a wolf?

Except you're not really a wolf! the inner voice scolded.

I am whatever I need to be.

If she kept the fight on the ground, Rhea had a chance. Losing the upper ground meant she was dead. They all were.

Rhea lowered her head and growled, perfectly imitating the wolf she'd met in the mountains last winter. Perhaps she could scare the lynx away and avoid confrontation. But such a predator as this must have been stalking them for days, waiting to sneak up on the cave unawares. It had been dreaming of that soft human flesh, depending on it, and would not submit now, despite the unnatural wolf in its way.

Wolf and lynx met in a clash of fur and tooth and claw. Growls and howls. Nothing strategic or methodical, but an all-encompassing tornado of want and need. Rhea lashed out in every direction. The lynx fought for food, but the wolf fought because she had no other option.

The lynx leaped on Rhea's back, clamped its jaws down upon her neck. She was trapped, with no idea how to free herself, and if she didn't move soon, those sharp teeth would sever her spinal cord, and if she didn't immediately die, she'd lie paralyzed, watching while the lynx devoured her children.

So Rhea, thinking like a woman and not a wolf, raised herself to her hind legs and slammed backward into the rock wall, smashing the lynx in between. It mewled in pain, relaxing its grip on her neck just enough that the wolf could fling it off. The lynx crashed into the dirt, and before it regained its feet, the wolf was upon it, biting the unprotected stomach, ripping it open with all her strength.

A lynx disemboweled, stomach and intestines in open air, steam rising.

She killed it. And then she ate it. Humans killed their enemies; animals ate theirs.

Afterward, the wolf limped back to the cave, a weary soldier returning home. But she was seriously wounded and wondered if she could survive these injuries without intervention. She was still able to nurse the twins, but it hurt to lie down, to twist, to move, to do anything or nothing.

The boys had no idea how close they'd come to an untimely end, nor did they recognize their mother's suffering. Children rarely do.

She stumbled from the den only to relieve herself. Already she could feel the wound festering and smell its rancid stench. Another battle had been won, but she was slowly wasting away to infection. Was this truly how she would die after everything? Inside, she nestled her boys against her while she panted, pained, feeling the manic grip of fever and the torturous itch of shredded skin.

In her mind, Rhea moaned. In the wolf's body, she closed her eyes, dozing in and out of consciousness for hours—for days—until she was pulled awake by her demanding thirst.

Water. Please.

And there he was, the river god, crouching beside her. He poured a vial of pellucid water into her wound, and she whimpered at its burn. But her body began to change, reacting to the magic, ejecting the infection as skin and sinew stitched themselves back together.

"I will have the lynx skinned, then bring back the fur for your sons."

Before he departed, he spoke softly to the boys. "Your mama fought bravely." He corrected himself, mouth twisting in a half smile. "No, your mama *fights* bravely."

Viridis cooed.

Rhea did not want him to leave but first they must speak properly about who he was.

Soon.

By morning, she was fully healed.

Chapter XLI

RHEA

IF SHE'D COUNTED the days correctly and her observation of the sky's passages was right, Rhea was due to become a woman again.

She would behold the new moon in her old body.

Because she assumed it would hurt, and that the transformation itself would be terrifying to watch, the wolf planned to be outside the den at sunset. She wondered how her boys would react when she reentered the den without fur or a muzzle.

Would they recognize their mother?

The sun moved westward, and the heavens bled pink and lavender into the river like maidens tossing flower petals in procession. Gorgeous cascades of color before the dark moon rose, a bare outline in the black-blue bruise of sky.

The transition was immediate and jarring. Rhea thought her heart might stop, that it might not be able to handle the incoming and outgoing energy as her form reconstructed itself, first with blinding heat then with freezing cold. She was transfigured, turned over, but she did not scream. She ground her teeth as they shrank and dulled, dug claws into the earth that became fingers and nails.

And then she was as young and human as ever, her hair back to its pre-Vestal length. She ran her hands down every bone and bend. No bruises, no breaks. She had all her teeth; her nose was straight. Was this proof of the empathy that exists between women, the solidarity and consideration? For Cybele had given Rhea a body before its violation—the fists and kicks and rope she tried so hard not to remember.

But Rhea was still very naked.

She crept back to the den, hoping no shepherds chose this exact moment to circle the Palatine. An unexpected item waited at the entrance to her cave, and that propelled Rhea forward. Had someone come by? Had they seen the boys?

And what was it?

A dress in fine blue-gray linen. She'd seen this material before—on the man from the river. She sighed as she fingered the fabric, then pulled it on. It fell over her skin like water, sensual and luxurious. Even as a princess, Rhea had never worn its like.

Between the clothes and her hair, she felt beautiful. When had she last felt beautiful?

Her babies waited in their basket. They stilled as she entered, but when Rhea leaned down to face them, it took only a moment for their smiles and gurgles to return. They saw something familiar in her, whatever that might be. She used her hands to repair the wear and tear on the basket, and to comb through the boys' hair with her fingers. Viridis had especially unruly curls. She nursed the twins, one at a time, with human breasts and treasured the feel of human skin touching. All the while, she told them meandering stories with no clear direction, making them up as she went.

Rhea had a voice. Let them hear it.

She wove tales with the borrowed structures of her father's histories, adding images from her own experiences, as well as transcendent themes—the patterns she saw in past and present, the imaginary and the real. Rhea spoke of an impossible love between a woman born from trees and a man who lived in his scrolls, a mix of fact and fiction. There was a brooch with three enchanted stones that became the first children, a flying horse named Hector, and seeds buried in winter that became wolf cubs in spring.

It felt cathartic to take the ugly moments of her own life and re-create them, even if they made little sense. Her audience didn't seem to mind.

She thought the boys might have fallen asleep. Rhea fell silent, letting her words linger in the air like stars in the sky, shimmering into a slow fade.

"Well, what happens? Between the wild woman and her scholar?"

Rhea's head whipped in each direction. In the darkness, she could not see him, for she never lit any fire, relying solely upon the sky to provide light. But as he came closer to the entrance, he seemed to glow. Backlit in blue luminescence.

"I don't know yet," Rhea admitted. "I'll work on the ending."

The river man sat in the dirt. "Would you tell us another?"

"My sons are asleep."

The man conceded. "For me, then. If you don't mind."

This time, Rhea was more direct, more intentional. "This is not one of mine, but it is quite famous. It tells of Aeneas reaching Latium."

He suppressed a smile. "Ah."

Rhea cleared her throat and began. "After consulting with the Sibyl in the Greek colony of Cumae, Aeneas headed north by sea. His men were so dreadfully tired and losing all hope, but Aeneas urged them forward. 'One more stop,' he promised. But the waters had been rough, unkind, and if they did not reach hospitable land soon, the Trojans would starve. As they approached the coast of Latium, however, the waters miraculously calmed, and in the gray-green mists of evening, Aeneas's ship passed from the sea into the great river, navigating—as if by some supernatural accord—toward its destiny. For though the men rowed, their arms did not tire.

"And Aeneas had a dream. In it, the god of the river—an old god, a Latin god—instructed Aeneas to continue to the place where a white sow with thirty piglets rested beneath an oak tree. And, once there, to make landfall and peace with the local king. He obeyed, and this is how the Trojans came to the Palatine Hill, where Aeneas sought out the friendship of King Evander in Laurentum and used that alliance to secure the hand of Princess Lavinia.

"Because of the river god's intervention, Aeneas found his homeland. And that same river god prophesied a mighty kingdom for Aeneas's sons, one unlike any before or after."

"Your imagination is a wonder."

"Is it?"

He chuckled. "That ending was even more absurd than the last."

Rhea lifted an eyebrow. "Tell me why."

"Because the river god was incorrect. His vision was limited." He held her gaze and the night, the moment and its anticipation, sparkled and crackled in the space between them. Rhea's heart raced. "The promised empire would come not from Aeneas's sons but from his daughter."

◆ ◆ ◆

TIBERINUS.

Father of the river.

God of the Tiber.

Spirit of the stream.

Protector of the Latin people.

It was almost inconceivable.

◆ ◆ ◆

RHEA FORCED HERSELF to swallow, to ground her flyaway heart. "Aeneas had no daughter."

"Some children aren't made manifest for many generations, until the right combination of elements is realized. You are more Aeneas than any I have seen."

"You have watched my family all these years?"

"Latium is my home. This land is my purpose." He looked outside the cave at the windless night. "I have long awaited its greatness."

"Alba Longa is great," Rhea disputed.

Tiberinus shook his head. "No, it isn't. Alba Longa will barely be remembered, but you, Rhea Silvia, are the origin point of an empire eternal. It will span the globe and the annals of history. It will be imitated, rivaled, discussed. It will never be forgotten."

"My sons are newborns, and I am a wolf." This was no frivolous conversation, and Rhea wasn't ready for its heft. She was healing, learning to be a mother and a wild animal. Vengeance and legend were a discussion for later, not now, not on her first new moon.

"Yes, and a woman, every now and then."

Rhea laughed, appreciating the moment of levity, and followed his pivot. "Thank you for the dress."

"The color is lovely on you."

Heat rose in Rhea's cheeks, and when Tiberinus continued to gaze upon her, she felt even more flustered.

"It's rude to stare," she admonished.

His forehead furrowed. "Why?"

"Because it's an invasion of privacy. Because it can imply . . ."

"Aggression? Attraction?"

His earnestness to understand made her smile. "Yes. Both. Either." Stars, when was the last time she'd smiled in genuine amusement? Rhea was surprised the muscles in her face recalled the motion.

"I was not trying to imply aggression." Tiberinus rose to his feet. He was far too tall to stand in her cave, so he crouched in a very ungodlike posture. "I wish you a good rest of your new moon, Rhea Silvia."

He left, walking a few steps into the night and then vanishing into the mist.

Once Rhea had been lovely and attractive. She thought that part of herself was dead, or at least dormant, but hearing these kindnesses from Tiberinus activated a hidden heartbeat, the pulse of the woman beneath the mother and the wolf.

A welcome vibration that warmed her the rest of the night.

Chapter XLII

RHEA

THE BABIES DID as babies always do: they grew.

First, they rolled over. Then they lifted their bellies and hovered. The wolf watched with proud excitement as they began to crawl—first Canus, then Viridis—one knee, then the other, coordinating little hands and chubby legs. Another miracle.

Their growth hastened a fresh set of fears. What if they left the cave while the wolf slept? How would a wolf teach them to walk upright? Use their hands? Speak? She had only one day—one *night*—of every lunar month to model human behavior. Would her sons be more wolf than man? And would it be so terrible if they remained something in between? For Rhea was an impostor herself—a woman in wolf's skin. She didn't belong with the wilderness or the people of the Seven Hills.

And nothing better embodied their halfway existence than their cave, a geographical representation of betwixt and between, the center point where mortal met nature. The verge. The threshold.

After feedings, the babies would climb on the wolf's back and head, pull on her nose and lips, sticking pudgy fingers into her eyes. They gnawed on her paws, squeezed her tail. Spit up all over her fur. They were an adorable menace, and Rhea loved them too much.

Loving someone, however, is an active art, for love is neither static nor stationary. Rhea thought she'd proven her devotion already, but life would force her to prove it again and again. Love is work—despite this, through that, overall.

Love is decision-making. Love is letting go.

For this is the point in the story when the good shepherd finds them.

He appeared at the den's opening as the wolf nursed—a bearded man, thin, with a forehead just slightly too large and dark eyebrows. He carried a shepherd's crook in his hand.

"Gods!" he exclaimed, jaw dropped.

The wolf snarled at him, urging him backward, but she did not rise, for her cubs—her *children*; had she truly referred to them as cubs?—were latched.

The man raised his hands peacefully as he retreated. "I am sorry I disturbed you."

Rhea worried, of course. She'd been discovered—a wolf nursing human boys!—but something about this man felt unavoidable. Later, when the twins slept, she went in search of him, easily tracking his scent from the cave to a shepherd's hut on the hill, eerily close to the fig tree on the Tiber. It was not remarkable, a hut like any other: circular, built of straw, a thatched roof.

Though it was nighttime and she made no sound, no sudden movements, a wolf is a wolf. The nearby sheep began to stir.

I'll only eat you if you can't keep quiet, she thought.

The wolf peered through the hut's open window. The shepherd and a woman ate dinner together, quietly conversing in easy companionship, in peace. There were no signs of children—no stuffed dolls or balls or sticks or mess. It was just the two of them and their animals.

The wolf studied the woman, assessing her in the petty way one woman regards another: How old? How pretty? She was older than Rhea Silvia or Antho, with a plain face and simple dress, but she moved with a lissome sensuality. Had she been a dancer? Even the way she brought food to her mouth or pulled back a strand of loose hair enchanted. And the way she looked at the man answered any questions Rhea had about their relationship.

He laid his hand atop hers as she spoke, as he listened. Loving her.

It hurt to watch.

The wolf retreated to her cave, to her snoring babes, and tried—in vain—to find comfort.

The man came again with gifts.

One time he left a leg of lamb. On another occasion he brought a clean blanket.

Rhea accepted his offerings uneasily. She did not growl, but neither did she allow him inside or permit him to touch her or her babies.

"The river told me to find you," he explained. "I am Faustulus."

A name. Another gift, perhaps.

And on his next visit, he carried some sort of crude handmade harp. Nothing like the fine instruments Rhea had seen at court. He stationed himself on the boundary of the cave's entrance and began to strum. A pleasant sound, one that brought her back to feasts with her family, to celebrations. Laughter and dancing. Memories she'd repressed after all the tragedy. Faustulus sang a silly song about turtles, light in tone and touch.

The babies were mesmerized. Viridis gurgled, and Canus scooted toward the man and his charming melodies. Alarm shot through the wolf as she leapt forward, grabbing her baby by the nape of his neck and pulling him proprietarily backward.

The music stopped. Faustulus withdrew.

"I apologize. I will not come again."

When he left, both babies wailed.

Their screams were Tiberinus's fault. He had sent the shepherd to her cave! He had overstepped, interfered, and Rhea was livid. On the next new moon, Rhea donned her dress and stormed down to the river to tell him herself.

"Did you send that shepherd to me?" she yelled into the water. She kicked a bare foot at the Tiber's surface, sending up furious splashes. "You coward! Face me!"

The river god rose from his domain, perfectly dry, as usual. He wore a frown. "I am helping you."

"You are meddling."

"I do what is right for Latium"—he lowered his voice—"but also what is good for you."

She stepped into the shallows and stabbed her pointer finger into his chest like a spear. "You think you know my family, but you do not know me."

He sighed, a rueful sound. "Then I can only urge you to adjust your thinking. I cannot imagine how it feels to be treated with such malice by your own kind, but you cannot live forever in a cave, licking your wounds. You were prophesied, Rhea Silvia!"

"I don't care about Latium," she insisted. "My sons are all that matter."

"How can you not see that the interests of your sons and Latium might be one and the same?"

"Leave us alone," she seethed. "I will kill that man if he comes again."

As she stomped up onto the riverbank, Tiberinus called out after her: "Parents send their young on apprenticeships, do they not? Mothers employ nurses. Children receive tutors. That does not mean they are not loved. On the contrary, it means their family cares."

"Do not speak to me of humanity, immortal."

Do not hate him for his honesty, rejoined her inner voice. *Tiberinus shows you what you need to see, tells you what you must hear. You think of Canus and Viridis as only babies; he considers the men they will become.*

But if Rhea could ignore an ageless god, she could certainly ignore her own mind.

Chapter XLIII

ANTHO

DAYS AT VILLA Flavius passed in dreary dullness. Calvus was very wealthy, and his two late wives had created a domestic system that ran on its own, leaving the mistress of the house with idle hands. Antho, however, had been raised by Claudia, who, despite her numerous faults, had instilled in her daughter a strong work ethic. Here, Antho was bored, and with no real tasks, she created hobbies for herself—cultivating a garden, building bird feeders, reorganizing already immaculate rooms.

Calvus did not come to her bed every night, but anytime he arrived at her door in his nightdress, it was more than she wanted. The first lesson she learned as a newlywed was how to make the marital act go faster. Because he found her thin body displeasing, she gained weight. She arrayed herself in the ways he enjoyed, murmured the compliments he craved, all to get him off her as soon as possible.

She knew his conjugal visits would not stop until she was pregnant; nevertheless, the moment he left her room, Antho jumped out of bed and cleansed herself with the ointments and tonics she kept hidden under a loose floor tile beside Jocasta's brooch.

She hoped her womb hated him as much as her heart did.

At breakfast together one morning, Calvus called for a carriage to be prepared. "I must visit the Regia today to counsel with the king."

"I would happily accompany you, husband. I wish to see my mother." Antho smiled shyly. "And the midwife."

The light in Calvus's eyes was not joy but avarice. "Prepare quickly. I leave at once."

She tried to keep her foot from tapping as the carriage passed through the Latin farmlands, but her eagerness to return was difficult to manage. There was no way of forewarning Leandros of her arrival; she could only pray that his duties were light and he could make space to be with her.

Antho prayed to Aphrodite.

At the Regia, Calvus gave his wife a curt nod. "We return home after dinner." He headed straight for the king's tablinum, where he and her father could argue over maps and numbers. Delighted to be free of him, Antho smiled at the servants she had missed, hugging many with teary eyes. She was engaged in a long conversation with Gratia, begging for recipes to bring to Villa Flavius, when she heard a cough behind her.

Antho turned.

And there he was—so handsome, so hers.

Leandros had grown a short beard, and she wanted to feel it on her skin. The thought alone made her knees melt.

"Welcome back, Princess," he said tightly, bowing.

Antho excused herself from the others. "Ah, Leandros, perhaps you can assist me. I want to have a decorative shield made for my husband as a wedding gift, but I know nothing about armor!"

"I would be happy to show you my own."

"How kind."

They removed themselves from the crowd, keeping an appropriate distance between them, but Leandros pulled her into the first empty room he saw, kissing her like a man deprived, irrational and impassioned, groaning and clutching her hair.

"Not here," she rebuked, barely able to extricate herself from his arms or his mouth.

They could not go to the larder during the day, so Leandros led Antho into the arsenal, where the soldiers stowed their weapons, and as they moved through the corridors, he was hard-pressed to keep his hands from her.

"Stop it," she hissed.

She loved it.

"Nobody comes here until the shift changes," he announced, but he barred the door regardless, moving a chest of daggers into its path. "We might have a few hours."

They did not move with the same achingly slow pace as their wedding night; this time, they couldn't remove their clothes quickly enough. Calvus only wanted to dominate Antho; he found his pleasure in making her feel small. But with Leandros, lovemaking was an act of give-and-take. They were both young and healthy and so very obsessed with each other.

She felt infinite.

"Antho," he moaned, "I am almost . . . Do you want me to . . . ?"

"Yes," she answered, understanding and gripping him tighter. "Inside me."

Afterward, as their breath returned and Leandros placed grateful, worshipful kisses on her neck and chest, Antho laid a hand across her belly.

"My children will be Greek," she murmured. "I will ensure it."

"And when your children have my skin? My hair or body type? I look nothing like Calvus Flavius."

"People will see what they want to believe."

Amulius had taught his daughter better negotiation skills than he realized. She understood the art of the deal. When she had promised to give Calvus a child and her father an heir, she never once indicated who would sire it.

◆ ◆ ◆

ON THE FLOOR, wrapped in Leandros's cloak, the lovers spoke of everything. For the first time, Antho spoke of the night in Rhea's cell, of all she had seen and done.

"The guards who captured Rhea Silvia are gone," Leandros said. "So is Petronius."

"Zea told me. My father must have killed them."

"He burned their bodies immediately, but I've heard rumors. Antho, people who caught a glimpse say all three were . . . slashed."

"Slashed?"

"Like they'd been attacked by something inhuman. And the prisoners who were down in the dungeon that night insisted they saw a beast."

Antho sat up. "You must interrogate them! What else did they see? Maybe Rhea somehow escaped!"

"The king had every inmate executed."

She pulled the cloak tighter around her shoulders as she shivered. All those men, murdered. For what? For being in the wrong place at the wrong hour.

"It must have been Mars," she said. "I can think of no other explanation. He came to rescue Ilia!"

Leandros pulled her gently back down to him. "My love, don't do this. You will torture yourself with hypotheticals. Rhea died that night, and so did the twins that only you, your father, and I know existed."

"It doesn't feel like she is dead," Antho confessed, sighing into his chest. "Gone perhaps. Hidden, definitely. But still alive. I would know, Leandros."

"A bond like the two of you had would be difficult to sever, even in death."

He did not understand, and she would not burden him with explanation, but Antho stored this conversation like it was its own type of arsenal. Information was just as powerful as gold or blade, just as fatal.

Something inhuman had killed Rhea's attackers, and her father had burned the evidence.

Maybe Rhea hadn't been on that pyre.

Maybe she had reached her sons on the river in time.

Maybe Leandros was right; Antho would go mad if she didn't let this go.

For the moments that remained, Antho pushed all conspiracies from her mind and filled her arms with her husband.

Chapter XLIV

RHEA

RHEA THOUGHT OF nothing except her conversation with Tiberinus, and the mental battle it had set in motion. She was of two minds:

I have to let my boys go.

I will never let them go.

What was the compromise?

As a wolf, she would stay by her sons' side for all the years she had remaining, watching and protecting, but Rhea had also made a promise to take down Amulius. If her sons were going to grow into men who would destroy their enemies, men worthy of a throne, then they needed to learn to be human.

Her father had been a good man, but he had stopped being brave once he suffered too much loss. She would have to trust that Faustulus would remain strong and true. And if he didn't, she could always eat him.

The wolf grinned.

In their remaining time together, she memorized her boys. Their tiny toenails. The thickness of Canus's hair and Viridis's curls. The shape of their lips, how their mouths hung open in sleep. Their skin even *smelled* soft. Was this what motherhood meant? To love every single aspect of a person? To ache in the most gorgeous way for their touch, their smile, the assurance of their heartbeat?

When Faustulus returned to the cave, as she knew he would, she allowed him inside. He sat and began to speak.

"I apologize for coming again after I said I wouldn't, but I needed to tell our story. You are a wolf, and it is crazy to talk to a wolf, but no less crazy than a wolf nursing human babies."

Fair.

"My wife, Laurentia, was a prostitute from Sabinum. She has only given me fragments of what happened to her there, but an incomplete picture is more than enough to understand why she ran away. I think she fears I would judge her if I knew it all. I never would. Or maybe she just wants to forget. I've accepted this about her, the parts she keeps hidden. Years ago, I found her wandering the Seven Hills, shunned by one community after another. But my lonely soul saw her lonely soul. Wolf, I married her.

"We thought we would have a family, but it never happened. Was it her body or mine? Our age? Our luck? We said we did not mind. We had each other and our life, our dogs and cats. Even the sheep.

"But maybe we did mind, because neither of us ever stopped praying for a chance."

Faustulus halted his story, squinted into the sky outside the cave. He stroked his long beard as he reflected.

"And then came this unusual dream. In it, I sat by the river, and a man's voice spoke to me of an important woman and her twin boys. He told me to search the Palatine Hill, because they needed a home. He failed to mention the wolf."

Faustulus smiled ruefully.

"I know there is something meaningful in all of this, and I'm not sure I'm worthy of playing a part. But if you allow me, I will care for these boys. My wife and I will honor them every day of our lives."

The wolf listened as she nursed. Canus fell asleep, but Viridis crawled toward the man, scooting naked through the dirt. Faustulus's eyes widened. "May I?" And because he asked politely, the wolf did not snarl. She lowered her head onto her paws, watching closely as the shepherd picked up her son and brought him to his chest. Faustulus massaged tender circles into Viridis's back.

Oh, Rhea remembered that feeling! Her mother's hand on her chest!

Her babbling boy reached for Faustulus's beard and tugged, which made the man chuckle.

"I promise you," he vowed, "I would give my own life before I let harm come to them."

Now that was a vow she understood.

And Rhea reminded herself that she wasn't losing her sons but sharing them. It was a transferal on her own terms, into a life and education she ordained. And the wolf wasn't going anywhere. She would remain in the Seven Hills, and she would be there when her sons learned to speak and swim, when they lost teeth and grew new ones. She would oversee their races through the pastures, when they tumbled in their first fistfights, when they stole wine and experienced clumsy first kisses.

Maybe she wouldn't watch that.

But they would always be safe; she would be their guardian, their avenger, for all her days.

The wolf purposefully rose to her feet, careful not to jostle the gray-eyed baby's sleep. She leaned down and gave her firstborn a lick across the top of his head. Then she padded toward the shepherd, who held the green-eyed baby out to her. Her second-born baby, her greatest surprise. She nuzzled her wet nose against his belly, and he giggled.

Rhea had done a fine job. She had kept them alive, despite all odds, despite every obstacle. They were healthy and darling. If she did not do this now, she might not have the bravery to do it again.

But that did not mean she could watch him take them away.

The wolf left the cave, and the shepherd man gathered her children. He would assemble their meager belongings—well-worn blankets from the woodcutter's hut, a basket, the lynx fur—and bring them to his home.

But until then, Rhea returned to the woods.

◆ ◆ ◆

THE SHEPHERD AND his wife named Rhea's babies Romulus and Remus.

Decent names, Rhea supposed, but not particularly memorable.

Chapter XLV

RHEA

IT WAS THE first new moon without her boys, and Tiberinus came to Rhea's den. He found her clothed in her one dress, tucked into a tight ball. Her eyes were closed, but she did not sleep. She was too miserable, too depressed, to achieve any rest.

"Come outside," he said.

"I would rather be by myself."

"Why?"

Rhea sat up in frustration. "When humans are sad, they like to be alone. It is called brooding."

"Does it help?"

She sighed. "Not particularly."

Tiberinus crouched and entered her cave. "Then you might as well spend the night with me."

"I suppose you can't make my life any worse than you already have." Rhea stood and brushed the wrinkles from her dress with her hands. They did not converse as he led her down to the river. A rowboat waited on the bank. Tiberinus entered first and offered her his hand. She ignored it, climbing in somewhat shakily on her own.

Her human body felt awkward after weeks with a wolf's agility. Even the balance of standing on two legs took a moment to recover.

Tiberinus dipped his hand into the water, and it hummed in return.

The river lifted the boat and carried it toward the spit of land at the center of the Tiber.

"Where are we going?" Rhea asked.

"To my island."

Tiber Island, of course.

"What if somebody sees us?"

Though Tiberinus did not answer, vapors rose from the river's surface, circling their boat in an effervescent, twinkling mist. Rhea took a deep breath, inhaling the heady and indescribable scent of night water.

After a short ride, they disembarked. The river god led her to the center of the island, where he already had a blanket spread and waiting. He knelt and opened a basket, pulling out a jug of wine and two cups, then bread and cheese and dried fish.

Rhea giggled but clapped a hand over her mouth when Tiberinus glanced up at her in obvious distress.

"Have I done something wrong?"

"It depends. What are you trying to do?"

He shrugged his shoulders. "Isn't this how mortal men entertain women?"

Rhea's heart nearly stopped.

"Well, I am not a woman anymore."

He slumped a bit, crestfallen, and Rhea bit down her grin.

"Grab the wine—just the jug is fine—and let's go back to your boat."

◆ ◆ ◆

SIDE BY SIDE, Tiberinus and Rhea Silvia lay on their backs in his rowboat, passing the wine back and forth as they watched the clouds pass over the stars.

"Why do you help me?" she asked. "Mars feared Jupiter's retribution if he supported me against Vesta."

Tiberinus scoffed. "I do not concern myself with those new gods and their squabbles."

"Just like Cybele," Rhea mused. It must be why Cybele wasn't afraid to offer her aid, either.

He nodded. "Cybele is her new name, but she is the mother. She has always been."

Rhea took the wine from him and drank long and deep.

"You are not saving much for me," he chided.

"Because you can drink wine every night."

"Yes, but not with you."

She bit back a grin but passed him the wine.

"No, you finish it."

Rhea raised an eyebrow, tipped the jug back and gulped down the rest.

"Is this how it was with you and Mars?"

Rhea spat out her drink. She leaned forward, coughing and choking.

"I apologize for the question," Tiberinus said worriedly, patting her on her back.

"No, I'm not offended. It's just . . . Mars and I were nothing like this." Rhea lay back down, and Tiberinus, following her lead, settled beside her.

"But he courted you?"

"No," replied Rhea. "I have never been courted."

"But then . . . how . . . ?" His voice trailed off.

"Mars and I together were just two bodies," she answered delicately.

"Ah." Tiberinus kept his eyes skyward. "He did not deserve you."

Rhea warmed—from the wine, from this indirect praise. "You hardly know me," she demurred.

"But I know him."

This was an opportunity to ask every question that had ever plagued her. *What have you heard of Mars? Has he spoken of me? Who are his other lovers, his other children? Was I wrong to make love with war, to bring his children to mortal life?* But knowledge would change none of her past choices, and might tempt her into regret.

Rhea despised regret. Avoided it like nightshade or scorpions.

"Mars and I were never friends," she concluded.

"Is that what we are, Rhea? Friends?"

She considered him in profile. Tiberinus wasn't conventionally handsome, not like Mars. But when he smiled, his whole face folded. She liked the wrinkles at the corners of his eyes.

Yes, he was undeniably charming.

He turned his head to the side and faced her. She saw the river itself in his eyes, and she wondered at all he had witnessed.

She also wondered if he might kiss her.

"Friends," Rhea agreed. "We can be friends."

Chapter XLVI

RHEA

FAUSTULUS DID NOT keep his new sons a secret. Nor did he disguise their provenance. They were an enigma worthy of celebration: Romulus, Remus, and their wolf, already the early makings of legend.

"Tell us again how you found them, Faustulus!"

And he would relay the dream, the den, the understanding in the wolf's amber eyes.

Then, quieter: "And you don't think they could be the children of . . . ?"

"No. Her body was still pregnant when they found it."

"More likely, some augur proclaimed twins a bad omen."

The hill people were outsiders, rejected by the more civilized cities of Latium; they kept to their own. Rhea's boys might have been famous on the Palatine, but not in the rest of King Amulius's kingdom. And the warm welcome of Romulus and Remus did not extend to Rhea. Though she was an interesting wolf, she was still a wolf, and they were a people who made their living in sheep and goats. Her presence made everyone uncomfortable.

"Just don't pet her," Faustulus warned the others with a chuckle. "She nearly bit my hand off."

Nobody shared his amusement.

For the wolf was no dog, make no mistake, and only Romulus and

Remus were allowed to touch her. Sometimes they rode together upon her back, as though she were a warhorse in miniature. They wrestled with her, tugging her ears and pulling her tail. The wolf would growl, even nip, to put them in their place, but she never hurt them.

This did little to ease the hill people's fears.

The people were suspicious of the wolf. It mattered not that Faustulus told his story to anyone who would listen; an education in warnings and folklore is difficult to unteach. *Wolves are big. Wolves are bad. Wolves are to be feared.* And Rhea was no fool. She saw how the villagers began carrying weapons, and she noticed the open hostility directed her way whenever she prowled down from her den. Rhea hadn't forgotten how ropes strangled and burned, how sword hilts broke bone. Rhea remembered kicks and punches. She had seen that same leery look—that human capacity for violence—in the eyes of the Vestals, the farmers, the soldiers, her uncle. She hadn't anticipated this response, had hoped for a wary acceptance of her presence, but as that was hardly her reality, it made visiting her boys both difficult and dangerous.

It was safest to visit her sons at night. She loved to watch them sleep, of course; she loved to watch them do everything, but she wanted more time with them in the day, in closer proximity to their childhood.

Children show time much differently than adults, and though Rhea was loath to admit it, her babies were rapidly becoming little boys. She watched from afar as they toddled around, played and fought and fell. Between the two, there was an endless litany of scrapes and bruises, and Rhea envied Laurentia every time she got to hold them and rock them and kiss away their tears. She was grateful, but she was so jealous.

Then came the day Faustulus taught the boys to swim. The wolf observed from a promontory above the river, nervous, because even though Tiberinus would never allow her sons to drown, they were too wild, too brazen. Misbehaving in dangerous ways. When Canus struggled to keep his head up, he clung to Viridis, and they would both go under. It took all Rhea's self-discipline not to run down the hill and pull them out by the backs of their necks.

"Romulus and Remus," Faustulus shouted, "kick your legs!"

Romulus and Remus, Remus and Romulus. She still forgot to use their proper names.

The boy they called Remus turned to splash his father but then spotted the wolf standing guard. He pointed excitedly to his brother. "Lupa!" he cried. "Lupa! Lupa!"

Lupa. She-wolf.

Romulus echoed his brother's calls, and then they pounced upon each other, rolling in the shallows like the cubs they once were, biting and growling, while Faustulus threw up his arms in frustration.

She was their first mother; she was their first word.

A euphoria that no suspicious villager, no substitute mother, and no forced distance could ever damper.

◆ ◆ ◆

THEN ONE NIGHT Rhea could find no comfort in her cave. She was racked by an unrelenting restlessness, invisible forces tugging at her mind and muscles. She needed to roam. The wolf skirted the edges of the Palatine Hill, heading northwest past Capitoline Hill and the oak grove and into the lowland Field of Mars. This was the best place to run.

A telling silence covered the land. The hares burrowed; the owls kept quiet. The turtles retreated into their shells. What did they sense? The wolf trotted down to the river's edge and listened.

Synchronized oars breaking the water, hushed human commands in even lower tones.

Raiders!

She needed to wake the Palatine.

The wolf bounded home, barking and howling, racing from hut to hut, not caring who might hate or fear her. Hysteria ensued as the herding dogs echoed her call to alarm and the sheep began to bleat. The wolf ended at Faustulus's door, pawing at the wood, whining and frantic.

"What is wrong?" he asked her, bewildered and half-asleep.

People rousted from their beds stormed toward Faustulus's hut in an angry mob.

"Shut your wolf up before I kill it!"

"Enough with this, Faustulus. That wolf is a menace!"

"We have humored you for too long."

"This is chaos! Look what she has done!"

Rhea spun; the villagers surrounded her, wielding torches and tools, spears and shovels and even a few swords. Faustulus, now joined by Laurentia, raised his arms and stepped protectively before his wife and the wolf.

"She is not like other wolves," he insisted.

The villagers shouted back and forth while Rhea panicked. All this time spent arguing was time wasted. Their enemies would reach their shores soon. Rhea shoved her nose into Faustulus's leg three urgent times, then turned and trotted toward the Tiber, begging for him to understand.

"I think she wants me to follow."

"She dies tonight, Faustulus."

"Give me one chance," he pleaded.

"He's lost his mind," a woman muttered, to much murmured agreement.

Faustulus left the crowd, following Rhea to the fig tree. She halted, faced north, and waited. By this time, the boats in the distance had rowed into full view. Faustulus cursed, then regarded Rhea with amazement. "Smart wolf." He sprinted back up the hill, sounding the alarm.

"Attack! We are under attack!"

They were Sabine raiders, come to the Hills for livestock and women. The people of the Palatine began their counterassault before the invaders could moor their boats. And the wolf fought in the vanguard along the riverbank, attacking any who dared come ashore. In the melee, she felt a sharp bite in her side. A rock crunching her ribs. She growled at the crude cruelty, ducking lower for cover as stones rained down like Jupiter's anger. A man waded through the Tiber, jeering.

"Come at me, wolf!"

The savage hatred in his eyes lifted Rhea from hiding, and she bounded forward to face him, ignoring the almost rhythmic pain in her chest, the sharp edge of breathing in a shattered chamber. She met the Sabine man at the water's edge. He pulled a coulter knife from a band at his thigh and slashed forward, cutting off the tip of her ear. Rhea howled but leapt forward, bullying past his bladed arms, aiming for his stomach. Her jaws met the taut muscle, snapping and popping through this abdomen.

They fell backward into the water.

The river took it from there. A wave resembling a familiar hand pulled the man's head under and held him. Drowning him in the blood-red water.

Fires erupted behind Rhea as burning arrows hit dry tree and brush. Though she scalded her paws and singed her fur, she continued to fight and rescue, retrieving fallen hill people and dragging them by their tunics, ferrying them behind the line of safety.

The Palatine won the battle that night, without a single death or abduction, but only because of the wolf's warning. Only because they were already awake, outside and armed, before the enemy's arrival. If they'd been taken unawares, asleep in their beds? Everybody knew how that story would have ended.

The debate over Faustulus's wolf was settled. The most ardent haters let her be, and she became a source of pride to the others, who composed the vast majority. Common Latin people didn't often feel exceptional, but now? *Oh, your city has marble? We have a* wolf!

The missing tip of her left ear became a poignant symbol of their mutual victory.

After the battle at the Tiber, offerings began to arrive at her den. *I am no goddess*, Rhea mused, *but only a fool would refuse a fresh meal.*

She was no fool.

She was the Palatine's wolf, and its people were hers.

She protected them all.

Chapter XLVII

ANTHO

AETIUS SILVIUS FLAVIUS, whom they called Ezio, was born to much pomp and falderal, to luxury unimaginable and all the very imaginable pressures. When Antho went into labor, Calvus had her loaded into a carriage—against the midwife's objections—and carted back to her parents' home so that his baby would be born in the Regia. She labored for nearly two days in her childhood room, and then . . .

A son.

After his birth, her parents almost didn't let her return to Villa Flavius.

King Amulius and Queen Claudia were stoic people. Severe. But they were doting grandparents.

It was one of the great surprises of Antho's life.

She had assumed they would treat Aetius with the same habitual disdain they had shown her, but no. Aetius was their Apollo incarnate, the golden son they never had. Claudia fussed over him, wove him blanket after blanket. She criticized how Antho wrapped him, how Antho held him. Antho wasn't feeding him enough. Antho laid him too close to the fire, then too far from the fire. Antho took all the criticism in stride. When the queen held baby Aetius, she was happy, and Antho could never begrudge anyone joy. For the first time, mother and daughter found equilibrium in their shared love of this boy.

And then there was Amulius, who had never shown any interest in children and seemed especially repulsed by the uselessness of babies. Her father demanded Aetius be handed to him anytime they were in the same room. He carried him everywhere, even taking him to council meetings. On more than one occasion, he made visiting dignitaries compliment his perfect grandson. Who was this man? Antho could almost forget he was a coldhearted murderer.

Almost.

But the time came when Antho had to return to Villa Flavius, and there was one person who had yet to meet the baby.

She placed the vase on the windowsill, just as she had in another life, and that night, Antho snuck down to the Regia's larder with Ezio in her arms. She kept him quiet as they waited and waited for Leandros, singing little songs and nursing. Hours passed, and Leandros did not appear. *He was assigned extra duties*, she told herself, but she was not placated.

"Next time, baby," she promised her son, who gazed up at her, all curious eyes and stunning eyelashes. Surely the most perfect boy in all of Latium. And as they made to leave, mother and child nearly bumped into the father as he finally arrived. Antho closed the larder door behind them, barely controlling her excitement; she had pictured this very scene so many times, and it was easily her favorite fantasy.

"Ezio," she cooed, "he's here. Your papa."

She presented the baby to Leandros only to be struck by a deep, disconcerting pain in her chest. Leandros would not touch him.

"Hold him," she urged. "He is yours."

"Yes, he is mine. And I am meeting him in a storage room."

Antho struggled for words. Leandros was withdrawn and distraught. Bitter. This was not at all how she'd imagined their family together for the first time; it was unthinkable.

"I heard you screaming the night he was born," Leandros continued, "and I could not come to you. I thought that you would die—that our child would die—and I could do nothing."

"It was always going to be this way."

"Well, it is too difficult."

She clutched Ezio to her chest, overtaken by an irrational fear that he might understand what they said. "Don't hold it against our baby."

"I'm not, Antho, but if I let myself love this child, it will only make it harder to watch him be raised by another man. I won't get to teach him Greek or how to ride a horse. I won't be there to help him learn right from wrong. I will miss all his milestones. And he will never know me as anything other than some guard who worked for his grandfather."

Antho began to cry. "You are my husband."

"I am sorry that this pains you." He kissed her on the cheek. "But I must protect myself."

She pulled down the swaddle around Ezio's head and neck, and held him up one last time. "Only look at him, Leandros. He has your face."

But he did not look.

"I must go, Antho."

And he hurried away.

Aetius Silvius Flavius, whom they called Ezio, born to pomp and falderal, to every luxury and pressure, watched his young mother sob amid the dried beans and wheat.

◆ ◆ ◆

THE SABINES HAD attacked one of the Seven Hills. Antho's father assembled an army to pursue justice at the border. Antho, in her new-baby stupor, barely paid attention. What did territorial squabbles mean in her maternity-centered world?

A lot, as it turned out.

During a visit to the Regia, she left Ezio with her mother, who was more than willing to oblige, and searched for Leandros. There had been enough time and space for her to process their earlier conversation, and she understood. She had ideas to mitigate his discomfort, to ease them into a semblance of family. She could fix this!

Leandros and Ursan were boxing in the courtyard beside the outdoor pool, and Antho took a seat. Watching her husband wrestle in minimal clothing was . . . well, her injuries from delivering Ezio were fully healed. When Leandros saw her waiting, he ended the bout prematurely. Ursan shot Antho a quick look, then nodded, and she wondered, not for the first time, how much the other soldiers knew, or at least suspected, about their relationship.

Did she care? To be honest, no.

He came to her, wiping his forehead and neck with a rag, sipping from a jug of water. Antho tucked her hands beneath her thighs, a physical reminder to keep herself collected though she yearned to leap into his arms, to kiss his mouth in front of everyone.

"We need to talk," he said quietly.

"I agree," she beamed. "I have been thinking—"

"Not of that." Leandros did not match her smile, and Antho's hopes dropped lifelessly to the ground like fallen petals. "You have heard of your father's latest war?"

She cast her eyes upward, squinting at the collected clouds. "Do you think it will rain tonight? It looks like rain."

"Antho." He sat beside her, on the same bench but at a distance. When he spoke, he stared straight ahead. "The king is sending me to Sabinum."

"He can't," Antho whispered. "We have an arrangement."

Leandros smiled then, loosing a low, sardonic laugh. "It is what I love most about you, Antho, but also what damns you again and again."

"What is?"

"Your belief that humanity is inherently good, that what we say matters."

◆ ◆ ◆

IMMEDIATELY AFTER, ANTHO strode angrily into her father's tablinum without invitation or formal presentation. "I provided a son," she declared, "and you send Leandros to his death?"

Her father did not look up from his work. "Oh, is that the Greek's name?"

"Do not pretend you don't know."

"It is no execution," Amulius answered mildly. "He is a soldier, and he has been reassigned."

"But you promised me, Father. In the dungeon with—"

He did not let her finish. "What will you do, Antho? Kill Ezio?"

There was no need to respond to such a ridiculous rhetorical.

"Be a mother, be a wife. Forget the Greek."

"Would it kill you to grant me one happiness? You have everything you ever wanted; can you not extend me this generosity?"

Amulius laughed. "You presume my character as a politician and a father. You only understand my roles." The king stood. "You know nothing about me as a man."

Even with his desk between them, Antho fought the instinct to shrink backward. But meekness would not merit her father's respect, nor save Leandros. She raised her chin. "Then tell me."

Never before had she been so forward, had she stepped so close to the brink of the personal. And Amulius hesitated. His shrewd mask slipped, and Antho glimpsed the pain beneath.

"Can't this end between us?" she pleaded. "Can't you be satisfied?"

"I have not been happy in a very long time, and because of that, I will never be satisfied."

Her father's deep, chilly voice usually echoed disdain, but now it spoke from the yawning abyss within him. He was an empty man.

"Reassign Leandros if you must, but do not send him to war."

"I do not countenance second thoughts. My mind is made up." The king returned to his seat and his correspondences. "You are excused."

Do not scream. I can fix this.

"There will be no more grandchildren until Leandros returns safely."

Amulius shrugged. "Ezio is enough."

"Oh, Father," Antho said, pausing in the doorway, "you of all people should know that a first son's kingship is never guaranteed."

Chapter XLVIII

AMULIUS

AMULIUS THOUGHT HE would think of Jocasta less as he got older. The opposite was true. The memories solidified over time, becoming monuments in his mind, built of the toughest metals, etched with diamond, filled with gold. An ever-present and immutable part of who he was.

After his daughter left, with all her youthful fury and self-righteousness, he remembered. He worshipped at his inner temple.

A second son, but no less a man, and *happy*.

When Jocasta lay in his arms, he felt worthy. He was tempted to describe it as a feeling of invincibility, but even at his age—which was still on the young side—he knew that wasn't quite right. No mortal man was ever indestructible, by nature of definition, no matter a god's favor or the love of a most perfect woman.

They lay together in the forest she loved. Personally, he despised the outdoors. Itchy and inferior. But it made her happy, and she possessed a happiness that was incandescent. A spectacle he couldn't tear his eyes from, even if he wanted to. Furthermore, he appreciated the secrecy of the trees, how they formed a wall between them and the others. Jocasta's people visited the Regia often, but their affair remained undiscovered. Soon he would ask his father to arrange their marriage. King Procas would consent, mostly because he cared very little about what

Amulius did. The younger brother, the spare heir. Only Numitor paid him any real attention.

Once their relationship became public, he would have to share Jocasta with the court and all the Albans. They would all see her smile, her laugh, her hair.

Gods, that hair. He would lay his face in it, inhale its jasmine. Twirl it through his fingers.

She was more than beautiful—she was beauty.

He would keep her hidden as long as he could. Even if that meant being outdoors. She was, after all, his one good thing.

"I can't believe you are mine," he murmured, afterward. But it was the wrong thing to say. She sat up. "I am no more yours than a tree is a bird's."

He snorted. "Birds are small and simple. If they had minds like ours, they would understand the necessity of ownership. They would defend their trees, not flit around." And then he placed his hands on her shoulders and pulled her back down into him. "They would find one place to rest and make it theirs. A good tree makes a good life."

Jocasta nestled against his bare chest. "But a bird has wings and must be true to its nature. They are not meant to settle."

"They are meant to fly, of course, but also to come home. To build a nest. To belong."

"But I am not a bird, and you are not a tree." She nibbled at his earlobe, and he laughed.

"No, Jocasta, we certainly are not."

And she whispered, "Trees can't do such delightful things with their hands."

He blushed—with pride, with happiness. She made him believe that being himself was enough, after all.

"Do you love me?"

"I love your hands and your . . ." She wiggled her eyebrows, making him grin. "And I even love your poor, tortured soul."

He felt content with her answer, but he also knew love came easy to her. It was the point where they split. She loved rain and strawberries and stray dogs and dancing no less than she loved her favorite humans. Her love was a net, widespread and expansive, while his remained always sharp and focused. Focused, poignant.

He kissed her lips, so softly, brushing wayward hair from her face, and she sighed.

"Nobody sees how soft you are," she began, "but I do." She closed her eyes. "Stay this way, Amulius. Stay soft."

"Then stay with me."

They fell into blissful silence. Light as a breeze through leaves, a susurration of the wind.

Amulius's hamartia: the decades passed, but he was still in love with his brother's wife.

His knotted feelings for his daughter were difficult to untangle. He didn't love Antho, nor did he hate her. By sending away the Greek, though, he did her a service—his fatherly duty so to speak—for he was setting her straight. Great love is destruction. Antho would be a better mother to his grandson without the distraction.

The most recent generation always believes they invented love, but Amulius knew otherwise. Nobody had ever loved like him and Jocasta, and if they could not end their days together, why should anyone else?

A knock at the door interrupted his reverie. If it was Antho returned to complain, he would not be so decorous. "Enter!" he called, already preparing his derisive response.

"My king." The augur bowed.

Relieved, Amulius beckoned Sethre forward. "I pray you disturb me because you bring results."

"I have loosed sacred chickens over maps of Latium and the greater world. Monitored the directions of birds in the sky, analyzing for patterns. I have rolled dice, checked the shoulder blades and entrails of sacrificial lambs, dissected liver after liver."

"Yes. And?"

The augur cast his eyes downward. "There is no sign of Rhea Silvia."

"Unacceptable."

The augur squirmed, frowned, sending that thick hairy eyebrow into a gross wiggle. Amulius sneered. He despised his dependency on this unsightly man.

"Dead bodies do not rise and walk away. Where did she go?"

"If you had some sort of relic, a baby tooth, her bone or blood, I could cast it into the fire and read the smoke and ash."

Amulius fingered the gold bracelet at his wrist, the band that covered his guilty treasure, a thin braid. "There might be something."

The night of Rhea's escape remained a violent mystery. After hours without word from Gnaeus or Xeno, Amulius stormed down to the dungeon to ascertain the news. Why wasn't that bitch dead yet? He couldn't relax until he knew. But instead of answers, he found his guards on the ground, gory and mutilated. Their bodies ripped open in a way no blade could ever replicate. And his niece? Vanished. The other prisoners cried out, proclaiming the arrival of a vengeful four-legged beast.

Amulius slit every throat.

Before dawn, Amulius enlisted Sethre and a few of his most trustworthy guards to transport the bodies onto pyres. Amulius himself walked through the dewy morn, tossing torches and fuming. She had evaded him again. Until he saw Rhea's corpse with his own eyes, Amulius would never know peace.

He would provide Sethre a lock of Rhea's hair, the hair he sent Helvius to steal from the Vestal pine tree years ago. The hair he kept on his wrist, in his trunk, at a hidden altar, not because of that damned, hated girl but because of her beloved mother.

"You shall have a relic by tonight."

Sethre brought his hands together in supplication. "My gratitude, my allegiance, belong always to you, King Amulius."

"Yes, yes. And Sethre, when you search the flames, watch out for wolves."

Chapter XLIX

RHEA

THOUGH THE SABINE attack had occurred at the Palatine, the hill people were the last to hear of Amulius's war. But they received the message, loud and clear, when a contingent of Latin soldiers and royal representatives marched through the Seven Hills. Their commander and the king's messenger ordered all men of fighting age to assemble.

Fighting age was an ambiguous designation. Was Faustulus, with his weak back and walking stick, of *fighting age*? According to the military commander, yes.

The wolf watched from one of her many hiding places as the men and boys assembled in a long line. The commander instructed them to count off by ten. When Faustulus called "five," Rhea felt neither sorrow nor celebration. What did it mean?

But then the ill-fated "tens" were called forward.

"All of you will record your names with the scribe, gather any belongings you can carry, and depart with our army tonight."

Screams and moans from mothers and wives and sisters and daughters coalesced in a jarring serenade. Older women, inured to life's injustices, offered their arms and shoulders to those wracked with wet, hot tears. Faustulus, serving as the Palatine's unofficial representative, stepped forward. "We cannot lose so many men, not before the season changes. We need all hands to prepare the sheep and pastures for winter."

The commander shrugged. "Wars do not stop for hay or harvest."

"King Amulius, in his infinite wisdom, has offered one provision," the royal messenger added slyly. "Any man selected for duty may donate ten silver denarii to the royal treasury in compensation for service."

Faustulus's face fell. "No man here can afford such a price."

"Then consider yourself lucky you didn't count 'ten,' old man."

But Faustulus did not relent so easily. "We defeated the Sabines on our own," he explained. "We have already fought and won for Latium."

"If you are such worthy warriors," the commander replied, narrowing his eyes, "perhaps I should take more of you."

Faustulus held his tongue.

"There is one additional matter to settle," said the messenger, hands behind his back as he surveyed the gathering. "The king has reason to believe a domesticated wolf frequents these parts. Who does it belong to?"

"A wolf does not belong to anyone," chuckled Faustulus.

The king's man stiffened. "Where is it, shepherd?"

"There is no wolf."

The messenger shouldered Faustulus aside to address the village. "Tell me about your wolf, Palatine! Such a beast would not only frighten our enemies but represent the might of our king and confederation!"

When patriotism failed to motivate a response, he pulled a coin from his bag and waved it in the air. "How much will it cost, then? A gold aureus to whoever shows me its lair!"

Gasps and whispers. A gold piece would transform the village.

Now was the moment Rhea both dreaded and awaited: the inevitable betrayal. She could always depend on people acting in their best interest, just as her family and the Vestals, even strangers like the farmer and his wife, had before. Loyalty mattered little beside cowardice or greed, and she was an animal now. Why would anyone care what happened to her?

One wolf stood no chance against an army. She would evade capture for days, maybe, and then she would not only be taken from her sons, she would be muzzled and caged, paraded through bloodshed as her enemy's trophy.

And when the new moon changed her into a woman, Amulius would experience the unique joy of killing Rhea Silvia a second time.

"Well?" shouted the messenger. "Who has information for me?"

The hill people frowned, traded guarded looks. And then a woman whose only son had just been conscripted raised her arm. "I am old," she began, moving forward as the crowd parted, "and I deserve a bit of luxury in my old age." The woman met the messenger with a sly grin on her face.

Run, you fool! chastised Rhea's inner voice, but two invisible lifelines had wound their way around the wolf's legs, holding her in place.

The woman's gaze passed from villager to villager, exchanging nods in discreet concordance, before she stood firm and finished: "There is not greater luxury than laughter, and certainly nothing funnier than a friendly wolf lying with lambs."

The people echoed her hilarity:

"Imagine! A wolf here? The king does know we keep sheep, doesn't he?"

"Only the city-born could dream up such a tale!"

"What will they say next? We keep elephants?"

"And they say the country people are superstitious!"

The king's messenger bristled, indignant and embarrassed. "Enough!" he bellowed, then he grabbed Faustulus by the neck of his tunic, hissing in his face: "King Amulius will not tolerate offense, and neither will I. Your inbred, ill-mannered friends have tested my patience. Bring the required men to my army by sundown or I will set each of your piteous hovels to flame myself."

"Yes, sir."

Faustulus appeared relieved, and Rhea? She was overcome with gratitude and astonishment and most of all, love. The love for her sons had deepened and widened her capacity for loving all, and she felt it most in these seven hills by the river.

I will die here.

A somber, striking thought, but it failed to frighten. There was nothing scary about belonging to a place, finally.

She had fought for these people, protected them, but now, most radical of all, she would let herself love them.

◆ ◆ ◆

IT WAS A quiet night on the Palatine as the conscripted departed with the army, some as young as thirteen years old. *Not men*, Rhea brooded, *boys*. If Romulus and Remus had been older, they would have taken their chances in that horrible lineup. It was unthinkable.

Quietness is often misunderstood, mistaken for submission or passivity. But quietness can also indicate rage. A simmering pot isn't loud, but touch it, and you will burn. Leave it long enough, and it will boil over.

The broken families and those who bore witness were all silent as the army marched northward, but the fire had been lit.

And when none of those men ever returned, the fire went ablaze.

Chapter L

LEANDROS

WAR WAS LOUDER than Leandros expected, and it reeked—of horseshit and human urine, sweat and blood and metal and ash. Leandros slept on the ground, wrapped in his cloak, and thought of his son. Ezio would never sleep on the ground, tucked into a cloak, coughing and pissing beside a tent full of army whores. Because Ezio would be king. He would wage the wars that sent common men like Leandros to their deaths. Inconsequential men. Fodder for the gluttonous hunger of the powerful.

His friends died in unspeakable ways, from immediate executions to drawn-out infections—those with amputated limbs in slow decomposition, still alive as skin gangrened and other organs shut down. Immolated men. Soldiers shot with poisoned arrows, fatal splinters in neck and chest and thigh. Thirsty men. Those with raving madness who slit their arms open with daggers or walked into the river after weighing themselves down with rocks.

Loss in incomprehensible extremes. Of bodies and resources, of trees and souls.

For what?

To push back the border between Latium and Sabinum a league or two?

Leandros missed Antho terribly and worried about how Amulius or

Calvus might hurt her while he was away. He had left the Regia with awkwardness between them, had pushed his only son away, and now he entered the fighting forces, tortured with regret. He heard how other men spoke of Antho around the campfire: *The little princess, so sweet and slender! Like a nymph I'd like to dance with—I'd like to bathe with!* Leandros maintained his stoicism, clutching the unappetizing bowl of rations to keep his fists occupied.

She was so much more than a face or body, than a position.

There are many sources of light in this world—star and moon, candle and flame. Antho, his wife, outshone them all.

◆ ◆ ◆

BATTLING IN THE rolling hills, painting the orchards in the palette of death, Leandros took an arrow to the heart. He lurched, stumbled, and collapsed beneath a fruit tree. Trembling hands gripped the shaft, and with a roar, Leandros pulled. Ribs split and shattered; hot red blood poured down his chest. He clutched the arrowhead in his hand, inspecting the gore, the grisly pieces of his pierced heart, as he slumped back against the trunk. Maybe it would hurt less with his eyes closed.

He didn't want to die without her.

"Open your eyes."

A woman's voice, but not hers. Still, he obeyed.

Leandros gazed into a haze, a shimmery countryside, rid of every soldier and weapon. Birds sang mellifluous melodies. And she was smiling, kneeling before him, this pale goddess with hair the color of strawberry wine.

"Am I dead?"

She shook her head, long locks swaying. "No, dear one."

"I should be dead. That wound . . ." But when he looked down, his chest was bare and healed. Only a small scar above his heart remembered where the arrow had hit. He regarded her with awe. "Why do you save me?"

"You remind me of my favorites. Romantic like Paris, handsome like Adonis. Strong like my son." She placed one soft palm upon his cheek, rubbed her thumb against the bone. "He also crossed the sea to Latium and married its princess."

Aeneas.

"I do not belong among such men."

Her perfect forehead puckered. "Why?"

"I am no hero."

"Every day you have loved your woman is an act of bravery. A weak man would have never chosen her and certainly never stayed."

"I would rather exist in her periphery, even at a distance, than live in exile."

The goddess beamed. She brought her other hand to his face, cradling him tenderly. This close, she smelled of sweet roses, and Leandros missed home so badly his chest hurt anew. When a tear broke loose, the goddess leaned forward and ate it off his skin.

Her hand lowered to his lips, holding a quince. "Eat this, and when you wake, you will live." He accepted the fruit, chewed and swallowed, never taking his eyes from her light-green ones.

"Will I make it back to her?"

"I don't know how your story ends, dear one, just that it could not stop here." She kissed his forehead, and at her touch, his mind filled to overflowing with images of passion and beauty from the whole of his life.

Boarding the ship to Latium, sailing on the winds of promise.

The first sight of a princess most enchanting.

His wife, moaning and gasping at his intimate touch.

In the darkened hallways, waiting and listening for his son's cry.

And then came the visions from his waking dreams.

Buying his parents' freedom.

A daughter, maybe two or three.

Their hands, veined and papery, still intertwined.

For all that once was and could be, Leandros would be restored.

The mirage faded; he fell out of the dream and back into the din of war. One hand slid up his toga and found the fresh scar. The arrow that had nearly killed him lay at his side, bloodless. Leandros brought it with him as he rose to shaky legs and tucked it into his belt.

"Hurry, Greek, while we have the advantage!"

Leandros rejoined the phalanx, stumbling to match the rhythm of the march. The infantryman to his left scowled and the one on the right teased: "You look like you've seen a ghost."

Not a ghost, a goddess full of grace.

Aphrodite.

Chapter LI

RHEA

SILENCE MUST BE learned.

Humanity is loud, even at birth—especially at birth—when body and soul both scream in ecstatic unison. From that moment until death, humankind yells, laughs, cries, talks, chatters, sings.

Whether in solitude or on the fringes of the Palatine, Rhea could not vocally participate. In the earliest years, this brought moments of torturous frustration. There was so much she longed to say, and as a wolf, Rhea was limited to the expressive capacity of a baby. She could growl and howl, whimper, whine—sounds of pain, of defense or offense. But she could not coo or babble. Happiness, contentment, even humor, she could only demonstrate with her body. (She did not wag her tail, however. Gods, that would be embarrassing.)

But as sometimes happens within constraints, Rhea discovered possibility.

Silence is a blessing. It does not need to be an agony.

Perhaps she was mute, but she wasn't deaf. Without the distraction of speech, she realized how much there was to hear, and her attention— like everything else about herself—transformed. In appreciating the sounds of silence, Rhea accessed wonder. She was humbled, awed, by the sentience of other beings, and by listening to them, she participated in their world.

In the before times, Rhea would have never considered the difference between a rock and a stone. When she was outside the Regia, she heard birdsong but little else—not the pop and stretch of the low plants, the wind playing the reeds and grasses like a stringed instrument, the shift of flowers to and from sunlight.

By becoming more aware of her world, she became closer to it. Rhea heard the heartbeat at the core of the earth, the interconnectedness of every breath and the concordance of things. In the quiet, she acknowledged the cycles she belonged to—sky and season and age—as well as the community—the tribe of trees, the interdependency of predator and prey. She watched the forest feast upon itself, subsist upon itself, and saw that this was unity.

Witnessing birth and death in their purest forms brought catharsis, but also broadened her capacity for compassion, especially in her role as a mother.

Creation is, at its essence, connection, and a mother's responsibility encompasses all.

In the sun-drenched, olive-hued landscape of the Hills, where yellow and green and brown met and blended in joyful trinity, hugged by blue arms of river and sky, Rhea thought, *All of this is love.*

And amidst all these revelations, as she recovered the joy of being alive, she was also relearning what it meant to be herself, who she was outside the walls and noise of human custom.

My words are precious. I will prioritize what needs to be said, what means the most. So different from life at the Regia, where small talk and gossip—culturally imprinted onto women—stole real cognitive energy.

She stored up ideas to share on the next new moon, when she would transform, brimming with theories and images and questions. For one night of each lunar cycle, Rhea regained her voice, and she shared it with Tiberinus.

What are the sanctioned stories I tell about myself?
Can beauty save us?
Must I surrender to mystery?

Am I only alive because I will die?

"I should feel voiceless," she confessed once, "but I do not. Because living this way, choosing this life, says something."

"I think it says everything," he concurred. "It is a brave thing to be alone."

Rhea trusted only the river god with her human form. Entering the village was non-negotiable. The wolf might have been accepted into their fold, but Rhea Silvia was a danger to all. Aiding and abetting a criminal would place the entire Palatine in jeopardy. Should Amulius discover where she was hiding, he would murder the village. Furthermore, if she was identified, Romulus and Remus would be suspected as well. As heirs to the Latin throne, they would never be safe—not just from Latins who might barter their location for royal advantage but also from assassins, domestic and foreign alike.

So, Rhea developed a routine. Every day of the month she was the devoted mother wolf, fully invested in her sons and the Hills, but then, on the darkest night of the lunar cycle, she became Ilia again. She enjoyed her time with Tiberinus; Rhea had never known anyone who could simultaneously soothe and challenge her mind like her immortal friend.

"What is happiness to a god?" she asked once.

She had recently taught him to play three pebbles. They had no board, but she drew a grid in the dirt with a stick and used small stones collected from the shore of Tiber Island.

He considered his answer, as she knew he would. Finally, he replied: "Like the idea of warmth to someone who has never known cold. I know it is a comfort, and I know it is good, but I've never had need of it."

"Everyone needs happiness. Even animals, even gods." It was her move; Rhea placed a pebble.

"Dolphins are happy," Tiberinus agreed. "They laugh."

This made Rhea laugh. "What do you need to be happy?"

Tiberinus frowned, his eyebrow tilting upward at the center. "I'm not sure I know. And you, Rhea Silvia, are you happy living like this?"

"Am I happy as a wolf? Am I happy in the Seven Hills?"

"Yes, all of it."

"I am happy I wasn't buried alive or murdered in a dungeon. I am happy to see my boys thriving." It was his turn. Rhea rested her hands in her lap. "But I have a wolf's years remaining. I will never get to love my sons as men."

He frowned. "Is it enough? To have known them as children?"

"No," she answered. "I will always want more of them."

And her words triggered some epiphany, for Rhea watched understanding dawn across his face.

"What is it?" she prodded.

"As an immortal, it is hard for me to comprehend time," he explained. "But with you, I finally understand. I could never get enough time with you."

"Oh." Rhea was certain she blushed, though Tiberinus didn't seem embarrassed. She picked up a piece to play her turn. "Thank you."

Ignoring the energy in the ether between them, the she-wolf and the river god continued their game.

◆ ◆ ◆

ANOTHER NIGHT THE boat traveled the Tiber all the way from the Seven Hills to the outlet at Ostia.

"Rhea Silvia, I present to you the Tyrrhenian Sea."

Rhea stood at the prow to get a better view of the horizon, of the thick, salty haze obscuring the lands beyond, so emblematic of her own future. The boat rocked but steadied with one wave of the river god's hand.

She sighed. "I always wanted to travel."

"You still could."

"A wolf boarding a ship? Depositing my bag of coin for a hammock and a bowl of porridge?

Tiberinus shrugged. "Life is strange."

Rhea gave him a hard look. "Not that strange."

He turned his palms up, conceding.

"Aeneas traveled," Tiberinus commented, "yet he only wanted a home."

"We always want what we don't have," she mused. "Is that a strictly human quality, or does it apply to the gods, too?"

He sat at the rear of the boat, staring up at her with such seriousness. "Oh, yes. I have always wanted a home in the desert, but I am a river god."

She laughed, and he smiled. Pleased to have pleased her.

Rhea again considered the sea, hands on her hips. It was neither friendly nor ominous, neither inviting nor terrifying.

"You know," she reflected, "when presented with sea or desert or river, I would pick river every time."

So much implied in such a statement.

"Should we return?" she asked gaily.

He nodded, and Rhea accepted his hand as she settled herself back into the narrow boat.

"You know, my friends, my family, they call me Ilia."

"Oh."

"You could as well. If you like."

Another "Oh," and then Tiberinus said, "I don't have a familiar name."

"My cousin Antho didn't, either, but she still called me Ilia."

"I will think on it."

As they reached the Palatine, Tiberinus remarked that the night was still young, and Rhea realized they were still holding hands.

The boat slowed to a halt and Rhea's eyes dropped to Tiberinus's lips. She wondered if they were warm like a man's or cool like the river. On an impulse, she bent her elbow, raising their interlaced hands, and she laid a kiss on his knuckles. He cocked his head to the side, watching her intently as she guided his hand to her chest, using it to slip the strap of her dress down her shoulder.

She placed his hand on the bare skin of her neck and closed her eyes. Tiberinus's fingers lightly traced the skin over her collarbone. When he rubbed his thumb at the dip beneath her throat, she let out a soft moan.

"There are other ways we could finish this night together." Her voice was low and raspy, catching on the intensity of its plea.

Tiberinus's hand passed around her neck, through her hair, and he brought their foreheads together, so gently.

Rhea trembled; she hadn't been touched like this in such a very long time.

"You mean . . . ?"

"Yes."

Tiberinus's mouth parted; she could taste his breath and she wanted him so ardently. But then he was pulling back.

"It will confuse things, won't it?" he said tightly.

"Not if we don't let it."

"Earlier we spoke of things we want but should not have . . ."

"No," she corrected, "that we *don't* have."

"Regardless, that is you for me. I don't and I shouldn't. Lying with a mortal is a boundary I have never crossed. With my age, my power, it wouldn't be fair to you."

"I don't care about any of that!" insisted Rhea stubbornly, but Tiberinus held up his hand.

"Let me finish, Rhea. Please." He cleared his throat. "If we do this, if I fall in love with you, it also won't be fair to me."

"Why?"

"Because I will have to watch you die."

He looked away as Rhea, confused and abashed, disembarked. By the time she reached the upper bounds of the riverbank, he and his boat had both completely disappeared.

She shivered. Had the night always been this cold?

For as long as she lived, Rhea would never offer herself to him again.

Chapter LII

ANTHO

WHILE THE LATIN League waged war on multiple fronts, Antho led her own campaign from her rooms at Villa Flavius. Her father had always boasted that Latins were at their best when at war, and wasn't Antho the ideal Latin in every other respect? One day she would expose her father, humiliate and overthrow him, then place her own son on the throne. To do that sooner rather than later required the support of the right people. Antho collected allies in the wealthy visitors to the Villa.

During dinners she hosted, Antho used seemingly innocuous conversation topics to suss out the like-minded. Easy, offhand references to Numitor's past reign:

Wasn't it glorious when . . . ?

Such peaceful times!

Remember the year of the grand harvest?

It was most often the wives who caught on to what Antho was doing, and afterward, when the men sought privacy to discuss business and brothels, they would find her, thank her for a lovely meal, and hint at their support.

My husband speaks often of your uncle . . .

We make sacrifices to Jupiter in your son's name.

I do hope to stay in your family's favor, whatever that might mean to you.

Antho kept meticulous notes and updated lists of which industries most benefited from her father's policies and which ones suffered. When the grain supplies ran low due to army conscriptions, she donated from her own stores in Ezio's name. "Prince Aetius, the king's heir, will never let you starve," she vowed as she personally delivered goods to homes across the region.

"Juno and Minerva shine brightly upon you, Princess Antho! And your son!"

Because kings were most often assassinated in their homes, the loyalty of the royal guard superseded even the allegiance of wives or daughters. Her father regularly executed soldiers who misspoke or made a misstep, whether those mistakes came with valid trespass or not. Kings were inherently distrusting, and none more so than a usurper. Antho preyed upon the Regia's pervading culture of suspicion, bred on its ruler's monomaniacal paranoia. Under the cloak of midnight, she carved graffiti into the walls of the compound: LONG LIVE NUMITOR and REMEMBER RHEA and JUSTICE FOR AEGESTUS. However, when Amulius began physically interrogating the servants, Antho ceased her acts of vandalism.

She could not permit harm to her staunchest allies.

Gratia and Zea became her first recruits among the Regia's help. In vague terms, Antho outlined her mission: building a hidden army of servants who would assist a rebellion, should it occur. Who had proximity to the king and queen and would be willing to spy? Who could watch the resident augur, Sethre? Who still believed in Numitor and would help wean him off his dependency on cretic wine?

The first steps in a long war, the internal siege.

After the domestics, she would begin approaching the guard. Which soldiers would stand aside and allow an army inside the walls?

Everyone Antho drafted received a fair wage—paid not only in coin but also in acts of consideration. She brought expensive oils for the laundress's chapped hands and feet, dandelion tea for a new mother suffering from constipation, and cherries for the royal chariot driver's gout.

Antho had been a girl, and things were done to her, but she was a woman now.

"You are our leader," Gratia said proudly. "When you say it is time, we will all fight for you."

"For Numitor," Antho corrected. "For Ezio."

Zea shook her head. "No, Princess. For you."

◆ ◆ ◆

YEARS PASSED. REPORTS from the war front were scarce and censored. Antho had no way to ascertain if Leandros lay dead in the woods—in an open-air tomb, slowly returning to the earth—or if he lived. Maybe he still fought loyally for Alba Longa. Maybe he had long since deserted the army and begun again. In another city, with another woman.

The hypotheticals were enough to make her delirious—with doubt and angst, with depression. She lit a candle for him every day. Made weekly offerings to the Greek pantheon. Prayed for her husband's survival on her knees before bed, while she walked her home and garden, in every quiet moment of her day. Without gentle Ezio and her quiet plans, she would have lost herself to grief entirely.

When the king summoned Antho to the Regia without the company of her husband or son, she assumed two possible reasons. The first? Leandros had made the official death toll, and Amulius wanted to personally witness her sorrow. The second? Her father had uncovered her many plots. Either way, Antho spent extra time dressing and attending to her hair and face. She would meet her fate at her finest. She kissed Ezio on both his cheeks, his forehead, and the tip of his nose.

"Be fearless in your kindness," she instructed him. "And keep asking questions."

Ezio, who had been building a castle with wooden blocks and stones, gave his mother a funny look. "You will be home soon, Mama."

She couldn't tell if it was a statement or a question.

One of her father's new guards met her at the entrance to the Regia. "The king expected you earlier. Make haste to your old quarters."

I'll get there when I get there, Antho almost said to this nameless upstart. She was getting too old for such nonsense, and she was certainly in no haste to accept her punishment. With his heir secured, her father could have her killed for treason. She kept her head up as she leisurely navigated the familiar halls of her former home. The door to her rooms was open, and Amulius sat inside, reading a scroll.

"Hello, Father."

As always, he made her wait.

Antho sighed; should she begin? "Father, I—"

"I want another grandchild by summer."

Antho reeled, thrown by his demand and taking a necessary step backward to reclaim her balance. Her mind spun through the various responses:

I don't care what you want.

I warned you this would happen.

I hope you are dead and gone by summer.

"The precision of your memory is well-known, my king," she responded lightly. "Surely you recall our past conversation."

Amulius stood, scroll under his arm. "I surely have."

Her father exited without explanation, closing the door behind him, revealing a man who had been hiding in wait. He was thinner and darker than she remembered, with a thick beard, and wearing a long arrowhead pendant necklace.

One hand rose to her mouth, stifling a sob, as the other gripped a table, and she barely caught herself before her knees buckled.

"You heard the king," remarked the man, a slight twinkle in his eye. "A grandchild by summer. Should we get started?"

Leandros had returned.

Chapter LIII

RHEA

RHEA'S SONS RECEIVED their education from the Hills.

Romulus and Remus were generally well-behaved boys who honored Faustulus and adored Laurentia. Even as children, they were revered among the village for their courage and capabilities. They were the most athletic, the most adventurous. Troublemakers who were, at the same time, the first to apologize and atone. With their disarming smiles and dashing good looks, they made it hard for anyone to stay mad. Besides, something about those twin boys seemed divine, like they were destined for more than huts and flocks.

They were rambunctious, with a permanent air of wildness, no matter how tightly their father reined them in. Always wrestling, racing, throwing, shooting, swimming, climbing. While Faustulus insisted they learn to read and write, they also received an education in nature: the Latin seasons, the Tiber's moods, how to forage, when to plant, the arts of calving and grazing and shearing and mating, the price of wool versus the price of meat.

Rhea so often imagined her own brothers in such a life. Lausus and Aegestus would have loved it.

Even the best childhood is only idyllic to a point. For Romulus and Remus, their innocence was lost when Laurentia died.

It wasn't a drawn-out illness or a fatal accident. She was kneeling in her garden one day, and then she was lying in the dirt, foam at her mouth. Something had snapped in her mind, and she was gone.

Romulus became morose and Remus full of rage. Romulus took to prayer; Remus broke things. But Faustulus held steady. He was the tether that sailors clung to on deck, riding out the storm. Rhea understood that role well.

She did not begrudge any of them their mourning. She could find no fault in Laurentia as a wife, a mother, or a woman. In another world, another life, they might have been friendly. But she did not attend the funeral. That moment was for the dead woman, her lover, and their sons.

But with Laurentia gone, the wolf came inside the hut.

She never had before. It had felt like a trespass on Faustulus's family, and Rhea could sense that the wolf's presence terrified Laurentia. Maybe she'd been a victim of one of those Sabine wolf cults, the ones where priests in wolf's clothing raped women. The possibility made Rhea sick, but mostly angry. How dare they hurt any woman in the name of their god! How dare those men disrespect such a glorious animal with their misguided religion!

She loved listening to her boys talk in the argot of young men. Bicker, joke, or debate—it didn't matter; everything amazed her. *These are my children, and they have their own marvelous personalities!* And she got to be present for it all.

Sometimes they argued about girls:

"Quinella definitely thinks about me naked."

Romulus, oiling a strip of leather, rolled his eyes. "She definitely does not."

"But she's beautiful," Remus argued, "and I'm beautiful . . ."

"She's too old for you. She wants a man with a beard."

Remus rubbed his bare cheeks. "I have hair where it matters."

Other times they discussed their dreams:

"The Seven Hills should unite and build their own city," Romulus mused. "Our own leadership, our own systems."

"We could do it, Rom."

"I know we could. Right here on the Palatine Hill."

Remus scoffed. "No. Aventine."

"Palatine is central."

"Aventine is southern, the first hill when you come up the Tiber from Ostia."

Faustulus was no help, refusing to choose between his children.

"Find a compromise," he said instead, rubbing the ache at his lower back. "The Capitoline Hill."

"Absolutely not," Remus retorted.

"Does it matter so much?"

"Where we build our empire?" Romulus asked, incredulous. "It matters more than anything."

And for the first time in a long while, the brothers agreed.

Faustulus sighed. "I am a common man with common thoughts."

Romulus frowned. "Do not disparage yourself. I value your opinion over any other."

"And I am getting old." Their father smiled good-naturedly. "A new kingdom will be the work of your generation, not mine, but if anyone can achieve such a place, it's the two of you."

While they argued, Rhea stepped up onto Romulus's pallet and curled into his blankets.

"Really, Lupa!" exclaimed Romulus while Remus laughed.

I nearly split myself in half giving birth to you, she thought crossly. *You can share your bed.*

The wolf was aging, still in her prime but not the boundless creature she'd once been. On the new moons, Rhea inspected herself in the river's reflection. Her human form aged as well, but the years affected her more subtly. When the wolf finally died, Rhea would not even be forty years old.

Younger than her father when she had last seen him.

The realization brought nostalgia, memories of Numitor when he was sound and sturdy, before melancholy and poppy seeds hollowed him completely. She spoke about it with Tiberinus under the next new moon, from where they sat beneath the fig tree, feet in the river, sharing new fruit.

"I think I want to see my father again, before he dies."

"The Latin Festival is soon."

It was a solid suggestion. Everyone who once mattered to Rhea would surely attend. She took a thoughtful bite. "Would you go with me?"

Tiberinus stiffened. "I will not trespass upon another god's celebration. It is uncouth."

"Mars did."

"Do not compare him and me, Rhea Silvia."

When I do, you always come out ahead. But she would not share such a thought aloud. Rhea still nursed the wounds of his rejection after their trip to Ostia.

"I will not dance around the fires at Monte Cavo," Tiberinus conceded, "but I will follow the rivers as far as they go. And I will be waiting there if you need my assistance."

Her foot found his in the water and she nudged it playfully. "Thank you."

The tradition of the Latin Festival began in the city of Aricia, where representatives of the thirty Latin League cities met and proceeded in a caravan up through the Alban Mountains. The wolf avoided the worn path, dashing and dodging through the dense forest instead, following the oscilla hanging in the branches to the Latin confederation's camp on the sacred mount. She stayed low and still and kept far away from the horses, who were most likely to frighten at her presence.

Yes, she had become the wolf lurking at the edges, just as Mars had been so many years ago. And this was, of course, the place where they had joined hands before the bonfire, snuck into the woods, and stolen a kiss. Would she have ended up this way—as a mother, as a wolf!—if she hadn't embraced the god of war so wantonly?

The Latins played their games and lit their fires. Young people danced, and the elderly reminisced. Milling about the tents were many people she did not recognize and many she had forgotten. She could not find Gratia but spotted Zea. Boys who had been friends with her brothers were now grown, many of them already bald. She noted members of the royal council, judging by their posture and their regalia, but who were these men? None of them had been in her father's assembly.

Except one.

Calvus emerged from a tent, leaning on a cane, and Antho followed, walking with effortless elegance.

Antho! Rhea's heart sang. Her cousin carried a baby in her arms, and there was a little girl holding on to her skirts. A handsome boy, olive-skinned and broad-shouldered, stayed by her side. These were Antho's children, her family, and they would not know Rhea from a stranger. The women had lost more than years; they'd missed moments. Rhea didn't get to attend Antho during delivery or decorate the vestibule of her home with laurel and ivy chaplets, welcoming the new life. Rhea wasn't there for any of the purification days, when Antho's babies were given their names. Rhea didn't even know their names.

And, naturally, Antho did not know Romulus and Remus had survived, were of a similar age to her own son.

Amulius had taken all of this from them.

And hatred, her old friend, resumed its war cry: *Eat his heart.*

Where was he? She needed to find her uncle. Now.

The wolf focused her hearing to the voice she could never unhear, loping around the periphery until her ears picked up the sound of King Amulius in a heated conversation.

With Numitor.

Father and daughter had not been face-to-face since he came to question her at the House of the Vestals, since the day he had refused to view her as a woman, only as a girl. What would he think of her as a wolf? If he looked in her eyes, would he see any glimmer of Rhea, or only a beast?

"You cannot invade the Hills, Amulius."

"It's not an invasion when they belong to us."

Mention of the Hills sent Rhea's heart lurching in her chest.

"The Seven Hills were Pallantium—distinctly Trojan, not Latin—for generations. Now they are their own people," argued Numitor calmly.

"They are incorporated territory. They are not independent."

"Regardless, taking their land will incite rebellion."

Numitor spoke truth. After forced conscription and hefty taxes to pay for Amulius's wars, the people on the Palatine would be furious if he attempted to commandeer their land. Losing their pastures, possibly their homes, would kill their livelihood and provoke revolt.

"Alba Longa runs low on gold. Sheep provide wool, milk, and meat, which all make gold."

Numitor groaned. "Spare me the lesson on the merits of sheep, brother."

But Amulius continued his pedantic discourse: "Sheep need pastures, and the Seven Hills have the best land. It is an untapped resource."

"You are oversimplifying a complicated issue. If you move your shepherds onto the Hills, you instigate territorial warfare. It will not end well for either side."

"There is only my side, Numitor."

Rhea dared to look up. The brothers sat before a fire outside the royal tent. In all the years, so much had changed, yet just as much remained the same. Her father and uncle bickered, continued to reside in fundamental opposition, but there was something more, something she had never noticed before. A fraternal bond. Maybe at the Regia, Rhea had been too involved in the dynamics—too biased—to understand. But she had been away for a long time, and she had grown up. At the core of Numitor and Amulius's knotted relationship was love.

Anyone else who pushed back against Amulius would be swiftly punished, but not Numitor. Why? Because despite all Amulius had felt and done, he still loved his brother.

It was a slightly upsetting but wholly interesting epiphany. She couldn't wait to discuss it with Tiberinus.

"I will take the Hills before summer. I've already drawn up the edict."

Rhea's father sighed. The fire crackled and popped between them as their disagreement settled into the silence.

The wolf slunk backward, overwhelmed by the need to return home and the instinct to protect. Alba Longa was coming for her sons, her friends. They would need her help.

This visit, despite the intricate emotional response it engendered, was well worth the exhausting trek.

There was a pleasant surprise: her father looked and sounded better than she remembered.

A vow: she would not leave this earth without revealing herself to Antho.

And an urgent reminder: for too long she'd let her enemy go unwatched, unpunished.

There was an undeniable awareness that Rhea's peace had expired. Fate—or whatever this very human mess they'd made could be called—beckoned.

Rhea Silvia, princess then priestess then mother wolf, would answer its call.

◆ ◆ ◆

THE ROYAL SHEPHERDS moved their flocks to the Seven Hills in slow, systematic batches, sowing discontent like millet seed. Amulius was canny, not pushing too hard too soon, so the hill people could not anticipate how bad it would get.

Amulius's men were invasive, a crop disease spreading in plain sight.

The wolf prowled the Palatine, keeping a watchful eye on her sons' flock. More than once, she caught royal herdsmen, empowered by dares and wine, sneaking over to catch a straggling sheep. She scared them off with well-placed howls.

They scattered. So simple and easy. So predictable and pathetic.

But the wolf had to rest. And when the royal men successfully poached one of Faustulus's sheep, the wolf reciprocated.

Caution be damned. Her boys couldn't be blamed for a mischievous wolf, could they? And Amulius's sheep were especially delicious.

Chapter LIV

ANTHO

WITH LEANDROS BACK in Latium and two daughters born in rapid succession, Antho's life became busy and full. Long gone were the days when boredom sent her searching for a hobby. Three children, a secret husband, and a coup kept her occupied from before dawn until well after dusk. Her girls were silly and fun; Antho loved to join their games. Ezio was an inquisitive soul. Sensitive. A bright student. Though he had the body of a soldier—the same build as his father—his mind was the sharper weapon.

And Ezio loved stories; he collected them. When her son was small, Antho would whisper bedtime tales about the cousins she grew up with: one a great hunter, one beloved by all animals, and one a girl she called Ilia, who was her soul's sister.

"What happened to them, Mama?"

"They are gone."

When Ezio got older, he understood that gone meant dead, but anytime he pressed for more information, Antho shut down the conversation.

"I would rather not speak of all that."

"But you used to!"

"It was a mistake."

For the more Ezio knew of Lausus and Aegestus and Rhea, the more trouble it might cause him with Calvus and Amulius.

The worst part of Villa Flavius was its patriarch. Calvus did not beat Antho, and after a childhood of slaps and pinches and bruises, that was a blessed relief. But he was not a kind husband, either. He called her names when she upset him, and he made crude comments. He treated their children as objects he could trade, which correlated with what he loved most of all: business. Calvus's greed consumed him—Antho believed it might even supersede her father's. Calvus still came to her room at night, but with far less frequency. She knew he visited brothels in the city but did not mind; to have done so would have been hypocritical, as she regularly lay with Leandros.

Antho maintained a pattern. When her family visited the Regia, she deposited the girls with her mother and Ezio with her father, then she sought out Leandros. Sometimes they only talked; other times they did not utter a word, needing only release: replacing clothing with the other's body. After their separation during the Sabine war, Antho and Leandros took no shared moment for granted; they found the spectacular in the simple. Leandros hadn't changed his mind about the children; he would not visit with them, but he did ask questions. He wanted to know everything, even if it hurt too much to be physically near them without betraying his true identity. And because Antho cherished him so much, she did not push the matter. Instead she regaled him with anecdotes of their son's brilliance and their daughters' spirit.

"They are the best of us, Antho."

When Amulius was occupied with closed-door matters, Ezio covered the grounds with his great-uncle Numitor. Those two would walk the perimeter of the Regia in all weather, discussing Latin history, the purpose of the League, goals for industry, and agricultural improvement plans. Numitor shared his scrolls, which held records of the Greeks and Trojans and Latins, as well as all the heroes and monsters. Hercules. Theseus. He drew constellations in the dirt for Ezio to memorize: Orion and Scorpius, Mars.

After one of these visits, Ezio told his mother, "Great-Uncle is the most learned man I know. Why isn't he king?"

She grabbed her son's hand, harder than she ever had, letting her nails dig into his skin. "Do not let these words leave your lips again."

Ezio grimaced and Antho, thinking of Claudia, released her grip, appalled with herself.

Her son massaged his wrist. "It was only a question, Mother."

"Kings have killed for far less."

On their next visit to the Regia, when Antho spied her son and uncle conversing beneath the bay laurel, she stopped to listen, hiding behind a column in the courtyard.

"Why don't you attend the king's councils, Great-Uncle? You have read more than any of the others, even my grandfather."

"Your grandfather is very smart," chided Numitor.

"Yes, but you are wise."

"I am educated. I used to think that implied wisdom, but I am not so certain anymore."

"There is much I wish to tell my grandfather about Latium, but I do not have your way with words."

"And what would you say to him, my boy?"

Ezio collected his thoughts, then took a deep breath. "To begin, his laws are increasingly exclusionary and aggressive. We do not need walls and wars to grow; we need mutually beneficial alliances and periods of peace."

Numitor nodded. "Yes, very good. Tell me more."

"A king should not seek to dominate his subjects but foster them. If Latium were a garden, I would prioritize supporting the flowers over ripping out every weed."

"Have you said as much to your father? Calvus holds the greatest influence on the council."

"I tried once," muttered Ezio. "He reminded me that I am but a child."

"Yes, but at fourteen, you are both educated *and* wise."

Ezio's frown shifted into a beam. "Nobody talks to me like you do, Great-Uncle. If I am to be king, I will need you on my council."

Numitor chuckled. "I am practically ancient."

"You judge yourself too harshly," scolded Ezio. "Your health is much improved! You are stronger than you think."

Not long after, the network of spies informed Zea that Numitor had almost entirely ceased his consumption of cretic wine, a victory she immediately relayed to Antho.

"It is for Ezio," Zea finished solemnly.

Antho listened, amazed, one hand over her heart. Her intelligent, empathetic son had done what nobody else thought possible. Ezio had broken through the fog of Numitor's addiction, hand extended, and Numitor had grabbed ahold. In slow beats and steady steps, the old king walked back into his life.

Chapter LV

From *The Political Histories of Latium* by
Aetius Silvius Flavius

The reign of Amulius Silvius was markedly different than the rule of his brother, Numitor. His harshest critics claimed he wanted to be king more than he wanted to rule—that he gained a title but forfeited his soul. Enemies of the new king tended to disappear. Those who criticized him fell sick. The Latin people understood that to plot against Amulius was to meet fatal consequences. Drusus was the first member of the royal council to go. His death hadn't seemed suspicious, considering his age, but then Messina died. And Gallus. All from similar illnesses, ones that came on quickly after a meal. They were mourned in grand public funerals and quickly replaced by wealthy Albans who were loyal to King Amulius and committed to his causes.

While many of the king's more nefarious dealings were pointedly ignored, he committed his gravest mistake in offending the people of the Seven Hills, for they were not the type to overlook an injustice. The king's constant wars with Etruria, Sabinum, and Latium's other neighbors had depleted the treasury, so in a quick grab for gold, the king fully relocated his royal flocks onto the prime grazing area of the Seven Hills, pushing out the local shepherds who had been there for generations. This was an area that had been informally independent since the fall of Pallantium.

Amulius had his shepherds assimilated into the Hills under armed guard. The guards left after a few days, passing along direct instructions from the king: *Do what is necessary to protect what is ours.*

If a royal human is better than a normal human, the same applies to royal livestock and their common kin. In Amulius's opinion, his sheep were simply more deserving of fresh grass and clean water.

The scuffles between the two sides began almost immediately, from territorial trespassing to taunts to outright violence. Dead sheep from the native flocks were left outside huts, usually in pieces, leaving the hill people with little option for retribution. Retaliation wasn't just futile, it was suicidal, for this was a conflict of opposing but inherently imbalanced forces. What is a common herdsman against a king?

The Seven Hills (Capitoline, Quirinal, Viminal, Esquiline, Caelian, Aventine, and Palatine) were a loose consortium of shepherds, small farmers, and foragers, a group of outsiders who preferred to handle matters in their own way. They consisted of exiles, runaways, the formerly enslaved, and even convicts. Theirs was a place of second chances, but also of separation. Of sovereignty.

The Seven Hills along the Tiber did not matter until they did, and then they became so important that Alba Longa was all but forgotten.

Chapter LVI

RHEA

RHEA AND TIBERINUS sat inside the wolf's den on a particularly stormy new moon. Down below, rain hit the river, water meeting water in elemental communion.

The question came out of her before she could stop it: "Tiberinus, am I a monster or a miracle?"

"Are you serious?"

"Quite."

"I think every mother is a miracle."

"But after all the feedings, all the killings . . ." She imagined the ghastly trail of corpses that had led to her current existence, a line of dead prey that began with the murdered guards in the Regia's dungeon. So many brutalized bodies. She shivered and wrapped her arms around herself tightly. "Can I still be delicate with a mouth full of warm blood? After what I've tasted and enjoyed?" Rhea had been a wolf for almost as long as she had been a girl. "Am I still human enough, woman enough?"

"I've never thought humans particularly delicate," Tiberinus remarked, "woman or otherwise."

"Well, I have yet to see a princess snap a rabbit's neck with her teeth," quipped Rhea.

"You are a princess and I saw you do that yesterday."

Rhea laughed despite herself.

"Maybe you are holding on to what they told you a woman is supposed to be."

She considered his answer, its easy sagacity. "How did you become so insightful?"

"Hundreds of years of observations?"

"You have had so much time," she mused. "I am a bit jealous."

"What would you do with immortality, Rhea?"

She leaned back against the rock wall, looking upward. "I would learn *everything*."

Tiberinus raised an eyebrow. "That would be a monumental task."

"The best ones are. I want to learn why mountains moan, why trees grow crooked, what makes lavender lightning. Why do eagles mate for life when sparrows are so promiscuous? How do the river otters sleep so easily while floating?"

"You have changed so much since I first met you," he marveled, shaking his head. "You traded resentment for curiosity."

"I still have a temper," she bantered back.

He held her gaze for a long moment; it stretched, silent and sweet. "You think you are bitter, but you are not. After all that was done to you, you wake each day and choose love. You are remarkable."

Everything about this conversation was remarkable, in a sense. Since her deal with Cybele, Rhea had experienced just under two hundred new moons. Just under two hundred nights with Tiberinus, less than a year and yet—

And yet . . .

So many ways she could end that phrase, but then a clap of thunder so loud, so immediately overhead, sent Rhea burrowing into Tiberinus's chest on instinct. Her heart pounded; his arms wrapped around her.

"Did I shriek?" she asked, mumbling into his toga.

"You shrieked."

The sky boomed a second time and Rhea gripped the river god tighter.

"Rhea Silvia is afraid of something. Unimaginable."

"It's gotten worse the longer I've been a wolf," she explained, peeking up at him. "The loudness makes me anxious."

He tucked her head beneath his chin and shifted his seat so he could hold her more completely.

"I'm not trying to disrespect your boundaries," she whispered. "Is this alright?"

"This is . . ." Tiberinus swallowed tightly. "I will not let go."

"And you will stay with me until it's over?"

"I am surprised you would need to ask."

His soft voice in a violent world. Rhea closed her eyes.

Outside, the rain continued to pour.

Chapter LVII

REMUS

REMUS WASN'T JUST fighting the royal shepherds; he was battling his own family.

For their land had been encroached upon, and Faustulus urged patience.

Alone with his father and brother, Remus ranted and raved. "You must allow us to carry better weapons!"

"No," Faustulus replied.

"But we need to defend ourselves!"

"We are losing ground to these royal shepherds," Romulus added with far more calm than his twin. "You should hear the insults, Father, the slurs. That our Latin blood is as muddy as the flooded river plains. That we are backward and stupid."

"You know you aren't," their father responded simply.

"You would let them call me a whoreson and have me not respond with my blade?"

Faustulus sighed. "You give them what they seek when you react."

"Romulus and I are the best fighters on the Seven Hills, even bare-handed. Just once let me show them what I can do! That will shut their mouths." Remus's fists clenched as he paced, and he swung phantom punches in the air.

"They will imprison you, or worse. I forbid it."

"I am no child."

"Exactly. And it is children who think with their fists."

"So do warriors. So do the gods."

Weary Faustulus rubbed at his temples. "The king's men bait you, and it is unfair. But if we respond in kind, the soldiers will return, and trust me, boys, all our people will suffer."

"They suffer now! Father, people are losing their homes! Not on the Palatine, not yet, but soon."

"It's true," Romulus concurred. "Balbus and Horatius were both 'removed' from their homesteads on the Esquiline."

"Swords will not return their homes."

"Then what will?"

Faustulus shrugged. "I am a shepherd; I do not know. Gold? Speeches before the royal council? Things beyond our reach."

"You would do nothing! This isn't patience, it's paralysis!"

"Remus . . ." cautioned his brother, but Remus was in no mood for a sermon on respecting his elders. He stormed from the hut, cursing, and whistled for the wolf. She arrived almost immediately, a sympathetic tilt to her head.

"Come, Lupa."

The boy and his wolf went down to the Tiber. She lay by his side, and Remus stroked the fur along her back until his breathing slowed and calm returned. Together, they watched a grey heron wade through the marsh, hunting for fish and insects.

"I wish you could tell me where you found us," Remus confided to the wolf, though his eyes remained on the bird, glazing over slightly. "I wish I knew where I came from."

Remus and Romulus were raised on village lore. They knew Faustulus found them in a cave being mothered by a wolf who must have lost her own pups. But this was an incomplete tale; it had never satisfied either of the boys. Even with loving parents at home, they wanted to know who made them and why they were abandoned in the wild in the first place.

Why weren't they wanted?

The wolf licked Remus's hand.

"You would fight, wouldn't you? If they took what was yours?"

And the glint he swore he caught in Lupa's eyes was more than enough of an answer.

◆ ◆ ◆

UNLIKE REMUS, ROMULUS was pious and found great solace in ritual.

"I'm going to travel north to Caenina and make a sacrifice to Pales."

Pales was the deity of shepherds and their flocks. Remus scowled. "That's your solution? Prayer won't change anything."

Romulus threw back his head "You don't think a divine force drives our lives? Remus, we were nursed by a wolf!"

Stubborn as a goat, Remus crossed his arms and pressed his lips together.

"I have to try," Romulus maintained. "I believe Pales will protect us."

"I know swords will."

But their father thought it a solid plan. "I will accompany you." And he assembled other elders from the community. "We are sending the correct message, to the gods and to the other cities. And if we have to fight, we will know that we arrived there by following the right path."

The men departed in the following days.

"Stay away from the king's men," Faustulus repeated, giving his son a hug.

"Don't be stupid," Romulus added, and then added more quietly: "Quinella can't lie with you if you're dead."

Remus grinned.

With the elders and the more temperate twin away, Amulius's men saw opportunity. It was their long-awaited opening, a chance to trick their main adversary into battle. For everyone stationed on the Seven Hills knew of Remus, of his legendary strength and agility, and of his equally legendary temper.

The royal shepherds set a trap.

Otho and Manius, two of Remus's boyhood friends, heard word that the royal flocks were relocating to the Field of Mars while the Alban shepherds returned to the city for a wedding.

"How did you learn of this?"

A convoluted story followed, tracing back to Otho's sister's friend, who was involved with one of the royal shepherds. But neither Remus nor his friends gave much credence to the situation's convenience. Why second-guess such a gift?

(Ask Aeneas and his fellow Trojans and they would surely provide a different answer.)

"Since so many of our men went to Caenina, they assume we are in a temporary truce."

"I saw them leave for the city this morning," added Manius. "Carrying their packs.

Remus considered. "And they left their sheep unguarded on the plains?"

"Watched only by a pair of their youngest. Can't be more than twenty years between them."

Remus whistled. "They must really think hill people faint of heart."

"We will show them how wrong they are." Otho grinned.

"It has to be tonight."

"We kill one sheep for every one of ours that has been slain."

"Fair is fair."

But Faustulus and Romulus appeared, unbidden, in Remus's mind. They would hear what happened and immediately know he had played a part. It wasn't difficult to imagine their disappointment, the disapproving looks; Remus's stomach turned over in premature shame. He must seek a way to compromise, to reconcile his own quest for justice with his family's commitment to caution.

"Another idea," he said slowly, the plan forming in his mind, "is that we steal as many sheep as they have taken from us, but we do not kill them. Instead, we hold them ransom until the king pays reparations on our lost flock."

Remus found a thin stick and, in the dirt before them, began to sketch a crude map of the Hills and grazing lands.

"We herd them from the Field of Mars," he began, drawing a path, "and move them eastward, out toward the Esquiline Hill, and hide them among the oak trees until we get our dues."

Otho crowed. "It's a heroic plan, Remus. By demanding coin, we demand respect."

"And maybe it will prompt other conversations, like the king paying rent on the Aventine."

"It is perfect," Manius agreed, nodding. "We will be heroes."

They plotted their attack based on stories they'd heard, for none of them had known real adversaries, and drank wine to bolster their courage. They laughed and imbibed and slapped one another on the back—because they were young and ignorant, because all of this was fun. Some part of Remus knew that playing with the king's possessions was serious, but it was a single scolding voice, simple to silence. And none of it felt real. Sneaking out late at night with his friends resembled some boyhood dare. The same games he had played with his brother throughout their childhood. *I dare you to climb that tree, swim to that rock, mount that horse.* Remus lived for those challenges. Romulus once did, too, but he had changed since the death of Laurentia. Romulus's mourning made him older, made him act like he couldn't smile anymore. Like it would hurt their father.

Tonight, nobody would stop Remus. He was free and, with his friends, would take back their hill's lost sheep—their honor, really—and set a shining new standard for their community.

"We're nearly there," Manius murmured as they moved north of the Aventine Hill. He lifted his arm and gestured to a light in the distance. "That must be the shepherd boys' fire."

Otho had suggested they attack the boys and tie them up while they stole the sheep, but Remus worried that such brazenness would hurt their cause. He offered an alternative: "You two approach the boys, talk to them. Claim you're interested in switching sides, in finding a paid position with the king's shepherds. Ask for details. Pour wine. And while you keep them distracted with what every man loves most—talking about his own opinions—I'll cut to the farthest side of the plain and move a flock out."

"Do we still have the wine?" Manius asked Otho.

He nodded. "Not much, but enough."

"We will meet you by dawn on the Esquiline, Remus."

Then Remus crouched down, watching and waiting as the other two neared the campfire. He monitored their voices—friendly, nonthreatening—and when it looked as though all four figures were seated, Remus double-checked that his slingshot and blade were both strapped to his waist, his crook at his back, then sprinted across the marshy expanse. Sheep dotted the Field of Mars in white bundles, making their sleep sounds, the music of his life.

The first rock was such a surprise that it hardly registered. What was that? A mosquito bite? Remus brushed it off. But the next volley came in such abundance there was no longer any doubt; he was under attack. Remus dropped down, throwing his arms up around his face and head as he took a beating of stones in every size and from every direction, knowing—not with a sinking fear but with bright red anger—that he had been deceived. Men emerged from the darkness, from around trees and behind rocks. Royal men with real swords and ropes.

Away at the campfire, Otho and Manius began to scream.

"Which brother are you?" an Alban man asked as he approached, beating a stick against the palm of his hand.

"The vengeful one," Remus growled.

The royal shepherd laughed, and a line of soldiers pounced upon Remus, who fought back with all the fire in his blood—biting, punching, kicking, stomping, and headbutting. He took down more than a few before they finally subdued him. Arms behind his back, wrists bound together. Another rope around his neck.

"The reckless one, maybe."

"Where's your wolf tonight?"

A soldier yanked Remus's head back by gripping his hair and sneered into his face. "You are under arrest for poaching. You face the judgment of King Amulius."

"I took no livestock. I have done nothing to the king," Remus replied, spitting blood at the soldier's sandals. "I went on an evening walk and was assaulted."

"An evening walk here? To check on the king's herd? Most unusual."

The soldier picked up Remus's fallen blade from the ground and grabbed the nearest lamb, slitting its throat. The bleating animal slumped to the ground. "This is your blade. That's the king's dead sheep. Now you've done something wrong."

"What do we do with his friends?" called another shepherd.

"Leave them. They are nothing but miscreants, half-drunk on piss-poor wine and their own stupidity. But they will spread word of what happens when you plot against the king and his property." The soldier sheathed Remus's knife in his own belt. "Load up. We return to Alba Longa immediately."

Chapter LVIII

RHEA

"WAKE UP, RHEA!" the river urged. *"They have your boy!"*

The she-wolf roused, rising, stretching from where she dozed by the Tiber. She slept there often; she liked being close to Tiberinus. It felt safer there, even out in the open, and cold was no bother.

But what had she heard? What had woken her from a dream?

A warning in the water.

Her boy.

Romulus was in Caenina with Faustulus, but Remus?

The wolf sprinted to the hut on the Palatine but found it empty. She raced from place to place, checking all Remus's usual haunts, tracking his scent. It brought her to the wet plains of the Field of Mars, where sheep rested and a few young boys gossiped over a fire. The wolf listened.

Her uncle's men had captured her son.

No, no, nonononono. This could not be happening. How had she been so negligent? Why was she sleeping when she should have been watching him?

This was her fault. She must find him.

It did not take long for the wolf to catch up with the royal procession. Among at least a dozen heavily armed Albans was Remus, bound hand and foot and neck. He was bruised and bloody but sneering.

Rhea seethed; they dared put their filthy hands on her son?!

She wanted to rip every man who touched her boy to shreds, but she was no rash fool. She paused and forced herself to consider the reality: Twelve men against one wolf? These soldiers carried sword and spear, and she was not the wolf she had once been. Heedless battle would only result in her death, and that wouldn't help Remus in the slightest.

Think, Rhea! There is a way to free your son. There is always a way.

The new moon would rise in the next day or two. The time had come—at long last—for Rhea to visit an old friend, her oldest friend.

Everyone she loved needed to stay alive for just a bit longer, and then?

Rhea Silvia would rise from the dead.

Chapter LIX

REMUS

REMUS ENTERED THE city of Alba Longa for the first time as a criminal. "Poacher!" the crowds jeered. "Thief!"

"The only thief is King Amulius," he shouted back, "who has stolen land from the Hills and stolen people for his pointless wars!"

But then a guard cracked a whip across his back, and Remus bit his tongue. Remus was no stranger to injury, but this was a fresh kind of hurt, an insulting one, malicious and insidious. It woke the animal inside him.

He was going to kill them all.

He thought they would lead him straight to the king, but he realized, with some disappointment, that his case bore little consequence. The soldiers brought Remus to a prison, dank and dark, below the Regia. Chained him to a wall beside others who looked far worse than he did. Men missing teeth and limbs. Men with crazy eyes. Men covered in feces.

It was a humiliation.

He worried about his father and brother, about what they would think and feel when they returned home and heard word of his betrayal. He feared what they would do. Would they fight for him? Could they raise enough support—or enough funds—to secure his freedom? Or would they abandon him here as punishment for his mistake? He hadn't listened. He had acted impetuously and fallen victim to an obvious ruse.

Remus sank against the wall and closed his eyes on a deep, pitiful sigh.

He was the stupid brother, the lesser twin. He'd always suspected as much, and now it was confirmed.

Rom, I'm so sorry, he thought, praying their mental twin connection hadn't been cloven by distance or duplicity. *Please forgive me.*

◆ ◆ ◆

DAYS PASSED IN a strange, torturous fugue, interwoven with states of agony and anxiety and an all-encompassing thirst. Moans then curses then cries for water on repeat. Remus's mouth ran dry, his parched body ached, and he panicked over the lacerated skin on his back growing infected from the moist and fetid dungeon air.

He'd visualized his brother rushing in with a mighty roar so many times that whenever he heard footsteps and a person who wasn't Romulus appeared, he sank even further into despair.

And then, at last, somebody did come for him, with a summons to the king's council.

Because of Remus's height and build, the guards did not remove his chains. Instead, they walked him like a dog up the narrow stone staircase, through the bare-bones servants' quarters, to the spacious upper levels and luxurious comfort of the Regia. *Rising up from the underworld to the realm of the gods*, he thought wryly.

Seven elderly men sat in a semicircle with the king on a raised dais in the center. One man couldn't stop coughing, another seemed half-asleep. These were the hallowed leaders of Latium? Could any of them still hoist a sword? Remus had heard rumors that King Amulius resembled a crow; it was true. A gray crow, now, aged but no less cunning, scrutinizing Remus with impossibly dark eyes.

An attendant to Remus's side read from a scroll. "Remus, son of Faustulus. A shepherd of the Palatine Hill. He has been charged with poaching off royal lands, destruction of royal property, and conspiracy to commit murder."

The king nodded, bored. "How do you plead, boy?"

"My name is Remus, and I am not your boy."

That certainly got the king's attention.

An adjacent council member stiffened. "Speak to the king in such a manner again and you'll feel the whip."

"By your arms?" Remus dared. "Or will you command someone else? When was the last time you held leather or steel in those soft hands?"

The man's jaw dropped, and the king chuckled.

"Hadrian, call off your dogs. Let this one talk." Amulius leaned forward in his chair. "How old are you?"

"Seventeen."

"Grave charges have been levied against you. Would you defend yourself?"

"I had no plans to kill anyone."

"But you attempted to steal my sheep?"

"I would only collect what I am owed."

Amulius sat back in amused disbelief. "What *you* are *owed*?"

Remus shrugged. A crown had never impressed him; he would say what he wanted to say.

"I should execute you immediately. You provide zero defense, are clearly guilty, and on top of it all, you're insouciant."

"It is against my nature to beg."

"I haven't seen your like in years," remarked the king quietly, narrowing his eyes. "It would be a shame to kill you."

"We agree there."

"Amulius!" interjected an especially feeble-looking councilor. "It is too much!"

"Oh, but aren't you entertained?" The king absentmindedly spun the gold bracelet at his wrist. "I have rescued others from your position before, Remus of the Palatine. In exchange for my mercy, they pledge their life to my service."

"A life as your slave would be no life."

"Kill him now, King," another councilor proclaimed. "Or allow me. My hands have yet to grow soft. And he could become a problem for Aetius."

"You, Calvus, have only grown harder. But my grandson will require soldiers one day, and I have found some of my best awaiting their deaths." Amulius stared Remus down with a cool intensity. "They will have you die—my council, my laws. But for twenty years in my grandson's guard, I will spare your life."

"I would rather lie on my sword."

The king chuckled. "You are so very young." He waved a hand at the prison guards, and they dragged Remus forward, trying to trip him, but Remus did not lose his footing. "In a few weeks, we will resume our talk. The prisons should have aged you by then."

As Remus entered a rebellious back-and-forth with his handlers, the bald man at the farthest end of the semicircle stood, his mouth slightly parted, and he stared, not at the tussle, but at the bulla around Remus's neck.

Remus stumbled as they regarded each other, and the guards regained control. They shoved Remus forward, but not before he snuck one last look over his shoulder.

The strange man remained on his feet, frowning.

Chapter LX

ANTHO

IN HER BEDROOM, Antho brushed out her hair, still long but thinner than it used to be. A by-product of three pregnancies. Each child had forever changed her body—thickened her middle, altered her sleep, even heightened her sense of smell. *It is wild how motherhood changes you*, she reflected.

And she was almost positive a fourth baby filled her womb. She knew the early signs well.

She hadn't mentioned her suspicions to either of her husbands. Calvus would react as he always did, with an approving sniff and then instructions: "Pray to Vesta and Juno for a boy." And Leandros? He would accept the news with happy sadness, lay a kiss upon her stomach, and pretend this whole arrangement didn't continuously break his heart.

Too often, Antho wondered if she'd made a mistake in asking him to marry her—not because she didn't love him but because she did. If she hadn't been so selfish, Leandros could have made a real family with children who rode on his shoulders and a wife who could hold his hand in public.

Antho sighed, laid her face into her hands.

But then she heard a rustle at the windowsill. A scrape, a grunt.

Antho looked up, and Antho screamed.

The dead walk on this darkest night.

Rhea Silvia sat on her windowsill.

"Antho!" her cousin scolded. "Hold your tongue!"

Antho put her fist in her mouth, bit down hard. A servant called from the hallway: "Is everything in order, mistress?"

"I'm so sorry," Antho answered, with a forced nonchalance that was surely suspect. "There was a large spider. It frightened me."

A pause. "Do you want me to remove it, mistress?"

"No, no, I am quite alright. Getting some rest now."

Rhea crept down from the window and entered the room. Antho stood, too, tempering her excitement until she finished her inspection and could confirm that yes, this intruder was truly her Ilia. Though Rhea was thinner than Antho remembered, her body far more toned, that thick dark hair remained unrivaled. A set of amber eyes monitored Antho in amusement.

"A spider, really?"

"Oh, now you be quiet."

Rhea smiled—or the specter of her, whatever she was, smiled—and Antho knew it was all real.

"Your eyes have changed color," Antho murmured. "Are you a ghost?"

"No, but I am different now."

"You are still so lovely."

"And you," mused Rhea. "You are even more golden."

Sweet lies, beautiful truths.

"I have missed you every day," Rhea added.

"If this is a dream, do not wake me. Oh, Ilia!"

They clasped each other, giggling and crying. Women who had found each other again, who had survived, who weren't warriors themselves—no Minerva, no Amazon—but had fought, too.

Oh, how they'd fought.

"You died," Antho insisted through tears. "I saw it."

"Almost died," Rhea corrected. "You were there that night?"

Antho wiped her cheeks. "I tried to save you and your babies. I failed. And I've gone over that memory a hundred times, trying to find a way I could have done better."

"No, none of that, Antho. We cannot amend the past." Rhea grabbed her cousin's hand, kissed it. "But perhaps we can change the future."

They climbed into Antho's bed and in whispers, Rhea told Antho everything that transpired on the night of her capture—Cybele, the wolf and the moon, the guards she killed, her escape to the Seven Hills.

"You have been a wolf all these years?" Antho wrinkled her pretty nose. "Living like an animal?"

Rhea grinned. "Howling and hunting and eating those who get lost in the woods."

Antho gasped. "No!"

"No," Rhea agreed, giggling. "I don't eat people, Antho."

"But why did you not tell me before? You could have come on any new moon."

"Because I know your father. Until he placed his hand on my wrist and confirmed my dead pulse, he would not stop looking for me or my boys. If he suspected you knew something . . ." Rhea shook her head. "I would not place you in harm's way."

"Then where do you hide on the new moon?"

"I have a friend."

Antho groaned. "The last time you made a mysterious friend you ended up pregnant."

And Rhea laughed so hard she had to bury her face in the blanket.

"All this time my father's maintained the lie that you are dead." Antho concluded in disbelief. "I doubt he has slept well in seventeen years."

Rhea sat up. "Good."

"Tell me about your sons."

They spoke of their children, divulging their names and ages, their likes and dislikes, but moved quickly into more serious conversations. There is a way of communicating, *The mother in me trusts the mother in you*, and if it is echoed in earnest, a shared space and language is established. Neither Antho nor Rhea had another woman in her life with whom she could disclose her most honest hopes and fears for her children, so this opportunity was a treasure.

"Romulus and Remus are better together than apart. What will happen if they turn against each other?"

"Calvus and my father already speak of Ezio's betrothal, but I know he does not desire women."

"I harbor a fear that Remus will die young."

"I worry that I don't give my daughters enough attention."

All of which meant: *I want my children to be happy, to be healthy. To know love and peace. Am I doing this right? Have I been enough?*

The cousins lay side by side beneath Antho's luxurious blankets. Rhea smelled different—like the forest, a dark, leafy aroma, a hint of citrus.

"Ilia," wondered Antho, "why are you here now?"

Rhea took a deep breath. "Your father's men captured Remus. I need your help to get him out."

"That won't be a problem. I have many friends in the Regia."

Rhea raised herself up on one elbow. "Your eyes may be the same color, Antho, but you have changed. I see it in the set of your jaw."

It would take more than one night to explain Antho's evolution: the abuse from her parents; a forced marriage to a mean man; her secret wedding; the loss of Leandros to years of war; the countless confrontations with her father in which she was forced to leverage her own children. And as Antho considered her own conflicted history, she wondered at the struggles Rhea also kept to herself—not because the cousins didn't love each other but because there simply wasn't enough time. Why waste it reliving the ugliest moments of the past?

Especially when there was a chance for a better future.

Antho left the bed and moved across the floor, tracing her bare foot along the tiles until she felt the revelatory crack. She lifted the loose piece and pulled out all the evidence she had amassed. Lists of names. Logs of dates and transactions and observations. Records of suspicious disappearances, of corrupt deals. A tally, corroborated by the royal treasurer, of Amulius and Claudia's extravagant spending. And the first piece in her collection, given to her by Leandros.

Antho carried it all to her bed, laying it before Rhea.

"What is all this?"

"Proof of my father's treachery." Antho had never felt so firm in her resolve. "I will be believed, Ilia."

"This must have taken you years!" Rhea sifted through the information, reading and marveling, until Antho set down the brooch. The color drained from Rhea's face. "Wh-Where . . . ?" she stuttered. "How?"

As delicately as she could, Antho explained her theory of Aegestus's death. Afterward, Rhea stayed silent for a long time, knees pulled to her chest, staring out the window at the vineyard in the fathomless night. "How can it feel like he died just yesterday but also in another lifetime?"

Antho wrapped an arm around Rhea's shoulders and leaned her head against her cousin's. "I miss him, too."

"Aegestus is not the only death on Amulius's hands. I'm almost certain he had Sethre poison a Vestal Virgin to free a position for me."

"And I have always wondered if Calvus and my father hastened the death of Calvus's wife to free a position for me."

Rhea's eyes glistened with tears. "You are showing me all this, telling me all this, because it's not just about Remus, is it? You have plans."

"Yes, Ilia."

"You want to overthrow the Regia."

A whisper: "More than anything in the whole world."

"But we only have tonight to plan. And there are so many people to coordinate. The timing will have to be perfect." Rhea exhaled loudly, then lay back on Antho's bed, closing her eyes and draping her arms over her face. "It feels impossible."

"For you and me?" Antho prodded. "Never."

"There is so little time . . . If I don't act now . . ." Rhea was mumbling, talking to herself, but then she smiled and gripped Antho's hand. "Yes, obviously yes. We do this together."

Before Antho could reply, Rhea held up a finger.

"One request: I do not want anyone besides you to know about my deal with Cybele or how I live."

"Why? It is extraordinary!"

"Because it is my story, but two boys nursed by a wolf is theirs." Rhea frowned. "It is difficult to explain, but I don't want to make their miracle about me. They will need it in the future more than I need recognition."

"To fortify their legend?"

"Yes."

"Then what will we say you are?"

Rhea grinned, and it was so wicked, so wolfish. "What I also am. A spirit of vengeance."

◆ ◆ ◆

"SADDLE TWO HORSES. We are going to the Regia."

"Now? Mother, why?"

"I must speak with my uncle."

Ezio raised an eyebrow, and Antho knew what he thought: she was often determined but rarely imperious. It was invigorating to surprise her son, to impress him, perhaps. They raced across the countryside at a warrior's clip, Antho feeling like some battle goddess of yore.

She dismounted, threw her reins at a stable hand.

"Keep up," she snapped at her son as they marched into the Regia and through its halls to her uncle's rooms.

Servants rushed to them. "Princess Antho! Should we alert your father? We were not expecting you!"

Antho ground to a halt. "Tell nobody I am here, especially not my parents."

Wide-eyed and similarly exhilarated, they backed away. Antho was well-liked in the Regia. Her parents were not.

Antho and Ezio burst into Numitor's rooms without preamble.

The old king was eating his supper alone but sat up straight when he saw them.

"My brother? Is he unwell?"

"Your brother—my father—is perfectly well, but perhaps not for long. There is something I need to tell you."

Numitor blanched. "Tell me, please. My heart cannot take too much stress these days."

Antho softened. She stepped forward and clasped her uncle's hand in her own, then reached the other out to her son. "There is something I need to share with both of you."

Both her uncle and son stared at her in wonderment.

"Rhea's sons are alive."

Chapter LXI

ROMULUS

THE VISIT TO Caenina had been fruitful. Romulus always felt reinvigorated by ceremony, and after these specific prayers and sacrifices, after speaking with others about the hard times in Latium, his sense of purpose was renewed. When Romulus's mind was his own, unoccupied by his headstrong brother and the flocks and their troubles, he dreamed of building a city. While Remus fantasized about girls and parties, Romulus imagined a new world.

He spoke of it often with Faustulus on their return journey to the Palatine.

"We could be independent of the Latin League! I have so many ideas, Father."

But all of that excitement was promptly curtailed when they arrived to an empty home. Otho and Manius, heads hung in shame, arrived at the hut only moments later to deliver the dire news. Faustulus asked them to repeat the story multiple times, maintaining a stillness that Romulus could not emulate. Romulus raged—in a way that no one had seen before. Traditionally, he was the more reserved brother, but without Remus, he became wrath incarnate. So it can be with bonded pairs. A delicate balance of personalities, once established, must be maintained, or the individuals are thrown into disequilibrium.

But Romulus heard the call of war in his blood as surely as Remus did; he was only better at ignoring it.

"We shouldn't have left him alone!" Romulus cried. "This is my fault!"

"It is your brother's fault."

"Remus was right—we should have stood up to the king's brutes long ago."

"They are making an example of your brother. We need to think, to plan, but you and I are not going to storm the Regia ourselves and free Remus."

"We can if we recruit the other shepherds and the people of the Hills."

Faustulus poured himself a cup of water and drank greedily, wiping his mouth with the back of his hand. "A revolution only works if it's supported from the ground up," he explained. "For the time being, we establish our base. We collect supplies and speak with our neighbors. That is all we can do."

Romulus knelt before his father, eyes glimmering. "He is my other half. I cannot abandon him. When the right time comes, promise me we will act. Otherwise, I will have to do this on my own."

His father laid a hand on his son's shoulder. "You must resist violence that comes from fear or anger."

"But I may act in just violence? Is there such a thing?"

"Yes."

Romulus lifted his eyebrows. "You are such a pacifist, Father. That's not what I thought you would say."

"Justice is not always supported by the law of the land. When those in power abuse it, we are forced to act."

"Forced to fight, you mean."

"Yes." Faustulus studied his son gravely, with determination, with promise. "And when we do fight, Romulus, we fight to win."

They were still debating next steps when the wolf arrived, carrying some sort of missive between her teeth.

"What is that, Lupa?"

Romulus took it carefully from her mouth and broke open the seal. Inside was a letter.

To the shepherd Faustulus and his son Romulus:

Before I begin, I must beg your discretion. Even if you choose not to answer my call, sharing this information with the wrong person could cost Remus his life. Should you trust me? Well, that's a tricky question. How do you put faith in one who has lain dormant for so long? Instead, I offer this: Do you doubt that Etna will erupt, no matter how many generations it lies quiet? Of course not. So, then, do I humbly compare myself.

I am Numitor. I've heard they call me the "old king," and that is fine. It is appropriate. I was the king, and I am old. The loss of my family precipitated the loss of my own identity. I sacrificed myself at the altar of grief thinking myself a tragic hero, and in my selfishness, I made many, many mistakes.

I hope to rectify some of those now.

If I am correct, you are all part of a wicked yet wonderful story.

Seventeen years ago, my daughter, Rhea Silvia, gave birth to twin boys. We were told they died with their mother, when in actuality, they were sent down the river in a basket by the former captain of my king's guard, a man named Petronius.

However, now I believe that a wolf pulled them ashore and kept them alive until they were discovered by a kindhearted shepherd. While the paternity of these boys has long been a subject of debate, you, Faustulus, are the man who raised and shaped them. You will always be their true sire. I honor you, and the boys who will represent you in manhood.

Remus is alive, rest assured, and under my limited protection. He waits in the Regia's dungeons for the king's next move—or, perhaps, for ours. On his person, I've

noted a bulla that belonged to my dead son Aegestus.
I believe that Romulus wears the other. A gold amulet
that once belonged to my firstborn, the prince
Lausus.

Rhea placed these bullae on her twins before they
were taken and she died.

Rhea Silvia, my daughter. A princess and priestess, a
sister and mother and warrior.

She was all these things. And more.

It must be quite staggering to open a scroll and learn
you are royalty. I promise to talk through all of it with you
soon, but first we must free the innocent and right
grievous wrongs.

If you are willing, there is a plan to both free Remus
and remove my brother from power, thereby restoring
sovereignty to the Seven Hills. If you agree, on the day of
the next new moon, here is what we must do.

The rest of the letter detailed a plan.

Faustulus set the letter down, and Romulus paced, fidgeting with the amulet at his throat, recalling memories he shouldn't realistically have—a woodcutter's hut, a dark cell, a basket, and a river.

Two wolves encircling him and his brother in the den.

"Could this be true, Father? Remus and I are"—Romulus stumbled on the words, embarrassed—"princes?"

"Yes, I think it might be."

Sometimes, when a person has undergone such a shock, when everything they thought they knew about their life has been deconstructed, they need to hear the truth again and again, albeit in different forms.

"My mother was a princess?"

"Yes."

"And a Vestal Virgin?"

"Yes."

"And she is dead."

A pause. "I'm sorry, my son. Yes."

"What do you think of this plan, Father?"

Faustulus set the letter down on the table after he had read it through a third time. "I think," he replied softy, "it is just violence."

Romulus considered the wolf, watching from her favorite spot in his bed. "Did you know?"

The wolf smiled.

Chapter LXII

FAUSTULUS

ALBA LONGA WAS a city under siege, but nobody in the Regia knew.

Faustulus arrived first, with the rosy dawn, as was their plan.

At the gates, he was stopped, as the letter said he would be.

The guards searched his person. The king was increasingly suspicious, the locals said. Convinced that the Latin people were aggrieved, doubted his decisions, and longed for his head.

"What brings you to Alba Longa?" the city official inquired.

"An audience with the king."

The men laughed. "Are you mad as well as old? Shepherds do not speak with kings."

"This one does. I have information he's awaited for nearly twenty years."

The official rolled his eyes. "And what would that be?"

Faustulus opened his closed fist, showing them Romulus's bulla. "I have the amulet of Rhea Silvia's son, the one she took from her own brother, the prince. And I think he might want to know why."

♦ ♦ ♦

THE GUARDS USHERED Faustulus into the king's private rooms, where he was dining with a man who must be one of his councilors. Neither of them could hide their annoyance at being interrupted.

"He is the king of Latium," the other man fumed. "My son is his heir. We have more pressing worries than another disgruntled shepherd!"

"This one isn't here about sheep."

Another soldier shoved Faustulus forward. "Come on now. Show him."

Faustulus brushed off their hands and salvaged his dignity. "I have in my possession the bulla of Rhea Silvia's son."

Amulius narrowed his eyes. "Rhea Silvia had no son."

"She did; she had twins."

Faustulus was always adept at spotting other men's tells—it was how he made a living in the gambling days of his misbegotten youth—and he caught the twitch, the recognition, in the king's left eye. The man who ate beside him did not seem to notice.

"Sit," the king ordered, then snapped at a servant: "Fetch this man some water and bread."

As Faustulus accepted his seat at the king's table, the other man snorted and rolled his eyes.

"Oblige me, Calvus," drawled the king, and Faustulus nearly shivered at the way Amulius made requests sound like threats. "I must hear why this man interrupts my breakfast with such an unhinged tale."

"I live on the Palatine Hill. About seventeen years ago, two babies were found in a cave, nursed by a she-wolf—"

"A wolf?" interrupted Amulius.

"Yes," Faustulus repeated, "a wolf."

"Continue."

"These boys are like no mortal I've ever known. Too tall and strong, too handsome." He paused, then lowered his voice conspiratorially: "People call them the sons of Mars."

"Outrageous," the king murmured in a cold voice, intentionally devoid of emotion.

"Why would rural gossip matter to the king or royal council?" added the man called Calvus.

"I am a simple man, my king. I do not have much, but I thought you might pay well to know that many people—not me, of course—consider these boys to be the lost children of Rhea Silvia and the rightful heirs of Latium."

"That is treason!" blustered Calvus. "Meaningless conjecture!"

"I brought proof." Faustulus laid the amulet reverently upon the table.

The king ran his tongue across his teeth. "Many children wear a bulla like this. This corroborates nothing."

Faustulus shrugged. "Perhaps, but people say it belonged to Prince Lausus."

The councilor slammed his fist against the table. "Amulius, can it be true? This could threaten Ezio's claim!"

"No, Calvus. Rhea was pregnant when we found her dead body. This is all ludicrous." The king studied Faustulus, seriously, ominously. "But any Latins claiming to be royal heirs deserve a meeting with me."

"I'll show you where they live, my lord, but I want ten gold pieces— per boy—for this information."

"I admire a man without scruples." Amulius stood and motioned for Faustulus to follow. "You walked here?"

"Yes. I own no horse or donkey."

"My personal bodyguard will provide you with a mare and accompany you to the Palatine." Amulius summoned a soldier to his side. "Escort my new acquaintance home and arrest the pretenders. Bring them to me immediately."

The guard nodded. "How many men should I take?"

"A dozen, at least. Your best fighters."

Faustulus, who never lied or pretended, had exceeded his own expectations. The king had not only believed Faustulus's mercenary act, but was voluntarily sending his most elite soldiers out of the Regia on a needless chase.

Laurentia, my love, the shepherd prayed, *you would be so proud to see me now!*

Remus, my son, the shepherd pled, *hold on! We are coming for you.*

Chapter LXIII

LEANDROS

LEANDROS'S HEART JUMPED in his chest with every measured step he took toward the dungeons. On the outside, he was precise, deliberate, but inside, his nerves were more wrought than they'd been on the Sabine battlefields. In the war, he only needed to keep himself alive. Today his whole family was at risk.

The other guards met his arrival with deference. He'd been a soldier of fine standing for longer than some of them had been alive, and he was a veteran. Despite his less than favorable Greek lineage, Leandros was commended for practicing keen judgment and rarely complaining. It was a solid reputation. When he explained to the head of the prison which inmate he needed, no further questions were asked.

Even after so many days, it took three guards to bring Remus forward. Leandros's memories of Rhea Silvia were fuzzy at best, but he recognized so much of her in this young man, who had that same spitting fire.

"I'll take it from here," Leandros said.

"Bring one or two of my men with you; this one's combative."

Leandros gave the prison lead a hard look and twirled his blade. "I think I can handle a half-starved kid."

The man shrugged but pressed the issue no further. He wasn't going to tangle with Leandros, and he also didn't care. Guarding the prison was a miserable job.

Leandros pointed his puglio into Remus's back. "Your time has come, shepherd. Start walking."

He bid perfunctory farewell to the other prison guards, then led Remus out of the prison depths and into the day. The boy flinched in the sunlight, so unaccustomed to its harshness. Leandros guided him away from the central rooms and toward the outer corridors, sneaking him through a servant's entrance to the outside of the Regia.

The same route Antho used to meet him at the ironwood tree a lifetime ago.

Remus looked around, completely disoriented and distrusting.

"I'm going to untie your hands and feet now," Leandros explained, quick and quiet. "Your friends are in the city, waiting for you."

He undid the ropes on the boy's wrists and ankles, grimacing at the flesh rubbed raw, and passed him one of his own daggers.

"Take this. Find your brother in the marketplace, and when the signal comes . . ." Leandros paused, sighed. "Well, I wish you the fortitude of Mars."

"What is happening?"

"Isn't it obvious? Tonight, we take back the kingdom."

Remus grinned, his split lips opening and fresh blood blooming. "Finally."

"Before you go, I need you to punch me."

Remus's smile slipped, but Leandros assured him: "The others must believe that you overpowered me and escaped. I can take it."

Remus nodded. "I understand. And I apologize."

And then he swung his fist into Leandros's eye, hard. The Greek soldier cursed.

"Nice," he said begrudgingly.

"Thank you, for all of it." And then, dagger in hand, the boy dashed off, blending into the crowds outside the Regia.

Leandros imagined Antho in his arms at the end of all this, no longer hiding, no longer stealing moments of joy. He had sacrificed a normal life to be her man in the shadows. And he would never renounce that choice, but he was tired. He wanted a home—to be with his wife, his children. He wanted to be whole.

If he survived this day, if Antho's mad plans came to perfect fruition, he would hold her every day for the rest of his life. He would teach his son to play astragaloi; he would carry his daughters on his back through the woods. Sing them songs in Greek. He wondered what their hair would feel like against his cheek, what their tiny hands would feel like in his own.

But when Leandros reentered the royal compound, two guards waited just past the doorway with their swords in hand.

Were they waiting for him?

"Where's the prisoner, Greek?"

Leandros swore, gestured to his face. "He ran. I think I lost consciousness for a moment."

One man frowned dubiously.

"Come with me," Leandros insisted. "We can still catch him!"

"Oh, we think we just did."

"There were no orders to move the shepherd."

Leandros drew his own sword, but two additional men jumped out from behind him, and then Leandros was surrounded, four on one. He killed two in the scuffle before they had him on the ground. The surviving soldiers tied Leandros's arms, kicked him senseless for their fallen comrades, then dragged him into a holding cell.

Leandros paced, unbothered by his injuries, consumed only with how his capture might affect Antho's plan. He hoped Rhea's boy reached his brother before the royal guard found him. He wondered if Antho's spies knew Leandros had been compromised. If only he could get a message to her! Frustrated, Leandros punched his fist into the wall—gratified, calmed, by the shock of stone against his skin and bone.

Soon enough, Leandros heard the unmistakable rhythm of Amulius's approach. The king entered the cell, tailed by the guards who'd apprehended Leandros, mouth twisted in bemused irritation.

"You have been so well-behaved for decades," Amulius began. "Why now? What changed?"

Leandros would gladly die one hundred deaths before he betrayed Antho. He faced her father and shrugged, refusing to speak. Irritated, Amulius questioned the others. "Which prisoner did he release?"

"The shepherd boy from the Hills."

"From the Palatine. How could I forget?" Amulius rubbed his forehead, muttering to himself. "The Hills, the twins . . ."

Leandros watched in fear, in astonishment, as Amulius connected the pieces. All Antho's careful plots laid bare by his own error. How had Leandros fumbled his part so badly? Could he have been more discreet? Should he have replaced Remus with a lookalike stand-in?

"Summon Numitor, Calvus, my daughter, and Ezio to the throne room. All of them. Now. And then bar the doors." The soldier left at a run.

"Something is happening today," Amulius reasoned, leaning closer to Leandros. "Tell me." And because the king had switched to speaking in Greek, Leandros answered in kind: "I am nobody. I know nothing."

Amulius chuckled, then he kneed Leandros in the stomach, an unexpected assault with unexpected strength. Leandros grunted, and just barely held down his vomit. The king gestured to the remaining soldier and issued one last command: "Fetch me a whip, a mallet, and knives. The Greek will share what he knows or I will take his tongue."

Chapter LXIV

RHEA

ON THE MORNING of the day that Alba Longa would fall, a wolf spoke to the river.

"If I die today," she said in her mind, knowing he heard, *"think of me on the new moon."*

"You are too stubborn to die."

"I did once already."

"This time, I'll offer you a better deal. Turn you into a fish so that you must stay here with me."

The wolf, in her way, grinned. *"Not a fish. Perhaps a shark."*

"A dolphin, for the happiness."

"I wish you could come with me." A wish made twice now.

"I will be here when you return."

Rhea headed east in the direction of Alba Longa, toward the city that had made her. She followed the scent of blood to her original wound, to face the injuries of her past, and fight.

The wolf was old now: her coat had gone gray and white; she had lost weight and muscle; sometimes her teeth hurt. She had outlived the sheepdogs and their litters and their litters' litters, yet she was not unscathed. Not at all. The wolf was marked by the scars of her wild life, but she bore those aches with pride. She had made it this long, empowered by magic, emboldened by lupine faculty, but mostly because of the tenacious woman beneath it all.

Still, there was more than a chance she would not survive this day and night.

The wolf quickened her pace.

She wished for Tiberinus by her side, but maybe this was something that had to be done alone.

(Not alone—with her sons and the good shepherd, with her cousin, her nephew, her father. Rhea was not alone.)

Rhea moved east. In return, in recompense, in revenge.

The trio of forces that finally brought her home.

◆ ◆ ◆

HOME.

A confusing, complicated word. The simplest, the heaviest.

Alba Longa was smaller than she remembered, flatter somehow. And though she noticed every difference as she trotted through its streets, it still felt entirely the same. How could it feel, after everywhere she'd been, like she had never left? Her body may have traveled and changed, but a piece of her heart had always been here. As trapped as it was preserved.

One last time in this city, and then never again.

She searched for her sons.

Chapter LXV

ROMULUS

ROMULUS ENTERED ALBA Longa shortly after his father with a cart full of wool and sheepskin to sell, his best weapons hidden beneath. And every hour or so, another set of men from the Hills came—to buy, to sell, to meet an acquaintance. And they assembled in various spots around the Regia, awaiting orders.

In the busy days since receiving Numitor's letter, Romulus and Faustulus had made endless visits to the people of each hill, speaking of King Amulius's crimes, Remus's arrest, and their plans to rebel. Exhausting, painstaking work. Repeating themselves over and over, approaching each conversation like it was the most important, earning trust, gathering support. The majority agreed to join the revolt. Others, well past fighting age, donated weapons.

He wondered how many other Latins lingered in the marketplace, prepared and expectant, ready for action. How many men, unknown to one another now, would fight side by side when the signal was raised, united by a common goal.

Numitor, I hope you have many friends.

For the Hills' men alone would not take down the royal guard, no matter their valor or just cause.

Tucked behind a food stall, Romulus kept his gaze trained on the Regia's entrance. Eventually, his father exited, riding a horse with a dozen armed men. It made him oddly proud—first, that his father had been able to pull off such a ploy and, second, that the king believed it would require so many soldiers to bring him and Remus down. Romulus barely breathed until his father officially left the city. Faustulus would not be present during the battle, and for that, Romulus would be eternally grateful. His father was rational, fair, and clever, but his physical prowess had declined over many hard years, and Romulus wasn't sure how effectively he would fight if he was worried for his father's safety.

On any other day, the aromas of the food stall would have gotten to him, and he would have spent more coins than he should have on warm bread and roast chicken legs, but today the scents only exacerbated his nerves. His senses were already heightened.

He'd never fought to kill before.

Would it feel the same as hunting a deer or boar? What if he liked it too much? Might he desire killing once he had a taste for it?

"Miss me, brother?"

Romulus whipped around, and there was Remus. Grinning Remus. Blood-encrusted and absolutely filthy Remus.

They gripped each other's forearms, brought the tops of their heads together as they had when they were babies.

"Gods, you smell foul."

Remus wiped his face against his brother's shoulder, leaving a smear of grease and sweat. Romulus pushed him off.

"Dirty dog."

Remus yipped.

"Have you heard? We are princes."

"Least surprising news I've heard today."

The best part of Remus was his indifference. Gods, Romulus loved him so much.

"Our grandfather is here," Romulus whispered. "I hope that before this day ends, I get to meet him." He eyed the dagger in Remus's hand and motioned toward the cart of lambswool. "Grab another. I have a speech to make."

As Remus selected a spear from beneath the stack of pelts, Romulus picked up his shield and sword and strode into the center of the square. He banged the blade against the shield again and again, calling for attention, turning in circles, looking into as many faces as he could. Onlookers hushed and pointed. Many backed away nervously.

"Latin people, hear me! I am Romulus, son of Rhea Silvia, grandson of Numitor, the true king of Alba Longa and Latium. This is my brother, my twin, Remus. Amulius tried to murder us when we were babies, but he failed, and we are here today to remove that kin-killing usurper and take back this kingdom."

Most Albans stared, gobsmacked, and a few snickered, but then the shepherds from the Hills began to shed their disguises, coming forward with weapons and absolute confidence in their leader. Romulus nodded to each man as they joined his side.

"Amulius has lied to you. Our mother, Rhea Silvia, was not pregnant when she died but a new mother. He had my brother and me ripped from her arms and thrown into the Tiber. But the gods decided we should survive."

And then Romulus produced a bag of ash that he had brought from home. He dipped his right hand into the soot, covering his fingertips, then dragged dirty tracks down the side of his face.

"The wolf is no tyrant and no more terrifying than a sheep who is blindly obedient to a false shepherd. Amulius has led us in the wrong direction for far too long. And I will no longer follow. Those of you who stand with us now, show us your sign, the mark of the wolf."

Remus came forward and performed the same ritual. Standing beside his twin, he twirled his spear artfully in his hand. "Fight with us now, or fight against us later." And then he howled.

The other men from the Hills howled in response and pulled back their hoods. All faces had been similarly marked, and the men held weapons above their heads.

"Why would I listen to a bunch of lunatics from the Tiber?" one woman shouted.

A man selling dried fish loudly agreed. "Amulius is the enemy I know, better than a wolfman calling himself a whoreson!"

Remus bristled, but Romulus placed a calming hand on his twin's arm. *Save that anger, brother, for the more deserving.*

A hush fell as a woman in white walked toward the brothers, crowds parting for her in reverence.

"A Vestal wishes to speak!"

"Not just any Vestal, the high priestess!"

At the center of the square, where she commanded the utmost attention, the Virgo Maxima spoke. "I have never met these men, but I was there when Rhea Silvia met her punishment. I doubted then, but I do not doubt now. Forces of the divine followed Rhea, and we sinned against them when we killed her. She and her sons are blessed, as surely as my name is Tavia."

Romulus had never heard of this person and didn't think she appeared particularly kind, but he could have kissed her on the mouth right then. The people hung on her every word; many began to nod.

Another stranger came forward, official looking and extremely nervous but edified by Tavia's confession. "I work in the royal treasury," he began, nose twitching. "There are things you should know."

The man might have lacked oratory presence, but he knew his numbers. In succinct terms, he explained to the people how Latium's gold had been mismanaged, directed into bribes and wars and personal funds when it was intended for the common welfare.

"There's nothing left," he concluded simply. "Amulius has spent it all."

"You have now heard testimony from the priestess, the mathematician, and me, the blood of Numitor!" Romulus yelled into the crowd that was quickly becoming a mob. "If you won't stand with us, then don't stand in our way!"

"To the Regia!" Remus boomed.

"Long live Numitor!" the men chanted. "Remember Rhea!"

As the war cries repeated, growing in volume, so did the excitement. More and more Albans entered the movement, grabbing whatever weapons they could find, caught up in the wails and bellows and wolf marks. And in the chaos, very few noticed the actual wolf who'd raced through the city gates, who'd joined the twins in the front line.

"Lupa!" Remus shouted over the din. "I missed you!"

She nuzzled his stomach.

Soldiers met them at the entrance to the Regia, where the royal command stopped their crushing momentum with a hastily assembled defense.

"Who is first?" Romulus challenged, banging his sword against his shield. Beside him, the she-wolf growled.

"I'm not afraid of you, baby wolf!"

A similarly aged soldier, eager to earn his fame, rushed forward, sword raised. Romulus sliced that guard's head from his body in one epic swing. Everyone, on both sides, held their breath as the head soared through the air, crashing into a statue of Jupiter and rolling to an inglorious stop in the mud.

Silence.

And then the clamor of every witness talking at once:

"How did he do that?"

"I've never seen such a strike before."

"The gods made that sword."

"Or the gods made that boy."

"That's my brother, Romulus!" shouted Remus. "Remember his name!"

"Let's go!" Romulus roared.

The charge. Metal hitting metal, hitting flesh, splintering wood and bone. Screams and spit and sweat.

Back-to-back, Romulus and Remus plowed through every soldier who dared to face them, sending most scurrying away in terror, splattering the front walls of the king's home in the art of war.

Remus whooped; the wolf howled.

Chapter LXVI

CLAUDIA

QUEEN CLAUDIA, WHO had observed the outbreak of violence from her upstairs window in abject horror, searched the Regia for her husband. She burst into the throne room.

"The city!" she shrieked. "It has risen against you!"

The king lifted one eyebrow. "You are hysterical."

It was true—she was gasping for air, and her husband despised strong emotions. Claudia forced herself steady. "There's been a riot in the marketplace. Armed men surround the Regia! The guard is holding them back for now, but Amulius, we must leave!"

"Leave?" snorted Calvus Flavius, who sat beside the king. "The Regia will not capitulate to a band of thugs."

"There are people dying everywhere!"

Numitor stood in the doorway, holding a jug of wine. "You called for us, Amulius?" He entered with Antho and sweet Ezio, closing the door behind him.

"I did. I summoned all of you."

Claudia stilled. He hadn't sent for her; she arrived on her own. Surely, she had missed the message. Claudia was important to Amulius. Maybe not at first, considering her many failures as a wife, but she'd proven herself a staunch ally, standing by him through every trial, defending every dicey decision he made, even in the most critical aftermath. Her loyalty was unquestionable and unrivaled.

And she was everything a Latin woman should be. Impeccably

dressed, her home managed to the most meticulous detail. Her daughter married to a wealthy man for whom she had borne three children. True, Claudia had needed to discipline Antho, but that was only a natural response to disobedience. Amulius taught her that in the early years of their marriage, and she had become a most devoted wife. Though her husband had not shared her bed with any joy or regularity, she had surely compensated for this disappointment, pouring herself into his many causes. She did whatever he asked and required no gratitude. Not that he would give it. Her husband wasn't a weak man.

"Bar the doors to buy us time," Amulius instructed the guards.

Calvus shot the king a furious look. "And you sent your best men with that fool shepherd!"

"They outmaneuvered me. That fool shepherd and his boys." Amulius relaxed into his chair, an odd smile across his face. "We will face what approaches together. All the key players in this tragedy."

Numitor sat on the other side of his brother. He poured them each a cup of wine, and they clinked the silver rims together.

Calvus and Claudia stared at them incredulously. "You're just going to sit there and drink?"

"Would you prefer we jump out the window?" Numitor asked, and Amulius laughed.

"You've both gone mad," Calvus spat. He cursed and flung an icon of Janus against a wall. He shattered a vase, broke a dish.

"Lausus used to do that," Numitor commented, "when he was a child."

Amulius laughed again. "I forgot how much I enjoy your sense of humor."

"Would you care for a glass, Calvus? It's one of your best."

Calvus swore but accepted a pour of his own wine.

Nobody offered any to Claudia.

Claudia took her place against the wall, tears streaming quietly down her cheeks as she longed for her loom, for the way it felt on her fingers, the way it lulled her mind into beautiful stasis. It was her only real peace.

A Latin Penelope weaving—not to extend time but to forget it, yet always waiting for her husband to finally see her.

Chapter LXVII

RHEA

RHEA FOUGHT BESIDE her boys as they broke through the Regia's guard, as her second family attacked the home of her first. There was a sad poetry here, but not one she was ready to consider. Probably one she would never enjoy.

In general, the royal soldiers were petrified by the wolf's presence. Not just because she was a notorious predator—a creature of children's nightmares—but also because her snarls resonated with preternatural force. Twin warriors and their allegiant wolf? It was a scene from a heroic poem.

Rhea was pummeled by foot and fist and object, punched and kicked and clobbered. More than one blade nicked her skin, drawing blood, but all the cuts were shallow, never striking a vein or artery. The wolf pushed through the pain.

If I can deliver twins by myself, I can do this.

I can do hard things.

It is almost over.

In striking parallel, the sun began its descent on Latium as the Regia's entrance fell to the rebels. Inside the capitol city's compound, insurgents clashed with loyalists—those people who, if not loyal to Amulius personally, remained loyal to the idea of him. Most of the servants, however, assisted the rebellion, proffering weapons and clearing routes.

"You go!" Romulus shouted to his brother, as he slammed a guard's head into a stone pillar. "Find Amulius."

Remus locked eyes with his twin. "Not without you."

Stay safe, my loves, Rhea thought. *Stay together.* For she felt the tug of the rising moon and needed to escape the melee.

She fled, racing to the kitchen's larder, where Antho had promised to leave her clothes. Above the ceiling and the tiled roof, the dark moon entered the sky and Rhea underwent the transformation, knowing it would be her last. The realization stole her breath, just as she shivered with an odd sense of omnipotence. She had nothing left to give besides this—this night.

Before she became nothing, she would release everything.

Rhea donned the waiting dress and an oak-leaf wreath. This was the civic crown, a military decoration for Latins who saved lives. Antho knew precisely what impact it would make. Rhea smiled as she fit it to the top of her head. Most importantly, however, she clasped her mother's brooch to her shoulder.

But you, Ilia, you are my center stone, my middle treasure, my moonstone.

The center of it all.

By then, the majority of the battle had dispersed into smaller scuffles, and Rhea knew were she would find her family. She walked barefoot to the throne room and over the remnants of a door that her boys had surely kicked down. And inside?

Everyone.

Nobody noticed her appearance, so Rhea watched the scene before her like an audience member at a play. There were Romulus and Remus, armed and bloodred, standing before the throne, where Amulius still clung to power. On either side of the king sat Numitor and Calvus, holding wine cups. Antho waited in the wings, gripping Ezio's hand. And, finally, her aunt Claudia on a far bench, weeping and apart.

Somebody was missing, Rhea realized, as she counted their numbers, but who?

The question flew from her mind, however, when her uncle addressed her sons.

"You are the other one," reckoned Amulius.

"I am Romulus."

"And you have come to kill me. Shall I kneel? Would you prefer my head? My throat?"

Remus shrugged. "I am impartial—I only want your death."

"And then what? The shepherd boys become kings of Latium?" Amulius took another sip from his cup. "Only one can be king, you know. It is hard with brothers; I would warn you."

"You must face judgment for your many crimes and return the throne to King Numitor."

Amulius laughed. "No, I don't think I shall."

But then his gaze drifted from the twins to the back of the room, and he was the first to see her. Amulius stood, black eyes wide against his pallid skin, one hand raised and quivering.

"Jocasta?"

Every person turned; every person watched with dropped jaw as Rhea walked down the central aisle, clothed in red, hair down beneath her wreath. A wild queen in a procession of one.

"No," Numitor corrected in a thick voice, awed and emotional. "It is Ilia."

Rhea smiled. "Hello, Father."

"What is this trick?" Amulius demanded. "What are you?"

"No trick but a revenant, made flesh and blood for one night."

"Impossible," he sputtered.

"You once found talk of spirits and the gods monotonous, Uncle. You told me they did not exist." She gestured to her body. "What do you say now?"

Her sons stared, and she approached them with her arms at her sides—the hardest thing she had ever done. She hadn't held them as a human in over sixteen years. Her hands itched to feel their faces, the hair hanging at their brows. But not here, before her enemies—and maybe not ever. There was always a chance they would reject her affection. To them, she was a stranger. So, as desperately as she longed to embrace them, she also wanted to run away, and she tried not to tremble, despite her overwhelming happiness, despite this ever-present terror.

"I remember," professed Remus. "But I thought you were a dream."

"Mama," Romulus marveled, eyes wide and wet.

She nodded. "Yes."

Later. I will hug you later. I will kiss your wounds and sing the old songs.

Rhea hoped the boys understood.

Amulius directed his discomfiture at his daughter. "I know you are somehow involved in this foolishness, Antho," rebuked the king. "Call it off."

"I cannot control a spirit, Father."

"Then you leave me no choice."

The king clapped his hands, and two soldiers emerged from a secret chamber in the throne room, dragging a man, mottled with purple bruises and red blood, between them. In such a condition, Rhea did not recognize him, but Antho screamed.

"I have your lover, Antho."

Calvus made a choking sound.

Amulius rolled his eyes. "Please, Calvus. Everybody knew."

"Leandros," Antho sobbed, "I am so sorry."

A moan escaped his broken lips, and Rhea swore she heard him say, "I love you."

"He will not survive another stroke of the whip. Call this off, girl, or watch him die."

Rhea interceded. "Tell your guards to walk away, Uncle, or my sons will make dog food of them. You know they can, just as you have always known their father is Mars." Rhea did not look at her sons, but she felt their shock all the same. "Your reign is over, Amulius. Stop using people's love as leverage. I did not rise from the dead to watch you play the same tired games."

"Then who will kill me?" Amulius challenged. "The twins? The forsaken princess, home at last?" He banged the bottom of his wine cup against the table. "Tell me! I am desperate to know how this will end, who will take the duplicitous honor."

So many with just cause.

Remus stepped forward, but Rhea barred him with her arm. "No."

Her other son offered her his sword, and she accepted it, lifting its blade to point at the king. "It should be me."

Amulius did not flinch. "I think so, too."

"You moved in the shadows for so much of your life, Uncle. Tricking and manipulating others to execute your darkest deeds." Rhea took a few more steps toward the dais; her arm did not waver. "Where is Sethre?" she demanded, looking around. "In what hole does that vile augur hide? How many has he poisoned for you? How many have fallen sick after inspiring your ire or blocking your schemes?"

Amulius shrugged.

"And how much did you pay Helvius to claim he was my lover? Or the mercenaries hired to be 'Etruscan bandits'?" She gestured to the brooch. "Thieves who would leave such a fortune behind? Sloppy work."

Still, Amulius offered nothing. No denial, no defense.

Rhea appealed to Numitor: "Ask your brother to confess, Father. This is your last chance. Ask him about Aegestus."

"There is no need," Numitor replied tiredly. "I have quit oblivion and accepted the truth."

The silence that followed his admission was nearly deafening.

"It was difficult for me to accept these truths about you, brother. It tore me asunder. The cretic wine and its potent poppy dulled my grief, but also the sting of your betrayal. I coped by disengaging." Numitor set down his cup. "I do not blame you for my addiction, though I know you fostered it. I did it to myself. But a question remains. One answer, I beg of you, and then we need never speak again."

Amulius's voice cracked: "I already know what you will ask, Numitor, and I didn't do it."

Numitor asked it anyway: "Did you poison Lausus and Jocasta?"

"No." A whisper, and then: "I would have never hurt her. It was a real illness. But her death was my signal to act. My fealty to her always held me back."

While Claudia cried and Leandros lay dying, the others paused, stunned, by this private reckoning between brothers made public.

"We lost our way so long ago."

"Because you took everything I ever wanted, Numitor."

"I am sorry, Amulius. I truly am. I understand how badly I have hurt you."

Amulius's face twisted with grief. "Jocasta loved me until the day she died."

"A life can hold many loves, of many kinds," responded Numitor evenly.

Even with his eyes shut, noiseless tears slid down Amulius's cheeks.

"A wound can be a source of power, but only when it is honest," explained Numitor, "and you've never been truthful with yourself. Jocasta did not leave you for me, she left because you refused to grow. Because love for you is possession. Absolute control. A straight path without dip or curve. When your own daughter diverged from your expectations, she lost your heart. And I pity you for this." In the way Numitor spoke, Rhea knew he was not angry but distraught. "For so long, too long, I could not acknowledge your capacity for evil. I can blame extraneous forces for my oversight, but it was my own obstinance. I saw you always as my little brother.

"Remember the day you broke your leg? You had to climb higher than me, had to prove yourself, and you fell. It was all for naught! I already knew you were the more daring! I admired that in you; I was even envious. Do you remember how I carried you home on my back? And I let you tell whatever story you needed to tell? Because I wanted you to feel big. I watched your path dip and curve, but I still cared. You are my brother, but you are horrible. And I love you—I will always love you—but you are horrible."

Amulius laid his head in his hands before his allies and his foes. Labels that no longer mattered at the end, and this was the end.

And Rhea, who had been tortured for years by this man, who had rehearsed in her mind all the things she would say on this day of judgment, stood by while her father eviscerated him with simple, careful honesty.

Amulius looked up at Rhea, who still held Romulus's sword.

"Earn that civic crown you wear, Rhea. Do it."

She swallowed tightly, fortifying herself. "I came here tonight to re-claim all you have stolen. My name, the name of my father, the names of my brothers and, most importantly, my sons."

Rhea closed the distance between them, lifted the sword above her head.

It is a crime against the gods to kill your kin.

Could she do this one last thing? Would she lose her last shred of humanity to outmonster him?

"No, Ilia," objected her father, and he stepped between his daughter and his brother.

"But, Father, he—"

"You misunderstand. It is already done." Numitor removed the sword from Rhea's hand and tossed it on the ground. He seemed so old and so very sad as he whispered: "It had to be me."

Amulius figured it out first. "The wine."

Numitor nodded. "Arsenic."

"How long?"

"With the dose I administered, a few hours."

Calvus began to shout. "And me?! You poisoned me, too?!"

"For your complicity, you are as guilty as Amulius."

"Antho!" shrieked Calvus Flavius, wealthiest man in Latium. "Fetch me a purgative!"

When Antho stood, Rhea noticed the telling swell in her belly. Her cousin dropped Ezio's hand and entered the scene. "No, Calvus," she replied calmly, "I will not." And then to the guards holding Leandros, she demanded: "Unhand my husband, or face the wrath of my nephews, Romulus and Remus."

Claudia, who everyone had forgotten, gasped. "Your husband?"

"Yes, Mother. I married him, in secret, before you sold me away to a man three times my age."

"You are a disgrace, Antho. You dishonor me and your father."

Antho laughed. "You think my secret marriage is what dishonored this family?"

Ezio rose, shaking his head. "Grandmother, with respect, she is braver than anyone ever realized. Maybe the bravest of us all."

"Such misplaced acclaim," lamented Calvus. "Yet, though I die surrounded by vipers, I will still live on in my son. My bloodline will rule this land for generations to come."

Antho shared an exasperated look with Rhea. "Will men never tire of this language?" She returned to Calvus. "You will die, and you will die. That's it. You will not 'live on in him,' whatever that means." And she lowered her voice. "He was never your son anyway."

Calvus gasped and sputtered. "Harlot! Whore!"

"One of the girls might be yours, I think." Antho's hands found the bottom of her belly. "But not this one." She shrugged.

Ezio came to Antho's side. "I would watch the words you call my mother. They will become my last memory of you."

At that moment, Calvus keeled over, clutching his stomach. "I feel it, Amulius, the poisons!"

And from the way Amulius's face shone with sweat, he did, too.

Romulus moved toward Numitor, knelt, and kissed the floor at his grandfather's feet.

"Grandfather, let me be the first to proclaim it. Long live King Numitor!"

Remus dropped to his knees beside his twin. Rhea stood behind them; she did not bow to anyone anymore.

Numitor placed a hand on each of their shoulders. "Latium was always meant to be yours. You are my direct descendants."

Romulus stiffened, so slightly that only Rhea noticed, and raised his head. "My king, we are outsiders in Alba Longa, unaccustomed to its ways or its role in the League. Why should its people accept us? But, also, why should we accept this place? We are half-wild, the people of the Hills. Our friends are outcasts. If we should rule any city, it must be theirs."

"Ezio is the rightful heir of Latium," added Rhea. "He is a testament to his noble parents."

Numitor beckoned Ezio to join them. "My boy, your cousins deny their birthright, preferring that it pass to you. Pretend you are my royal councilor. What advice would you offer me?"

Antho's son considered. "I would say, 'My king, send these warriors home to the land they love. Offer them a pledge to support the building of a new city, one worthy of our shared history and their unique causes.'"

Numitor nodded, eyes twinkling. "Romulus, Remus. How would you respond if I extended such an offer?"

"The city of the Seven Hills would be a forever friend to the future king Aetius," replied Romulus.

"And very grateful," chimed in Remus.

A duumvirate, a double rule. An ideal future where both Rhea's sons and Antho's son could exercise power and execute positive change.

Sometime during these negotiations, Calvus had slid from his chair to the ground, where he groaned in misery. Antho appraised him with disgust, then stepped over his body to reach Leandros.

It was time to leave the dying men to die.

Romulus and Remus leapt up to help Antho carry Leandros, but Ezio insisted: "He is my father, after all." And the shy smile between mother and son nearly broke Rhea's heart anew.

Seven people left the chamber, ready to face the aftermath, to confront the myriad of problems and injuries, the death and destruction, that waited in the Regia and city at large.

While the others were distracted, Rhea snuck back to the throne room. Calvus lay in the fetal position, pink foam at the edges of his mouth. She did not speak as she slit his throat.

Amulius surveyed Rhea's every move from the other side of the room, where he rested, slumped against the wall. "Will I also receive a mercy killing," he managed to say, "or do you hate me too much?"

"That depends, Uncle," answered Rhea, making her way toward him. "What were my mother's last words?"

He smiled, blood from his stomach just beginning to fill his mouth as the poison did its deathly work, then he chuckled at the cruelest irony:

"Love my children."

Rhea lowered the knife.

Chapter LXVIII

RHEA

THERE WAS MUCH to discuss and so little night left.

Into his private rooms, Numitor welcomed his family: Rhea, Romulus, and Remus.

"Is it true we will only have you until morning?" her father asked in sad wonderment.

"Yes. I am no longer what I was, Father. I exist on borrowed time."

Romulus clasped one of Rhea's hands, and Remus took the other.

"Where do we even begin?" Numitor mused, the old king made new again.

"My sons will rule, Father, and I will not be there to offer counsel. I must know that you will be present when they need you." Rhea hoped that the way she articulated *present* made her feelings on cretic wine clear.

"I thought I would never be a grandfather. Your sons are a revelation." His whole face lit up. "In the coming days, I will prepare a gift to aid your city. Stone and timber, oxen, mules, men, and tools. All my resources will be available to you, my histories and philosophies, for there are many questions to be considered in such an undertaking."

"Questions like which hill should center our city?" interjected Remus slyly.

Numitor raised an eyebrow. "I sense this is an ongoing debate?"

"We have different preferences," explained Romulus. "And have never reached consensus."

Numitor's eyes took on the foggy gleam of reflection and recollection, the evidence of his mind traveling through everything he had ever read or heard or seen. Rhea recognized the look immediately and wondered again at the parts of us that never change.

"I have seen this in a dream," he began, "and I know what you must do. The hill will be chosen by the gods, by Jupiter himself. When you return home, you must each make an appropriate sacrifice, then depart for your respective hills. All night you will stand vigil, and when morning comes, watch the skies. The birds shall have your answer."

"But what are we looking for?" Remus pressed. "To see the first bird? To see the most birds?"

"When you see it, you will know."

Her boys were decorous and thanked their grandfather for this foresight, but Rhea knew them better. Romulus was already worried, and Remus found it all ridiculous. She gave each of their hands a light squeeze. *I understand.*

"Of course, there is another way to settle this predicament," Numitor considered. "Ilia, do you know which of them is the elder?"

Rhea froze. She hadn't anticipated this query—although she should have—and had not strategized a response.

"The day of your birth was . . . hard. I was alone and inexperienced. I nearly bled out." She stopped, choked by the memory. "I cannot recall much before I awoke in the dungeons."

Her boys, her good boys, quickly suppressed their disappointment.

"Do not feel bad, Mother," Romulus urged.

"It's probably me," Remus said with a wink.

They hugged her, and her heart swelled, despite her lie. Canus was Romulus, and Remus was her green-eyed Viridis. She knew who came first, but she would not be the one to dictate that course.

She would leave that to the mix of fate and free will called life.

♦ ♦ ♦

THE TWINS LEFT to find food and water, but Rhea remained with her father. He studied her like he was trying to decipher her mystery. Finally, he divulged what he saw: "I see your fear for them in your face."

"I am their mother."

He ceded her point, eyes closed. A nod, a slight smile.

"You fault my advice about the birds."

Yes. You are as fallible as any. And I dread our family's curse, which saw brothers ripped apart by ambition, by love and ideals. Would Lausus and Aegestus have ended the same way if they had lived long enough?

But she said none of that.

"No, I fault obscure answers to direct questions."

"But that is what makes us unique. We interpret, make mistakes, and reinterpret. It's the process for our evolution, individually and collectively."

Rhea was not sure that she agreed. Maybe humankind just made simple things difficult. In nature, growth was far more practical. At this point in her life, Rhea's identity intersected oppositional worlds, the city and the wild. Her father might talk in circles, but Rhea spoke with a lexicon he wouldn't understand.

You cannot relay the wisdom of the forest to one who has sheltered indoors for too long.

"I do not take the poppy anymore, Ilia."

She heard the apology beneath his words. Rhea did not hate her father for his struggle with dependency, but neither could she forgive his abandonment.

"I am glad for you, Father, and I am proud of you."

"I like to think that everything we've been through has prepared us for this, for our reunion today and our victory."

This was where Numitor lost her.

Rhea would never diminish her family's tragedies by relabeling them a life lesson. She worried that her father would soon commence with platitudes, preaching the merit of her trials and their beneficial impact on her character. She wasn't grateful for all the hardship she had endured; a person should not have to be brutalized to be considered strong. Besides, it was too neat an ending. Too easy for Numitor, the father who spent years in willful oblivion while she suffered.

But her damned heart still loved him.

Numitor no doubt watched the emotions warring across Rhea's face.

"Will I ever earn your trust again?" he asked—he begged—in a low voice.

And she softened her face. She lied. Because Rhea was still part human, and that is what humans do for family.

"Yes, Father. You have always had it."

He wept.

♦ ♦ ♦

THE BOYS REGARDED their mother like both a goddess and a ghost.

"One night with you could never be enough," Remus mourned, reminding Rhea that her sons were only seventeen years old.

"Let me show you something."

She brought the twins through the courtyard to the bay laurel, pointing out the branchy path to the roof.

"Shall we go up?"

They nodded.

Rhea was relieved that she could still make the climb look effortless, and sat between her sons as they admired the view. The darkness hindered detail but emphasized the enormity of the Regia and Alba Longa.

"Our city will be even grander," Romulus promised.

"Yes, but how will you rule together if you cannot agree on a site? There will be more problems, harder questions . . ."

"We have our grandfather here and our father at home. They will both provide sage counsel."

"Remember this, both of you." She turned her head both ways, meeting each boy eye to eye. "Do not let the animosity between Numitor and Amulius trickle down into you. Remain brothers first, kings second."

Romulus stared at her, aghast, and even Remus recoiled.

"Never, Mother."

She had done all she could; she had to believe them.

"Faustulus will always be our father, but did you mean what you said to Amulius? Is Mars . . . ? Did you and Mars . . . ?"

She answered instantly, without hesitation. "Yes."

Remus swore, then coughed into his fist. Rhea gave him a hard look. "I'm sorry, Mother, I'm just . . . impressed."

She rolled her eyes.

"I wish you two could have had more time together." Concern tugged at Romulus's brow. "You deserve great love."

And, oh, if images of Tiberinus didn't come pouring through her mind! All the nights they spent conversing and laughing, playing games, riding his boat up and down the river. Rhea thought of him standing guard over her babies in their basket, bringing her a dress on the first new moon. Holding her, healing her. She missed him. She wanted him here to share in her accomplishment.

"I have known great love," Rhea answered in a shaky voice, as she both consoled her son and confessed to herself. "Do not worry for me."

"Ilia?"

And with just one word, one swish of leaves brushing the wall, Rhea was thrown back in time. Antho was climbing over the roof ledge, and she was both a teenage girl and a grown woman. Had they done this so many years ago or was it yesterday? Time became more difficult to determine and differentiate once you reached the end of it.

Ezio followed. "I've never been up here," he marveled.

Remus chuckled. "You know we haven't."

They made space for the new arrivals, and Ezio passed Romulus and Remus a wine jug.

"How is Leandros?" Rhea asked Antho.

"He will live, but oh, Ilia, for a moment I thought . . ."

Rhea wrapped her arms around her cousin, bringing Antho's head to her shoulder. "I know," she murmured, and then she sighed. "But we did it, Antho."

"We did it."

The women held each other, and their secrets, so tightly. There were sons in their lives—lovers, husbands, fathers, and brothers, too—but there was always *this*. This unspeakable, unshakable sororal bond in which understanding is a given, as is loyalty.

And look at all they had done.

Five people sat on a roof, occupying the space between earth and stars, slumber and dreams. Three young men, suddenly tasked with kingdoms, and their mothers. Two generations of cousins. They finished the jug of wine together, talked some, sat in rich silence, and eventually fell asleep.

But not Rhea. She would not lose a moment. She would stay as long as she dared, guarding her people, her precious, beautiful family.

Just before the sun rose, in the particularly vivid and special blue hour, Rhea felt a warm wetness seep across her body. She peered down the top of her dress and watched her skin split open in fresh wounds. These were her injuries from the rebellion. Rhea ran her palms across her arms and legs and shoulders, finding scars everywhere.

The lynx. The Sabines.

Rhea took a deep breath, lifted her hand to her left ear, fingertips confirming the missing tip.

The veil between the wolf and woman was thinning, and she needed to leave.

She kissed her boys' cheeks.

"All I ask is that you remember me as loving you."

Then Rhea Silvia, half woman and half wolf, slunk down and away, trading places with the sun.

Chapter LXIX

ANTHO

THE REGIA WENT down with limited bloodshed, a monster felled by a mere stone.

But there were some who had to die; the latest members of the royal council were first, as those were the men who had most enabled Amulius's crimes. Romulus and Remus summarily executed each man as quickly and humanely as they could—if there can be any decorum in execution.

The augur, Sethre, vanished without a trace. How he managed to escape, nobody knew. Dark magic, perhaps, or just excellent timing.

Numitor organized the immediate aftermath, issuing clear, time-sensitive orders that redirected the rebels' bloodlust into productivity. He made up chores and errands: *Protect this room. Calm the horses. Deliver messages of the coup to the townspeople, to the farms, to all the estates.*

After the private funerals for Amulius and Calvus, Antho found a home for her mother in the city. The fomer queen had requested to join the Vestal Virgins but was denied by the high priestess, Tavia. On the day of her relocation, all Claudia took from the Regia was her loom.

"We are both widows now, daughter," Claudia said in farewell.

"My husband lives."

But Claudia pretended she did not hear. She would never regard Leandros as such, never recognize her grandchildren as his.

Antho refused to let it bother her.

There was so much work in rebuilding the city. Numitor and Ezio began by establishing a new council, enlisting honest men to whom they could delegate tasks: conducting inventories and assessing damage. Amulius had decimated Alba Longa's treasury and destroyed its relationships—both inside and outside Latium. Ezio and his great-uncle spent hours together each day, creating plans for reparation but also improvement.

The young prince was impressing everyone with his endless energy and acumen.

Antho left Alba Longa to the others. She had enough to manage with her younger children and a rapidly progressing pregnancy. Furthermore, she had Leandros transported to Villa Flavius—now called Villa Silvia—to recuperate and reside permanently.

"People will talk about you," cautioned Numitor, as they made to depart the Regia. "Can you handle their judgment?"

"The people who consider me a bad woman for 'remarrying' are the same ones who condoned my father's beatings and Calvus's humiliations." Antho stood tall. "I no longer concern myself with the opinions of such people."

"Be happy, Mother," Ezio urged, and he offered Leandros, his father, an awkward but respectful bow. It would take time for the two to establish a bond and ease commensurate with their blood, but both men were willing to put in the work, if for no other reason than their mutual adoration of Antho.

And then, finally, Antho had Leandros all to herself. Because his injuries were so intense, he spent the first few weeks in Antho's bed recovering. But he was never alone. She tended to each of his wounds herself. And she knew he was recovered the day he pulled her into his arms and kissed her.

"Am I home? Is this home?"

"Yes."

"You were always home for me, but now we have walls."

"And a bed."

"No more hiding."

"Never again."

The door opened, and their three children timidly entered.

"They've been asking if it was time," apologized Zea, who had come to Villa Silvia with Gratia.

Antho sat up, patting down her disheveled hair. "It is the perfect time."

Ezio pulled a chair over to the bed, and both the girls followed.

"What do you want to say?" Antho asked, prompting the conversation she had practiced repeatedly with her daughters.

"Can we see your scars?"

Leandros laughed out loud.

Antho sighed. "That's not what we discussed."

"She was supposed to say, 'I hope you are feeling better,'" the older one tattled.

The younger girl lay her hand against Leandros's face, tickling her tiny fingers into the gray of his beard. He found his wife's eyes. "I am now."

Chapter LXX

RHEA

FROM HER DEN at the base of the Palatine, the wolf dreamed herself back into the moment that forever changed her life. She returned to the cave, the great in-between, where Cybele and her lion emerged for those who made themselves worthy.

"Is this my mind," Rhea questioned, "or is this real?"

"After all these years, you still have to ask?"

Rhea conceded.

"I summoned you this time, Rhea Silvia," professed the Great Mother.

"Whatever for?"

"You know why."

"Because the wolf is dying."

Cybele nodded. "Yes, but child, you did well with your time."

At the edge of the cave, at the edge of the fantasy, Tiberinus appeared. "*Did well*, Cybele? She was perfect."

Delighted, Cybele clapped her hands together. "You came for her! Mars never did." But then she pouted. "Oh, do not look so cross with me, Tiberinus!"

"Rescind the deal," he demanded, coming to Rhea's side. "Return to Rhea her human body."

"I cannot unmake a sacrifice. She chose to become wild; I cannot reverse a woman who has taken back her nature and owned it."

Rhea laid a hand on Tiberinus's arm, murmuring his name. "I am not afraid."

His eyes glistened as he covered her hand with his own, running his thumb back and forth across her skin.

And then, from the other side, entered Mars. "I heard my name."

Cybele laughed, as entertained as she was annoyed. "Your impact, Rhea Silvia! Two gods!"

Mars ignored the goddess. He pulled Rhea away from Tiberinus and toward him. She had forgotten his height, how he had to slouch to come close to her. Funny little memories.

"Is it true? You are dying?"

Rhea lifted a shoulder. "Every warrior has her day."

"I told you once that you weren't like other mortal girls."

"And I warned you not to underestimate us."

The corner of Mars's mouth turned up in a half smile. "Rhea, those boys are unlike any before or after. And it's all because of you."

Rhea nodded. She accepted his compliment, but gently removed his hands from her body. "I know."

"It might have been different if we were different," he said more quietly, not wanting the others to hear.

"If you didn't love war and I didn't love home?"

"Yes, exactly."

For that was their conundrum, why Rhea Silvia and Mars were never meant to be. He would always be called away, and she would always be called back. Their paths shouldn't have crossed, but they did, and it had produced something unprecedented. They had made Romulus and Remus to transform the world, and then their purpose to each other had been fulfilled.

"And you still do not regret me?"

"I only regret the things I haven't done."

He grinned.

Tiberinus said nothing but monitored their interaction closely. Mars nodded to him once, respectfully, before vanishing.

Rhea returned to Tiberinus's side. "How much time do I have left?" she asked Cybele.

"A day or two."

Tiberinus closed his eyes, and Rhea laced her fingers into the river god's own. "Come with me; come back with me. I need to say goodbye."

◆ ◆ ◆

THE WOLF WOKE soon after, and it hurt too much to move. Her injuries had compounded since her two selves had begun to merge. Since the rebellion and the return to the Seven Hills, Rhea typically spent her days listening to her sons in their planning councils outside Faustulus's hut. Today, however, she could hardly stand. The wolf heaved herself up onto all four legs and immediately fell over. She whimpered, tucked her body into a ball.

Would she die alone in this cave?

But then her boys arrived with a jug of water and meat.

"Oh, Lupa," Remus moaned, dropping to her side.

Her sons hand-fed her, then lay down on either side of her body. She had become so thin, so frail. Her sons curled around her, keeping her warm, and their arms held her tight, fingers burrowing into her fur just as they had done when they were babies.

Physical sensations between mother and child are stored in the body; in the circular rub on a chest, the rhythm of fingers in hair. It was a wild language, sensory, inarticulate in the words of humankind.

"We know who you are, Mama."

"We've always known, Lupa."

"Rhea Silvia had your eyes."

"Like amber."

Her mind saw their eyes. Canus and Viridis, gray and green.

She remembered how she'd first won control of the wolf's body.

Ours.

One word. One love.

They would always belong to each other, and she would become part

379

of their legend. Maybe not in the way it truly happened, but the wolf would be there, keeping those boys safe and alive, the way she had always wanted.

She was their mother, and she had lived.

"I don't want you to die," cried Remus.

"No," admonished Romulus, breaking. "Don't say such things. Just hold her."

"We love you."

I love you, too. I love you more.

As she drifted to sleep, she thought she recognized shapes in the cave's shadows: a bear, a crocodile, a spider, and a lion. The communion of mothers come together once more to honor their wolf.

Chapter LXXI

RHEA

AS ROMULUS AND Remus slept, the wolf rose from the cave for the last time. She dragged herself down the familiar path to the river, to the fig tree, to the breaking dawn and all that was to come. She could not pass on in front of her sons; it would make leaving this world even more impossible.

Rhea's soul flickered within the wolf, desperate for freedom. She was both a woman watching and a wolf on her way. Visions blurring and conjoining. Together. Reunited. But also separate and slipping.

A dark, shadow heart, shared between wolf and woman, struggling to beat.

The wolf made it to the riverbank and lay in its silt, covered in scars from old battles, tortured by aches from new ones. She panted. It hurt her chest, this agony of breath, this valiant effort to keep going. She looked at herself in the water's surface and watched, mesmerized, as Rhea was fully released from her form—a human spirit hovering above an ancient wolf.

And standing before her?

Tiberinus, waiting, as she knew he would be.

"I wonder," she said aloud, thrilled to hear her human voice in the daytime, "does the river stare at the sky, or does the sky stare at the river? For I see heaven in the water."

"More of your questions, Rhea Silvia?" Tiberinus glided through the stream and out onto the riverbank.

"No. I came to thank you, and bid you farewell."

"I cannot watch you die," he demurred.

"Then leave," she replied, with thinly veiled disappointment. She had hoped he would at least hold her. "I will not fault you."

"That's not what I meant." He lifted his arms, gesturing to the land around them. "You belong here, Ilia, in your sons' empire, the one you fought so hard, so long, to give them."

"You called me Ilia," she murmured, smiling.

"It felt appropriate, considering what I ask."

"I don't understand."

"You have already lived two lives, but would you live again? For me?" Tiberinus extended his hand. "I cannot spend eternity without you; I'm afraid I've grown quite attached."

She laughed, softly. "After so many years of 'not now, not yet,' you finally want me?"

His eyes flashed. "I have always wanted you."

"But you are too late, I am dying."

"Say you'll be mine, and when your soul leaves your body, I will catch it. I'll make you as immortal as the river."

Rhea paused. "You are serious."

"Become my Queen of the Tiber."

She trembled with feverish hope, because her greatest wish wasn't to escape death, it was to be with him. "And we would be together forever?" she managed to ask.

"Not if you don't decide soon." And Tiberinus motioned impatiently at the prone wolf, panting and unstable.

Rhea resisted. "We haven't even kissed. What if we don't—"

But she was cut off by his mouth on hers. Their lips met, then their tongues, and as her soul sang, *At last!* Tiberinus was bringing her body—part spirit, part flesh—into his arms and Rhea wished she was more substantial so that she could do all the things she'd imagined doing with him, right here on the riverbank in the morning sun.

Her fading heart could hardly stand it.

Rhea faltered, and her knees gave out, but Tiberinus held her tightly.

And she wanted more of him, all of him, in whatever form that meant. He was delicious, and it was no secret; she had always known.

Why not? After it all, why not become a goddess?

"If I stay with you," she murmured, their foreheads together, both breathing rapidly, "then you will become mine, as well."

"I already am."

Below them, the wolf's throat rattled; a cracked, wet inhale. Her body shook.

Rhea Silvia, in the dawn of her death, thought of wolves and kisses.

Her mouth found Tiberinus's again, but she kept her eyes open, absorbing everything with this last, exhilarating breath—his smell and taste and hands, this sky and ground and air. Overwhelmed by the beauty of it all, by her love of it all. And when the wolf succumbed, her severed spirit rose even higher, but Tiberinus caught her as he said he would, as she knew he would. He crushed her against him—with want and need and hope—and then pulled her beneath the water.

If this was death, it was gorgeous.

They emerged, and she examined her body: shining, strong, whole, complete.

Beside her, Tiberinus's face glowed with joy, and his eyebrows arched upward in that adorable way of his. "I think we will be quite happy, my queen."

Princess and priestess, wolf and woman. Mother of Romulus and Remus, of Roma, of everything it would one day be.

Crowned in water, the lifeblood of her precious land, and hand in hand with the god who had always loved her, Rhea Silvia ran like the river.

EPILOGUE

From *The Early Histories of Roma* by Aetius Silvius Flavius

Romulus and Remus found their wolf's body entwined in the roots of the fig tree, and they had her entombed within the den beneath the Palatine. Quietly, and without fanfare.

Romulus would build his city, but Remus would not be there. Nor Faustulus. Because although Rhea Silvia had raised her sons to be better brothers, she could not control the actions of others.

No mortal can; perhaps no immortal, either.

But Romulus's city, which shared his name, was everything he wanted it to be, at least in the beginning. He offered asylum to the exiled, and established the early laws of the kings, which granted common people the right to select their patron.

He also forbade any child under three years old be put to death.

In the years that followed, many strange occurrences were reported along the Tiber. Many claimed to glimpse a family in the waters. These people were dismissed as crazy, as seeing things, as staring too long at the in-between. Others began to avoid Tiber Island, not because it was haunted, but because this was where the river god made nightly love to his wife.

The locals learned to welcome the noise with a wink and a shrug for every time the river queen moaned or cried out or giggled, new life burst into the region.

Rhea Silvia came to be remembered as the guilty woman of the forest, with only a select few understanding how she found asylum in a wolfskin. It is easier to think of what happened to her as a punishment rather than a choice, but sometimes, to heal, we must be reborn.

Listen. Mark the sound. The wolf's howl is its own song, full of tenderness, full of rage. It is a soul shared with the world.

Wild. Alive.

AUTHOR'S NOTE

I am a storyteller, not a historian, but to plan and produce *Mother of Rome*, I relied heavily on these primary sources:

- *Roman Antiquities* by Dionysius of Halicarnassus
- *The History of Rome* by Titus Livius (Livy)
- *Roman History* by Dio Cassius
- "The Life of Romulus" from *The Parallel Lives* by Plutarch
- *Fasti* by Ovid

These texts tend to agree on three central facts: (1) Rhea Silvia (called Ilia) was the daughter of Numitor, a Latin king overthrown by his brother, Amulius; (2) Rhea Silvia was a Vestal Virgin raped by the god of war, Mars; and (3) Rhea Silvia bore twin sons, Romulus and Remus, who founded the city of Rome in 753 BCE.

Ovid calls Rhea's brother Lausus; Dionysius names him Aegestus. Both, however, agree that Amulius had Rhea's brother murdered in a fake robbery. Dionysius also writes of a Vestal Virgin named Aemilia, famous for rekindling the lost flame of Vesta, but she was a priestess of Rome, not Alba Longa. The good shepherd Faustulus and his wife, Acca Laurentia (who might have been a prostitute), are named in almost every version of the Romulus and Remus myth.

Claudia, Jocasta, Calvus, Ezio, and Leandros are my creations.

In a familiar trope, the babies are taken from Rhea after their birth, placed in an ark, and set upon the river "120 stades" from Alba Longa. But sources differ on what ultimately happens to Rhea. Does she meet the Vestal Virgins' capital punishment? According to Plutarch and Dio, she is condemned to death but spared due to an intercession by her cousin Antho. Others say she throws herself into the river, either in a desperate act of suicide or by invitation of the river god, Tiberinus.

There is no suggestion that Rhea Silvia and the wolf who nurses Romulus and Remus in the Lupercal on the Palatine are the same entity.

I also relied heavily on the story of Aeneas in Virgil's *Aeneid*, particularly books seven through twelve, where the Trojan hero arrives in Latium, meets Tiberinus, and marries Lavinia. Aeneas did rescue the Penates from a burning Troy and bring them to Italy, but there is no evidence that his household god was singular and Cybele.

Lastly, the research of impeccable historian Mary Beard in *SPQR: A History of Ancient Rome* was an absolute godsend in composing this story.

Are you not entertained?

ACKNOWLEDGMENTS

This book, for whatever reason, for a million reasons, has been my Sisyphean task. I would not have gotten this boulder up the hill without my agent or my editor. Jane, my cheerleader, thank you for your relentless support and advocacy. And Anne, my coach, thank you for the guidance and advice, time and time again, no matter how many times I fumbled the ball—"Pivot! Keep pushing! Lift with your knees, not your back!" I adore you both. Go, team! (Okay, I'll stop mixing my metaphors now.)

Thank you to Dystel, Goderich & Bourret, the premier literary agency, and the enthusiastic, expert teams at Ace/Berkley and Titan Books. The best in PR and publicity, the best covers, hands down.

Entering the "book world" has introduced me to some incredible people. To every writer and reader who has supported me with kind words, posts, and messages, THANK YOU. You keep the impostor syndrome at bay. We ride this tide, we *rise*, together.

I must always thank my people. My friends from Long Beach and Los Angeles and Seattle, my book club, the St. Joe's mom crew. My extended family, my cousins who are more like siblings, Rachael—you fill my heart.

For my dad, who first taught me about ancient Rome and raised me on sword-and-sandal epics. For my brother, who makes me laugh harder than anyone else and continues to be the coolest person I know. And for my mama, who always knew I would write books. I know you are proud of me.

My mother gave me the greatest gift when she believed in my voice. Tell your children they have a story worth telling. It might make all the difference.

For R, D, and S, my three cubs. In *Hamnet*, Maggie O'Farrell writes of Anne Hathaway: "She will place herself between them and the door leading out, and she will stand there, teeth bared, blocking the way. She will defend her three babes against all that lies beyond this world. She will not rest, not sleep, until she knows they are safe." You have given me the fiercest love, have shown me what it means to be a wild woman. As Queen Jocasta says, "To be a mother is to be alive."

Dan Bear, you signed up for a party girl but ended up with a moody creative in Fruit of the Loom sweats. You always make the coffee. You are my Greek soldier, my river god, and my hero. I love you.